Carib

Lutchmee and Dilloo

A Study of West Indian Life
Edward Jenkins

Edited and with a new Introduction
by David Dabydeen

CARIBBEAN CLASSICS

Series Editor: John Gilmore

Titles already published:

1. Frieda Cassin, *With Silent Tread: A West Indian Novel* (first published Antigua, c. 1890). Edited and with a new Introduction by Evelyn O'Callaghan. ISBN 0 333 776070

2. J. W. Orderson, *Creoleana: or, Social and Domestic Scenes and Incidents in Barbados in Days of Yore* (first published London, 1842) and *The Fair Barbadian and Faithful Black; or, A Cure for the Gout* (first published Liverpool, 1835). Edited and with a new Introduction by John Gilmore. ISBN 0 333 776062

CONTENTS

Textual Note

In the original edition of the novel, the governor of the colony is sometimes called "Walsingham" and sometimes "Walkingham," though the former is more common. In this edition, the name is given as "Walsingham" wherever it appears.

Macmillan Education
Between Towns Road, Oxford OX4 3PP
A division of Macmillan Publishers Limited
Companies and representatives throughout the world

www.macmillan-caribbean.com

ISBN 0 333 91937 8

Typeset by EXPO Holdings
Cover design by AC Design

Printed and bound in Malaysia

2007 2006 2005 2004 2003
10 9 8 7 6 5 4 3 2 1

THE early literature of the Anglophone Caribbean, that is, of the generations before the great rebirth and transformation of this literature in the 1950s and 1960s, remains little known, even though it is slowly beginning to attract increased scholarly attention. Many people would be surprised, for example, to be told that published poetry by an author born in one of the former British Caribbean colonies can be found as early as the 1680s. Leaving aside the many histories, travel narratives, sermons, and ephemeral publications of a polemical character, there is a considerable body of poetry and fiction in English from the eighteenth and nineteenth centuries by writers either born in the Caribbean or intimately connected with the region by family ties or prolonged residence. Some at least of these works are of considerable interest for the insights which they offer into the history and culture of the Caribbean, but nearly all of them remain little known even to scholars specialising in the region's literature.

The reason for this is a simple one: people cannot read or appreciate books which they cannot get hold of. Many of these early works of Caribbean literature are now extremely rare and difficult to find even in the largest and best known research libraries.

The purpose of the Caribbean Classics series is to make some of these books available again, in the belief that they are of more than historical interest. Some of them certainly count as 'a good read' – and we hope this is true of all those selected for inclusion in the series. At the same time, while it has to be admitted that this early Caribbean literature is very much an elite literature – nearly all of the poetry and fiction produced in the Caribbean or by writers of Caribbean origin during the eighteenth and nineteenth centuries is by whites rather than blacks; nearly all of it is by men rather than women – these works can offer much that is of significance for an understanding of Caribbean culture as a whole, and they should be seen as part of the heritage of all Caribbean people today.

Edward Jenkins' *Lutchmee and Dilloo* is in many ways a good example of this literature. Unlike authors such as J. W. Orderson (whose *Creoleana* and *The Fair Barbadian and Faithful Black* are reprinted in a volume in this series), Jenkins was not born in the Caribbean. But his origins symbolise the way in which the region has for centuries been intimately connected with the rest of the world: he was an Englishman born in India, and he came to write a novel set in what is now Guyana because of his concern for the Indian indentured labourers in British Guiana and other British colonies. *Lutchmee and Dilloo* is in fact the earliest novel of Indo-Guyanese life; that it should have been written by someone like Jenkins rather than a Guyanese should cause little surprise. Most Afro-Guyanese and Indo-Guyanese had at this date only the most limited access to educational opportunities, and it was not until the twentieth century that a more open educational system came into being and allowed Guyana to produce writers as distinguished and diverse as Wilson Harris, Martin Carter, Edgar Mittelholzer, A. J. Seymour, Jan Carew, John Agard, Grace Nichols and Mahadai Das. There were some nineteenth-century Guyanese writers, such as Michael McTurk, a member of the white elite who wrote with a degree of sympathy of the lives of Afro-Guyanese in the Creole verses he published under the pseudonym Quow (1899). However, most nineteenth-century Guyanese, whether locally born or long-term residents, who possessed any significant level of education were too involved directly or indirectly in the plantation system to be able to view Indian indentureship with any objectivity, or to feel any sympathy or understanding for victims of the system. In this respect, the pseudonymous "West Indian" who published a pamphlet rejoinder to Jenkins' *The Coolie: His Rights and Wrongs* seems to have been typical of his class.

Jenkins' sympathy for the indentured labourers is unquestionably genuine, as is his outrage at the way in which the indentureship system which was supposed to provide real benefits for the labourers as well as the planters had been perverted into a one-sided scheme of oppression, supported by flagrant class bias in the colonial legislature and judiciary which pretended to represent the highest ideals of British justice. His sympathy and his radicalism take him only so far, however; he does not question the concept of 'superior' and 'inferior' races, or see it as anything other than part of the natural order of things that the British should rule India, British Guiana, and large parts of the rest of the earth. He denounces the 'Local Aristocracy' of British Guiana for their oppression of other races in the narrow-minded pursuit of their own self-interest, and suggests that other white colonial oligarchies behave in the same manner by adroit references to the then-recent Confederation Crisis of 1876 in Barbados (a subject well covered in Bruce Hamilton's *Barbados and the Confederation Question*). On the other hand, as an author Jenkins' own treatment of his non-white characters leaves a lot to be desired – with the exception to some extent of Drummond's 'housekeeper', Missa Nina, his portrayals of Afro-Guyanese and Chinese are grotesque caricatures.

His main Indian characters are more successful. In Lutchmee, Jenkins creates what we feel is a real human being and it seems that, like his character Craig, with Lutchmee Jenkins manages to overcome the all-too-common belief of white Victorian Englishmen that difference necessarily means inferiority. The entirely innocent relationship between Lutchmee and Craig produces, not understanding – the politics of race and class are too much for that – but some striving towards it, some beginnings of hope for the future. If the lecherous and revengeful Hunoomaun is a bit of a one-dimensional villain, there is considerable subtlety in Jenkins' description of how the kind and loving Dilloo is transformed by the injustices he experiences into a morose individual who seeks some kind of compensation for his own sufferings by beating his wife and who comes to share Hunoomaun's obsession with vengeance. While the rebellion never comes off, the very planning of such a thing elevates the Indians above the status of passive victims. Whether intentionally on Jenkins' part or not, the dying Dilloo's defiant refusal to be baptised, to be received into the faith of 'Massa Drummond's God', echoes the defiance of one of the Caribbean's earliest anti-colonialist heroes, the Amerindian cacique Hatuey, who refused the offer of baptism as he was about to be burnt at the stake by the Spanish, saying he had no wish to go to the Christian heaven if he was likely to meet any more Spanish there.

Other aspects of the novel are well handled. The plantation manager Drummond is not a bad man, but he is led into bad acts out of self-interest; moneyed British readers of Jenkins' time would perhaps have been more willing to have their own consciences pricked by this characterisation than if Drummond had been an out-and-out figure of evil. The gradual emotional and political awakening of Isabel Marston and her education of her father make her an attractive figure, while Jenkins shows perhaps unusual restraint for a popular novelist in leaving the inevitable marriage between her and Craig to take place in the reader's expectation rather than in the pages of the novel itself. There is real humour as well as social commentary in the Intendant-General's failed orphanage scheme, while the vacillating Governor is drawn with some skill as a man hopelessly out of his depth rather than a simple cartoon incompetent. Jenkins is good on descriptions of scenery, and his pictures of life and work on the sugar plantations are drawn from personal observation. The Tadja ceremony and the final battle between Dilloo and Hunoomaun are wonderful set-pieces.

Lutchmee and Dilloo is now reprinted with an introduction by David Dabydeen, himself a distinguished Guyanese novelist as well as a scholarly interpeter of the Indo-Caribbean experience. His introduction offers modern readers an erudite and perceptive commentary on the context of Jenkins' novel, the nature and extent of the novelist's achievement, and what *Lutchmee and Dilloo* can tell us of the system of Indian indentureship which effected such a major transformation in the culture of much of the Caribbean.

John Gilmore
Centre for Caribbean Studies
and
Centre for Translation and Comparative Cultural Studies
University of Warwick

A NOTE ON THE TEXT

In this edition, the spelling and punctuation of the original edition (3 volumes, London, 1877) have been followed. A few misprints have been silently corrected.

For the Anglo-Indian vocabulary which Jenkins occasionally uses, the reader is referred to Sir Henry Yule and A. C. Burnell, *Hobson Jobson: The Anglo-Indian Dictionary* (first published 1886; facsimile reprint of 1902 second edition, Ware, Hertfordshire: Wordsworth Reference, 1996).

INTRODUCTION

I

On 4 January 1836, John Gladstone (father of the future British Prime Minister), owner of two British Guianese sugar plantations, wrote to a firm in Calcutta seeking a supply of labourers under a contract of indenture. Two years later, the first batch of 396 Indians arrived, and between then and 1917, when the system of indentureship ended, more than 238,000 'coolies' were shipped to British Guiana, in excess of forty per cent of the total number of indentured Indians taken to the region.[1] The only reason for their presence was to maintain the plantation system by their labour. The newly emancipated African slaves abandoned (or were threatening to abandon) the plantations in droves, leaving behind them the great symbols of tyranny, the canefields, canals and sugar factories. They settled in free villages, the names of which expressed their idealism and aspirations: Better Hope, Good Fortune, Friendship, Perseverance. Those who made their labour available to the likes of Gladstone wanted proper wages and employment rights. The plantocracy, accustomed over the centuries to dealing with an enslaved labour force, would not countenance such and sought workers who could be coerced into productivity by whip, Law, Bible or whatever means lay at hand. And so began what the British Secretary of State, Lord John Russell, called in 1840 'a new system of slavery.'[2]

The Indians came from different castes, though the majority were from the lower end of the scale, people specialising in fieldwork and agricultural cultivation. The overwhelming majority came from the United Provinces (Uttar Pradesh and Bihar), with a lesser number from Madras (Madrasis were seen as 'inefficient labourers, with reprehensible social customs' and recruited only when there were insufficient North Indians available).[3] A very high proportion were Hindus, the rest being mostly Muslims. Whatever their linguistic, religious and social differences, they were lumped together as 'coolies' and packed off to the Caribbean:

> In the same manner that slavery brought together Africans of different religions and linguistic affiliations, so did indentureship create a mélange out of Bhojpuri speakers and Tamils. Beef-eaters were bundled together on the same ships and on the same estates with those to whom this practice was abhorrent. Low castes now became *jahagis* (shipmates) with twice-born brahmans, and Aryan-descended North Indians rubbed shoulders with Southern Dravidians with whom they had little intercourse in India. On this later re-visit to the middle-passage, a melting-pot was created which broke down some of the barriers existing in the homelands. In the new environment, Hindus could be found celebrating the Muslim Shia observance of Muharram in which even Afro-West Indians participated vigorously.[4]

Several factors led to the Indians signing indenture papers, leaving their homeland and crossing the *kala pani*, the dark ocean, which was forbidden territory, since the crossing meant a loss of caste affiliation, a loss of the security of community.

Undoubtedly many villagers were fooled by the *arkatis* (recruiters) who spun tales of fortunes to be made in a new, nearby place (for the *arkatis* would certainly have kept quiet about the *kala pani*). Walter Raleigh's ancient description of Guiana as El Dorado would have been evoked, consciously or unconsciously, to excite their imagination, the possibility of glittering wealth in powerful contrast to the drabness of their existence: 'It have so much gold there that you don't have enough hand and neck and foot to wear bangle. You wish you have ten hands like Lord Shiva, and even then you run out of skin.'[5] The majority however emigrated for very practical reasons. They were fleeing from natural calamities which bred famine or epidemics such as cholera, smallpox and the plague. Or else they were fleeing from man-made adversities of economic, caste and gender oppression, from

> landlords, moneylenders, husbands, wives, or mother-in-laws, or from some task or family obligation [...] women did have solid reasons for wanting to migrate, and consequently made a conscious

decision to leave, to escape painful, empty domestic lives, economic hardships, the social stigma of early widowhood, the odium which descended upon those who had brought inadequate dowry.[6]

It would have taken little effort for the *arkatis* to persuade such people to abandon their villages and seek a new and better life elsewhere, a life unencumbered by debt, the burden of caste and other stigmas.

The immediate challenge facing the migrants was how to make accommodation with the new landscape whilst maintaining aspects of social, cultural and family structures which created their sense of Indian identity. The numerical disparity between the sexes led to new stresses on family life. The immigration ordinances stipulated a 2:5 ratio of females to males, but in practice women were extremely scarce. In 1851 for instance, the ratio was a shocking 23 females to 100 males. The sexual imbalance led to crimes of passion including wife murders in extreme cases. The Agent-General's report of 1875 states that:

> The disproportion of the sexes is the great exciting cause of the deplorable large number of wife murders which are perpetrated notwithstanding every precaution being taken to by removal or otherwise which can be taken to prevent them.[7]

The new practice of polyandry (sometimes forced upon women by estate managers in the hope of keeping the peace) invariably led to outbreaks of jealousy accompanied by violence. But women were not unremittingly victimised in the plantation environment. Some used their scarcity value to negotiate better conditions for themselves in the domestic sphere, threatening to leave their husbands for a male partner should their material ambitions remain unfulfilled.[8] Sometimes, their voluntary association with white overseers sparked off riots by Indian men:

> The withdrawal of even a single woman from the Coolie dwellings to the overseer's lodge is regarded with jealous eyes by her fellow countrymen, and when it was remembered any female over childhood was already the actual wife of one of them, it is evident that no surer way could be found of sowing the seeds of discontent and riot.[9]

The trauma of accommodating to the new environment was deepened by the hostility of the black population who attacked the newcomers as scab labour. Afro-Guyanese argued that the Indian presence depressed wages, and the Indian habit of frugality and asceticism gave them an advantage since they were willing to survive on very little. The Afro-Guyanese had absorbed the consumerist ambitions of the British. They had been brought up to live in a 'British fashion', which was relatively costly.[10] Moreover Indians had been given land in lieu of a return passage home upon expiration of their indentureship contract, to encourage the retention of their seasoned labour. The freed Africans however had to purchase Crown lands, the cost of which was prohibitively high. Hospital, housing and schooling provisions on the plantations, albeit rudimentary to say the least, also created resentment on the part of the Africans, who under slavery had lesser privileges and as free men and women were left largely to fend for themselves. In short the Indians were seen as stealing their rightful inheritance, newcomers and interlopers accorded legal protections and material privileges denied to slave and ex-slave populations. That Indians were mere pawns in an Imperial economic enterprise, wholly powerless to address, much less remedy, black demands and aspirations, did little to stem ethnic hostility. And apart from linguistic and cultural differences which impeded dialogue, the very self-contained structure of the plantation prevented fruitful and satisfying intercourse between Indians and Africans. The plantation, within whose boundaries Indians were effectively imprisoned, and the free African villages, were worlds apart. Maintenance of difference was a central strategy of British administration of its subject peoples, since one group could be played off against the other in a system of 'divide-and-rule.'

Many factors sustained Indian communities against despair and disintegration in the hostile new environment, but two were outstanding. Firstly, their psychological sense that the period of indentureship was relatively short, and that in five years' time, they could either return home as moneyed people, or acquire land and become property owners. Hence their extraordinary feats of sacrifice in terms of severely curtailed expenditure and

patterns of consumption. Every member of the family worked at
every opportunity, and the saving of wages for future investment
was a supreme Indian discipline. Secondly, their stubborn refusal
to surrender the ancestral religions and convert to Christianity.
Henry Kirke echoed the opinion of several other missionaries and
observers when he wrote that 'the attempt to convert the Hindoo
and Mahommedan immigrants to Christianity has been an utter
failure.'[11] Muslims established mosques and continued the practice of teaching Arabic to their children, so that the Holy Koran
remained central to their lives. They continued to celebrate their
traditional religious festivals. Hindus regularly enacted the stories
of the *Ramayana* in popular folk festivals, stories they knew by
heart since it was related to them constantly by their pandits in
temple settings. If the Holy Koran provided an ethical framework
within which Muslims could conduct their lives, irrespective of
place of settlement, the *Ramayana's* power was the power of the
mythical. Its story of banishment, exile, displacement and
perilous new encounters amongst strange and hostile tribes; and
the eventual, if arduous triumph of good over evil and the usher-
ing in of a Golden Age, nurtured the imagination of Hindu
Indians, providing them with the symbols to sustain their spirit in
the midst of plantation miseries.

II

On Christmas Day 1869, George W. Des Voeux, former stipendiary magistrate in British Guiana, then Administrator of the
Government of St. Lucia, wrote a lengthy letter to the Earl
Granville, Secretary of State for the Colonies, detailing abuses in
the indentureship system which needed urgent remedies. The
134 numbered paragraphs of Des Voeux's submission called
attention to various malpractices, ranging from inadequate
medical facilities for Indians to the authoritarianism and bullying
tactics of planters in the legal administration of justice. Without
specified reforms, Des Voeux argued, the colony would suffer
labour unrest and erupt into violence. A year later, a Royal
Commission of Enquiry was set up to investigate the substance of
Des Voeux's criticism of the indentureship system. John Edward

Jenkins, a radical young barrister, was sent to British Guiana by the Aborigines Protection Society and the Anti-Slavery Society, to observe and report on the proceedings of the Royal Commission.

Jenkins, the son of a Wesleyan Missionary, was born in Bangalore, India, in 1838, the very year that the first batch of labourers left India for British Guiana. His family emigrated to Canada, and Jenkins was educated in school and university there, first at Montreal High School and then McGill University. He moved to Britain in the 1860s, qualifying as a barrister in 1864.[12] He soon became involved with the National Association for the Promotion of Social Science, an organisation which was 'truly mid-Victorian in spirit: zealous, enquiring and humane [...] an effective pressure group as well as a vigorous forum for social discussion.'[13] In 1866, Jenkins presented a paper to the Association, on the legal aspect on Sanitary reform. Two of the hallmarks of Jenkins' political and writing career over thirty years were first revealed in his paper. Firstly, his concern for the plight of the common people, exposed to diseases because of the apathy or intransigence of Local and National authorities, is linked with a range of other social causes: in the opening page he places the agitation for public health improvements in the context of other reformist movements – 'emancipating Negroes, enfranchising householders, and abolishing oppressive taxations.'[14] Such connection between national and international issues was to recur in later writings, showing the breadth of his reformist vision. In 1872, in his *Discussions on Colonial Questions* he linked the suffering of the English agricultural class to that of African slaves, Indian indentured labourers, child workers in South Africa and Polynesians exploited by their English masters.[15] Two years later, contemplating the conflict between capital and labour which threatened to engulf Europe and its Empires in social conflagration, he wrote:

> This portentous question is beginning to shake the very pillars of society in every part of the civilised world. The Coolie, the Negro, the immigrants in the Western lands, the English artisan and peasant, the French and German workman, all alike are conspiring together to demand for labour a larger reward, a better coparcenary with capital.[16]

Secondly, the tension between the rational and the emotional, between the documentary and the literary. His paper on sanitary reform was closely argued; as befits a newly qualified barrister on his first major public brief, various statistics and tables were marshalled to give objective support to his opinions. Jenkins however on occasions could barely contain his feelings for the victims of neglect, and his anger at the inaction of the authorities. In these moments, his mood found literary form and his prose swelled with pity and outrage:

> The stench from the watercourse was at times unbearable – there were some houses and stables round which the overflowing feculent matter of dungheaps and *cloacae* lay in stagnant pools, not only sending up a continuing miasma, but being absorbed into the walls of rooms in which human beings were living, eating and sleeping.[17]

Pity and outrage were the features of his first novel, *Ginx's Baby,* published in 1870, the very year he set off for British Guiana to investigate the coolie condition. The novel, 'a pathetic satire on the struggle of rival sectarians for the religious education of a derelict child',[18] was a vast success and Jenkins became a controversial figure overnight. It was a Victorian best-seller, running into thirty-six editions by 1876, making it as popular as Edward Bulwer-Lytton's *Pelham* and Thomas Hughes' *Tom Brown's Schooldays.*[19] O. G. Rejlander, the renowned studio photographer, made a photograph of a howling and destitute baby which sold 60,000 prints and 250,000 cartes-de-visites in 1870.[20] The Education Act of that year, arguably the most important piece of social legislation in Victorian Britain, was influenced by Jenkins' novel. Given his fame, his interests in international affairs and his commitment to the destitute, it is no wonder that the Aborigines Protection Society and the Anti-Slavery Society chose Jenkins to report on indentureship. That he accepted the brief was testimony to his idealism and to his moral and physical courage. 'I was going alone beyond seas for indefinite months, into strange regions, with black reputations in health matters, and on business of deep importance', he wrote.[21] His statement echoes any number of descriptions in Victorian imperial fiction of the English hero embarking upon an epic

adventure on behalf of race and nation, but Jenkins was no clichéd
Imperialist. When he composed his statement he was confessing to
the anxiety and pain of leaving his family behind, especially his two
infants. And his intimacy with health issues meant that his fears of
malarial Guiana were dreadfully real rather than a matter of
Imperial rhetoric.

III

The Coolie: His Rights and Wrongs, published in 1871, was a work
of monumental detail, its 446 pages the most comprehensive account of the indentureship system in the nineteenth century.
Specialist readers – members of the Aborigines Protection
Society, the Anti-Slavery Society, the Colonial Office and the like
– would have found in it very substantial material for consideration, but Jenkins' work was also aimed at the general public.
Hence the inclusion of two woodcuts and commentaries in the in-
troductory chapter, summarising in easily graspable pictorial
form the grievances of the labourers.

The first shows the manager's house and compound. The manager and his attorney, two fat characters, are seated on the veranda, drinking the blood of labour. At the foot of the stairs, on either side, is a Chinese and Indian worker, both being bled by drivers [sub-managers]. A boy takes a glass containing their life fluids to the manager and attorney upstairs. The manager's fat wife and children look out of the window at the coolies huddled in misery and anxiety. The coolies' hands are bound, signifying their status as 'bound labourers' [that is, labourers bound by the terms of indentureship], but also their servility. On the right of the veranda are the plantation's 'happy and healthy owners in England',[22] seated before the ledger book and cash-box. To their right are two aged coolies, witnessing the abuse of their relatives, and weeping, the broken fence behind which they stand representing the collapse and dereliction of moral values in the plantation environment. A huge tree in the shape of a crucifix is a silent commentary on human suffering and the absence of Christian values. The house, in the light of the tree, becomes a grotesque temple of Pharisees or moneylenders, and the blood-letting a degraded version of the celebration of the Eucharist. The rigid spatial divisions (Indian labourers on the left, Chinese on the right; the fat cows in the foreground, and the fat wife and children in the mid-ground; the coolie being beaten on the right edge of the print, and the horse eating contentedly on the left) echoed in the solid and rigidly geometric pillars, stairs and roof of the house, tell of the absence of moral communion (or community) between the various ethnic groups. Only the tree, its fluid shapes echoing the contorted limbs of the indentured labourers, offers relief from the grim and heartless geometry of the plantation house.

The second print is a picture of misery. The setting is the plantation hospital, a place of cruelty rather than healing. On the left are two patients in stocks. Next to them are a row of sick and neglected patients. As Jenkins explains, 'the nearest, a Chinaman, is just expiring, spite of the chicken soup – *vide* the chicken in the basin – which has been supplied to him *in extremis*. The question of the actual supply of nourishing food in the hospitals when

ordered by the doctors was another point raised by the
Commission.'[23] The manager kicks down the steps a meagre
wretch, too weak to be worth curing. The doctor's horse is well-
fed and the manager's pigs are contentedly fat compared to the
bony workers hoeing the ground. Hung mockingly above them is
the diet-list in Chinese and Indian, detailing the instructions
given by the doctor for the nourishment of patients. Obviously the
list is for show purposes since very little food is served to the patients. One hangs himself from the veranda, his gaping mouth signifying hunger. His suicide is in abject and moving contrast to the
family of chicks scooting about the yard in innocent freedom or
the two fighting cocks confronting each other in masculine po-
tency. If in the first print, the top windows of the house alluded to
an altarpiece (a religious triptych), in the second, the window is a
star, but it is a star that looks down upon an inhospitable manger
of decay and death.

    Jenkins' attempt to make his work accessible to the reading
public is also evident in the literary style of his writing. His report

is part travelogue, part adventure tale, Jenkins' seeking to give character and idiosyncratic qualities to the people he encounters. He casts a novelist's eye over his fellow passengers, seeking out particular details:

> The poor French lady who sat moaning in the cuddy, the stout Dutch dame who, for forty-eight hours, rested her double chin on her ample bosom in a state of adipose imbecility, the pretty Hamburg girl, belle of the voyage, whose pink cheek faded for a short time […] [24]

He records with a novelist's ear particular conversations on board ship, catching the individual idioms of speech:

> Last time I came out – eh? there were three Bishops and about twenty ecclesiastics – eh? going to the council. There was great fun – eh? The Archbishop of L ----- was one – eh? He was a comfortable little man – eh? He liked well his glass – eh?[25]

As he sails through the Caribbean sea his pen grows excited at the exoticism of the island:

> For three days we steamed past the wondrous islands, furrowed, ribbed and riven, lifting up their shaggy heads into the clear sky, whilst below they nourished here and there in pretty laps an exquisitely bright green vegetation.[26]

Finally there are the picturesque descriptions of the lush strange landscape of Guiana and finely drawn portraits of the coolies:

> Down the trench comes a coolie wading to his breast, dragging a load of floating brushwood for his home fire. The sun flames upon the water and glints over his slippery limbs. Next an Indian woman, choosing the same damp causeway, who, with pretty modesty, dips up to the neck in the brown water, and watches us soberly with her great black eyes.[27]

Woven into these novelistic passages are details of wages, the diet of workers, acreage under cultivation, hospital conditions, and statistics of how many hogsheads of sugar are produced, how many puncheons of rum, casks of molasses, bales of cotton, cubic feet of timber. The effort to give literary colour to social and economic data ultimately fails: although the prose is at times heightened by exquisite descriptions of plantation life, it finally succumbs to the weight of documentary detail. The shift is sometimes abrupt, Jenkins reining in the momentum of his literary sensibility, suddenly bringing a fine description of landscape to documentary closure:

> Round the corner of the wall and past the lighthouse we glide into a river – the broad, brown river – and at our left reach away the flats, the stellings, the stores and sheds, the low white jalousied houses over which, everywhere, graceful cabbage-palms spread their green wings. This is Georgetown, Demerara. Thermometer 85 degrees Fahr., time 5.00 P.M.[28]

Such shifting between styles is not evidence of flaws in composition; the whole of Jenkins' writing career was to seek a marriage between the modes of literature and reportage. He is 'a writer inhabiting the important no-man's-land between fictional and documentary writing',[29] and as such belongs to an honourable tradition originated by the 'father of the English Novel' and professional journalist, Daniel Defoe. At the time of writing *The Coolie: His Rights and Wrongs,* Jenkins belonged to a group of socially committed authors, under the publishing house of Strahan and Company. Alexander Strahan had gathered under his wing novelists and periodical writers like William Gilbert and poets like Alfred Tennyson. As Strahan put it, his aim was

> supplying such literature as will not ignobly interest or frivolously amuse, but convey the wisest instructions in the pleasantest manner, and supply it in such form that it will find its way to tens of thousands of British homes to be well thumbed and dog-eared by the children and the grown people, on the journey and at the fireside.[30]

The use of illustrations and the insistence upon literary quality to excite the imagination of readers, especially when the subject was potentially as dry and specialist as labour reform and sanitation, were the distinguishing features of Strahan's publishing house. Jenkins' *The Coolie* is an exemplary Strahan publication in its conscious mixing of the genres of travel writing, adventure story, comic caricature, economic tract, legal report and socially concerned journalism.

IV

It was to be expected that Jenkins' *The Coolie* would provoke hostile responses from apologists for the plantocracy. His book was criticised for 'containing much grotesque sensationalism and spurious sentiment, many baseless insinuations, and misrepresented facts.'[31] The anonymous author ('West Indian)' of the pamphlet *The Coolie in Demerara* goes to great lengths to counter the charge that indentureship amounted to a new system of slavery. Checks and balances instituted in India, he argues, involving Emigration Agents, the Protector of Emigrants, magistrates, medical doctors, and other officials of government, mean that indentured labourers were afforded proper protection against misrepresentation, fraud and forcible removal. 'The regulations are so elaborate and stringent that it is a sheer impossibility for a single coolie to find himself on board ship and bound for the British West Indies except by his own free will and consent'.[32] As to the highly emotive charge that mortality aboard the coolie ships was excessive, he conceded that a couple of ships did fare badly in 1869, but no more so than ships bound for Australia with white emigrants. In any case, lengthy sea journeys are inevitably perilous, so deaths are inevitable, whatever preventative measures are put in place. Furthermore, it may well be, he proposes, that the emigrants are carriers of all manner of diseases contracted in India from the effects of famine, hurricane and other natural disasters. 'The influence of these dreadful visitations might be lurking unseen in a number of emigrants before departure, to be developed during the voyage; thus causing a comparatively large number of deaths, which mortality would, in all human probability, have taken place among the same people had they remained at home.'[33] All in all, the deaths are a drop in the ocean considering that the majority of emigrants arrived safely at their destination.

'West Indian' attempts to negate other attacks on the plantation system by evoking the plight of Englishmen back home. In this respect, his tactic is reminiscent of that of the pro-slavery lobby who

had argued earlier that enslaved Africans were materially fortunate when compared to the English labouring classes. The fifty
dollars given to the coolie as bounty money in re-indenturing is a
veritable fortune, 'West Indian' argues, compared to the penny-a-
day increase in wages awarded to English soldiers, and the foun-
dation of future wealth if invested wisely in the purchase of a cow,
or re-lent to other labourers at a high rate of interest. As to the
question of wages, the indentured labourer, with his 'simple
wants, both of food and dress', and with the privileges of free
housing and hospital facilities, was much better off with his five
shillings a week than the 'Dorsetshire hind'[34] whose nine or ten
shillings were depleted by the need to pay for housing, heating,
medicine and the 'heavy food and warm clothing' rendered necessary by the climate. The 'Dorsetshire hind' in his relentless
poverty, had only the workhouse to look forward to in which to
end his days, whereas the coolie could return to India with healthy
savings. Jenkins' concern about the mortality rate in the plantation is countered by the comparison with the death rate among
the English labouring classes. Moreover, Jenkins neglects to take
into account that coolies 'are of a race not the most sensitive to
cleanliness, nor the easiest to manage in regards to sanitary considerations.'[35] 'West Indian' ends his pamphlet by attempting to
deflect what is arguably Jenkins' most powerful appeal to
Victorian mores, the appeal to family values. This he does by simply blaming the Indians for innate moral deformity. It is not the
disproportion of sexes in British Guiana which creates the condition for wife-murders and sexual debauchery, but the temperament of the Indian. 'In his own country the Hindoo is extremely
jealous; his passions are as strong and his sense of injury are as
great as any that possess the European, whilst his regard for the
sanctity of human life is very much weaker.'[36] No amount of
Christian tutelage and not even the most stringent laws can moderate his brutal instincts and natural propensity for sexual callous-
ness. He is what he is. To be sure, heinous crimes of passion occur
in England, but those of 'heathen immigrants' are the norm,
rather than the exception. The plantation system is innocent of
Jenkins' charges, 'West-Indian' concludes.

V

Jenkins, by all accounts a forceful and confident campaigner, would have shrugged off 'West Indian's' criticisms for what they were – sophistry born of smugness, 'West Indian' blinded to moral values by the dividends to be reaped from the sugar plantation and the immigration system. The remarks which would have stung Jenkins, given his literary sensitivities, would have been those relating to the aesthetic merit of his writing. 'Social characteristics have presented', 'West Indian' writes, 'a ready field for the satirists of every age and time, from Aristophanes to Jenkins, and it was not to be expected that the latter would refrain from using his tremendous power of adjectives in regard to the general condition of the people on the estates of Demerara.' Such bracketing of Jenkins with a revered Ancient like Aristophanes is obviously sarcastic, and there is the added charge that coolies are not worthy subjects of proper literature (which in any case Jenkins cannot achieve since he is so excessively wordy and hyperbolic). Jenkins, 'West Indian' continues, is deemed 'by some of his friends [note the malice of the qualification, 'some'] with much good nature and unconscious sarcasm, the Swift of the nineteenth century, and he manages to make good his claim to the title by forcibly-feeble writing.' The pun on force-feeding would have been a potentially withering criticism, especially given the effortlessly biting wit of Jonathan Swift. Compared to Swift, Jenkins is accused of being a bore: 'when he is not sensationalist he is dull, and it may very well be said of his work, "one half will never be believed, the other never read".'[37]

Such scathing criticism, however, rather than routing Jenkins, only provoked his resolve to press home his case, in literary form. In the Preface to *Lutchmee and Dilloo,* he admits with characteristic modesty and sensitivity that his report on coolies had a certain 'natural dryness', and that what is needed is to express the problems of indentured labour in a 'concrete and picturesque form', giving flesh and heartbeat and animation to otherwise dry data. To write a novel on coolie life would be an audacious project since, Jenkins himself observes, 'The field is a new one for fiction.' The great challenge would be to persuade the Victorian reader that the coolie was a subject worthy of literature. Jenkins squares up firmly to this challenge:

> The life of a Coolie man or woman, with its simple incidents, its petty cares and vexations, its occasional events of terror or sorrow, and all the various feelings, sentiments, and impulses that sway an existence passed amidst the relations of a bond-service, these and their peculiar influences on the higher and more cultivated race, do not at first sight present an attractive ground for fiction. Besides, the subjects and interests seem to be too remote. But happily the ties of universal brotherhood are ever drawing men more closely together. The sorrows of Dilloo or Lutchmee are the sorrows of humanity, differing only in their conditions and their relations from the tragedies of our own homes.[38]

Such conviction created ground-breaking work, one in which the Guianese coolie in particular and the Indian diaspora in general are for the first time in English fiction portrayed with a degree, however limited, of psychological realism and aesthetic artistry. The Indian enters English literary history in the characters of Lutchmee and Dilloo, a young married Bengali couple, who, through adventure and misadventure, find themselves in British Guiana as indentured labourers. Their relationship in Bihar, India, is an idealistic one. Lutchmee is a picture of physical symmetry, with her 'light-brown oval face, with its regular eyes, arched eyebrows, delicately-chiselled nostrils and well-turned mouth and chin'. Jenkins' interest in the Victorian pseudo-science of phrenology is evident in the way he links Lutchmee's outer beauty with her inner character. Dilloo is suitably presentable, his handsome and manly features reflecting nobility of spirit. Their physical and spiritual characteristics are Europeanised,[39] in terms of ideal beauty, but equally their qualities are derived from Hindu religious texts. Lutchmee is an image of the *Ramayana's* Sita, in her loyalty and her devotion to her husband, whose prowess and courage make him a Rama figure. Their spiritually pure love is threatened by the ugly, uncouth and dark-skinned Hunoomaun, a Ravana figure who lusts after and will abduct Lutchmee given the chance. Jenkins reconstructs Hindu scripture with breathtaking audacity, for in the *Ramayana* it was Hanuman, the monkey-god,

who rescued Sita from Ravana and returned her unblemished to
Rama. Hindu mythology is also paralleled with Greek mythology:
Hunoomaun resembles Ravana but is also described as a satyr intent on chasing and raping a nymph. Jenkins' reference to ancient
Hindu religious texts may be fleeting or indirect (he quotes from
the *Gita Govinda* and mentions the laws of Manu) but in the context of Victorian celebration of Indian culture they are of considerable significance. Victorian scholars like the Oxford don Max
Müller, wrote glowingly of India's ancient civilisation, drawing
parallels between Eastern and Western classical achievements, in
art, architecture and literature. Max Müller wrote of a common
origin for all Indo-European languages, relating Sanskrit to Greek
and Latin. He summarised his appreciation of the Aryan heritage
of India thus:

> If I were asked under what sky the human mind has most fully de-
> veloped some of its choicest gifts, has most deeply pondered on
> the greatest problems of life, and has found solutions to some of
> them which well deserve the attention even of those who have
> studied Plato and Kant – I should say India. And if I were to ask
> myself from what literature we, here in Europe, who have been
> nurtured almost exclusively on the thoughts of Greeks and
> Romans, and of one Semitic race, the Jewish, may draw the cor-
> rective which is most wanted in order to make our inner life more
> perfect, more comprehensive, more universal, in fact more truly
> human, a life, not for this life only, but a transfigured and external
> life – again I should point to India.[40]

Jenkins was of course hardly as adulatory of India as Müller, but
he was obviously as aware of India's rich literary heritage and
artistic equivalences and relationships with Western classical
traditions. Lutchmee and Dilloo may be nineteenth-century
indentured coolies, but they are descendants of High Civilisation.

The British governing class of India and the Guianese plantation owners paid no heed to such heritage. Jenkins details various
malpractices in India which converted the indentureship project
into a system of financial abuses. In Guiana itself, the plantation
environment destroys the idealised love between Lutchmee and
Dilloo. Dilloo grows furious at the constant cheating of his fellow

labourers: they are given extra work, their wages are unjustly reduced, they are cheated of adequate housing and medical provisions, they are subject to the whims of managers and magistrates. Dilloo degenerates into an angry, murderous character, beating his wife and threatening to chop her to pieces with his cutlass. The plantation treats him like an animal, and he becomes one. Jenkins writes, with scathing passion:

> It is hardly possible to conceive how the scientific or unscientific – it matters little what we term them – arrangements of an artificial system of indenture, with the laws that defined and regulated it, had succeeded in moulding out of a manly, tender, generous and loving character, a hard, unnatural and ferocious savage. We have not been without instances in Christian lands where circumstances and conditions have thus distorted most promising natures.[41]

The achievement of *Lutchmee and Dilloo* however is not the detailing of social and economic injustices but the revelation of emotional, psychological and philosophical shifts in the character of the Indians. They are not wooden stereotypes but people who respond vividly to their changing conditions. If Dilloo's nature is constrained by bitterness and hatred, Lutchmee senses the possibility of an existence above and beyond domestic chores, wifely duties and the closed ghettoised space of the plantation. Her intimacy with the overseer Craig whom she nurses back to health, provokes a radical awakening of spirit. The passage deserves quoting in full since it reveals a nascent feminism, a nascent defiance of patriarchal structures, whether those of the plantation system or inherited from India.

> The life was new. It brought into her life fresh human elements, feelings she had never experienced before: ideas – novel, sweet, piquant. Very pure, very simple, even very holy seemed this time to her – and yet, to the least worldly observer, how charged with peril was the atmosphere of these halcyon days! Dilloo's sudden hint to her to prepare for her return home struck in harshly upon this contented, delightful peace. It woke her up to the fact that the agreeable season must soon close – it brought her back to common life and to her wifely duties – and, *though she could not analyse the meaning of the feeling*, Dilloo's request disquieted her with a

conscious unpleasantness. She would rather not have been reminded by him that he had a claim on her superior to the charming engagements of her recent life. The immediate feeling passed away, but, for the first time in her experience, there had crossed her mind an idea like a shadow of regret or of resistance towards the supremacy of her husband in her heart. [my italics][42]

And yet, Jenkins himself is not radical enough to give Lutchmee her own voice, her own emotional and intellectual control over the narrative of her experiences. Hence 'she could not analyse the meaning of the feeling.' Earlier in the novel, Jenkins, writing of Lutchmee's nursing of Craig, had also denied her agency: 'this strong youth [...] excited in her mind a sort of fascination which it would be hard to define [...] She was too natural to attempt to define these feelings to herself [...] Had Lutchmee been able to analyze her own feelings [...]'[43] In other words, whilst Indians are subject to sympathy, subject to admiration, subject to psychological growth and moral enquiry, that is what they remain in Jenkins' novel – subjects, albeit rebellious ones.

VI

In his own time, Jenkins was attacked for being a communist and a revolutionary. He was plainly not. He was, instead, a social reformer, a defence barrister for the underdog and prosecutor of the governing class. He is certain, in *Lutchmee and Dilloo,* that it is 'European energy'[44] which brings order and civilisation to the jungle environment of Guiana. In his *Discussions on Colonial Questions*, he stated unequivocally that the colonies could be productive and Empire flourish only if 'organised and applied under the direction of Europeans'.[45] His overriding concern was the elimination of the injustices which corrupted the ideals of Empire. His limitations are obvious in his depiction of Africans. He wrote of Guiana's 'large, lazy, prodigiously sensual and fecund black population'.[46] In *Lutchmee and Dilloo*, he reduces the African character to brute stupidity, his descriptions of their behaviour being as objectionable and vile as any found in the racist rantings of his Victorian contemporaries. Sarcophagus for instance is a brainless animal, incapable of intelligible speech, much less writing: 'If you tossed him a bundle of words, he used them as a gorilla would use a bundle of sticks. He unaccountably mixed and twisted them up together, he tore them to shreds between his teeth.'[47] Indians fare better in that they are sometimes given ornate speech indicating lofty feeling. Ultimately, however, they are denied the capacity to fictionalise their own world, Jenkins remaining steadfastly in charge of the narrative. The recruiter who addresses the villagers at the beginning of the novel is of dubious literacy, for all of his pretensions. His relationship to English paper, or English letters, is comic and squalid. The official document authorising his role as recruiter is literally close to his head but metaphorically distant from it:

> Presently he took off his turban and slowly extracted therefrom an envelope, out of which he produced a piece of paper, well saturated with oil and other exuded matters, and browned by constant handling with dirty fingers. This he opened and proceeded to read with great solemnity, as he did so rolling round his eyes to mark its effect upon his hearers. It purported to be a declaration by a great personage, entitled "the Protector of Emigrants" at Calcutta, in the name of Her Majesty the Queen [...] [48]

Later in the novel, Jenkins dismisses some coolie complaints against the plantation as 'obviously ridiculous fictions.'[49] In *The Coolie: His Rights and Wrongs*, Jenkins had made a similar charge against the Indian and Chinese labourers giving testimony before the Committee enquiring into their affairs. Their petitions are

> written on all sorts of paper – brown, straw, candle-box, cartridge, etc., one on a tiny slip of scarlet torn off a wall or cut from a book [...] Asiatic ingenuity and craft were sometimes plainly written between the lines, and although some of them may have been based on facts, the Commissioners found on testing them that many were built upon fiction.[50]

Jenkins' accusation is that they 'enhance the effects of their narrations'[51] by colouring and dramatising their grievances, but is this not what Jenkins himself is doing in his own ways in writing his novel? The fact is that the coolies were *writing* for the first time, thus authorising their lives. If they fictionalised their lives, it was an attempt to give such lives the kind of psychological nuance and depth and drama that Jenkins declared to be his intent in writing the novel. Jenkins however will not give credence to their 'narrations,' much less space in their novel for their expression. *His* is the masterscript. *He* writes of and for them. They remain indentured to his authorial voice.[52] It is deeply ironical then to learn that Jenkins' novel was soon forgotten and Jenkins himself written out of the history of Victorian literature. The only aspect of him which survives in the English language is the word 'jinx', from *Ginx's Baby*, but even this fact has been hitherto unrecorded by etymologists.[53] As a descendent of one of Jenkins' indentured coolies it is now my curious privilege to make this fact known, to recover his voice and to bring him once more into print, into the life of English letters.

David Dabydeen
Centre for Caribbean Studies
University of Warwick

NOTES TO INTRODUCTION

1   D. Dabydeen and B. Samaroo, eds., *Across the Dark Waters. Ethnicity and Indian Identity in the Caribbean* (London: Macmillan, 1996), p. 1.

2   D. Dabydeen and B. Samaroo, eds., *India in the Caribbean* (London, Hansib, 1987), p. 25.

3   C. Seecharan, *'Tiger in the Stars': The Anatomy of Indian Achievement in British Guiana 1919–1929* (London: Macmillan, 1997), p. 6.

4   Dabydeen and Samaroo, *Across the Dark Waters,* pp. 3–4.

5   D. Dabydeen, *The Counting House* (London: Jonathan Cape, 1996), p. 4.

6   Seecharan, *'Tiger in the Stars'*, p. 31.

7   Dabydeen and Samaroo, *India in the Caribbean,* p. 30.

8   F. Birbalsingh, ed., *Indo-Caribbean Resistance* (Toronto: Tsar, 1993), p. 46.

9   Dabydeen and Samaroo, *India in the Caribbean,* p. 124.

10 Dabydeen and Samaroo, *Across the Dark Waters,* p. 32.

11 Henry Kirke, *Twenty Five Years in British Guiana* (London: Sampson Low, Marson & Co. Ltd., 1898), p. 212.

12 J. Poynting, 'John Edward Jenkins and the Imperial Conscience', in *Journal of Commonwealth Literature,* Vol. 21, No. 1, 1986, p. 211.

13 A. P. Stewart and Edward Jenkins, *The Medical and Legal Aspect of Sanitary Reform* (Leicester, Leicester University Press, 1969), p. 21.

14 Stewart and Jenkins, *op. cit.,* p. 80.

15 Edward Jenkins, ed., *Discussions on Colonial Questions* (London, 1872), p. 8.

16 Edward Jenkins, *Glances at Inner England* (London, 1874), pp. 75 ff.

17 A. P. Stewart and Edward Jenkins, *op. cit.*, pp. 82–83.

18 *Dictionary of National Biography,* 1910.

19 G. C. Kinnane, 'A Popular Victorian Satire: *Ginx's Baby* and its Reception', in *Notes and Queries,* Vol. 22 (1975), pp. 116–7.

20 Brian Maidment, 'What Shall We Do With The Starving Baby? – Edward Jenkins And *Ginx's Baby'*, in *Literature and History,* Vol. 6, No. 2 (1980), p. 163.

21 Edward Jenkins, *The Coolie: His Rights and Wrongs* (London, Strahan & Co. 1871), p. 15.

22 Jenkins, *The Coolie: His Rights and Wrongs*, p. 9.

23 Jenkins, *The Coolie: His Rights and Wrongs*, p. 12. The Chinese presence in the Caribbean is a greatly neglected subject in Caribbean scholarship. See W. Look Lai, *The Chinese in the West Indies 1806–1895* (Mona, Jamaica: UWI Press, 1998).

24 Jenkins, *The Coolie: His Rights and Wrongs,* p. 21.

25 Jenkins, *The Coolie: His Rights and Wrongs*, p. 23.

26 Jenkins, *The Coolie: His Rights and Wrongs*, p. 26.

27 Jenkins, *The Coolie: His Rights and Wrongs*, p. 51.

28 Jenkins, *The Coolie: His Rights and Wrongs*, p. 27.

29 Brian Maidment, 'Victorian Publishing and Social Criticism: The Case of Edward Jenkins', in *Publishing History,* Vol. XI (1982), p. 42.

30 Maidment, 'Victorian Publishing', p. 46.

31 'West Indian', *The Coolie in Demerara* (London, 1871), p. 5.

32 'West Indian', *The Coolie in Demerara*, p. 15.

33 'West Indian', *The Coolie in Demerara*, p. 16.

34 'West Indian', *The Coolie in Demerara*, p. 24.

35 'West Indian', *The Coolie in Demerara*, p. 26.

36 'West Indian', *The Coolie in Demerara*, p. 27.

37 'West Indian', *The Coolie in Demerara*, pp 21–22. For Jenkins' sensitivity to literary criticism, see Brian Maidment, 'What Shall We Do With The Starving Baby?', p. 161.

38 Edward Jenkins, *Lutchmee and Dilloo* (3 vols., London, William Mullan & Son, 1877), I, x (this edition, pp. 29–30).

39 See Jeremy Poynting, *op. cit.,* p. 214.

40 Clem Seecharan, *India and the Shaping of the Indo-Guyanese Imagination* (Leeds: Peepal Tree Press, 1993), p. 14.

41 *Lutchmee and Dilloo*, III, 275–276 (this edition, p. 331).

42 *Lutchmee and Dilloo*, II, 70–71 (this edition, pp. 155–6).

43 *Lutchmee and Dilloo*, I, 265–6 (this edition, p. 128).

44 *Lutchmee and Dilloo*, I, 101 (this edition, p. 69).

45 Jenkins, *Discussions on Colonial Questions,* p. 8.

46 Jenkins, *The Coolie: His Rights and Wrongs,* p. 243.

47 *Lutchmee and Dilloo*, II, 10 (this edition, p. 134).

48 *Lutchmee and Dilloo*, I, 21–2 (this edition, p. 39).

49 *Lutchmee and Dilloo*, I, 138 (this edition, p. 83).

50 Jenkins, *The Coolie: His Rights and Wrongs,* p. 149.

51 Jenkins, *The Coolie: His Rights and Wrongs,* p. 153.

[52] The two drawings reproduced in *The Coolie: His Rights and Wrongs* are woodcuts made by a Chinese artist. Jenkins will allow the coolie to sketch out but not *write* or articulate in words his/her story, the pictures being immediate, simple, lacking intellectual depth and subtlety, overstated.

[53] The *Oxford English Dictionary* gives an early twentieth-century American usage for 'jinx', but is unaware of the fact that there were at least five pirated American editions of *Ginx's Baby* by 1876. See G. C. Kinnane, *op. cit.*, pp. 116–117.

Although vastly popular for many years, *Ginx's Baby* eventually went out of print and was forgotten. Jenkins himself suffered a waning of popularity and his subsequent novels never achieved the same success. He turned to politics and journalism, becoming M. P. for Dundee between 1874 and 1880, and editor of the *Overland Mail* and *Homeward Mail* from 1886 onwards. He died, a relatively neglected figure, in 1910.

SELECT BIBLIOGRAPHY

Adamson, A. H., *Sugar Without Slaves*, (New Haven: Yale University Press, 1972).

Birbalsingh, F., ed., *Indo-Caribbean Resistance* (Toronto: Tsar, 1993).

Bronkhurst, H. V. P., *The Origin of the Guyanian Indians* (Georgetown: The Colonist Press, 1881).

Dabydeen, D., *The Counting House* (London: Jonathan Cape, 1996).

Dabydeen, D., and B. Samaroo, eds., *India in the Caribbean* (London: Hansib, 1987).

Dabydeen, D., and B. Samaroo, eds., *Across the Dark Waters. Ethnicity and Indian Identity in the Caribbean* (London: Macmillan, 1996).

Hamilton, B., *Barbados and the Confederation Question, 1871–1885* (London: Crown Agents, for the Government of Barbados, 1956).

Jagan, C., *The West on Trial* (London: Michael Joseph, 1966).

Jenkins, Edward, *The Coolie: His Rights and Wrongs* (London: Strahan & Co. 1871).

Jenkins, Edward, ed., *Discussions on Colonial Questions* (London, 1872).

Jenkins, Edward, *Glances at Inner England* (London, 1874).

Jenkins, Edward, *Lutchmee and Dilloo: A Study of West Indian Life* (3 vols., London and Belfast: William Mullan & Son, 1877).

Kinnane, G. C., 'A Popular Victorian Satire: *Ginx's Baby* and its Reception', in *Notes and Queries*, Vol. 22 (1975), pp. 116–117.

Kirke, Henry, *Twenty Five Years in British Guiana* (London: Sampson Low, Marson & Co. Ltd., 1898).

Klass, M., *East Indians in Trinidad* (New York: Colombia University Press, 1961).

La Guerre, J., ed., *Calcutta to Caroni* (2nd ed., St. Augustine, Trinidad: University of the West Indies, 1993).

Look Lai, W., *Indentured Labour, Caribbean Sugar: Chinese and Indian Immigrants to the British West Indies, 1838–1918* (Baltimore: Johns Hopkins University Press, 1993).

Maidment, Brian, 'What Shall We Do With The Starving Baby? – Edward Jenkins And *Ginx's Baby*', in *Literature and History*, Vol. 6, No. 2 (1980).

——————, 'Victorian Publishing and Social Criticism: The Case of Edward Jenkins', in *Publishing History*, Vol. XI (1982).

Mangru, B., *Benevolent Neutrality: Indian Government policy and labour migration to British Guiana* (London, Hansib, 1987).

Poynting, J., 'John Edward Jenkins and the Imperial Conscience', in *Journal of Commonwealth Literature*, Vol. 21, No. 1 (1986).

Rodney, W., *A History of the Guyanese Working People* (Baltimore, Johns Hopkins University Press, 1981).

Seecharan, Clem, *India and the Shaping of the Indo-Guyanese Imagination* (Leeds, Peepal Tree Press, 1993).

Seecharan, Clem, *'Tiger in the Stars': The Anatomy of Indian Achievement in British Guiana 1919–1929* (London: Macmillan, 1997).

Seecharan, Clem, *Bechu: 'Bound Coolie' Radical in British Guiana 1894–1901* (Mona, Jamaica: The University of the West Indies Press, 1999).

Scoles, Ignatius, *Sketches of African and Indian Life in British Guiana* (Georgetown: The Argosy Press, 1885).

Stephen, Leslie, and Sidney Lee, ed., *The Dictionary of National Biography* (63 vols., London, 1885–1900, with later editions and supplements).

Stewart, A.P., and Edward Jenkins, *The Medical and Legal Aspect of Sanitary Reform* (Leicester: Leicester University Press, 1969)

Tinker, H., *A New System of Slavery: The Export of Indian Labour Overseas, 1830–1920* (London: Oxford University Press, 1974).

Vertovec, S., *Hindu Trinidad* (London, Macmillan, 1992).

'West Indian', *The Coolie in Demerara* (London, 1871).

Yule, H., and A. C. Burnell, *Hobson Jobson: The Anglo-Indian Dictionary* (first published 1886; facsimile reprint of 1902 second edition, Ware, Hertfordshire: Wordsworth Reference, 1996).

LUTCHMEE AND DILLOO

A STUDY OF WEST INDIAN LIFE

BY

EDWARD JENKINS

PREFACE

IN my account of the results of the Commission of Inquiry in British Guiana, entitled 'The Coolie: his Rights and Wrongs,' I tried to inform the English public of the gravity of the issues that arose in that inquiry. Flattering as was the reception of that book by the critics, the public little cared to read it. However impartial or exact I had striven to be, it was no wonder that a statement which the desire to be just very likely made too long and detailed should fail to attract popular attention, or to arouse popular sympathies. Not to speak of the natural dryness of the subject, the character of the wrongs complained of was rather practical than sensational – arose rather out of a permanent process of treatment than from extraordinary outrages, or more often from incompatible relations than from direct collisions between the planters and their Coolies. Meantime I have waited, hoping that those in power whose consciences have been made alive to the necessity of action, *would act* promptly and effectively.

But now I feel the subject to be altogether too important to let it sleep. Another Royal Commission has inquired and reported at prodigious length about the system of Indian indenture in the greatest of the Coolie colonies, and has exposed a state of things in the Mauritius which may well startle the Colonial Minister, and excite the alarm and watchfulness of the British people. What right have we hotly to discuss slave circulars, and the inviolability of our ships of war as refuges for foreign slaves, or to proclaim our sympathies with Bosnian rayahs or Bulgarian Christians, until our own Mauritius and British Guiana are swept clean and garnished?

These vast blue-books issued by Parliament often entomb and hide away from public eyes the injuries of Government. I am going to try in this tale to disinter the real wrongs and difficulties, and to present them in an appreciable form to those who are ultimately responsible for British honour and British fame – I mean the British people.

I have long since expressed the opinion that a Coolie system, under proper supervision and restraint, could be made a system of incalculable benefit to Asiatics. But the sole condition on which we can allow it to exist within our dominions is that our Government shall exercise over it, in its inception and continuance, ceaseless watchfulness and most rigid control. One need hardly insist that we can only insure justice now-a-days by ourselves watching the Government. The worst of the whole matter is that officials seem always to be convinced of the satisfactory nature of an argument when it can be shown that any pecuniary loss or benefit to Englishmen depends upon it. It is only occasionally that we get at the head of an office like the Colonial Office a Carnarvon, who unites a conscience and a heart with a clear head and a firm will. I say this the more freely and cordially since the Minister concerned works with a party with which I have no association.

There is the greater need for vigilance in the present case, because a body of merchants enriched by the labour of the people whose life I have here faithfully depicted, are organized, astute and powerful in the defence of their interests. I do not assail them for that. They are exercising an undoubted right, many of them conscientiously. I simply call the fact to mind, to show how necessary it is that philanthropy should be equally organized, watchful and astute on the other side.

It therefore occurred to me that I might try to throw the problems of Coolie labour in our Colonies into a concrete and picturesque form. The life of a Coolie man or woman, with its simple incidents, its petty cares and vexations, its occasional events of terror or sorrow, and all the various feelings, sentiments, and impulses that sway an existence passed amidst the relations of a bond-service, these and their peculiar influences on the higher and more cultivated race, do not at first sight present an attractive ground for fiction. Besides, the subjects and interests seem to be too remote. But happily the ties of universal brotherhood are ever drawing men more closely together. The sorrows of Dilloo or Lutchmee are the sorrows of humanity, differing only in their conditions and their relations from the tragedies of our own homes.

I have endeavoured in these pages to reproduce with exact fidelity the picture of a Coolie's life. Thus I thought I could more clearly show what are the difficulties and perils of the system of indentureship of Indian and Chinese immigrants in English colonies. Even should I fail from the artist's point of view, which it is to be hoped is not a necessity, I may yet enable many persons to understand the subject better, and that must lead to a more earnest consideration of the questions it involves.

One word of explanation is necessary as to the details of the story. Though it contains no fact which could not be verified in some Coolie-worked colony under the British flag, I wish it to be understood that I do not credit British Guiana with all the evils here represented. I have not in any instance, unless I say so, drawn a character from life, nor have I described under another name any particular scene or estate. My object has been rather to embody many aspects of character and varieties of incident, the more picturesquely to bring out the lights and shadows of the system. I was obliged to select some colony as the scene of the tale, and naturally selected the one with which I was familiar. But upon this scene will be presented phases of the question which are only to be found in other colonies.

To give greater variety and reality to the tale, to display the system fairly in its proper setting, and above all to make the story a wider and therefore, I hope, a more interesting study of human life, I have not confined its incidents to one race, but have brought into view the whole of that strange mixture which constitutes West Indian society, from the Queen's representative to the African Creole.

The field is a new one for fiction, but human nature still bears out the wisdom of the poet who declared that it does not change with clime. The loves, the hopes, the envies, jealousies and fears, the superstitions, the mutual wrongs, the goodness and wicked-ness of the human heart, bloom everywhere with similar blos-soms, developing into the same fruits of life or death, of sorrow or of joy.

LUTCHMEE AND DILLOO

CHAPTER I

A RUDE SURPRISE

Down behind the far-off western hills the flaming sun had dipped
gently, and while their bluish outlines were emblazoned with a
fringe of fire, a soft, misty glory hovered over the Bengal landscape to the eastward. A few minutes sufficed to deepen the
lustrous cloudiness into denser shades, and ere long the pall of
night was rapidly drooping down upon the scene. In the glooming
air began to flash frequent and bright the restless gleams of the
fire-flies; through the silence sounded far and clear the late croak-
ings of some unsettled crows, or the sharp shriek of a kite; and now
a jackal in the neighbouring jungle, or the pariah dogs in the
village, shrieked or barked a welcome to the incoming night.

Half-reclining on the grass-grown slope of a tank, whence, with
her face towards the setting sun, she had been gazing at the mist-
veiled rim of the vast sleepy orb as it sank into the lap of night, was
a young Indian girl, whose loose white robe and jacket of coloured
cotton scarcely hid one line of the delicate mould of her form,
displayed, as it was, by the *abandon* of her posture, in all its grace,
litheness and perfection. The long hair from which she had been
but lately wringing the water, wherewith her pretty play in the
tank had saturated it, hung black and dishevelled from the
symmetrical head, leaving her light-brown oval face, with its
regular eyes, arched eyebrows, delicately-chiselled nostrils and
well-turned mouth and chin, in fine relief as they were irradiated
by the parting glow of the sun. She seemed half-dreaming – a
pleasant dream; for now and then a sly movement in her eyes,
which, in cunning changes, flashed with dark fire or became
gentle as a summer lake, betokened some lively or genial thought.
So she lay, reclining on her elbows; joy-lit and dreamy, unconscious of the rapidity with which the shades were deepening

round her, unaware of two flashing eyes that were fixed upon her from the shadow of a small palm-grove, not twenty yards away.

Presently she began, in a low, sweet monotone, to sing a simple ditty, rather a rude and free paraphrase of a passage in the *Gitagovinda*:–

> 'Gentle, sandal-scented air,
>   Blowing love-sighs from the south;
> To my open bosom bear
>   Aëry kisses from his mouth.
>
> Yet oh give me more than this is!
>   Bring him to me face to face,
> Let me feel his burning kisses,
>   And sweetly die in his embrace!'

As in soft, listless cadence the song rose and fell, the fiery eyes in the tope grew more bright, and presently a black shadow glided stealthily towards the singer, until it stood behind her, looking down on her unwary figure. It was the form of a tall, powerfully-built man, of extreme darkness of skin, with a shaggy head of hair and a moustache and beard that added their bristly terrors to a face naturally ugly and deeply pitted with small-pox. Large plain rings of gold decorated his big ears. He wore simply a 'dhotee,' or loin-cloth, with a short coat thrown over his shoulders and buttoned at the neck.

As the girl ended her song, the man, stooping quickly, pinioned the arms on which she supported herself, and then, leaning over her, pressed his rude lips against her smooth forehead. Loud and long was the shriek that startled the night; but he was not disconcerted

'Lutchmee,' he said, in a deep guttural voice, whilst his features were twisted into the caricature of a smile, 'why are you here so late? Has Dilloo deserted you for Putea? I thought he never left you alone. How long have I watched for such an opportunity as this! The sun is down, the fireflies are flashing in the air, and the bark of the jackal is angry in the jungle. Do you not hear? Ah! Were you waiting and singing for me? Did you linger here to tell me you would at last change your mind, and be more friendly to me?'

Reference to mythology

Perhaps this foolish hope had really passed through the satyr's thoughts, for his eye grew softer as he spoke, and he relaxed his grip upon the delicate arms. The answer to his address was a sudden and violent jerk of the girl's head into his face and the slipping of the two soft arms from his fingers, as his prey sprang to her feet, and, with another loud shriek, darted away. The blood came from the ruffian's nostrils, and he was for a moment confused; then rapidly wiping away the red drops on the sleeve of his jacket, he pursued, with an oath, the flying elf. She would have escaped him in the dusk, for the village was not far away, had not the surprise unnerved her, but, mistaking her steps, she suddenly tripped over a clump of grass, and came with violence to the ground. There she lay senseless. The man, who could just distinguish her as he came up, kicked her over with his foot in the madness of his fury, until her pretty little face was turned upward to the sky. Then, with a muttered curse, lifting his heel, he was about to dash it into the delicate features, when a very respectable blow on the side of the head sent him bleeding to the earth. This blow was delivered with the aid of a long smooth stick, by a young fellow of moderate height, but, for a Hindoo, of unusually fine development. He immediately stooped down, and endeavoured, in the gloom, to examine the young girl's face. Then he wrung his hands and broke out in reproaches on the groaning foe. Then he rose, and taking his stick, played it with remarkable vehemence and skill all over that person's body. Again he knelt beside Lutchmee, and placing his hand on her heart and his ear over her mouth, waited for tokens of life. In a short time she began to respire, then to recover, and, at length, she sat up.

'Lutchmee, Lutchmee!' said the young man; 'wake up! I am here. It is Dilloo!'

'Oh, Dilloo!' sobbed the girl, putting her arms round his neck, 'is it you? I have had such a frightful dream. I thought that wicked creature Hunoomaun laid hold of me at the tank: then I got clear of him, and ran away, but while I was running, I tripped and fell down. Oh, I was sure he had me at last!'

'It was not a dream, Lutchmee: 'twas well I heard you scream, my darling, I can tell you. Look there! do you see that dark heap?

That is Hunoomaun. I came upon him just in time to save you, and I have drubbed him well with my stick. Do you not hear him groaning? That's fine music, my good fellow!' cried he to the peon. 'I'm glad, my Lutchmee, I came up when I did, or your pretty face would have lost its beauty for ever.'

'But oh, Dilloo,' she said, clinging to him, 'what will he do to you? He will kill you. Let us go away.'

'No fear,' said the sturdy Dilloo: 'he is a big fellow, 'tis true, but an arrant coward. Get up, you bully,' added he, giving his prostrate antagonist a kick: 'get up, and be off with you to Rumcoary or Noonda; they are the sort for you. And listen to me: if ever you come frightening the wife of Dilloo again, I'll finish you with a knife, and not let you off with a beating. You know I always do what I say. Come, my Lutchmee, let us go.'

The manly fellow wreathed his arm round the supple waist of his wife, and, half-supporting, half-fondling her, led their way to the village. The baffled ruffian followed as best he could, dragging his stiffening limbs, and vowing a frightful vengeance on the young pair.

CHAPTER II

THE WATCHMAN

OF the Bengal village in Behar, where the hero and heroine of our story were born and had lived, the only other character yet presented to the reader, Hunoomaun, was the 'chokedar,' or watchman; a character, at the time we are writing of, found all over Bengal. The chokedars were not Government police. To them, under the old village system, were assigned, on behalf of the community, the general oversight of the precincts. They were paid by a local rate, or sometimes by the principal zemindar. These officials were of a low order, both of caste and of merit, and their most active occupation consisted in winking at the operations of the rural dacoits (or robbers), and in lending themselves to the corrupt designs of one villager or village family upon another. Hunoomaun was a chokedar of more than usual ability; as avaricious, sensual and dishonest as any Indian in the province. Prowling about the village at night, on the pretences of his duty, he had innumerable opportunities of gratifying his envy or his passion; and his remarkable cunning, and the invariable retribution that fell upon any persons who in any way crossed him, had created a very real dread of him through the whole community.

Dilloo was a tenant, under one of the zemindars, of a very small plot of ground, on which there stood a hut of mud and wattle, which Lutchmee kept in beautiful order; while her husband tilled the ground with an assiduity that secured a very fair return. K——— contained about four thousand inhabitants within its bounds. It was near one of the largest villages in the district, which, as a convenient centre of a very populous portion of Behar, had been selected as the head-quarters of a deputy magistrate; in this instance, a European. The vicinity of this magistrate, with his sub-officials, the darogah, jemmadars and burcandazes, rendered Hunoomaun's office extremely unnecessary, and, indeed, exercised over him a somewhat wholesome restraint, while it made him more cunning and cautious in his proceedings. He had many times looked with an evil eye at the bright, lissome young wife of the ryot; and, with the confidence of a villanous experience, had again and again attempted to get her into his power. But her husband, Dilloo, was a formidable obstacle; he happened to be very fond of her: and he was a fine, strong, ready young fellow, with a taste for athletics and adventure. In his village he was regarded with a certain respect. His performance on the crowns of venturesome rivals in the favourite exercise with the long *lattey*, or single stick, which had proved so fatal to the chokedar's designs, were famous over the whole plain, among villages where not a few skilful players with the same weapon were to be found. In wrestling no one could excel him. His thrift and industry had given him a respectable position. Altogether, therefore, Dilloo was a man, as Hunoomaun felt, not to be openly fought; and he had accordingly been very cautious in pursuing his infatuated fancy for Lutchmee.

Lutchmee and Dilloo had, by the conventional arrangement between their parents, been betrothed before they knew what love was, or, indeed, before they had ever seen one another. But in this instance, when at twelve years of age the pretty girl was married to the boy of seventeen, the mutual liking that had before sprung up between them grew into a genuine and pure affection. It could hardly be otherwise. Both of them of unusually handsome make, of open dispositions and simple hearts, they seemed to have been fitted by nature for each other's company. Lutchmee almost idolised her strong, active husband: he dwelt with constant pride on his wife's beauty, her obedience, her humility, her love and attention. There are many Englishmen with the improved modern wife who will be inclined to envy the idyllic charm of this old-fashioned simplicity of things. But as for Dilloo, he, a man of low caste, had, without his own choice, been fortunate enough to attain that which, by the ordinances of Menu, the sacred acolyte was instructed to seek.

'Let him choose for his wife a girl whose form has no defect; who has an agreeable name; who walks gracefully, like the pheni-copteros, or like a young elephant; whose hair and teeth are moderate respectively in quantity and in size; whose body has an exquisite softness.'

When, on a gala day, Lutchmee's hair was oiled and braided, shining with a silver pin athwart her well-formed head, and her body, duly anointed, was clothed in a short-armed, slight cholee or jacket, of bright silk, a petticoat of calico, and over all, co-quettishly wreathed, a white muslin chudder, the scarf of Hindoo women; and her ears were laden with silver rings, and her arms and ankles tinkled with bracelets and bangles of the same metal; as she walked with the gentle lissome motion of refined indolence, the phenicopteros or the young elephant could hardly have excelled her in grace, and, but for her caste, she might have satisfied the most bigoted disciple of the great lawgiver. Dilloo was proud of his wife, and Lutchmee was proud of her husband – conditions such as may, even in India, bear fruits of happiness. This happiness had been alloyed by the death of Lutchmee's only child a few weeks after its birth, and by the occasional unpleasantness to which the young wife's attractive beauty exposed her, from Europeans and from men of her own race.

Hunoomaun had been the most persistent, as he was by all odds the most disagreeable of all her admirers. Her detestation of him was extreme. He had annoyed her now and again with stupid compliments, and had surprised her into interviews which, for the sake of peace, and to save the fellow's life, she had hidden from her husband. But the chokedar had never so far committed him-self as in the scene we have related, and probably would not then have gone so far but for a dose of arrack with which he had fortified his courage. Hitherto Hunoomaun had carefully shirked a collision with the husband of the girl whose beauty had so wrought upon him. The first occasion was a discouraging one. But he knew well how to revenge himself.

Dilloo soon began to know something of the watchman's resentment. His fowls disappeared, his rice was trampled and destroyed. One night there was a dacoity* in his house, evidently managed with great skill, by which he lost part of his savings. Strong as were his suspicions, he could not bring home these crimes to the chokedar, and he dared not act upon them without confirmation.

*Robbery.

CHAPTER III

THE RECRUITER

NOT long after the events we have narrated, there one day arrived in the village of K—— a stranger, a Bengalee, arrayed, save as to his turban and paejamas, in an imitation of a European uniform. Across his shoulder and body on a belt he wore the chuprass, the badge of official employment. He had the air of a man shrewd and travelled. There was a touch of town-culture about him, and when he began to talk, as he very soon did with the ease of one to whom that was a vocation, he spoke with extreme hyperbolism even for an Asiatic. It was not long before he was sitting in an open space in the middle of the village, surrounded by a group of curious natives. Could it be possible that this was their old friend the pilgrim-hunter from Jaganath, adopted for some fresh purpose of State by a paternal Government, and turning up here in a new guise? Hitherto, from their somewhat sequestered situation, such a visitor as the present had never been known to these villagers.

He had taken his seat with great dignity, and now calmly surveyed the gathering audience, which sought to penetrate him with its keen glances. Presently he took off his turban and slowly extracted therefrom an envelope, out of which he produced a piece of paper, well saturated with oil and other exuded matters, and browned by constant handling with dirty fingers. This he opened and proceeded to read with great solemnity, as he did so rolling round his eyes to mark its effect upon his hearers. It purported to be a declaration by a great personage, entitled 'the Protector of Emigrants' at Calcutta, in the name of Her Majesty the Queen and by authority of the Government of India informing all mankind that Dost Mahommed, the bearer – who bowed to his own name with deep respect – was, by the aforesaid Majesty and august Government, duly licensed to seek for and recruit in the district of B———, persons who were willing to emigrate as labourers to other parts of Her Majesty's dominions; that is to say, to British Guiana, or Trinidad, or Jamaica, etc., etc. This license, moreover, as he showed them with many flourishes of the paper, had that day been countersigned by the resident, Reginald Howard Walter Wood, Sahib, not unknown by disagreeable personal experience to some of those now listening to him. When he had concluded the reading, the traveller demonstratively folded up the document, placed it in its envelope, restored it to the fold of his turban, and sat silent, with the air of a man who deserved well of his kind. Hindoos are courteous. They admire one who has a good estimate of himself: they hesitate to break the illusion. So there was a pause.

Among those who had gathered to see and hear the traveller, and had listened to his recital with interest, was Dilloo. He manifested, with those around him, wonder as to the meaning of this mysterious document, and anxiety to hear it explained. But due time must be allowed to the stranger, who meantime sat silent, in order to give to curiosity a stronger incentive. At length an ancient Brahmin of the village, who sat by, opened his mouth:–

'O Baboo,' said he, 'we have heard with interest your recital of that long and grave document, by which we learn that you are a messenger of the great Queen and the most august Government at Calcutta! I gather from it that you are directed to go about the country in quest of men and women who may be inclined to take the risk of leaving the land of their birth and the society of their own people to be carried over mountains, rivers and seas, and to labour for Englishmen in far-off parts of the world, as they do in the Indigo districts. Can this be so? Wherefore should you, a Bengalee, be found helping to persuade your people to desert their own land, and engage in adventures they know not how perilous, and the end of which they cannot foresee?'

'Ah, you are right, sir! But, listen, O friends!' said the wily Dost Mahommed, taking off his turban again, and reproducing the dirty envelope, which he held between his thumb and finger high in air. 'This is the command of the great Queen to me, Dost Mahommed, one of the meanest of her servants, to travel about and inform my countrymen of inestimable benefits, boundless riches, and unalloyed happiness which await them, if they like to seek them, in other parts of her wide dominions. It is my duty to tell you, by authority of the Queen and Government of India, that it is open to any one who hears me to become as rich as a zemindar. Is everything so golden here that you should not do like the English themselves – take your journeys in search of riches and happiness? Look around you! You see how poor millions of our Indian people are! Everywhere the fields are small, the wages are low; everywhere the land is crowded with people – too many mouths and too little money; too many taxes, too much government. Most of you have hard work, bad food, and very little of it. Look at your clothes! I see some of you only with a coarse dhotee: you are obliged, many of you, to be content with the meanest garments. You see me! I am dressed like an Englishman: I wear good quality paejamas and a European coat. You may, if you like, every one of you, do the same!'

A delighted buzz came from the throng as this dazzling prospect was held out to them. It must be true, they thought, for there was the chuprass on the breast of the speaker to vouch for it! Dost Mahommed pursued his advantage, and condescended to particulars.

'All this you may have, and much more, in lands where the sun is warm like the sun of Bengal, and the water is plentiful and pure like the streams and tanks of India, and the earth is richer and more productive than ours; where the mango and banana, and breadfruit and rice, and sugarcane and cotton grow. Great English sahibs own these lands, and want labourers like you to cultivate them. They are rich and they are generous. There a man may get every day of his life as much or as little as he likes. The work is easy, like your own garden work, and for such labour a man or a woman can make easily from ten annas to two rupees' – he deliberately counted this extraordinary sum on his fingers as he uttered the magical promise – 'for every day's work. See: here is the proof!'

The crowd eagerly leaned forward to look at the paper which he now produced from the breast of his uniform. It was in English, but he gave a very free translation of it. Representations were thereby made that there was a great scarcity of labourers in the West Indies; that thither emigrants would be carried for nothing; would receive a bounty of one hundred rupees; would be indentured to kind masters; would get house-room for nothing; when sick would be admitted to an hospital, and there be provided with a doctor, medicines, and food free of charge. All this was vouched by the authority of the Governor and Legislature of British Guiana, and certified by a sahib at Calcutta, who dated from Garden Reach on the Hooghly.

It may easily be inferred what curiosity and surprise were awakened in the minds of the ignorant but subtle Indians by this story, afterwards embellished by many additional illustrations from the recounter's vivid fancy. The novelty of the proposal, the romantic halo which invested the unknown possibilities of such an enterprise as he suggested to them, the tempting bribes of a heavy bounty, easy work, plenty of food, and good wages, excited the imagination of the natives to a high pitch. The great sahib at Calcutta loomed up before their excited vision as a kind divinity, proffering to unworthy wretches entrance into a Paradise of labour. Yet there were not wanting in the crowd timid sceptics whose faith was apt to be regulated and restricted by sight, and who hinted at contingencies quite unworthy of the high authorities by whom these solemn statements were vouched.

'Bah!' said a shrewd vendor from the bazaar, with native sophistry: 'if the great sahibs were desirous to give us all these good things, would it not be cheaper to send them to us than to take us to them?'

The fickle crowd admiringly adopted the transparent fallacy, and looked to the recruiter for an answer. It came, however, straight and sharp, from Dilloo.

'Nonsense!' said he: 'Samânee knows he is talking like a fool. The baboo tells us we are offered work in a distant country at good wages. Does Samânee wish the Government to carry the country here, and drop it down in Behar?'

Dost Mahommed led the laugh which rewarded this refutation of Samânee's quibble. The tide turned again in favour of the recruiter. He, however, understood his business too well to press the matter any further at that time. He knew that he must do his work in detail, – in this following the example of his prototype the pilgrim-hunter. So he arose and announced that he proposed to spend the night in a neighbouring village, but that he would return next day to talk with any one who desired to ask him any questions.

Dilloo had listened to the man's words with peculiar interest. The natural energy of his character, his taste for adventure, and his imagination were all appealed to by the recruiter's language. Here seemed to be an opening for a new and prosperous life. His relations with Hunoomaun, now his sworn enemy, were likely to render his life in the village unpleasant, even if it were not dangerous. A man in the chokedar's position in India has so many ways of working out his vengeance and forgiveness is not a Hindoo virtue.

No wonder Dilloo's brain was on fire as he extricated himself from the crowd, and slowly paced in the direction of his home.

CHAPTER IV

A LONG FAREWELL

WHEN, the next day, Dost Mahommed came back to the village, Dilloo was among the first to seek him out. Again the recruiter expatiated on the promises of the Government, the bounty-money of fifty dollars, the high wages, the free medical care, the light work. He said nothing – indeed probably had not himself been told – of fever-swamps, of liabilities, under rigid laws, to fines and imprisonments for breaches of the proposed contract, of labour in crop time for as long as twenty, twenty-five, or thirty hours at a stretch, and sometimes without extra pay – a not universal, but frequent incident of a Coolie's life in the West Indies. Dilloo's mind was gradually won over, and the only remaining doubt was concerning his wife. 'Could she go?'

Oh, yes; the recruiter was only too anxious to procure women. They were in great demand. She should have the same bounty and the same wages as he.

But on consideration, Dilloo began to doubt whether he ought to entertain this kind offer. He loved his wife too well rashly to permit her to share what he felt by instinct to be an uncertain experiment; and he was perplexed between his own desire to venture it, and the perils to which she would be exposed were his protection withdrawn from her. This difficulty was, however, a few days afterwards removed. Mrs. Wood, the wife of the deputy-magistrate, happened to require a maid, and being rather particular, had caused considerable inquiry to be made for the sort of person she wanted. Dilloo took his wife to the magistrate's bungalow at T——. The lady was at once struck with Lutchmee's cleanliness and good looks, and offered to engage her. Dilloo, like most impetuous men, too readily satisfied with temporary solutions, considered that this sufficiently ensured his wife's safety, and urged her to accept the offer. She, while her heart trembled with painful forebodings, was too lovingly obedient to her husband's will to question his desires.

When the day of parting came, Dilloo held Lutchmee in his arms a long while. They could scarcely speak. The pangs of an adieu amongst ourselves are keen enough, but they are mitigated by the knowledge that intercourse is easy and information certain, however far in space hearts may be sundered. What, then, to our young lovers must have been the moment of separation which rested no hopes on certainties or possibilities of communication, which knew only that years must elapse before they could meet again, and that perhaps from parting to meeting no single message could pass between them?

'Lutchmee!' said the young man, 'I go away, thinking of you only. I will love you faithfully all the time I am away. I am promised that in a few years* I shall be able to return with all the money I have made, and then you and I will be well off. We shall be still young, and can spend our lives in prosperity and happiness.'

'Ah, Dilloo!' said the girl, with a sob, 'how much this is to pay for a hope: is it not?'

Then, feeling that this was half a complaint, and ashamed to raise a doubt which might, at so sore a moment, begloom her husband's heart, she checked herself, and tried to smile.

'I shall be as happy as I can,' said she; 'and the time will run quickly when I think of you. And you will not be afraid that I shall not continue to love you, will you?'

A tender pressure to his heart was the pledge of Dilloo's trust.

'Do your best,' said he, 'to win the good-will of the Mem-sahib; and if Hunoomaun tries any more tricks with you, go at once to her and ask her to protect you. These English are sometimes cruel and harsh themselves, but they won't allow Hindoos to commit

---

* The promise authorized by the Government is ten years; but it is not the re-cruiter's cue to be too specific in his representations. That this is not an exaggeration is proved by the fact that an order issued to the Indian magistrates to be careful to explain the exact incidents of the contract seriously diminished the immigration to the West Indies, and led to a protest from the planters of British Guiana.

injustice. Be very wary of that rascal. Never go out alone, if you can help it: always go to the tank in the morning in company with the other women. It is well he does not live in the village with you.'

Thus in simple talk these simple hearts prepared for a parting to them so appalling; and at length, with manly tenderness on the one side and tearful struggles for fortitude on the other, they bade each other farewell.

CHAPTER V

A NARROW ESCAPE

NEARLY two years have passed since Dilloo's departure. From the recruiter, when he returned next year to the district, Mr. Wood, whose wife had taken a fancy for Lutchmee, learned that her husband had sailed in good health, within three weeks of their parting. The graceless Dost Mahommed elaborated a fabulous message from the emigrant, descriptive of his well-being, his happiness, and his bright assurances of success, concluding with a hope that it might be possible for Lutchmee to join him in a year or two, should she not hear from him to the contrary. This message was joyfully received by Lutchmee, to be pondered and dreamed of with unceasing pleasure.

For more than a year Hunoomaun, seeing the young woman to be under the protection of the magistrate's wife, and, indeed, as he had, owing to the distance between the two villages, but slight opportunities of meeting with her, left her undisturbed. She rigorously attended to Dilloo's injunctions, and never went beyond the grounds, to tank or temple or bazaar, unless accompanied by some of her fellow-servants. At the time when we resume her history, one of those rumours that are periodically current in India, of a projected rising of the Mussulman population, had excited alarm among English residents. Mr. Wood was a brave man, and really gave no credit to the rumour, but he thought it right to appear to be on the alert, and appointed several of the most trustworthy Hindoo peons and burcandazes to act in turns as armed guards of his house at night. There were always plenty of these hanging about it by day. Among those selected from the neighbourhood was Hunoomaun, who had cleverly managed to give the magistrate the idea that he was a very trusty and effective fellow. At regular intervals he took his station during the night on

the verandah in front of the deputy's house, armed with a cutlass
and prepared to give warning to the more reliable force, consisting of Mr. Wood, his clerk, and an English servant, inside. In separate buildings were the justice-rooms, and there the Darogah
and some peons were stationed. The verandah covered in three
sides of the bungalow: on the right side were the reception-rooms;
on the other, those for sleeping and dressing. A lattice, pierced by
a door, shut off the verandah leading to the latter from the one in
front. Lutchmee preferred sleeping outside her mistress's room,
in the side verandah, and Mrs. Wood being attached to the girl,
and often needing her attendance in the night, made no objection
to it. The chokedar now had occasional opportunities of seeing
and addressing Lutchmee. He pretended to have a fancy for another of the women, and treated Lutchmee with distant courtesy.
He professed himself pained by her aversion, again and again begging her not to be afraid of him, to forget the past, and to believe
that he no longer entertained any evil designs against her. In this
way Lutchmee's apprehensions were gradually soothed, and she
allowed herself a little more freedom in her intercourse with the
man. When he was on guard, he would peer through the lattice at
the young girl as she disposed herself to sleep on the verandah;
but he dared not venture within, for he knew the magistrate's ear
was quick, and his revolver always ready. One night, however,
when it was his watch, after he had had recourse to his old
prompter arrack, his quick perception informed him that
Lutchmee was restless and awake, – he drew her by a gentle
whisper to the lattice.

'What is the matter?' he said: 'you do not sleep.'

'I have some foreboding,' replied the girl timidly. 'Did you hear
anything like a woman's cry a long way off? And just now I thought
I heard a rumbling as of carriages or of a troop of horse.'

Hunoomaun started, and listened attentively a full five minutes.

'No,' he said, 'it was some distant thunder, or the murmuring of
the heavy air over the house and through the trees; and the scream,
no doubt, was that of a paroquet or a monkey in the wood.'

'I cannot rest,' said Lutchmee, 'I am so frightened. It seems as if
some dreadful thing were going to happen. How hot the night is!'

'Come and sit down awhile and talk with me,' said the peon: 'it will make you sleep. You are quite safe,' he added, judging instinctively that she hesitated, though he could not see her face. 'Sahib and Mem-Sahib are close by, and can hear us.'

Lutchmee for the moment felt half ashamed of her suspicions, and slipping back the wooden bolt of the door, stepped out on the front verandah beside the dark shadow of the chokedar.

'See,' he said, 'we will go away from the Sahib, and sit on the seat at the end of the verandah until you get sleepy.'

As they took their way along the verandah, their shoeless feet passing silently over the smooth hard clay, Hunoomaun rapidly estimated the opportunities of the situation. Could he not carry her off? She was slight, and he was a powerful fellow. The thing he had so long desired seemed at length to be nigh, and yet so difficult of attainment. Unobserved by Lutchmee he had, in closing the lattice door, slipped the bolt back again with his finger. The front door opening on the verandah was, at that time, bolted. This verandah measured sixty feet from end to end, including the width of the two side verandahs: no one slept on the right or west side of the bungalow, which was also the farther side from the magisterial offices. In the middle of the verandah on that side there was an opening in the lattice, from which steps led to the compound towards a shrubbery. The rascal's plan was soon formed. He extended their walk from the front verandah as far as this outlet. Quietly placing his cutlass on a window-sill as he passed it, he unbound the puggery from his head, and, snatching Lutchmee's hand in his right, suddenly thrust the cloth over her face with his left, while he said in her ear, -

'Do not call out, or I will kill you.'

He thus stifled her first cry, and after a minute removed the cloth from her face. But poor Lutchmee was unable to call out. The suddenness of the attack and the deprival of air, had produced the effect which had probably been calculated on, for she fell flaccid and insensible into Hunoomaun's arms. Pressing her to his bosom, he was in the act of carrying his inanimate burden off to the shrubbery, from which he could have escaped towards his own house, when Mrs. Wood's voice was heard shrilly calling out the girl's name. A disturbance immediately followed, assisted by the bass voice of the magistrate. The ruffian was completely disconcerted. He was well aware of Mr. Wood's promptitude of action. If he carried the girl back he would probably be met by the magistrate, and his villany was certain to be exposed; if he left her where she was she would, on recovering, call up the household. While he hesitated, he heard Mr. Wood unfastening the door, and saw the flash of a candle; at the same moment his burden began to revive. There was no time to retrieve and use his cutlass, with which no doubt he would have revenged upon her his disappointment; so, venting an oath at his ill-luck, he flung her down with all his force, and darted away into the night. When the magistrate, whose quick eye had detected the guard's weapon, reached the place where Lutchmee lay groaning, he found her bleeding severely from a wound in the head, and with her shoulder dislocated. The peon was nowhere to be seen. After shouting for him in vain, and firing two chance shots in the direction of the shrubbery, the resident called his servants and proceeded to treat Lutchmee for her injuries. As soon as she was able to relate her story, Mr. Wood, satisfied of the chokedar's guilt, issued a warrant for his apprehension; but that wily Hindoo had already adjudicated on his own case and condemned himself to a period of exile.

As Lutchmee recovered from the illness consequent upon this adventure, her mind turned more and more to the absent Dilloo. She felt that there was for her no real safety away from him. Two years of patient resignedness might well have made her weary of the separation, and she recalled with increasingly glad recollections the terms of the fictitious message delivered by the recruiter. At length she decided to make a bold venture and follow her husband. The kind dissuasions of the magistrate and his wife fell on unwilling ears. When at length he saw that grief and suspense threatened to affect her health, Mr. Wood consented that she should join a party of emigrants that happened to be passing the village. He wrote to the depot at the Hooghly stating the circumstances of her case, and asking for her, as a woman of respectability, the special attention of the doctor who might have the conduct of the voyage. In the end, Lutchmee, with four hundred and thirty-three others of different ages, sexes, origins, and castes, embarked on board the good ship 'Sunda,' bound from Calcutta for the port of Georgetown, Demerara.

We have now done with India; the scene changes to other and far different circumstances and conditions of life.

Show how crowded the ships were.

CHAPTER VI

'WHERE IS HE?'

THE good ship 'Sunda,' after a voyage of ninety-three days, was standing in before the warm, light, north-east breeze, towards the Georgetown lightship. Little could be seen beyond the expanse of yellow-tinged water, – coloured by the mud of the far interior brought down by the vast rivers which discharge themselves into that sea; the lightship gently rolling in the swell; in the distance a dark line of shore, from which here and there rose slender shafts that looked like reeds – the lighthouse at Georgetown, and the chimneys of the coast estates. From galley to forecastle the deck was crowded with Coolies; some eagerly scanning the horizon; others entertaining their comrades with childish exhibitions of joy and curiosity, or with their lively babble; others crouched on their hams, their heads bowed down to their knees in an attitude of despondency.

Lutchmee, whose pretty face and coquettish ways had during the voyage won upon the rough English and foreign sailors, was standing well forward on the forecastle near the look-out, who, with grotesque English and uncouth gestures, tried to make her understand their progress. It was three o'clock in the afternoon. The sun, nearing a level, shot its hot beams sidewise on the Asiatics, nearly all of whom showed signs of weariness. Lutchmee alone seemed animated with joy. She was looking forward to the meeting with Dilloo, and her little heart beat, and her eyes were shining with a hopeful light. The sailor noticed her gladness.

'Aha, Lutchmee!' said he, with a voice like a rusty coffee-mill, – they had found out that the pretty Hindoo was journeying to meet her husband, – 'you glad, eh? You go see Dilloo? Bah! Dilloo marry 'nother woman. Ha! ha! what you do then, Lutchmee? Come back to me, eh?' – putting his hand on what he supposed to be his heart.

Lutchmee understood the good-natured banter, for she had already made herself a little familiar with English. She tossed her head, and laughing, in a silvery tone, put her hands together and bowed towards the shore. The pantomime was pretty, and modest and sincere withal.

'No fear Dilloo: all true Dilloo.'

'Hem!' said the sailor to himself, winking his eyes very hard, for the glare was strong: 'I only hope so, for the poor wench's sake. If he's true; he's the first honest copper-skin I ever come across. Where's that clumsy tug a-drivin' to?'

The steamer thus spoken of soon approached and hailed the ship. As it was getting late, the captain resolved to engage her to tow his vessel into the river; and before long the 'Sunda' was more rapidly cleaving the muddy water. Gradually the long line of shore began to grow clear; then could be discerned the fringing palm trees and the scraggy bush along the bank: then the wooden houses, here and there; and at length, just in front, the mouth of the river. On the left ran a strong sea-wall, at that hour the promenade of the fashionable world of Georgetown: fatigued officials with their cigars, pale ladies languidly sauntering, children in their perambulators, and the dark buxom nursemaids, gay with their bright-coloured turbans and white dresses. Up and down walked many a wealthy planter, – one, a grand old figure, erect and haughty, with stick on shoulder, a Scotchman who had spent forty-five years in the colony, the Nestor of the planting community. At the corner of this promenade towered up the lighthouse. On the right entrance of the river the low flat banks were maintained by a short piece of sea-wall; and out from the small village protected by it there stretched in lengthy skeleton the Pouderoyen Stelling, or wharf, which was the landing-place of the ferry for the west bank of the Demerara river. Between the banks flowed the stream, silent, smooth, and muddy; sweeping by many ships and schooners, steamers, barges, and boats, anchored or moving on its ample bosom.

By this time the Coolies swarmed to the sides of the ship, and eagerly peered over the taffrail as the great vessel swung round the corner and disclosed to their eyes the flat site of Georgetown – with its huge sheds of merchandize, its white houses and green blinds, and the familiar cocoa and cabbage palms, lifting their high, graceful heads into the clear air; while in front, on the yellow banks and by the stellings that jutted out into the river, there went on the work and bustle of a thriving port. Before the strangers could take in all these features, the rattle of the running anchor chain told them that their voyage was at an end, and that now for them a new life had begun. It was the rough knell that marked off their native existence from an experience to these poor, simple creatures, more than novel, unexpected, inconceivable; an experience for not a few of them to be embittered with intensifying and hopeless aggravation until death should become their truest friend.

Scarcely had the anchor sunk into the muddy bottom, when a boat pulled by four powerful blacks in sailors' uniform came alongside: and presently there stepped on board the health-officer of the port, the immigration Agent-General, and an interpreter. The latter salaamed right and left, and the people delightedly returned the welcome of a countryman. The ship's doctor showed his books. The health-bill was declared satisfactory. The Agent-General, a grey old gentleman of considerable activity, passed round the vessel to take a survey of the new arrivals, here and there putting a kindly question through the interpreter.

'This lot,' said he to the captain, 'is not a very promising one. I don't believe thirty per cent. of them ever did any field work.'

The captain shook his head.

'A whole lot of them were sent aboard not fit to travel. You'd have thought they'd have shaken the life out of themselves the first time they were sick. We had forty or fifty cases of disease among 'em. Look there, now, there's an idiot; and here are two lepers, – there are more below. How your agent in India comes to pass such creatures as able-bodied, beats me to understand. It don't require a doctor to tell me such a fellow as *that* ain't worth his salt,' said he, pointing to a little dark, unhealthy looking man, who, in the favourite sitting posture, was vacantly regarding them.

'Ask him how old he is.'

It turned out he was nearly sixty.

'It's a shame!' said the Agent-General, angrily. 'If I had my way, I would send half this lot back again. I see by the list five idiots are reported by Dr. Chandle. But there is such a demand for labour, that the planters can't afford to send them back, and so they must make what they can out of them. This bad selection is the beginning of every sort of wrong and evil.'

'I' ll tell you what,' said the shrewd captain, 'my opinion is, those Indian recruiters are a set of scoundrels. They don't honestly go up the country and get people really fit to work: they just pick them out of the slums of Calcutta and the large towns; and your agents aren't over particular either about their examination. You should see them passing them at the Hooghly depôt. The examination is a farce: Dr. Chandle will tell you so. But what can I do? I must bring 'em, you know.'

Probably every one concerned would have asked the same question, and shrugged his shoulders, and, in the same way, shifted the responsibility on some one else. The cunning Indian recruiters would have shrugged their shoulders, and asked, 'What can we do? We must make a living.' The colonial agents would have shrugged their shoulders, and asked, 'What can we do? The colony must have people, good or bad.' The highly-paid officials of the Indian Government, whose business it was to superintend the emigration, and who were supposed to be responsible for the character of the recruiters, and the condition of the people permitted to emigrate, would have shrugged their shoulders and asked, 'What can we do? The people want to go, they understand they will be better off in the West Indies, and, at all events, they can be spared.' The Indian Government, the British Government, and the Colonial Government would each have shrugged their shoulders, and said, 'What can we do? The evil consequences are much to be regretted; but, really, no pains are spared to avert them!'

Thus responsibility floats *in nubibus*, while the realities of wrong and sorrow come cruelly home to the victims of a complicated system of shifted obligations.

How many evils of this sort remain in the world unredressed only Heaven knows; but they are often infinitely more pestilent, more difficult to remedy, than the direct and concrete efforts of deliberate tyranny.

Mr. Goodeve, the Agent-General, had noticed Lutchmee, who, clothed in her finest, with her hair daintily dressed, stood curiously watching the small group of gentlemen, as they passed, among her country-people.

'That is a fine young woman,' said he, stopping to look at her.

'Yes,' said the surgeon; 'and she has behaved very well on the passage. She is superior to any woman I ever saw coming over. She says that she is married to some man who emigrated two years ago.'

'Ask her who it is,' said Mr. Goodeve to the interpreter. The answer was rapidly obtained.

'Dilloo!' said he. 'Why, if we have one, we have fifty Dilloos on the estates. What ship did he come in?'

Lutchmee did not know. She could tell the year he left her, and the village he came from; but, as the latter information was not kept on record by the Immigration Department, identification by those particulars was impossible. Nor was it of any avail to attempt to describe her husband's appearance.

An agent, with thirty or forty thousand people under his care, could not recall every face that passed under his notice.

'Can I not see him?' inquired the simple woman of the interpreter. 'Where is he? I want to find him.'

The interpreter shook his head.

'There are many Dilloos,' he said. 'They are scattered about over a great country. How shall we know the Dilloo whom *you* seek?'

Lutchmee clasped her hands, and the large drops stealing from her eyes jewelled her dark cheeks, as she went on her knees before Mr. Goodeve, and poured out in her own language a passionate appeal to him to take her to her husband. The long-tried patience of years, the ever-pleasing dreams of day and night throughout the voyage, had tended towards this hour as one of unmixed joy; and the sudden eclipse of her hopes extinguished her fortitude. She had never forecast the disappointment of this moment. Mr. Goodeve was affected, and the sailor who had been watching the interview turned away with a dry cough. The Agent-General took her by the hand and spoke kindly to her, promising to do his best to find her husband, 'before she was allotted.' Lutchmee had little or no idea what this meant. To her the contract she had made in India was a matter of form – a means of reaching her lover. She had not taken the trouble to think of the nature of her engagement, so absorbed had been her mind in the one aim of affection.

CHAPTER VII

A DANGEROUS ADMIRER

THE next day the emigrants were disembarked in boats and conveyed to one of the stellings, whence they marched to the Immigration depôt, a wooden barrack situated at the end of a flat marsh behind the sea-wall. At the other end of this marsh were the garrison barracks, inhabited by some companies of one of the West India regiments. The whole of the buildings on the ground were below high-water mark, and lay between open trenches. Arrived at the depôt, the people squatted quietly about the house and beneath the verandah. Then the Agent-General, assisted by sub-agents, classified them, as required by the local law, according to relationship, and, as far as possible, by placing together friends or fellow-villagers. Subject to this, allotments were then arbitrarily made of batches of them to various estates, in proportion to the number for which the proprietors had applied. Looking forward to this contingency, it was usual for the planters to apply for more than they needed. In due time the agents of the estates, or overseers, attended at the depôt to receive their quota, and the Indians were marched off in bodies, some to the steamers for the Arabian coast, or the Islands, or Berbice, others to the east and west coasts of Demerara. Along with the five idiots who were retained by the Immigration Agent-General to be sent back to India, Lutchmee was kept at the depôt. She saw her fellow-travellers disperse with a heavy heart, and sadly, through the long hot days, she sat on the verandah, gazing listlessly at the few acres of grassy swamp, watching the morning and evening evolutions of the troops; or in the afternoons, as the sun declined, and the pale people of Georgetown gathered to catch the incoming breeze, she lay upon the grassy bank, looking at the yellow waves or observing the gloomy gaiety of the strollers on the wall.

Thus a fortnight passed, and the sub-agents, though they had made active inquiry, had been unable to identify the missing Dilloo. Six Dilloos had arrived in the ship which, as they judged from the information Lutchmee supplied, had brought her husband. One would have thought that nothing could be easier than to write to the employers of these six Coolies and request them to ascertain whether their servant of that name had been married to a girl called Lutchmee. And, in fact, Mr. Goodeve directed the sub-agents to write to the masters of the six Dilloos; but they were not bound to reply, and only one found it convenient to do so. His Dilloo had only one eye, and hearing a wife had arrived to claim a husband, pretended to have once married a Lutchmee, but she declined to believe in him. Mr. Goodeve was perplexed. He had now retained the woman, without allotting her, an unusual time. Experience had made him suspicious of the excuses of wily Hindoos, and he considered that possibly, nay, in spite of himself he was beginning to think *probably*, her story was untrue. Fortunately he had the Governor's approval of what he had done; for, indeed, Her Majesty's representative in British Guiana follows with all the minuteness of a tradesman the movements of the Immigration office; and the Agent-General, instead of being a departmental minister, with a seat in the Court of Policy, is practically degraded to the level of a petty clerk, waiting on the nod or the wink of the Viceroy.

One afternoon Lutchmee, as was her wont, strayed to the embankment. She had arrayed herself with her habitual neatness and elegance. The western end of the promenade was frequented by a few of her countrymen, who had interested themselves in the subject of her anxiety. They were 'unbound,' that is, freed from their indenture, and one or two of them were wealthy. A lithe little Madrassee pedler and usurer took special notice of her, and, having dealings with most of the estates in the colony, had caused her story to be pretty generally circulated. He held out the hope of being able to find Dilloo. This afternoon, as she was sitting waiting for him, a tall, sharp-eyed man, of middle age, with the dark face and hair and strongly-marked features of a North Anglian, who was taking his afternoon constitutional at a pace rather more energetic than was common among promenaders, suddenly caught sight of her, and, stopping, conned with the greatest coolness and deliberation her features and figure.

'Hum,' said he, aloud, with unconcealed satisfaction, 'that's a tidy young girl. The handsomest Indian I ever saw. Where did she come from? – Whose wife you, eh?'

'Dilloo, massa,' said the soft voice.

'Dilloo? Who is Dilloo? Where Dilloo live, eh?'

'No sabby, massa,' replied the girl, adopting the Creole *patois* of her new acquaintances on the wall.

'No sabby? What estate?'

She shook her head: this was Greek to her. Just then her Madrassee friend, who knew her questioner too well, came up.

'Salaam, massa!'

'Salaam! Look here, Akaloo, just ask this girl what estate she's on, will you, or who she is living with?'

'She no on any estate, massa. Stay Goody office. No bound° yet. Just come.'

He gave a jerk of his thumb over towards the river, where the 'Sunda' was still lying.

'Not bound yet? How's that? All the last lot have been on the estate weeks since. What an old rascal that Goodeve is to keep such a fine girl hanging about the depôt! I shall apply for her at once.'

He said this out loud, indifferent to his Indian audience. Akaloo, however, who had been keenly watching him, struck in, –

'No, no, massa. She go look for 'usbaun; left her in India: come here. No found 'usbaun estate yet.'

'Oh, nonsense: she might look for him till doomsday. Tell her he's dead, or married to someone else. There are four Dilloos at Belle Susanne, one is very likely hers, and tell her she can have any one of them she likes – eh?' said he, laughing, and patting her cheek.

Lutchmee, half gathering the meaning of his words, indignantly turned her face from his touch, and the ready tears rolled down her cheeks. The gentleman looked at her with some astonishment.

° 'Bound,' the pigeon-English term for 'indentured.'

Your regular planter has no faith in a Coolie's feelings. To him every act of an Indian, however natural, is acting. But Drummond shrewdly suspected the acting to be this time genuine.

'What,' he said, 'you love Dilloo? Much want Dilloo?' She nodded assent.

Akaloo explained that she was inconsolable from her disappointment, and that Massa Goodeve was doing all he could to find her husband. Mr. Drummond, after a cheering word, took his way along the wall to where he knew Mr. Goodeve would at that time be found taking the air, if, indeed, breathing a half-furnace blast may be so favourably described.

'I say, Goodeve,' said he, abruptly, 'what are you keeping that pretty girl at the depôt for? This won't do: I must report you to the Governor.'

'Very well,' said the Agent-General, smiling. 'Do it in writing, please, and I shall forward a memorandum in reply. But the fact is, that girl is giving me a great deal of anxiety. I have been looking for a man she says is her husband. But, from her story, I shrewdly suspect she is not sure he is here at all. He may have gone to Trinidad or St. Lucia. He left India, she says, two years ago.'

'Pshaw!' interrupted the other: 'it's a cock-and-bull story. You ought not to keep her here any longer. She must be allotted. Send her to me at Belle Susanne: I'll find a husband for her. I must see old Tom about it.'

I regret to say that the 'Old Tom' here referred to was no other than His Excellency Governor Thomas Walsingham, who had certainly not won the sobriquet by his cat-like vigilance, or because his spirits were sweet and above proof. He was one of those steady-going mediocrities whom a grateful Colonial Office is apt to value in such inflammable quarters as the West Indies, where the least spark of originality or independence may, in certain conditions, set fire to a whole community. An estimable, good-natured, easy-going man was Thomas Walsingham, who, never too active a friend of the Coolies, and never too stern a reprover of the planters, retained an imperial reputation for humanity, and was lucky enough to hold one of the richest governments at Her Majesty's disposal.

As Drummond turned away, the Agent-General looked after him doubtfully. This was one of the most powerful planters in the colony; a member of the Court of Policy, and noted for his determined will, strong passions, and practical ability. Mr. Goodeve held a good opinion of him as a master, though he was rather doubtful of him as a man. In the present instance his mind was divided between his suspicions of Drummond and his own growing distrust of Lutchmee. If she were telling the truth he could do nothing less willingly than to put her in Mr. Drummond's power for five years. Were her story untrue, even his mind was not able to overcome the natural race indifference to what became of her. He knew too well the ordinary and inevitable fate of the small proportion of Coolie women then in the colony; without clear evidence that this one was unlike the rest, – her good looks, indeed, being rather against her, – how could he be expected to get up any special interest in her fate? Subtle, indeed, but powerful are the influences upon the calmest and most honest mind, in those peculiar relations of a superior to an inferior race, of which terms of bondage or terms akin to bondage form a part. If they are difficult for an analyst to define, they are certainly too real and strong for the persons concerned to resist.

CHAPTER VIII

THE RECOGNITION

MR. DRUMMOND was as good as his word. The next day he applied to the Governor in writing, informing him that 'he had ascertained a Coolie woman, *ex* "Sunda", still remained at the depôt unallotted; and begging to state that as she appeared to be a respectable person, and he was desirous of securing as many women of that kind as possible on Belle Susanne, he asked that she might be allotted to that estate.'

The Governor had hardly ever been on an estate in his life. He was personally incurious. Faith, to an official who must write home long despatches about his proconsulate, is superior to sight. He could affirm that the general condition of the immigrants was satisfactory, and the Coolie system a great success, if he only came in contact with the subject in letters, minutes, or despatches, or only saw the people in holiday attire in the course of his afternoon drives. Had he been challenged to say whether he thought Drummond a fit and proper person to whom to deliver up a handsome young Indian woman, he would have said that 'he had no reason from any official memoranda to doubt that she would receive at Belle Susanne the same satisfactory attention and care which the reports he had received of the estate led him to believe were characteristic of Mr. Drummond's management.' The man who can at once satisfy his own conscience and his official superiors with negatives of that sort saves himself and them innumerable inconveniences, and is deemed a most valuable person.

The Governor had already been informed by the Agent-General of the reason why Lutchmee had not been allotted, and had approved of her retention. But there are limits to governmental kindness. Mr. Drummond was too powerful to be disregarded. The matter would get talked about, and talk in a small colony must be avoided. Accordingly a 'despatch' was written by the Government Secretary to the Immigration Agent-General, two hundred yards off, stating 'that he had the honour to enclose a copy of a letter received from the Hon. C. C. Drummond, and that His Excellency the Governor recommended that the woman "*Sunda*, 330", should be allotted to the estate of Belle Susanne.'

Mr. Goodeve's humanity never slept. Whatever doubts had sprung up in his mind, he still desired to act the part he deemed the law had assigned to him, of Coolie protector, – a part which the planters thought he acted too extravagantly.[*] He sent for Lutchmee and told her, through the interpreter, that as her husband had not been found, the Governor had ordered him to allot her to an estate where she must discharge the obligations of her contract made in India, but that if her husband should be found she would be placed wherever he was.

Lutchmee had gained from her countrymen on the sea-wall some inkling of estate life. They had described to her the work in the field and the 'megass-yard,' the houses, the hospitals, and the general conditions. For this she was quite unprepared. The whole impulse of her engagement and voyage had been to regain her husband. To lose him, and find herself bound to perform labours she had never thought of, almost crushed her. She implored Mr. Goodeve to find her husband, or send her back to India. The terrible unfriended desolation of her heart excited her to a loud outburst of grief. The Agent-General was moved by her agitation, but was obliged to return a decided answer. She must go to Belle Susanne.

The poor woman sat down, and covering her head in her chudder, rocked herself backward and forwards, moaning piteously. The interpreter vainly tried to comfort her. Mr. Goodeve went to her, and put his hand on the bare arm that clasped it, to remove the drapery from her head. The skin was dry and burning.

'Ha!' said he, 'she has fever, and very badly, too. Sammy, she must go to the hospital.'

[*] There is an official who has sat for the portrait of the Agent-General in the text. I need not mention his name, but it is well known and greatly respected in the West Indies.

The way from the immigration depôt to that admirable public institution, the Georgetown hospital, lay along a road that traversed Eveleery, the garrison fields, and turning at the end of the east coast 'dam,' or high road, which was cut short by those fields, passed over a wooden bridge that led across a creek to one of the principal streets of the town. Beyond the garrison, right and left of the east coast dam, was a wilderness of unoccupied land, and on either side of the dam a broad canal, which required every few weeks to be cleared of its weeds. The property belonged to Government, and afforded occupation to a number of short-time convicts, who were led out to their work in gangs of about a dozen.

Lutchmee was borne along in a low handcart covered with an awning of cotton, her whole frame burning with fever, and her eyes restlessly wandering over every object they could reach. As the cart reached the bridge, it passed a file of prisoners going out to work, who looked with interest at the sick woman. Before any one could interfere, one of the prisoners, suddenly exclaiming, 'Lutchmee!' darted from the line and clasped her in his arms. Her quick eye had taken in the familiar though altered features, and she had half risen, but the joy was too great, and she lay senseless in the embrace of Dilloo. He was instantly seized and pulled away by the foreman of the gang, who took the strange act of the convict for a sudden frenzy. Dilloo's teeth ground together, and a fierce fire was flaming in his eyes. Fortunately the interpreter had accompanied the party, and after exchanging a few words with the prisoner was soon able to explain his singular conduct. Meanwhile Lutchmee began to recover, and, opening her eyes, stretched out her arms towards her husband, repeating his name. The warder let go his hold, and in a moment, Dilloo, his face wet with tears and his whole body trembling with excitement, sat upon the edge of the cart, and lifting the sick woman on his knee, laid her burning head on his shoulder, and unmindful of the gathering crowd of Blacks, Indians, Portuguese, and Whites, soothed her with eager words of affection. Among the spectators was Lutchmee's friend the sailor, who happened to be lounging on shore. He drew the back of his hand across his eyes, – he was idiotically soft-hearted.

'Blow me,' said he, 'if this ain't too much for me! I never see two copper-skins go on so like human bein's afore in all my born days.'

At this moment a light covered waggon drawn by a spirited horse, and carrying a gentleman with his Negro servant, came swiftly along the road from the east coast. The spectators blocked the bridge.

'Get out ob de way!' shouted the black fellow, glad like all his race to domineer when well supported. 'What you stop up dat bridge for?'

The horse came on, the crowd gave way, shouting to him to stop, and disclosing the pathetic group in its midst; but the Negro never drew rein, and would have seriously if not fatally damaged the interesting scene, had not our sailor jumped forward and seized the horse's head.

'Stop! you black fellow,' he cried. 'Would you bear down at ten knots on human bein's like a shoal of mackerel?'

The Negro gave one cut with his whip over the sailor's brawny neck. Before he could repeat it, he was seized by the collar, dragged from the waggon, and pitched neck and crop from the bridge into the muddy water beneath. The previous movement had turned the horse round and broken a shaft. Half a dozen hands held the animal's head.

'There! you wretched black-skin,' said the sailor, looking down upon the mud-covered object that was scrambling out of the shallow creek, 'that will teach you to keep your fins off an English tar if ever you're tempted to try it again!'

The gentleman had jumped out of the waggon, and in his turn now collared the sailor, amid dangerous murmurs from the crowd.

'What do you mean by stopping my horse and assaulting my servant in that way, sir?' said Drummond, for it was no other.

It was white man against white man this time, and Drummond was powerful and accustomed to command. The sailor, though not alarmed, was subdued.

'Well, you see, sir,' he replied, touching his cap, 'your servant warn't over polite to me for a black-skin to an Englishman, as you'll admit; and moreover he was about to drive over this young couple, that haven't spoke or signalled one another this two or three year; and the poor wench too under the weather, and being hauled into dry-dock for repairs.'

Drummond's quick eye rested on the couple, and he recognised both of them immediately. Dilloo was too well known to him. He was one of the ablest of his labourers, and, in his opinion, one of the worst of his servants. He did his work rapidly and well, but his independence, energy, and capacity gave him great influence among the estate's people. Instead of using this in the ordinary Indian manner, to curry favour with his master and advance himself, he rather employed it in organising and aiding the Coolies, against any wrong on the part of their superiors. Upon an estate worked by indentured labourers, that such a man would be likely to become an intolerable nuisance to the manager would not be doubted by the most partial philanthropist, though he and the planter would not draw identical conclusions from the circumstance. Dilloo was now suffering three months' imprisonment for an alleged assault on the very groom of whose condign punishment he was as yet unconscious. That was the first time the cautious Hindoo had given Drummond any legal hold upon him, and indeed his conviction was undeserved.

Drummond was naturally a kind-hearted man. The hardness that had grown in him towards the dark races by whom his wealth was made for him had sprung out of the nature of his relations to them, and somewhat against the grain. In his mind it was based on justice to himself, for he had succeeded in convincing his conscience that their interests and his were rarely compatible, and that when there was collision *they ought to give way*. This is the inevitable tendency of these relations. The glance at Dilloo and Lutchmee touched a soft place in his feelings. He loosed his grasp on the sailor, and at the apparition of Pete, his servant, in the natural dress of a crocodile, chuckled so maliciously, that the crowd gave vent to an inordinate chorus of delight.

'Well, you're an object, Mr. Pete. You will have to walk home, and get dry as you go. Keep your whip in future for horses and black men – though,' he added, significantly, 'you have not found that answer, either.'

The discomfited groom made off amidst the jeers of his countrymen, whose huge lips and shining teeth exhibited the keenest
relish of his misfortune.

Drummond meanwhile turned to the young couple. The fore-
man of the convict gang was getting impatient, and ordered
Dilloo to return to his place. The Coolie did not hear him.
Drummond put his hand on his shoulder.

'Is this your wife, Dilloo?'

The Indian looked up boldly into the planter's face, and said, –
'Iss, massa.'

'She's a fine young woman, then. She is coming to my estate –
bound to Belle Susanne. I wish for her sake you were out of gaol.
What's the matter with her?'

'Fever.'

Drummond's experienced hand sought her pulse, and felt the
burning skin.

'She's very bad. You had better let her go to the hospital at once.
When she gets out, I'll take care of her. How long have you been
in gaol ?'

'Two mons.'

'Well, it won't be long before you get back to her. She shall live
in the hospital till you come home; and I hope, now, after this,
you'll keep quiet and get into no more scrapes.'

It was with difficulty that Lutchmee could be parted from her
husband or he from her; but she was at length removed in a paroxysm of the fever, while Dilloo, resuming his place among the convicts, went on to complete the imprisonment, of which the
monotony had been so sadly yet so excitedly broken. When
Drummond turned round to his carriage, he found that the sailor,
using his knife and some tarred strain from his pockets, had very
neatly spliced the broken shaft. As he thanked him the man took
off his cap.

'Lookee 'ere, sir,' said he, drawing a gold coin from some mysterious hiding place beneath his belt, 'I'm afeard that there young
Injin woman's a-going to be very cranky this long while, and
mebbe they ain't over partikler how they overhaul and caulk 'em
in that there 'orspital. Will you kindly take keer 'o this, and mebbe

'twill get her some extra stores and better handling, and I couldn't do no more for my own sister?'

'You're a good fellow,' said Drummond, kindly taking his hand. 'I'll see she is well taken care of. She is my servant now, you know, and I am bound to look after her. Good-day.'

CHAPTER IX

BELLE SUSANNE

THE estate of Belle Susanne lay a considerable distance up the east coast of Demerara, the central county or district of British Guiana. Vast as is the country known by that name, extending deeply into the South American continent, only a selvage of it has been rescued from wilderness by the hand of civilization. The interior consists of impassable swamps, open savannahs, tropical forests where the gigantic trunks of the Mora or Simiri, amongst which rise here and there the slender shafts of the graceful Eta or Turu palms, are festooned with vast, embowering creepers, while every nook and shoulder of their massive branches is gemmed with rare orchids. Beneath their shadow, great spreading ferns and huge-leaved shrubs exhibit the perfection of tropical vegetation in a soil and climate most favourable to exuberance. In these almost impenetrable scenes, the reign of nature is disturbed only by the wild animals and a few thousands of wandering Indians – Caribs, Arawâks, Acawoios, and Macusi. These people, of light copper skin, short well-made bodies and agreeable countenances, range the endless hunting-grounds, where nothing more dangerous than the deadly Labarri snake, and perhaps nothing more disagreeable than the vampire-bat is to be found: a harmless people, in a perfect state of nature, both bodily and mental.

It is the flat alluvial land along the banks of the great rivers Demerara, Essequibo, Berbice, and Corentyn, and a strip bordering the sea-coasts of the colony, that have alone been won from nature by European energy. To bring even these parts into culture, the Dutch, who first occupied the country, were obliged to undertake such vast works as were familiar to them in their native land, but they had to carry them out under a burning sun and in a horrible climate. While they erected dykes to shut out the sea and the rivers on one side, or the vast overflowing waters of the inland swamps on the other, they were obliged to create a system of canals and drains to relieve the occupied parts from the too-domineering water, and to facilitate the conveyance of the produce down the long lines of their estates. The shore or river fringe varies in breadth from two to six miles, and is divided by parallel lines into the various estates, some being not more than a hundred yards wide. The road to these estates is the top of the dam protecting them from the sea, to which joins at right angles the 'middle-dam' or centre road of each estate, which runs back as far as the inner boundary, and is drained on either side by navigation and drainage trenches. Looking from the top of the dam across the vast flats, the eye lights only on an occasional tree and on groups of estates' buildings.

Belle Susanne was a long way from Georgetown, but it would scarcely have mattered up which of the branching dams we turned to find its counterpart. We should discover the same general features and economy on all the estates. Some buildings are distinguished from others by greater neatness, better machinery, and the evidences of more business-like conduct. And Belle Susanne was conspicuous amongst Demerara estates, both for handsome buildings and good management. As you approached the white-painted bridge which connected the front dam with the estate road, the canes along on the right looked tall and green and juicy; and, if you noticed the cane-hills, you saw that they had been weeded and hoed with industrious care. Through such fields on either hand were at length reached the manager's house, in its neat garden; the hospital, a handsome wooden barrack, erected for a hundred patients; the overseer's quarters: all these buildings elevated on piles, with broad, latticed verandahs, and long-sweeping shingled roofs. Past these the road led straight to the megass-yard, shut in on three sides by its corrugated iron sheds, some hundreds of feet in length, where the dried refuse of the sugar-cane was laid up for the fires that were to boil the next year's crop. To the left was an irregular pile of wooden buildings, over which towered a tall brick chimney, the erection whereof in that fierce sun-glow must have been a

Tartarean business. To-day it is vomiting forth abundant smoke, the noise of machinery rumbles within the vast wooden shells, the yard is alive with active men, women, and children; the smithy, with its white head-blacksmith and his Chinese aids, is wheezy with the blowing bellows and resounding with rapid hammers; for it is crop time, and no idle hand can be allowed to exist out of the hospital. The soil of the megass-yard is almost as black as ink, spongy to the feet, and offensive to the smell. The lees of the rum-still in the corner, which we had forgotten to mention, are discharged incessantly upon the surface, and fermenting the damp mass of earth, produce a foetor that fouls the air to leeward sometimes for miles. Yet it is beyond and to leeward of this place that lie the eighty or a hundred cottages, huts and barracks, that constitute the 'Negro-yard' – an old name, which still lingers, recalling old memories, though Negroes now rarely inhabit any of these estate houses. No grass surrounds the rows of wooden sheds. They are irregularly placed: here a line of thirty or forty, recently built after a Government pattern on a slight elevation of hard earth; there some two-storied barracks, erected on piles, relics of the Negro-time, when scores were penned together in their numerous rooms; there again a few Hindu-built huts of wattled palm, on a hard mud floor – the Coolie's palaces. By these places are open ditches, some dry and some half full of foetid water. Their use is misunderstood, or certainly not much appre-ciated, for everywhere one can see the evidences that the surface of soil nearest the houses is considered the natural and proper receptacle of refuse. Constant must be the vigilance, and heroic the sanitary zeal of the manager who would attempt to enforce on his ignorant people the simplest health laws.

At Belle Susanne, the manager's house was exceptionally clean and comfortable. Mr. Drummond was not married, but a nice-looking Creole woman of about thirty years of age served him as housekeeper, quite as faithfully as she would have done had she been his wife. The sitting and dining-room which occupied the first floor were coolly and simply furnished with a few easy-chairs, dining and card-tables, manager's desk, and a settee. A table crowded with chemicals proved that he understood the scientific parts of his business. At one end of the gallery swung a fine grass hammock. A large side-board graced the dining-room, where the table was long and flanked with a dozen chairs, for the overseers were provided with their meals in the manager's house. Missa Nina, the housekeeper, looked well after all these things, took charge of the stores, dispensed from them to the hospital-cook the daily supplies and, above all, superintended the preparations of the substantial meals wherewith Europeans fortify themselves against tropical deterioration. Mr. Drummond prided himself on his liberality to those in his employ.

Upstairs, the manager's bedroom was a lofty and roomy place, under the unceiled rafters. One side of it was occupied with pegs, whereon hung every description of male garment, giving it the aspect of an old clothes' shop. Rows of boots ranged beneath increased the resemblance to a Dudley Street warehouse. In the middle of the room stood a great iron-bedstead covered with its mosquito-netting. A plain deal table, a capacious wash-stand, a shaving-glass, a chest of drawers, some trunks, and two chairs completed the furniture. The floor was left uncovered, and afforded no lurking-place for centipedes or scorpions, though it was the constant foraging ground of innumerable ants.

Under the netting, one morning, at five o'clock, lay Drummond, having just been waked by the attentive Missa, who had lit a candle, and bore in her hand a cup of coffee with a small slice of buttered toast.

'Nina,' said the manager, taking the cup as she raised the netting, 'there is a girl at the hospital called Lutchmee, landed from the last ship. She is the wife of that man Dilloo, who was sent to gaol for licking Pete. Egad! you should have seen Pete, in the mud that time!' he interposed, with a chuckle. Pete, being a Methodist local-preacher, was a sort of favourite with Nina. 'She's a young handsome girl, and needs to be looked after.'

He was intent on his coffee, and did not see the sudden lustre that lit up the dark eyes of the woman, who had been standing looking with admiration at the broad muscular neck and chest which the unbuttoned shirt, with its corners thrown back, exposed to view.

'You had better send for her over here and ration her from the house for a few days. – Halloo! what's the matter with you? Do you mean to say you are jealous?'

'O no, massa: I ought to be used to your ways by this time.'

'There you go again! What do you mean by that? See you do what I tell you. I want to do the girl a kindness, and you'd like to prevent it? Go away: I'm going to dress.'

'What does the woman mean?' said Drummond to himself, turning uneasily in his bed. 'She's like all those niggers, jealous and conceited. "Ought to be used to my ways by this time!" What does she mean?'

The fact was, the covert hit in this simple sentence had gone further home than Missa Nina could have expected, or than Mr. Drummond would admit to himself. This creature, whom he had taken as a young girl from her mother's house, had ministered with the fidelity of an animal to his weaknesses, his appetites, his passions. She had nursed him through a dangerous illness; and her devoted attention to his comfort, and patient obedience to his slightest command, had made her a necessity to what he called his home. But he had long ceased to derive pleasure from her companionship, or to give her his confidence. After all, what was she?

As for her? Her poor mind had few ideas, – her simple nature had early been absorbed in the one passion for this great and glorious being, whose strength, manliness and spirit seemed in her eyes so god-like. The few vague notions of religion she had gathered at the village Sunday-school years ago, and in some occasional paroxysms of religious excitement at the meeting-house in Guineatown, seemed to have awakened in her mind no suspicion that she stood in any other than a proper relation to Drummond: the relation proper for nuch a person of such a race as she was to such a being of such a race as his. Indeed, her shallow piety ran towards him, and circled round him, and he was the chief subject of her rare and simple prayers. She was conscious he regarded her rather as he regarded his dog and his horse, as a part of his establishment, and she felt that she ought not to expect to monopolise the entire affection of a man like that; yet, there was something in her which flamed up with fierce, volcanic energy, when she saw him confer on others the favours she had once arrogated to herself. There are few more puzzling psychological studies than these stunted mental and moral natures, embodied in whole races of mankind, and seeming to stand half-way between the Adamite ideal and the pure, unspiritual brutism of lower animals!

As Missa Nina went downstairs from Drummond's room, the tears were running down her cheeks in a tropical shower. 'Azubah! – Desolate – a woman forsaken and grieved in spirit!'

But she would sooner have lost her life than have disregarded Drummond's slightest fancy. Accordingly, by breakfast-time – that is to say about eleven o'clock, when manager and overseers met after several hours' round of the estates – Lutchmee was sitting on the grass under the manager's house, and receiving some kindly attentions from the poor Creole. The latter had no sooner seen the Indian woman than she was attracted by her beauty. Lutchmee looked doubtingly at the brown, well-formed face of the other, but after a while surrendered to the gentle marks of favour which were shown to her, and though she was unable to exchange many ideas with her hostess, began to feel at home. She tried to express her thanks to Missa, who at once, angrily, repudiated any generosity on her part.

'No *me* like you; Massa Drummond,' she said, pointing to the house above. 'Your massa, who live here. Massa tell me do this, tell me send for Lutchmee.'

'Too kind,' said Lutchmee.

'Yes – too kind – much – much kind to Coolie woman. Good man to Coolie woman, Massa Drummond.'

Nina brought this out rather convulsively, and her tone was slightly satirical. Lutchmee started and gazed in the other's face, but the woman avoided her glance.

'You stay here all day – stay here all time,' said Nina at length. 'Massa Drummond take good care of Lutchmee.'

'No, no!' replied the Indian woman, her heart divining some perilous mystery in this arrangement. 'Me go live where all Coolie women live: too, too kind, Massa Drummon'.'

Nina's woman's instinct told her that this girl was shrinking from something to which she had herself readily yielded. If it were a pleasure for a moment to feel that here she had no rival, it was, on the other hand, a somewhat displeasing reflection upon her, that Lutchmee should be superior to so overwhelming an attraction. So Missa said sharply, –

'You Massa Drummond's Coolie woman; do what Massa Drummond say. Else Massa Drummond beat you, kill you!'

'No!' cried Lutchmee, now thoroughly alarmed. 'Massa Drummon' too good hurt Coolie woman. You too good, too. You good woman – me good woman. You help me. Me go back now to other Coolie women. Please, please.'

Lutchmee softly touched the other's cheek, and then gently leaning over, after a moment's hesitation, kissed her on the forehead. Nina's eyes suddenly filled – it was the first pathetic chord that had been touched in her heart for many a year. Often had she wept the tears of passion and grief, but that was the malign tempest: this was the soft and blessed April rain. She held Lutchmee's hand in her own, and silently let the showers come. The Indian, with her delicate, child-like courtesy, took the end of her muslin scarf, and gently wiped away the trickling drops. She began dimly to comprehend something of Nina's relation to Drummond, and of the reason why she wept. O divine innocence and purity, so often obscured, yet never wholly left without a ray, in the densest and most eclipsed of human souls!

'We two friends,' said Lutchmee. 'Lutchmee wife of Dilloo. Missa wife of Massa Drummon'. Me, no, *no* go to Massy Drummon'.'

As she said this with an energetic elevation of voice, Drummond, who, having dismissed the overseers, had lounged down the back stairs with a cigar in his mouth to take a look at her, and had overheard her last words, struck in with his deep rich voice: –

'Nina, what have you been doing? Setting this girl against me, eh? Now look here, I have a good mind to horse-whip you. You're the most ungrateful vixen I ever knew. You have everything a nigger like you could wish, and you're as well off as any woman of your sort in British Guiana, and yet you must strike in with your infernal jealousy between me and my servants, and try to set them against me. Go up stairs.'

'It's not true,' said Missa, facing him with flashing eyes. 'I was doing my best for you, when this woman declared she would have nothing to do with you, and was so gentle and kind, I couldn't stand her – indeed, indeed I couldn't, Drummond,' said the poor woman, sobbing.

'Massa, massa,' cried Lutchmee, with her hands together, – she had half gathered the meaning of the conversation, – 'me talk Missa, say me Dilloo woman, no want leave my man. Massa keep Missa: send Lutchmee dis time to 'ospital.'

She went on her knees and wrung her hands and beat her bosom in true Indian fashion. Drummond was touched. In the pursuit of his whims, the remains of generosity and justice in his nature had always hitherto restrained him from any forcible assertion of his wishes. Nor did he meditate revenge. He was good-tempered, easy going, morally indolent. As soon as he saw that Lutchmee showed a determination to be true to her husband, one which he knew an Indian woman rarely affects unless it is real and earnest, he good-naturedly acquiesced.

'O yes: no hurt Lutchmee,' said he, smiling at what he thought to be the absurdity of the scene, and patting her on the shoulder. 'Lutchmee have good food here, but go back to Coolie women each time. Lutchmee, trust me, eh?'

It would have been hard, even for the suspicious Lutchmee, looking into the fine open face and clear eyes of the manager, to believe that any dangerous cunning lurked behind them, or that his word was a fraud. She breathed a new breath, and smiled most charmingly as she took his hand from her shoulder and naively kissing it, bowed low to her master.

CHAPTER X

SIMON PETY

'SIMON PETY,' as he was usually called among his friends and relatives, was a Creole African of perfect type. High and receding was his forehead, crisp and close the wool that clung like a black cap about his conical head; huge were his ears, well capable of supporting the massive rings that strained their enormous lobes. Beneath the prominent brows which stretched like a rugged bow across his front, the small dark orbits of his eyes, set in their pinky whites, rolled restlessly, cunningly, quizzically; and the crows'-feet on either side trembled with incessant motion. From between these quaint orbs came down a nose the exact resemblance of a top split in half, turned upside down and glued upon the face, with the similarity enhanced by the appearance of two deep and rugged holes, pegged, as it were, into its larger end. Then the descending eye of the observer lighted on a pair of lips brown-red, and full, – lips of a satyr, yet soft and mobile in their motion, and, when open to their full extent in the agony of a great cachinnation, disclosing an Acherontic gulf, with cliffs of rocky ivory shining far within. If we add to these the half-grizzly forest of beard that grew untended on Simon Pety's chin, can our reader believe us that the being we have been describing was a man of gallantry and one of the lights of Mount Horeb Chapel, at Guineatown, the adjacent Negro village? Yet it was so. More than one damsel of dusky hue – not to mention a certain widow, who, having a house of her own, and a capital plantain-plot, was deep in Simon Pety's regard – had evidence too damning of his indifference to moral laws.

Such a character as that of Simon Pety is an interesting, if also a painful, study in psychology. All sense, instinct, and emotion, combining the shrewdness of some of the finer brutes, with an

intellectual power of the narrowest capacity, – nay, seeming rather
to be endowed with an intelligence than an intellect, – this strange
being, half man, half animal, now and then showed himself capable of spiritual apprehensions far beyond his mere intellectual
understanding, and could at intervals be swayed by moral emotions to which conscience and not reason gave within him any
force or vitality. To do or abstain from doing a thing because it was
right and approved itself to his mind, as abstractedly the good and
right thing to do, was, so far as you can judge, for Simon Pety an
impossible thing; but if you touched his religious emotions, it was
a fair chance that in some of his moods you would be able to incite
or deter him in a certain course of action. In nine cases out of ten,
the animal within him was stronger than the spiritual, – passion
surprised and confounded devotion and conscience; and the rally
was simply a violent spiritual emotion in the direction of penitence. What missionary who had for the first time heard Simon
Pety praying at Mount Horeb, with florid imagery, vivid eloquence, and pathetic voice, amid the sobs and exclamations and
beatings of the breast of the seething congregation, could have
believed that, on a summary of Simon Pety's life, any impartial
fellow-man must have declared him a hypocrite and a scamp?
But, since a being of such mysteriously anomalous construction is
to be found, on the whole one must hold with the missionary who,
through many failures and discouragements, has been able to
redeem from inhumanity worse subjects than this, and who
bravely sticks to Simon Pety as a brand yet to be snatched, not
utterly to be abandoned as hopeless until he has taken his last
breath of earthly air.

On the evening of his misadventure at Georgetown, Simon
Pety, who had walked home, a good five hours business, in his
clay-covered suit, and had, indeed, in the process managed to
divest his mind of the humiliation of the morning so far as to convince himself that he had been a martyr for some truth unmen-
tioned and unknown, was sitting in the house of 'Missa Sankey,'
the widow aforesaid, eating voraciously out of a big basin of fou-
fou soup, – the thick mucilaginous mixture of boiled plantains and
gravy, which is the delight of Creole Africans. The spoon was large

and wooden, the soup was sticky, and as Pety's capacious under-
jaw dropped down to admit the generous instalments of food, his
beard received fresh contributions from moment to moment.

In an old rocking-chair, watching him with keen enjoyment, sat
Missa Sankey. She was a comely black, of shining face, neat figure,
and, just now, of cleanly dress, – for she had on a tight-fitting calico,
on the bosom whereof just then Pety's progeny and hers, aged two
years, was being rocked to sleep. On her head the invariable
bandanna, of flaunting colours, diversified the monotony of her
own hue. She was, as we have said, a comely woman, and a pleasant withal; and when she spoke her mouth seemed always to smile,
as the regular rows of white teeth glistened inside the ruddy lips.

'Poah Simon Pety!' she said, at length, after watching for some
time in silence his greedy efforts; 'dat dere white fellah ought to
be shot: go and serve de good man so.'

Simon Pety was getting near the bottom of the bowl, and was
correspondingly satisfied. He paused, after a huge gulp. Like many
good enthusiasts, Simon Pety was accustomed to air his shallow
Scriptural knowledge without particular regard to its relativeness.

'Susan Sankey, de Lord hab said, If you am smote on de right
cheek, turn round de left. I'se been maltreated dis day by de enemy
of mankind. Dat dere sailor, Susan, he'm a miss'onary ob Satan sent
to buffet me. Ha!' said Pete, swallowing another spoonful, 'if dine
enemy hunger, feed him – it shall be an exc'llent ile dat shall not
break his head. I'm sartain dat dere sailor fellah go to de debbil.'
Another spoonful. 'But de Lord keep us from presentiments!'

'But, Pety, why Massa Drummon' let you go be treated dat way?
Why he no lick de saila man?'

'Susan Sankey, you kent adop no conclusions 'bout de rules ob
action whereby dese yere European whites will registrate dere
conduc'. Deys like de 'guana.* You'm got 'em yere, dare you
haven't. Massa Drummon' any oder day 'd a knock dat ere sailor
man into chips – dis day take a huma de oder way. It's all de debbil,
Susan. Massa Drummon' he not one ob de Lord's people; and de
way ob de wicked am turned upside down.'

* The Iguana, a huge and very active lizard, which is very good eating.

Here he heaved a deep sigh, but whether it were at his master's depravity or at the empty state of the calabash from which he had been eating it was difficult to guess. He then rose, and, approaching Susan Sankey, stooped down to give her a kiss. It was ill requited.

'Dere, you nassy man, go 'way! Wash your face. Cober my face all over wid de fou-fou soup!'

'Mos' extremely beg pardon, Susan,' replied Simon Pety, meekly, for he could not afford to fall out with her. 'Dese yere imperials am berry awkwid and imposing. Dey ain't conducted to de consumption of fou-fou soup. I'll cut 'im off if you wish,' added he, gallantly.

'Go 'way, you foolish niggah! Go cut off de most butiful features ob yer face. Der ain't sich a whiska in Guineatown. Heah! I'll wash him for you.'

And rolling the naked youngling on the ground, Missa Sankey proceeded to wipe Pete's beard with a wet towel, and then to brush it with the remains of a hair brush; and when this was concluded, she pushed him into the rocking-chair, and, sitting down on his knees, gave him a kiss.

'Ya! ya!' said a shrill voice, which was immediately followed by a small chorus of two or three others: 'dere's de preacher and Missa Sankey kissin' in de rocking-chair!'

The sounds came from the cracks of the half-open door, where three or four village juveniles, without a scrap to cover them, had been amusing themselves by watching with their dark eyes the whole of the scene we have been describing. Pete jumped up incontinently, rolling his burthen on the baby, and rushed out after the impudent cynics, who tumbled off the high stairs into the mud without hesitation, and were out of sight in a twinkling. He was brought back by the united screams of Susan Sankey and her baby, the former having suffered as much in her dignity as the latter had in its feelings.

'Get away, you awkwid niggah,' she shouted, shaking the child at him in her passion. 'You'm a'mos' kill de baby an' me too. You call yourself a gen'leman, throw me 'bout in dat impropa way. Dere ain't no Christianity in dat dere sort ob rudeness.'

'Susan, I hab done wrong; my wrath and anger was 'cited by dose juvenile youngsters protruding on our sacred privacy. I ought to hab born wid meekness de scorning ob de proud and de laughing ob de simple.'

'You bigga fool than eber! What you come back for? Why you no go catch the little debbils? You 'spose I ain't got no character to lose!'

And here Susan swept off into her kitchen with the squalling baby, slamming the door in Pete's face. He knew it was useless to invade that sanctuary, so, taking up his old hat, Pete ruefully departed homewards, his awkwardness having cost him the glass of rum which invariably solaced his parting moments with the widow. He knew she would not hold her anger long, but he felt grieved that he had lost an opportunity for one more drink.

'Oh!' said Pete, to himself, apropos of nothing, – 'O dat I had wings like a dove, den would I fly away and be at rest.'

CHAPTER XI

THE OVERSEERS

AT Belle Susanne there were seven overseers, young men of ages varying from thirty to twenty, and no two of the same country. One was a Creole white; another, the eldest, a coloured man; another was the son of an Englishwoman by a Madeiran father; the three younger had been sent from England by the proprietors, and represented the three kingdoms; the last was a Barbadian Negro. Taken generally, they were men of energy, and one or two of them of considerable ability. Their duties were onerous and responsible; their life was nearly the most penal that could be devised for any man who is not a slave or a prisoner in a penitentiary. Separated, except in one or two cases, from any society but that of their colleagues – thrown simply, for amusement, upon the wretched resources of an estate, and generally so hard-worked that the zest for amusement was gone; constantly suffering from attacks of fever, in the intervals of which they pursued their occupation, and, debarred from the engaging and civilising influences of female society, one can scarcely imagine, outside a penal establishment, a more dismal post than that of an overseer on the sugar estates of British Guiana; unless, perhaps, when it is mitigated in the case of those who are fortunate enough to be within easy reach of Georgetown, and are privileged to enter its society.

At an early hour of the morning these young men turned out of their quarters, to see that their gangs went off to work. Crampton, the senior, looked after the buildings, the rest took charge of the various gangs in the fields, such as the gangs for weeding, shovelling, or hoeing. Each had his book, wherein he noted the names and the time and quality of the work of each person in his gang, and made his remarks thereon. Were any of them absent it was his duty in the afternoon to compare his list with the hospital entries, and ascertain whether sickness was the excuse. In cases of absconding and laziness he was to inform the manager, who forthwith summoned the delinquent before the magistrate, and, at the hearing, the overseer was expected to attend to prove the case. So much was this a matter of course that Mr. Drummond rarely took the trouble to ask his overseers whether they were able on their own evidence to convict the culprit. They on their part never hesitated to supply it if it were wanting. The defendant rarely understood what was going on, and the mysteries of cross-examination were Sibylline to him. The most conscientious magistrate could hardly be expected to weigh the evidence of Coolie companions who eked out their small modicum of fact with obviously ridiculous fictions or exaggerations, but he too often received with placid confidence any relation the overseers chose to inflict upon him. One overseer at Belle Susanne, a young Scotchman, named Craig, had given Mr. Drummond some trouble in this respect. He was stupid enough to decline to swear to matters not within his own ken, and in consequence of this had put the manager in one or two cases to the expense of fresh summonses, or had obliged him to drop a case. Drummond pointed out to him that, on the whole, general justice was done, and that to fail in a charge against a labourer was injurious to the discipline of the estate, but Craig was too Scotch to see the humour of this demonstration.

The first business of the morning for the overseers was to go the round of the Negro-yard and rouse the people, and if they proved, or were known to be, refractory, to enter their dwellings and turn them out. In cases of sudden resistance they sometimes handled the Coolies very roughly. It may be imagined that this often made whole gangs turbulent for the day. In British Guiana I believe the custom has been abandoned.

The most powerful of the overseers was the youngest, whose name we have already mentioned. His ability and spirit had gained for him the manager's good-will. An inch over six feet in height, with broad shoulders, strong frame, bold regular features, of blonde complexion, Craig would have been remarked by any one seeing the overseers together, to be as superior to the rest in

tone and manner as he was in appearance. He came from
Ayrshire, where his father was a well-to-do farmer, who had given
his son as good an education as was attainable before he reached
the age of seventeen. His mother would have made a minister of
the really clever stripling, but to the youth himself the 'call' was far
from clear; and hearing of openings in the West Indies, he had
prevailed on his father to procure him from the friend who owned
the estate the offer of an overseer apprenticeship at Belle
Susanne. Little had young Craig conceived of the true nature of
the work to which he had engaged himself for five years, and he
often chewed bitter thoughts over his experiences. But a natural
buoyancy of disposition, gradual acclimatisation, and the prospect
of advancement had somewhat reconciled him to his lot.
Drummond naturally took much to this powerful and diligent
youth with his ingenuous face and marked character.

In one point Craig was peculiar among his companions. They
were nearly all the children of adventure and misfortune. For
them in their young days there had been little experience of
domestic happiness; whereas he recalled with the deepest affection a mother of handsome and kindly face, of gentle life, somewhat of an 'enthusiast,' as the world would take her, strictly true to
the principles of Free Kirk and shorter Catechism, a Puritan, but
withal a mild one. At her knee he had listened to the simple and
devout eloquence with which she spoke of the principles and the
example of the noblest life of which we have record; and from her
he had imbibed a gentleness and conscientiousness not seldom
found combined in some of the manliest and most rugged Scotch
natures. The same creed which in many minds developes the
narrow rigidity of the Covenanter, is in other natures found to be
consistent with the tenderest spirit and the broadest sympathies.
Some of the mother's devoutness, of her superstitious respect for
the very words of Scripture, had been transfused into the son's
being. He never professed to emulate her piety; but he had a
reverence for the Sabbath, and adhered regularly to his solitary
though lamentably brief 'diet of morning and evening worship.'
In these habits his physical superiority secured him against the
open ridicule of his mates. They regarded these things with much

the same astonishment as was manifested by a professed infidel at
one of our Universities, who, declaiming against prayer at the
table of one of the most licentious of the undergraduates, was
rebuked by the latter, and assured that he, for his part, could never
begin or end the day without 'saying his prayers!' The result, however, of Craig's education had been to give him a horror of the
grosser vices; to ground him in principles of honour and virtue;
and to leave generally upon his mind an indefinable but real
influence of Calvinistic religion.

To a youth of such a mould, the characteristics of West Indian
life were sometimes revolting. In a community where everything is done for one race and class, and where, with slavery
disowned, the relation of the larger portion of the community is
that of contemptuous patronage on the one hand, and of sullen
self-defence on the other; where the morality of the superior
race is, except in a very select portion of the community, un-
fettered even by the ordinary restraints of civilised societies;
and where, among the inferior races animal instinct is too much
the overmastering power, – the first sensation of a pureminded
man, in Craig's situation, is one of repulsion from the tone and
manners of his associates. They were of that low type of Briton
and half-breed, common in tropical latitudes: their morality
was only restrained by the capacity of their desires, or by
considerations of opportunity and safety. Craig, with a large-
hearted wish to be on good terms with every one, could scarcely
govern his repugnance to the language, ideas and acts of his
fellow-overseers.

A fortnight after the meeting between Lutchmee and Dilloo, as
the young men were returning to their quarters from the evening
meal at the manager's house, Martinho, he of Portuguese blood, a
lithe, dark, small-faced fellow, who at that time was hospital overseer, said, –

'I discovered something this morning at the hospital, – the
prettiest Indian girl that ever I saw. I believe Drummond spotted
her somewhere, and insisted on getting her here. But what do you
think? She says she is the wife of that rascal Dilloo.'

'Nonsense! It's a make-up, of course,' said one of the others.

'There is no doubt he knew her. They recognised each other in Georgetown the day that our psalm-singing Pete had so good a ducking. But these Indian marriages mean nothing, as we very well know.'

'Yes, but Dilloo is a determined man,' said the Barbadian Chester: 'the most dangerous man on the estate. He would kill you or get up a row on the least provocation. I always give him a very wide berth. He's a good workman, too.'

'I don't think I have seen much of him,' said Craig, whose curiosity and spirit were excited by any hint of danger.

'He has been away since you came,' said Chester: 'we were obliged to get him three months at Georgetown gaol for that shindy with Pete, though I believe the old scamp was trying some of his tyrannical tricks on the Indian, who is a perfect demon when he gets in a rage. He shall go to Massaruni next time he breaks out.'

Massaruni is a penal settlement on an island some distance up the river Essequibo. In this strong and isolated place convicts for serious crimes expiate their malfeasances in the ordinary routine of English gaols the world over. For an obstreperous Coolie your manager could desire no fitter mode of sequestration than this well-guarded home of the condemned. Within sight of it, at the junction of the Massaruni and Essequibo rivers, is another asylum of outcasts, – the lazaretto of British Guiana; where (in spite of the Report of the Royal Commission against such isolation) those whose physical corruption has made them intolerable to society, surrounded with what alleviation their hopeless state admits of, sullenly drain in each other's companionship the wretched dregs of life. How well were it if from our social life we could thus ex-clude its physical and moral corruption, sequester and localise them in lonely spots, and hold society safe from their contagion! But alas, they are sinks that never dry up: the foul scum of hu-manity rushes up again from below, so soon as we think the horrid outflow has been staunched, and again and again must justice and charity set to work with unflagging efforts to skim it away! …

The overseers pursued their conversation.

'This woman,' said Martinho, 'is of a better class than we usually get here; and a real devil for temper, I should say – as bad as her husband. I gave her a pinch of the arm and a pat on the cheek, and she was as savage as Miss Marston would be if I were to take the same liberty with her, – eh, Craig?'

He looked at Craig, but something in his eye warned the Portuguese not to pursue this line. The fellow would not have dared even to address Miss Marston, still less to pinch her arm or pat her cheek; so he went on about Lutchmee.

'She jumped up and faced me like a tigress, and said, "Massa no put hand on Coolie woman: Dilloo wife!"'

'Ah, she'll soon get over that!' said Loseby, the Englishman, a heavy, sensual-looking youth, of unwholesome colour, who was wont to regard the world in general with cynical stolidity. 'Virtue is not an Indian woman's best reward in these regions, – eh?'

He chuckled quietly over his own joke, which one or two of the rest received with appreciative laughter.

'I would recommend any one to let her alone while Dilloo has charge of her,' said Chester.

'Why, one would think you were afraid of this fellow Dilloo,' put in Craig, himself fearless of anything but dishonour.

Chester repudiated the impeachment; but, in truth, he had good reason to be timid of the Hindoo. We have explained that the estates of British Guiana extend in the rear for a great distance: hence the inner portion is always spoken of as 'back.' The back-dam of Belle Susanne was three miles and a half in a straight line from the buildings: the labourers, in its furthest fields were far from sight or sound of other men. Out there one day with a powerful gang, Chester, who was riding on a mule, had found Dilloo surrounded by a small crowd of his 'matties,' or *mates*, whom he was excitedly haranguing. Work had so far suffered. The Barbadian, in a rage, raised his whip to cut the Indian over his naked shoulder; but before it had descended, the latter had avoided the stroke, and, leaping up on the mule behind the over-seer, clasped his strong arms vigorously round the latter's neck. But for Dilloo's companions, Chester might have been before many minutes ready for unceremonious burial in the adjoining jungle. They pulled the two on the ground, and drew off their angry comrade; but, holding out a threat of instant vengeance in case he should be so unwise as to tell, they exacted from Chester a solemn promise of silence. He was too great a coward to face the horrible prospect of assassination, or the chances of an application to the Obe man to poison him; and had held his tongue about the affair, – not only because he knew that it would lower him in the estimation of the manager and overseers, but for the sake of his life: he was glad, therefore, to change the subject. The languid interest of his colleagues in Luchmee had been satisfied for the present.

In a short time, as night had closed in and their work called them up before the sun, they had all tumbled beneath their mosquito nets, and were enlivening the night and the watchful peon under their verandah with a chorus of snores.

CHAPTER XII

AT HOME!

A FEW days after the scene between Drummond and Missa, let us pass through the Negro-yard to a wattled hut beyond its extreme end – a house well-built of its kind, its roof of Eta palm leaves, rising to an apex, its floor of smooth well-hardened mud, its interior divided by a light bamboo and leaf partition into two rooms or stalls, the whole illuminated and ventilated only through the small doorway. Outside is a limited terrace on which deft hands have moulded a clay fireplace. This tabernacle, a daring Hindoo had taken advantage of the leisure hours of a single Sunday to uprear, without leave asked or given; thither he had removed his household gods, and out of it, the manager, who knew it to be as good and healthy as any dwelling he could provide, did not care to eject the tenant. That daring Hindoo was Dilloo; and here, to-day, in a neat white vest and skirt, Lutchmee was sitting in the cool interior, rubbing, in a sort of mortar scooped out of the hard floor, the rice for their evening meal. She was humming to herself in low tones, but neither with the animation nor the joyous lightness of the song she was singing when we first surprised her in her native home far away. Only the day before yesterday had Dilloo, released from his imprisonment, brought her to his house. He was loving and tender as ever. When, taking her hand on the verandah of the hospital, and bearing her little bundle of clothes, he led her to the hut of which he had never expected to see her a tenant, there was a touch of sadness about the joy with which, secure from human eye, they indulged the transports of affection. Lutchmee saw and felt that there was a change in her husband. Not only did he look older, but he was graver and more stern in manner. Moreover, she remarked in him a novel habit of reserve. You will say this was quick apprehension, but it was the intuitive intelligence of love. Just then, however, they were very happy.

'Lutchmee,' said he, 'I rejoice to see you here, my lily, and to clasp you once more in my arms. But this is not the kind of place I had hoped to find when I listened to that cursed recruiter, and came away here in search of riches I shall never win. My poor Lutchmee,' he said, stroking her hair with his supple hand, 'you know not what you have come to in looking for your lost Dilloo. How unhappy you will be!'

'Dilloo, why do you talk so? I am always happy with you. With us, so loving and true, hard times cannot make hard hearts. I cannot be sad so long as I can see you and follow you about and work for you.'

'Ah! my darling, that is not all you will have to do. You know you are "bound" now to this estate. Massa Drummond has you in his hands for five years. He and six or seven other sahibs can almost do what they like with you – *unless I watch them closely!*' said he, in a grim undertone, as he clenched his hands and teeth. 'You must work every day in the megass-yard, carrying your burden swiftly, under a Negro-driver, and for very poor wages. And you are pretty, you are graceful and sweet as ever, my own Lutchmee,' – with softening eyes he drew her to his bosom, – 'and scoundrels of every race will have opportunities of tempting you and threatening you, and even me.'

'No fear of that!' replied Lutchmee, forcing a smile. 'I am true to you, Dilloo, and you are true to me, are you not? I was true to you all the time we were apart. Do you know, that vile Hunoomaun again attacked me, and I was only saved at the last moment by Wood Sahib. He was driven away from the country, and sometimes I tremble to think he might have gone to bind himself and come here.'

'What do you say?' exclaimed Dilloo, with some excitement; 'Hunoomaun went away from K——— ? Then I think he really is here! When I was being taken to Georgetown prison, I met a body of newbound men coming along the road from the ship to one of these plantations; and I thought I saw him among them, but could not believe it; yet I thought I knew the villain! He must have come in the ship before yours. He may even be on this estate or the next one.'

Lutchmee's heart grew cold with apprehension as she heard this, and she clung tightly to Dilloo's shoulder, not as of old, freshly oiled, soft, and springy as the shoulder of a young deer, but dry, toil-stained, and hard. In an instant there flashed through her mind all the possibilities of this unwelcome conjunction.

'Never mind,' said Dilloo; 'see! I have the means of defending you.' Placing his hand down a crevice formed by the meeting of the wattle and the low mud wall, he drew forth a cutlass, about two feet long, made in one piece, and used for cutting the canes in crop-time. 'Do you see that?' he cried, in a loud determined voice: 'I always keep it well sharpened: It shall protect my honour and yours, my Lutchmee, and, if not, we shall die together.'

As he stood up there in the dark hut, fierce and glowing, Lutchmee shrank before the fire in her husband's eyes. It was not so much like the frank lionhood of his former days, as it seemed to her to resemble the sullen savagery of a tiger.

'O Dilloo,' she said, covering her eyes with her little hands, 'you frighten me!'

He dropped the weapon into its hiding-place; and coming back to her side, wound his arms around her, but said nothing.

Thus it was that Lutchmee and Dilloo met in the golden fields and paradisiac working-grounds of Dost Mahommed, the Government recruiter!

CHAPTER XIII

A VISITOR

IT was on the second day after Dilloo's return that, as we have said, Lutchmee was sitting in the house preparing the evening meal. Outside, in the fireplace, the brushwood crackled and smoked beneath the pot. As she energetically worked the wooden pestle, the doorway was darkened by the figure of a woman.

'Salaam!' said the woman.

'Salaam!' replied Lutchmee very quietly.

The woman unceremoniously sat down and watched Lutchmee, who, with Eastern gravity, went on with her work. Her visitor had a not displeasing face, though she was evidently much older than Lutchmee, and her teeth, when she smiled, showed gaps in their blackened rows. She wore a very limited jacket, exposing her plump shoulders; a not over-clean calico skirt; and she was without a scarf. But round her neck were two heavy necklaces – one, a solid collar of silver, the other formed of florins linked together. In her ears, which were pierced with many holes, were rows of rings. Her nose was decorated with a gold ring set with a doubtful stone; and her arms and ankles were loaded with silver bangles.

'Where did you come from?' said the woman.

'From Behar,' replied Lutchmee.

'Oho! then you are from the country – a real villager?' exclaimed the woman, scrutinising Lutchmee's face and dress. 'We get very few of your sort here, I can tell you,' she added, when she had concluded her survey. 'How pretty you are!'

'Why, who are you?' inquired Lutchmee, innocently.

'Well, I *was* a dancing-girl when I was younger,' replied the other, laughing. 'You know, what that means, even at K——,

don't you? But, you see, I was born in Benares, and lived there all
my life. Then I went to other places and lived as best I could. It is
very hard living in great bazaars, so I was glad of the chance of
coming here as a respectable woman' (she laughed shrilly), 'when
I fell in with a recruiter who offered me bounty-money and so
many good things.'

'And do you like this place?' asked Lutchmee.

'I should think so; I have good reason. The voyage was pleasant.
I was sent to this estate – one of the best in the country. I soon
found I could have my pick of a husband, and plenty of money
besides. See!' she added, with feminine vanity, 'I have had all
these given to me: they are worth three hundred dollars. I have
five cows, and I pay a man to keep them.'

'Who gave you all these: your husband?'

The woman laughed again at Lutchmee's simplicity. She had
exceeded the woman of Samaria in the number of her husbands,
though she was unlike her in a sense of shame. A husband,
among Coolie women in British Guiana, is a varying factor. You
cannot understand much that takes place there without knowing
this.

Lutchmee's ideas of modesty and sense of delicacy were, no
doubt, far inferior to those of an English girl; yet she, by some
God-given instinct, shrank from her visitor's bold confessions. She
knew not what to say, so she said, –

'What is your name?'

'Ramdoolah. Tell me, is Dilloo really your husband?'

'Yes; – why?'

'I did not believe he was married at all, though he used to say so.
He is a close, clever man; and so handsome! Any woman on the
estate would have married him. I know I wanted to; but he never
would look at me.'

Lutchmee sprang to her feet, her eyes aglow, her lissome body
trembling with passion.

'Stop! you vile woman!' she cried. 'Hold your abominable
tongue! You speak of my husband, who is a man too good and
noble for such carrion as you even to look at. Begone, or I shall
tear out your eyes!'

Ramdoolah, also, had risen. She was not a woman, after her experiences, to be afraid of the nails or the tongue of a young girl, and was certainly not moved with bodily fear; but the moral air and posture of Lutchmee were too commanding to be matched with any weapons at the disposal of the bazaar-woman. So she tried to laugh it off.

'Ha! my fine girl,' said she; 'you are too good for this place, I see. I wouldn't be you for a good deal. Your pride will soon be taken down, or my name is not Ramdoolah!'

By this time the younger woman, in uncontrollable fury, had rushed to the place where the weapon was hidden, and drew forth the cutlass, at sight of which Ramdoolah beat a retreat. Outside the hut she met Dilloo.

'Go in, my handsome lad,' she cried, smiling maliciously; 'go in, and look after your princess! She's a fine girl to put on such airs. Won't they be taken out of her before long, that's all!'

When Dilloo, without replying, hastily entered the hut, he found his wife there, standing flashing and furious as a Pythoness, with the cutlass in her hand. In a moment the weapon dropped on the floor with a clang; and she hung, sobbing, on his neck.

'O Dilloo! Dilloo! That wretched woman has been speaking to me about you, as if you were a common fellow that would speak to the like of her. To think you should have been even named by her lips! I could bear it no longer. Have I done wrong?'

'Lutchmee,' replied Dilloo, gravely, sitting on the floor, and making his wife sit beside him, 'hear me. There is not one woman on this estate who came of a respectable stock. They were poor creatures from great cities, like Lucknow, Benares, or Calcutta. We should think of them pitifully. I should say they are better here than they were there. They get married, some of them many times over; and a few happily forget their old condition and become better women. I would never have anything to do with them. They cause nearly all the trouble among Coolies in this place. Two men on this estate have been hung for murdering women who were not faithful to them. But you must not quarrel with anyone. We are now obliged to live among them, for five years, and your peace and our safety depend on our being on good terms with these people.

They are Indian, after all, you know; and we have far more dangerous enemies in the English. Once give this woman a chance, and she might ruin us both. She is the most treacherous woman on the estate.'

'O Dilloo! I cannot bear this any longer. Let us run away from this dreadful place.'

'There is no running away from this place, my Lutchmee. The interior lands are wild and swampy, full of snakes, and no runaway could live there. The roads are all kept by Negro police, black people, who hate us. They stop any Coolie travelling without a written pass from the manager. No: our plan is to be patient, watchful, careful of our money; and, perhaps, in a year or two we may be able to buy our freedom and go back to India.'

'I will do anything you tell me, Dilloo,' said his wife, with her head on his breast; 'but, please, put away that cutlass where I cannot find it.'

CHAPTER XIV

MEETING – BUT NO GREETING

DILLOO had been working for nine hours, and was hungry. His
little wife soon quelled her apprehensions and set to work with
recovered spirits to prepare his meal. He meanwhile went out to
the trench, not many yards off, to wash away the thick clayey soil
which coated his legs and hands and arms. Dilloo was one of two
or three Coolies on the estate who were able to make wages
approximating to the promised *two rupees a day*. It was by hard
work, however, though work of which both immigrants and
Creoles are very fond. For trench-digging the highest wages was
paid. Eighty or ninety cents for twelve and a quarter feet of trench
twelve feet wide and five feet deep was the usual remuneration.

Standing nearly naked, the labourer digs out the soft wet clay
with a long-handled scoop by the sheer strength of arms and
shoulders, and then throws it out of the trench some three or four
yards. Negroes, being generally more powerful, are preferred for
this work, but few of them could surpass at it our lithe and brawny
Bengalee. There was this difference between them, however, to
the planter. Scarcely any Negro would work more than two days a
week, at most three, while Dilloo's indenture, spite of the law, was
held by manager and magistrate to bind him to at least five days'
labour, and he often was obliged to work six. In fact, by the system
in vogue, the more a Coolie did the more he was compelled to do.
The Negro thus had the advantage, for after making an effort for
a day or two, he could lounge for the rest of the week. It spoke
well, however, for the effect on Dilloo's constitution, of his steady
work, that he was rarely in the hospital. One good result of his
industry was a handsome hoard of silver pieces, two cows, and a
wonderful conglomerate dress, which he had purchased of a
Georgetown dealer, and which looked like the cast-off garments

of some stage-strutting monarch. At the Tadja festival it was his wont to come out conspicuous in this gorgeous attire. Quite a trade is done among Coolies in ancient uniforms and coats of many colours, which you may see them carrying on their heads until they approach their own homes; and then, vanishing behind a hedge, they will reappear in a state of decoration that ravishes their friends.

As Dilloo, now of course wearing nothing but his 'babba' or loin-cloth, was washing his feet in the canal, a knot of the new-service immigrants who had been employed at the 'back' came along the dam. They looked weary. They had been working in the sun from early morning, and had walked three miles out and three miles home. One man among them was remarkable for his height and size. The villager from Behar stood above the poor weavers and sweepers of Delhi or Calcutta. It was Hunoomaun. Dilloo recognised him in a moment, but preserved his composure. Hunoomaun was more surprised. Though he had been three months on the estate, and knew that one, Dilloo, among others, was in gaol at Georgetown, it had not occurred to him that it was his old antipathy at K——. He therefore lifted up his hands, and cried, –

'Dilloo?'

'Yes,' replied the other, drily. 'Hunoomaun, you see Dilloo! You have followed me to this place. We live together on this estate.'

'Is it peace or war?' inquired the other, looking doubtfully at the fine limbs of Dilloo, which glistened in the afternoon sun.

'I hold no grudge,' replied Dilloo, cautiously. 'Years have come and gone since you by your evil-doing made me your enemy. Since then you have been more base and brutal than ever, and my wife, who is with me here, has told me of your wickedness and flight. I had a mind to kill you,' – Dilloo looked straight at the chokedar, and his eye glared a moment so fiercely that Hunoomaun went back a pace, – 'but I am willing to forget the past if you will do so. You must confine your attentions, though, to the other women on the estate. Any one who troubles Lutchmee I will cut into pieces!'

Hunoomaun read a determination in Dilloo's eyes that could not be misinterpreted. He was too cowardly to challenge it just then.

'I will be friendly,' said he.

'No,' said Dilloo, 'we can never be friends: let us agree not to be enemies. It will be better for you! Do not cross my path, and I will not cross yours. That is my house; do not go near it at your peril. We are obliged to live on this estate together, and all Coolies should agree to help each other, and not quarrel among themselves. All the Coolies here look upon me as their leader,' he added, more loudly, with an Asiatic touch of self-assertion.

Some of the others who had listened to this conversation with curiosity testified their assent to this.

'All Coolies trust Dilloo.'

The chokedar's overbearing nature, though he was a coward, resented Dilloo's tone, but he held his tongue, while he mentally resolved that the eminence of his foe should not be unassailed if he could help it. Hunoomaun was a man of great acuteness and tact. He had managed, during the voyage to Demerara, to win the good opinion of the officers of the ship, and was formally reported as a good immigrant. Among his countrymen on board he had gained some respect. About forty Coolies from his ship, the 'Benares,' were allotted to Belle Susanne. He had not spent many days on the estate before he began to acquire a very fair idea of its economy, and of the means by which he might better his condition. He found that, as a rule, there were placed under the overseers, in immediate charge of the gangs, persons called 'drivers,' – a name of no small significance, which had come down from the old Negro times, but was used now to indicate a person acting in the capacity of a foreman. Almost universally these drivers were Negroes. They were with the gangs all day. They watched the men at work. It was their duty to see that the task was properly done. They took notes mentally, for none of them could write, of the amount of labour done by each person in their gang, and the accuracy of their memory in these particulars was astonishing. Their reports about the individuals in their charge were listened to with attention by the overseers, consequently they wielded a great deal of influence in the estate community. They could play all sorts of tricks with a man's work; could get him sent the long three miles 'back' to reach it; or, on the other hand, could favour him by keeping him nearer the buildings, or assigning him lighter tasks: could help to cheat him out of his wages; in fact, they could either make a man feel the full weight of his obligation or reduce it to an agreeable load. Hunoomaun's quick mind at once fastened on this office as the key of the position. It could be made by an unscrupulous man even more powerful than that of an overseer. He inquired if it was ever held by a Coolie, and found that the Dilloo, who was then in gaol, had held it a short time, but had been degraded because he had taken the part of his former 'matties,' or companions. This was a misuse of power of which the former chokedar was not likely to be guilty. He ascertained, also, that there were other Coolie 'sirdars' on the estate, and resolved to give all his efforts to the attainment of this position.

His plan was to retain the influence he had won on board ship over his fellow travellers. For the first week of their arrival they were allowed to lounge about the Negro-yard and do as they pleased, getting rations from the hospital. Each man then received from the stores a cutlass, which he was instructed by the old hands how to sharpen and to smooth at the handle. They were then set to carrying megass, and afterwards to weeding and clearing brush. This is the rank and rapid growth of reeds, bushes, creepers, and weeds which in the tropics a very short time suffices to produce on a fallow field, and it presents the hardest and most tiresome of all the labours to be performed on an estate. Hunoomaun soon learned how to do this work, and made it his business to help his companions to become adepts at it, in this way securing their good will at the same time that he gained the approval of drivers and overseers. Hence the "Benares' lot" pleased Drummond vastly. They were every way the best addition he had made to the *personnel* of the estate; and all this was due to one clever man among them, who produced this result in pursuing his own ends. At the time when Dilloo and Hunoomaun met, the latter had already won a place in the esteem of his employers and the regard of the people. The more galling, therefore, was Dilloo's patronizing air to the wily chokedar. However, he and Dilloo managed to exchange 'salaams' without any further indication of feeling for that interview.

CHAPTER XV

AGREED

On the Sunday succeeding the day when Dilloo and Lutchmee had encountered Hunoomaun and Ramdoolah, the two latter, invested in their cleanest and brightest garments, were sauntering together, in the sultry evening, along the smooth, sandy shore, which the ebbing tide had left in front of the fringe of brush to the edge of which it used to flow. The Coolie gentleman, nominally occupying the position of Ramdoolah's husband, was at that moment engaged at a little opium shop in the Chinese quarters, kept, with an affectation of secrecy, by Ching-a-lung, the ugliest Chinaman outside his own country, – a hopeless dead-weight to managers and overseers, by whom, from mistaken motives of kindness, his illegal traffic was winked at. Achattu, the husband in question, was one of the earlier importations from India, and a Madrassee. At one time he had by thrift and cleverness, as an able-bodied Coolie may do in the West Indies, made a considerable sum of money. He became the owner of three or four cows: he paid a Negro man to look after them, – a change of race relations not unknown in British Guiana. But Achattu had one want – a wife. The number of women on the estates was at first so limited that it would have been impossible for him to get a wife for love or money. As the proportion of female immigrants increased through the exertions of the Colonial Government and its officials, more opportunities were afforded the wealthier Coolies to select partners, too seldom for life. A curious circumstance was wont to diminish their chances: the long sea voyage worked miraculous results upon the affections. On the discharge from a ship of a cargo of immigrants, sometimes as many as thirty or forty couples were found to have made engagements on the voyage to tie their fates together; and in order that the rule of allotment of

relatives to the same estate might be applied to their case, the
immigration depôt at Georgetown became the theatre of a comic
scene. The Agent-General caused the aspirants for matrimony to
be arranged in two Roger-de-Coverley lines, the women on one
side and the men on the other, each, it is to be hoped, facing the
desired partner. Between the lines passed the Agent-General,
accompanied by an interpreter, haranguing the parties on the
duties, temptations and perils of matrimony. Since many dialects
were represented, and the interpreting resources of the
Georgetown depôt are limited, the pertinency of this performance must often have been a puzzle to those concerned. At the
end of his exhortations, the official, by a single and simple ceremony, made the forty couples happy or miserable, as chance
might develop. When so many of the single women were withdrawn from competition before they reached the estates, it may
be imagined that the residuary chances left to the older and richer
Coolies were neither extensive nor brilliant. Hence Achattu had
lived to himself. He lent money to his needy brethren at astonishing rates of interest; he kept silver dollars in a large chest in his
room carefully locked, and secretly disposed of some of his specie
in unfrequented parts of the estate; he did not care to let the
officials know how rich he was, by depositing it all in the Savings
Bank. But a subtle Chinaman, suspecting Achattu's wealth to be
greater than was known, made it his business to study the latter's
habits for some months, and followed him till he had discovered
the closest of his hiding-places. One day Achattu found himself
poorer by several hundred dollars than he had been the day before. All the hair he forthwith pulled out of his head and beard, –
all his exertions in dancing a regretful fandango about the outraged spot would not assuage his grief. He took to arrack, and
made himself drunk: he sought out the bench of the opium shop,
and made himself terribly sick, and, finally, he came across
Ramdoolah, who knew all about him, and willingly undertook to
soothe his sorrows. He gave her a necklet and a cow: he paid her
existent husband another cow and thirty dollars to purchase a
voluntary divorce, *a mensa et thoro*, and took Ramdoolah to his
heart and home. Through these combined influences Achattu's

wealth dwindled away. Ramdoolah soon carried about on her person, in the shape of armlets, necklets, and bangles, most of his secret hoards. The big chest yielded up its deposits, and became an insolvent bank. His debtors were pressed to return their loans; and, as these came in, Ching-a-lung, or the gambling-room of Chin-a-foo – another institution on the estate – swallowed them up. It can hardly be wondered at, therefore, that Ramdoolah was looking out for another engagement, and was now coquetting with the gallant Hunoomaun; for her practical shrewdness told her that at Belle Susanne he was a coming man. Let us conceal ourselves in the brush and overhear a little of their conversation. Ramdoolah is speaking:–

RAMDOOLAH. There is a beautiful country-girl who has come here lately, named Lutchmee, who is the most respectable Hindoo woman I ever saw in this place.

HUNOOMAUN. I know her well. She came from my own village: she is a great fool, and I owe her a grudge. If it had not been for her, I should not have been here.

RAMDOOLAH. You did not care for her, did you ? Was she ever a friend of yours?

HUNOOMAUN. No, no. A friend of mine, a peon, took a violent fancy to her, and tried to make too free with her. She declared, most falsely, that I was the person. That cursed fellow, Dilloo, believed her, and collecting a number of his friends, gave me a beating. He is my enemy till one or other of us dies. As for the girl, he left her behind him; and she, out of sheer spite at my taking no notice of her, denounced me to the magistrate with whom she lived, and I was obliged to fly from the place.

To a woman of Ramdoolah's character, it seemed so natural for another Indian woman to behave in the manner described by the peon, that she gave a ready belief to his story, and hastened to take advantage of the information.

RAMDOOLAH. The little slut! I went in to see her one day, and indeed she is very pretty, but I found her as proud as a bird of paradise, and as haughty as the highest Brahminee. She treated me as if I were the filth of the streets, and when I talked of Dilloo – who, as you say, is an ill-conditioned brute of a fellow – as he deserved, she seized a cutlass; and, had I not escaped, would have wounded me.

HUNOOMAUN. Oho! She did so, did she? The creature! Then you and she are enemies, of course. You see, our interests are the same. We must agree to live together, and then we can help each other to work out our revenge. How are you to get rid of Achattu?

RAMDOOLAH. Oh, you must manage that! You have only to fill his stomach for a few weeks, lend him a little money, encourage him to drink and gamble, and he will be in your hands. He will then readily sell me to you.

HUNOOMAUN. (In reality caring little for Ramdoolah, but having arrived at the belief that she was the cleverest woman on the estate, and would be a powerful ally in working out his various plots.) Well, my sweet one! delight of my heart! and lustre of my eyes! I will do all that is necessary to win possession of one so handsome, so clever, so desirable. With your help I can secure the highest position of any Coolie on the estate, and all my wealth shall be thrown at your feet.

RAMDOOLAH. It is a bargain, my friend. Give me ten dollars as the earnest of it, and then I shall be yours!

The shrewd Hindoo showed no hesitation, though he inwardly felt some chagrin, as he disengaged, from a fold in his babba, ten silver dollars, part of his bounty money, and counted them into the outstretched hand of his business-like *fiancée*.

CHAPTER XVI

LOST*!*

IN accordance with his engagement with Ramdoolah, the peon had now to wind Achattu in his toils, and bring him to a state of mind in which he would consent to part with his wife. Poor Achattu had been indentured three times on as many different estates, and had also spent an interval of several years as a free man. His talents and wealth had procured him a good name and position among his countrymen. He was well known on both the coasts, as they are termed, of the Demerara county, in Berbice, and even on the less accessible Arabian or Aroebisce coast, beyond the river Essequibo. The place he had once held as a banker and money-lender had been more than filled by Lutchmee's first friend in the colony, Akaloo, who was a free man and travelled from estate to estate in the pursuit of his business. It is from new Coolies that these money-lenders chiefly derive their profits. In the process of acclimatisation, the poor people, from their awkwardness at the unaccustomed labour, or from sheer physical incapacity, often fall behind in their receipts, in spite of the bounty-money with which they begin, and find that they cannot live on their earnings. Though they were at the time when these events occurred, by the law and by its administration kept strictly to their part of the contract, made in India, and forced to work at least five days a week, the corresponding promise of ten annas to two rupees a day, offered by authority of the Governor and Court of Policy of British Guiana, was not recognized as a contract in the colony, and could not be enforced. A more singular instance of Christian and official easiness of conscience could scarcely be cited than this fact. The legislature of British Guiana, with the connivance and sanction of Her Majesty's representative, passed resolutions affirming a statement of current rates of wages, at a time when it was well known that scarcely an immigrant in the colony was earning anything of the kind. Nay, the recurring injustice of enforcing one side of a contract and overlooking the other was alike disregarded by Governor, legislators, and administrators of the law, so that, as a fact, Coolies who, disheartened by the fraud, failed or refused to work for the indifferent wages available to them, were again and again brought before the magistrates to be fined and imprisoned.

It was in such cases as these that men like Achattu and Akaloo proved to be, to their own profit, real benefactors to their fellow-immigrants. They lent them money to pay off their fines, or to procure the food they could not earn. By this means new Coolies, becoming gradually acclimatised, were at length able to do more work, and thus to earn enough to pay off their debts. Many remained hopelessly in debt during the first five years of their indenture, and upon re-indenturing themselves for another five years were obliged to sacrifice to their creditors the greater part of the bounty-money they then received. Though these Indian money-lenders were avaricious enough, they performed many acts of forbearance and kindness to their needy brethren, and were by no means commonly regarded with the aversion that attaches to such tradesmen elsewhere. If a Coolie with twenty-five dollars desired to purchase a cow worth fifty or sixty, he could get the necessary sum, at a certain rate of interest, from Akaloo. Various shops were kept on some of the estates, and to their adventurers Akaloo frequently furnished the capital. On occasions of some particularly unjust decision by a magistrate, involving a fine, both Akaloo and Achattu had been known to pay it off gratuitously.

But, as we have seen, poor Achattu had long given up the pursuit of business. Dollars and 'bitts', or fourpennies, as soon as they were earned, now went directly to the opium-shop, or were more rapidly lost in another Chinese den, the gambling-house of Chin-a-foo. This estate 'hell' of Mr. Chin-a-foo was a queer place. It was on the westward border of the village, an old tumble-down tenement, ostensibly forbidden to the Coolies by the manager, who to an inspector would have shown surprise at the discovery that anyone professed to inhabit it, or would have alleged that immigrants preferred that sort of tenement, and that it was impossible to keep them out of it. A simple expedient open to the manager in such cases appeared never to have occurred to him, namely, to pull down the house.

However, here, in a room which the injurious Chin-a-foo had enlarged by a low half-underground out-building of wattle and mud, with door and windows carefully closed; lit by a wretched petroleum lamp, that threw out a dismal glimmer in the reeking atmosphere, there squatted on the floor fifteen or twenty Coolies, most of them Chinese. The Hindoos, at the time of which we are writing, rarely indulged in either of the Chinese dissipations of opium-smoking and gambling, though since then there is no doubt that these vices have largely bitten the Indian immigrants. On a low bench of boards, two Chinese and an Indian – a woman – lay in the helpless torpor that had succeeded their inhalation of the horrible narcotic. Round the lamp the rest squatted or stood, pitting their bitts on the throw of some bamboo dice; eager, yet silent, the strange, unimpressive faces of the Chinamen contrasting with the starting eyes and clenched teeth of the two or three Hindoos. In the midst, most excited of all, was the Madrassee, who, when first he entered that place, had been received with surprise and respect, but who was now regarded with contempt, even by Chin-a-foo himself. That gentleman was an old gambler from Hong-Kong, with a face it would be a work of art to describe. The lines in its bleared and yellow surface were marked out by long-established deposits of dirt. It seemed to have been crumpled and kneaded and flattened by one of the grotesque idol-makers of his own country into the nearest possible resemblance to a broken-nosed monkey that could be reached by any human artist. The leery slits he used as eyes were only opened sufficiently to let in the knowledge which their owner wanted, and to give no clue to the observer of the emotions or thoughts of the spirit – if there were a spirit – within. In the combination of his features his gums and teeth appeared to have been a matter of difficulty to the designer, and to have been fortuitously placed in the least appropriate relation to his other features. The blue shaven head, with its short grey pigtail, was in harmony, if I may so say, with the grotesqueness of his countenance. Thick was his neck; short, sturdy, and powerful his body, which was clothed in a dirty blue blouse and paejamas of cotton. In a belt round his waist, but concealed under the wide paejamas, was a knife about two inches broad and fifteen long, tapering to its end, and kept in a state of suspicious brightness. There were few men on the estate who would have tackled Chin-a-foo. He was considered altogether a dangerous problem to solve, and no attempt to solve it was made by any one. Drummond had observed him. He could, when he chose, be a good worker; and when his earnings at the gamblinghouse failed, as they sometimes did, he took his share, with great address, in the labour of the sugar-house. But more frequently he wandered away to the back of the estate, or a short distance into the savannah behind it, and sometimes brought home birds or snakes, or the iguanas he had caught. Drummond knew that the immigrants at Belle Susanne would find some means of gambling on the estate, or would go to the next estate for it, so he directed the overseers not to see too much of Mr. Chin-a-foo's business, at the same time warning the sullen rascal that any breach of the peace occurring in his hut would be followed by instant punishment.

To-night, having thrown off his upper garment, thus disclosing from the waist upwards his muscular trunk, the Chinaman glided softly through the place, bearing a coarse jar and a half-cocoa-nut, offering to his patrons and guests some of the illicit arrack which he kept concealed in a corner of his hut.

'Arrack, Achattu!' said he, with a motion of the face intended for a grin, and shaking his diabolical head at the rest of the company, as he stopped at the Madrassee, whose heavy eyes betokened that he had already had enough, though they were still fixed on the fatal pieces of bamboo with their rude marks; and he was staking his last coins on the chances. Achattu shook his head.

'No.' He showed his empty hands. 'Trust me?'

Chin-a-foo was decided in his negative.

'You owe me seven dollars. I cannot trust you any more.'

Achattu hung down his head. It was a shame, indeed, to have fallen so low that Chin-a-foo would not trust him.

'How much do you want ?' said a deep voice from the door-way.

Every one started. The voice was a strange voice in that company: it was, indeed, that of Hunoomaun. He came forward towards the light.

'I am going to try my luck with my friend Achattu,' said he, sitting down beside him. 'You do not seem to have done well to-night, Achattu?'

Achattu recognised the peon as a new Coolie, and Chin-a-foo, who, when first startled by the interruption, had looked round nervously with a quick glance, immediately began to play the host to the new-comer with many professions of respect. The fellow had made himself an adept in the language of the Indian Coolies.

'Will my friend drink to the good of my house, since he has placed his worthy feet inside my door?' said he.

Hunoomaun took the cocoa-nut, and, nearly filling its bowl, drank off the stinging liquor at a pull. It seemed to have no effect on him, and the boldness of the act was noted with more admiration by the guests than by their wily host, who had conscientiously watered the spirit in rather excessive proportion.

'Now,' said the chokedar; 'I, and my friend Achattu, are going to play together against the whole company, if they like. Achattu,' he whispered, 'I will lend you five dollars.'

The Madrassee's face brightened up, and he called for more liquor. The half stupor of his drunkenness seemed to pass from him. He again exhibited the keen, eager frenzy of a gambler's hope.

The two won. Hunoomaun was cool and apt, and evidently acted upon calculation. The other had the usual gambler's superstitions, and would fain have pressed them on his wily partner, but the latter would not listen. After an hour's play there were four dollars to be divided between them. Achattu was in an ecstasy. He drank again and again; he placed his arms around Hunoomaun's neck, and covered him with maudlin caresses. The peon rose as if to go, when Achattu challenged him to a few farewell throws.

'No: I cannot stay. You play for too small stakes. I must go to sleep.'

'Wait,' said the other, feverishly, holding out the dollars which Hunoomaun had lent him and the two others he had won. 'I will toss you for any stake you like; one dollar, two dollars, if you please.'

The peon instantly sat down and took up the box. The Chinese and Indians, to whom such high play was a rare sight, leaned forward over the pair in great excitement.

'Let it be two dollars, then,' said Hunoomaun. 'Now, what do you say?'

'Three!' cried Achattu.

'Six!' said the peon.

He threw five. It was nearer his guess than the other's.

'You have lost'.

The Madrassee seized the box with a trembling hand. It was made from a thick bamboo. He gave it a flourish.

'Seven!' said Hunoomaun.

'Three!' cried Achattu, again.

It was his favourite number. He had thrown it exactly. The excitement grew hotter. The lamp was dying out. The circle pressed forward so eagerly that there was scarcely room on the floor between the players. Their half-naked bodies glistened with the dew of heat. The dim radiance played weirdly on the strange countenances about it. From the doorway, against which he was leaning, lowered the sweating face of Chin-a-foo, to whom these last moments were always periods of anxiety. The next throw was won by Hunoomaun; the next, and the next. In ten minutes the Madrassee's hand was empty. He seized his hair and cursed his fates, and took another pull at the cocoa-nut.

'Lend me one ten dollars more!' he cried.

The chokedar coolly counted them into his hand, and said, 'I will throw you five times for the ten dollars.'

He won three out of five throws. Achattu threw down the dollars. As he made an effort to rise from the squatting posture he had maintained for three hours, he stumbled, and fell down insensible. The Chinaman, after coolly examining him, without a word picked him up and, with the assistance of two others, proceeded to carry him to his house.

As the men lifted their senseless burden, a woman, who, through a crevice in the wooden wall, had been closely watching the scene, glided swiftly away and ran before them to Achattu's house, which she reached and entered unperceived. It was

Ramdoolah. The bearers deposited the Madrassee silently on the bank, outside his hut. The woman inside, breathless, listened to the whisperings of the men

'Shall we call up Ramdoolah?'

'No,' replied the Chinaman, coolly: 'he will soon come to himself and go in.'

Ramdoolah was of the same opinion, and, after listening a few minutes, without hearing any movement on Achattu's part, she fell asleep.

CHAPTER XVII

CHANCE-MEDLEY

THE overseer who, the morning after Achattu's unlucky 'corro-boree,' went the rounds to wake up the Coolies, found the Madrassee lying on the bank as he had been left by his companions. He was stiff and cold. The fact was that the wily Chinaman had the night before discovered the fatal issue to his customer of the last throw, but he kept the information to himself.

Ramdoolah, on being awakened, proceeded to fill the village with her ululations. These, however, were regarded with great stolidity by the crowd of males and females who soon gathered to look at the body. Hunoomaun, always an early riser, was one of the first to arrive on the scene, and he slipped away to warn Chin-a-foo. That gentleman, looking more dirty and ghastly than usual, then appeared, pulling violently at his pig-tail, holding up his hands, giving vent to nasal and guttural exclamations of great variety and force, and meantime, as they came up, whispering to any of the spectators who had been present at his house the evening before that they were to know nothing about Achattu's last moments. For the poor Madrassee there was a general expression of sympathy. He had once been a head man among them, and few creatures are so degraded as to be insensible to the reverses of fate in the case of a life that is familiar to them. They recalled the wit of the lively Madrassee; his once genial, easy manner, his strength and aptitude, and his occasional acts of generosity. The feeling gradually grew stronger and stronger against the influences which had brought the poor fellow to his fate, and sarcastic exclamations were uttered by the crowd to the disadvantage of both Chin-a-foo and Ramdoolah.

'She may well cry! See all those silver ornaments he gave her!' said a woman.

'Ah! she'll get over that,' said a man, – no other than Nobbeebuckus, who had once made a futile attempt to seduce her from the dead, ' as soon as some one else is kind to her.'

'I expect he died in good time for her,' said another; 'she is making too much noise to be in earnest.'

By this time three or four overseers were on the spot. Ramdoolah, who, her head wrapped in a chudder, was sitting on the ground beside the body, still exhibiting considerable animation and vigour in her grief, was sternly ordered to adjourn her lamentations to a fitter season; an injunction she obeyed with admirable self-command.

'Do you know how he came to be lying dead outside your house?' said Crampton to the woman.

'No, massa; no see my man last night. Me go sleep – no see him.'

The overseer did himself the credit not to believe a word of this.

'Well,' said he, 'any other Coolie see him? Chin-a-foo, you sabby Ingliss, sabby Indian talk; ask any Coolie see Achattu any time?'

The Chinaman, peering through the slits in his face, and preserving an impassive aspect, pitched his voice in the key and tone of a question, but really instructed his matties not to know anything about the dead man's business last evening. Every Coolie present instantly shook his head: Chin-a-foo also opened his palms, and half-shrugging his shoulders, expressed a regret that he had not seen Achattu the night before, since he had apparently been so ill. The Chinaman professed to be something of a doctor. Hereupon Drummond, who had been sent for, arrived. He first of all carefully examined the man, and ascertained that there were no marks of violence upon him. He took note of the fact that he had been drinking. And lastly, opening the clenched hand, he quietly slipped therefrom the die which the poor fellow had thrown in his last bout with fortune. Drummond's suspicion was that the man had been poisoned.

'Ha! Mr. Chin-a-foo, this Coolie go your house last night, eh? Who put 'ee here?'

'No, massa,' replied Chin-a-foo, with exemplary calmness. 'Achattu no money, no trust 'im: no come to Chin-a-foo house diss too long time.'

'Look here, sir! Do you see that? I just found it in the man's hand.'

The face and hands of Chin-a-foo displayed the most grotesque astonishment.

'Yours is the only gambling place on the estate, you know,' continued Drummond, talking ordinary English in his excitement, 'and the last thing the man was doing was evidently gambling. Lay hold of that fellow, Craig!'

Craig's powerful grasp was on the Chinaman's shoulder in a moment. The next instant there was a flash of steel in the morning sun, and a knife was driven into the side of the young Scotchman, – driven by a steady and accustomed hand. Before the villain could repeat his blow, Drummond's fist had felled him to the ground and his arm had caught the fainting youth. Two overseers disarmed and secured the Chinaman.

All this passed too quickly to be told, but its effect on the Coolies was extraordinary. At sight of the blood on the one hand, and of their 'mattie' in the hands of the overseers on the other, the Chinese, especially, became hysterical in their excitement, and loud cries arose on every side. The pigtails brandished their knives, the Hindoos ran for their latties.

There was a Babel of outcries. 'Well done, Chin-a-foo! Take him from them,' and the like.

Some pressed forward on Drummond, who supported Craig on his left arm, as he shouted to the overseers to stick to the Chinaman at all hazards. At the same moment his right fist levelled a too-audacious Coolie who came within reach of it. The mob closed about him and the overseers, and began to use their sticks. The noise brought out the whole village. The women, with loud shrieks, encouraged the men to the attack. Simon Pety, bravely running to the rescue, excited the mob to such frenzy that he was fain to cut and run for his life, pursued by some infuriated Chinese females. All the pigtails turned out of their quarters, flourishing their knives; and the rest of the overseers arriving on the scene did good service with both sticks and fists. But Indians and Chinese in a fury are not easily quieted. The Coolies not only held their own, but were getting the better of the Whites. Two overseers were seriously wounded. The Negroes on their way to work watched the fray at a safe distance. Drummond, hampered by his burden, could scarcely keep up under the storm of blows that now rained upon him. At this juncture, Dilloo, with several others, arrived from the extremity of the village. Seeing Drummond nearly overpowered by the numbers who pressed upon him, and observing, in a moment, that the row was over the Chinaman in custody, the Hindoo, without asking a question, dashed into the *mêlée*, and with his redoubtable lattey began to play about among the Chinese in a way that soon cleared a circle round the manager. His companions seconded him, at the same time calling upon their matties to stop fighting. Hunoomaun, who, to tell the truth, had been standing aloof from the fight, meditating which side he should take, was now seized with a sudden zeal for law and order, and took his place by Dilloo. Nothing could stand before those two men. The immigrants, finding themselves opposed by their own friends, began to fall off, and in a few minutes, carrying off their wounded, retired to the Chinese quarters, where they prepared for a desperate resistance to the now inevitable visit of the police.

Craig was removed to the manager's house and laid on Drummond's own bed. The loss of blood had rendered him insensible; but Drummond, having stripped him and examined the wound, came to the conclusion that it was not mortal, though he saw that the youth had had a narrow escape. The gambler's nerve and quickness had been trained to a nicety, and his blow was aimed with devilish skill. The doctor, who arrived an hour later, confirmed Drummond's opinion. Any wound is dangerous in that hideous climate, but with rest and quiet and incessant care, he hoped to be able to save the life of the strong and healthy youth.

A force of police soon arrived from the police-station at Guineatown, marching with their rifles to the front of the manager's house, where the inspector in command drew them up in military line. Order is maintained in colonies where Coolies labour and black men are citizens as it is in Ireland, by constables armed with rifles and muskets. There was some hesitation about the course to be pursued. The noise from the Negro-yard indicated a continuance of the excitement. It was clear that the advance of the police would give rise to a serious riot. Drummond was anxious to avoid a collision, and proposed to go down and address the men. This was immediately objected to by everyone but Dilloo. He offered to accompany the manager, and assured him of his safety.

'You, Dilloo!' said Drummond, looking into the Indian's open countenance, and at a dull bluish mark in his brown forehead, where a lattey had left the record of its visit. 'You fight for manager this day, kill manager to-morrow!'

'Massa,' replied the other, proudly, 'me no want massa die, cos Dilloo go prison. Too much Coolie fight massa: Dilloo help him.'

'Ha! Then a Coolie may have some sense of honour and fair play!'

Here, Hunoomaun, who had been closely watching the conversation, struck in.

'Hunoomaun too – new Coolie – fight too for manahee. Me and massa go to Coolie people.'

Dilloo looked sardonically grave, but said nothing. He felt sure the peon would not risk his skin among the Coolies just then.

'Then shall we all go?' said Drummond.

'No,' said Dilloo. 'Massa Drummon' and Dilloo one; Massa Drummon' and Hunoomaun one.'

Hunoomaun clearly shrank from facing those with whom he had been fighting, unless he were covered by the rifles of the police.

'Very well,' said Drummond. 'Look here, Dilloo, I'll trust you. My life will be in your hands, you sabby.' The Indian nodded. 'But you fought bravely, just now, and saved my life, so I will trust you again.'

The police were ordered to withdraw into the road. When Drummond and Dilloo appeared boldly advancing towards the Chinese quarters, where three or four hundred immigrants, of whom thirty were Chinese, were assembled, some excited by arrack they had plundered from the cellar of their hero, Chin-a-foo, the enterprise seemed to be one of no little danger; but Dilloo, holding up his hands, explained in a word or two that they had come unarmed and unaccompanied with any police, to talk with the people; and he asked them to sit down and listen. After a few minutes' hesitation the influence Dilloo had gained among his countrymen told. They squatted on their hams, or lounged against the buildings, and the Coolie and manager walked among them.

'Now,' said Drummond, characteristically swearing at them, 'what has taken you all to get up a mutiny in this way? and over that scoundrel Chin-a-foo, of all others! Am I not kind to you?'

'Iss, massa,' was the reply of those who spoke; the rest nodding their assent.

'I never beat you?'

'No, massa: ovaseah beat Coolie.'

Drummond winced at this naive rejoinder.

'Well, what possessed you to beat *me?* Overseer beat you, tell me, – every time tell me. You know Chin-a-foo rascal. Eh? look here!' He took off his hat and showed them blood on his forehead, and held out his arm, which was also bleeding. 'Coolie do that.'

There was a dead silence. The manager could not have produced a better effect by the most elaborate argument than he did by this illustration. The gentle-hearted people, now that a break had been effected in the torrent of their excitement, were completely transformed: they hung down their heads ashamed, all but the Chinese, who remained sullen and angry: Drummond might count that he would never make it up with them. Dilloo took advantage of the moment: he spoke in a language common to both the parties.

'Massa no punis Coolie, s'pose Coolie all still, go work, all shaky hand, no more fight, no more bad heart. Massa and Coolie friend.'

As Drummond nodded assent, the Coolies rose, and, crowding round him, put him through a course of hand-shaking worthy of an American President at his installation; and then quietly disappeared along the dams to their work.

In a short time, Mr. Chin-a-foo having been handed over to the police, and the overseers having received directions from Drummond as to their conduct towards the rioters, the manager and Missa devoted themselves to the wounded overseer. The scalp and flesh wounds of the others were treated by the doctor, and formed the subject of lively conversation at breakfast. It was a curious proof of the confidence that a manager may acquire among his people, that, after they had received Drummond's pledge of forgiveness, those Coolies who had been wounded in the affray came freely to the hospital to be treated, and made no attempt to conceal their complicity in the disturbance.

CHAPTER XVIII

AN ENGLISH JUSTICE

THE house of the magistrate of the Macusi district was situated on the other side of Guineatown, about two miles from Belle Susanne. Keeping along the monotonous road, after one had passed the flat swamps, the dirty drains, the jagged and rutted dams, amidst which there seemed to stalk about in straggling discomposure the timber-legged huts and hovels of the villagers of Guineatown, you came upon a barn-like building, shingle-roofed, of unpainted wood raised upon very lofty piles, and with a steep flight of steps leading from the garden to the verandah.

The garden that surrounded this ugly tenement was really one of great beauty. Divided by clipt hedges of thorny orange, its squares of black rich soil were gay with varieties of shrubs and flowers, some of which were not to be matched even in Guianian gardens; in the forks of the branches of shrubs and trees, such as the Frangipanni, the Cannon-ball tree, the Guava or the Tamarind, grew precious specimens of the orchids, with which, in infinite variety, the trees of the interior forests abound. In a broad trench at the end of the garden floated sleepily the great cups of the Victoria Regia and its mammoth prickly rafts of leaves. The long line of cocoa-palms beyond, the lime and orange trees with their shining leaves and fruit, the arbour where no one would have dared to sit, for marabuntas, and ants, and centipedes, and those tiny scourges, the *bêtes rouges*, had long since established their kingdom there, and resented the intrusion of foreigners; the straggling, overpowering Stephanotis, with its wealthy festoons of ivory bugles, sharing with a great Passion-flower the decoration of the entire verandah, made altogether an embowering Paradise for the homely though comfortable barrack which was the head-quarters of justice in that neighbourhood.

Here, shaded from the level rays of the early morning sun by the jalousies of the wide verandah, with its rocking-chairs, the invariable hammock, one or two small tables, on which appeared tokens of feminine occupancy, sat, at a large secretary-table, a man of about fifty years of age. Stout, but evidently quick and energetic, from the way in which he turned and spoke when interrupted by some one who suddenly emerged from the dining-room, he was a man on whom time had written the marks of care and disappointment. The dark, wiry hair on head and chin and cheeks was beginning to change its colour, and there were wrinkles on his low, broad forehead – the hieroglyphs of old troubles and passions. As he sat in his shirt-sleeves, his portly form was well displayed in the white-duck waistcoat and trousers it so neatly filled. You would have said, at the first glance, that his face evinced firmness and resolution; but, had you watched him shrewdly, you would have detected that the resolution was that of a ready, impulsive man; that about the well formed though too full lips there played the movements of doubt; that the eye was uncertain and fitful in its gaze, varying, indeed, with rather extraordinary changes of expression; and, as he sat at his work, the real nature of the man would have discovered itself to you in his movements. Sometimes he laid down his pen in the middle of a sentence, when his eye had lighted on something in his previous manuscript, or one of the books that were open about him; or perhaps to throw himself back and yawn, and dream a moment about some matter plainly disconnected from his occupation. Once he half rose to pursue a mosquito, more intemperate, keen, and pertinacious than its fellows; and then, suddenly changing his mind, took up his pen and rattled off with renewed application. Or, again, he leaned back in his chair and watched the impudent marabuntas, as, with loud trumpet accompaniment, they built their clay nests under the joists of the verandah. In fact, Mr. Marston, except for the lack of that element of energy which not only makes a man resolute to begin but to persist in every work he undertakes, might, with his abilities, have raised himself to an almost distinguished position at the English bar. But his study, as well as his practice, had been fortuitous and capricious, whence he had found it convenient to offer to his country talents that seemed incapable of supporting himself. The Colonial Office, that last refuge for mediocre and distressed rank or genius, with a charity that, to begin with, hopeth all things, though it is ofttimes not so enduring as many of its clients would desire, had given him the appointment of a stipendiary magistrate in Demerara, where he had now spent, with few intervals of absence, nearly twenty years of his life. Five years before, he had lost his wife, who left him six children, – a terrible charge upon a man in his position, with an Englishman's notions of his duty to them in the matter of education, and an Englishman's ideas of what was due to himself in the way of living.

How much trouble and sorrow their proud, but unpractical and extravagant views bring upon fellow-countrymen of ours in all parts of the world it would be hard to estimate, if not, indeed, to exaggerate. The struggles to make both ends meet, the thriftless and unheroic heroism of many a poor gentleman and lady, brought up in luxury, and schooled, after they have left school, in repression and want, and an economy they never know how to apply, would form a story, the satire of which would need no added bitterness from the pen of sarcasm, so strong is the gall of actual facts. It would be a tragedy none the less real because it was not intensified by its murders, suicides, and fatal passions. This is not the time or the place to consider how far this might be remedied, how far it is possible to change in whole classes of society unpractical ideas and the results of foolish upbringing for a training in the school of utility and restraint. Those who neglect to instil the principles of common sense and economy in earlier years pass on their wards to an academy of adversity, wherein the scholars too often ignominiously perish.

The person who, as we have said, interrupted the magistrate in his vigorous physical and mental exercitations, was a young girl of slight figure, which happened, on this morning, to be well shown off in a plain white dress, involving from neck to feet the symmetry of her form. She was not tall, but was moulded in the exquisite perfection of outline and proportion whereof tropical countries sometimes give such fine specimens in the earlier stages of life.

Her delicate features seemed to shine with a glorious light. The dark hair, smoothed over the ivory forehead, and braided in a coronet on her head, – the pencilled eyebrows, – the large, deep, lustrous eyes, fringed so coyly by the long lashes, – the slightly aquiline nose, with its chiselled nostrils, – the tender, small, sweet, cherry lips, the little dimpled chin, that curved, in magic beauty of outline, – and the neck, whereon this perfect mask was lifted up – an alabaster tower so small and yet so grand in its proportions – altogether gave Isabel Marston a loveliness lily-like and attractive beyond the play of words to picture.

'Bell,' said her father, glad of the interruption, – he suffered from endless *ennui*, – 'why are you so restless? You have been going in and out all the morning, and you know how important it is I should have this minute finished. The Governor requires me to send it in by to-morrow.'

'That is very cool of you, you naughty justice, when you know that if I sit here you talk to me every five minutes, and work far better when I am away. There!' said she, pulling back the big, grizzly head, and printing a kiss on the man's forehead, 'that is a fine for my absence; and now I want to tell you about something.'

'Gonzales sent for his bill again, I Suppose. Is there no one who will rescue me from the fellow, and do to death

– That valiant but ignoble Portuguese?

Why, these Madeirans are worse than Jews! Ay, and confound it, worrying a *magistrate* for money! I'll commit him for contempt – I'll imprison him – I'll give judgment against him the very next case he has before me – I'll send him to Massaruni – I'll – '

'Hush! you know perfectly well you won't do anything of the kind, papa, and he knows it too, or he would never bother you; but someone might overhear you, and take some of your jokes in real earnest, you know.'

'Ha! ha!' laughed the magistrate, revelling in the impossible idea. 'It would be fun to see Gonzales' face if I were to pay him off every "bitt," and leave him without a grievance! The fellow imagines he gets some benefit in his petty-debt cases in my court, because I am obliged to be civil to him; but he *doesn't*, you know.

I am always on my guard to give the poor devil he sues the best of justice – treble X. Ah! by the way, did Cumming Brothers send that bottled ale yesterday? We'll have some for breakfast…. Yes, the best of justice. I tell you what, I very nearly convicted him that time the bottle of rum was found in his bed.'

At this moment, after a preliminary knock, not at all of a ceremonious character, on the post of the open doorway which led from the verandah to the steps, a short, sturdy man, dressed in dark clothes and wearing a Panama hat, stepped into the gallery. His straight hair, dark eyes, and brown face, with the ruddy tint in the cheeks, discovered the Madeiran, the identical 'devil' of the conversation.

'Good-morning, Gonzales!' cried the volatile magistrate, while Isabel drew back with a scarlet face. 'What are you doing in this neighbourhood, and so early in the morning? Do you want a summons against anybody, or are you stripping some poor nigger's plantains?'

'No,' replied the other, speaking in tolerably good English, and very deliberately; 'that is not the cause of my visit to-day. I have been at my shop in Guineatown, after visiting my cattle farm at Mahaica.'

'Ah, you lucky Portuguese! You are buying up the whole country.'

'And the magistrates too – eh! eh!' replied the other unadvisedly, as he rubbed his hands together and chuckled to himself.

The Englishman's blood flushed to his face. It is dangerous for a foreigner, especially if he be a creditor, to rally a Briton on his debts! Marston, however, restrained himself, and said, with dignity, –

'Well, Mr. Gonzales, we poor officials are put in your hands by the Government, which refuses to give us the necessaries of life. They forget that we may be tempted to sell justice to make it up! But you must remember, too, this is an English colony, and your claims are protected by English laws. Don't be too grasping, my friend.'

'Eh?' said the other, shrugging his shoulders good-humouredly – he could afford to be genial; 'the protection of English law is a very fine thing, eh – eh? This planters' government swindles me at every turn! I am obliged to hide my money to save it from them, – in America, you know,' he added, feeling he had admitted too much.

'Oh, don't be afraid of me, Gonzales; I'm not the Inspector-General of Police! It is no business of mine to inquire into your resources.'

'Well, let it pass. Protection – eh? They charge me, for instance, five thousand dollars for my spirit licence in Georgetown; twelve hundred dollars at Berbice. I have to put twice as much water in the rum since they passed the new ordinance. I can't keep a drop of spirits or wine in my own house. Always those sub-inspectors, because they get half the fine, and divide it, mind you, with the magistrate, – keep still, sir: not you – you have not the chance! – are coming into my place, turning my wife out of bed, shaking up the mattresses and pillows, looking into – '

'I know all about it. But, Mr. Gonzales, not to refer to your own unspotted honesty and notorious integrity, some of your country-men are great scoundrels. I admire the candour with which you own to me, as a magistrate, to watering your rum. You cheat the excise and the public too, and no one can catch you. The Government must raise a revenue.'

'Yes: out of Portugee and Coolie. Planters' goods, machines, guano, hogsheads, all come in for nothing; but Coolie rice, ghee, salt-fish, American pork, rum, everything we eat and drink, heavy duty. Ah, you precious English: your protection is expensive, my friend!'

'But what did you want with me?' said the other, rather offended at the familiarity of the Madeiran. 'You did not come here to talk about this.'

'No, I forgot,' said the other, glancing at the young lady; 'I drove back from Guineatown. There has been a row at Belle Susanne. One overseer nearly killed and several wounded: all the police out.'

'Indeed!' cried the magistrate, getting up excitedly.

The young lady turned pale and red by turns.

'Who was hurt so badly, Mr. Gonzales, did you hear?' she said.

'Yes. The best man on the estate: a fine young man, very fine young man, name of Craig, stabbed by a Chinee… . Eh, eh! look here! What is the matter with the young lady, eh?

The father and visitor ran together to Isabel, who lay back in the cane chair, with an ashen face, quite motionless. There was the hubbub usual on such occasions. Servants came, water was brought, and presently, after a decent suspense, Isabel opened her eyes: she was carried away in her father's strong arms and laid on a bed. He satisfied himself that it was only a swoon caused, as he imagined, by a sense of the danger; and, assuring her they were quite safe, he returned to his visitor.

'This young man, Craig, is a friend of your young lady, eh?' said the acute Gonzales.

'We know him. He is a respectable youth, and comes here sometimes: a Scotch farmer's son.'

'I am sorry I spoke his name so quick: the young lady perhaps likes him. No? Pardon. Ah, you English are very funny about those things! Well, let me tell you he is the best young overseer in the colony. Never do for this colony. Mister Drummond soon gets tired of him. He has spoke to you about the treatment of Coolies, eh?'

The magistrate turned round sharply.

'Gonzales, you are too inquisitive: you have no right to ask me about private conversations. What are you driving at?'

'Eh, eh! Well, no matter. Look here, Mister Marston,' – the Portuguese put his finger on Marston's arm, and commanded his attention, for he now spoke in a low, serious tone, – 'there is danger: I came to warn you of it. This is not the last row there will be. I travel all over the colony: I know every estate. All Coolie shopkeepers buy my goods; and I tell you things look very bad : bad hearts, bad looks everywhere.'

'Yes: these Coolies are never satisfied.'

'If you spoke to your young friend, Craig, he will tell you why. Overseers interfere with wives, drivers beat Coolies, swindle in hospital, cheat at pay-table; all which Mister Drummond pretends not to know. But I know he does.'

'Hush!' said the magistrate, getting up and looking out to see that no one was eavesdropping. 'I cannot hear anything against Drummond. He is a friend of mine. Besides, he is a plaintiff or defendant in every court I hold.'

'Yes, yes, I understand. Well, I only say he gets the money they cheat the Coolies out of.'

The Portuguese put his fat forefinger on his lip and nodded, as if to hint more than he said. 'The same on many other estates. Manager cheats Coolie, cheats owners too. Makes money both ways, eh?'

'And you grudge him the opportunity, eh? Trust a Portuguese if he could get such a chance.'

The other gave a shrug of his shoulders. He did not pretend to peculiar virtue. He was not ready to proclaim himself insensible to temptation. The man was as queer a mixture of cunning and good-heartedness as could be found among the wonderful variety of incongruous natures in this medley of a world.

'Coolies they are all unsatisfied, Mister Marston, from end to end of the colony. Berbice, bad hospitals, stopped wages; Mahaica, stopped wages, bad hospitals; same in Demerary, same on East Coast, same on West Coast, same at Essequibo, same at Wakenhaam and Arabian Coast. All this is very dangerous. If these people rise nothing will be safe. All our property and lives go.'

'Oh! then the Portuguese are getting frightened, are they? Well, if there is a rising, we shall have twenty thousand of you on our side, and all the blacks'.

The other shook his head.

'No, sir. Portugee will not fight against the Coolies for you English. We have some spite for you. You are a magistrate and my friend. Let me tell you not to trust that. No Portugee, no black men will help you. But I must go. 'Spose you will ride over to Belle Susanne. Eh?'

'Ah! yes, I forgot, I suppose I must. Well, good morning. By the way, I am going to pay you off that loan. The interest is too heavy.'

'Eh?' The Portuguese shrugged his shoulders slightly, stretched out his hands in deprecation, made a grimace, silently raised his hat, and went away.

CHAPTER XIX

A PLEASANT NURSE

CRAIG'S wound for a day or two progressed favourably. Drummond watched at his bedside day and night. The doctor came twice a day. Every appliance that could mitigate the tendency to inflammation was used. Early each morning Pete drove into Georgetown for ice. Missa devoted herself to the sick-room, and quite fell in love with the strong, brave youth who lay so helpless and was yet so patient. On the fourth day the doctor saw with alarm symptoms of inflammation. The feverish heat, quick pulse, and wandering eye of the sufferer told a story of danger. Drummond's anxiety increased. He would have remained by the young man's bedside all the time, but it was impossible to neglect the estate, and, strong as he was, he could not afford to lose his sleep. It was necessary to find someone to help Missa. After a short consultation, they jointly decided on asking Lutchmee to undertake the duty. When Dilloo had been sent for, and had heard the manager's request, he readily yielded to the proposal, and Lutchmee herself, no longer afraid of her employer, agreed at once to act as an assistant-nurse. She accordingly took her place at the bedside of the overseer and hardly ever left it. Though entreated to take certain periods for sleep, she refused, and sat upon the floor hour after hour, watching all the changes of the wearisome fever that now set in. She seemed always fresh and always on the alert, possessing that faculty invaluable in a nurse, of being able to take her snatches of rest unobserved.

Thus it was that in his delirium Craig seemed to become conscious of a gentle presence continually moving about him with noiseless ease; and with the softest and deftest of hands placing the ice on his burning brow, or fanning his fevered face; or, anon, holding down the blankets over his chill-stricken limbs. He could not see its features or distinguish its voice, but he called it 'mother.' And often, during his wild wanderings, Lutchmee stood with clasped hands and palpitating heart to hear him address to her as 'mother' a torrent of affectionate phrases; or when the infinite longings of his excited heart to be once more at home expressed themselves in peevish reproaches to the absent one for ever letting him out of her sight, though Lutchmee could not understand him, many a flood of pure, strange sympathy poured from her eyes.

But, in more lucid moments, Craig's mind, now somewhat awakened to the danger he was in, turned back to the serious lessons of his early boyhood. Several exclamations which Drummond overheard induced him to send across the next estate to the clergyman in charge of the parish church. British Guiana was, after its English occupation, divided into parishes, in each of which the majority of parishioners were permitted to choose a parochial form of religion. Hence, in some parishes Anglicanism, in others Presbyterianism, had the superiority. It was scarcely of much consequence, since all religious bodies are equally endowed by the colony.

Mr. Telfer, the incumbent, was an Englishman, a Cambridge graduate, of indifferent origin, whose plodding zeal had won him a respectable degree at the University, but was unequal to advancing him in the carnal world. Hundreds of such men, reasonably polished by education and the moderate contact they have had during their College career, with a better society, and who, adopting the Church as a profession, do by and by succeed in working themselves into something of a clerico-spiritual frame of mind, are scattered here and there in the rural districts of England, and dispersed among our colonies. If they are rather insipid, they discharge the formal duties of their office with neatness and dispatch. An ingenious use of a few familiar rhetorical *formulæ*, of conjunctions and interjections, and of Bible texts, enables them to construct a sermon. They are always respectable units at a provincial or colonial dinner-table, where they generally contrive to obtrude as little as possible of the clerical element. Beginning their earthly walk in a cottage, or a garret, or a four-room flat, or the back-room of a tradesman's shop, they start on their heavenly career from college halls and cloisters, under the benediction of a Bishop's hands. The work is respectable, though the pay be small. They are content to achieve all possible distinction at one leap, by the simple process of ordination, and they quietly roll along a narrow-gauge tramway which appears to have been expressly constructed for them to the top of Pisgah. It is fortunate for the Church of England that she leans not on such slender ministers as these, – that she is able to appeal to higher and nobler classes of men as the apology for her existence.

Mr. Telfer was a fair specimen of the sort of clergyman we have been describing. His father had been a successful shoemaker at Cambridge. It was because the old man's affectionate pride would not allow the fact of his relationship to be idle or silent that the son found it convenient to change the scene. He accepted a living in British Guiana, whither it was scarcely probable that the senior Telfer would, in face of yellow fever and mosquitos, extend his too demonstratively paternal regard.

The Reverend Adolphus Telfer's charity was suited to his mind, – it was narrow. He rigidly restrained it within the bounds of his own communion. Presbyterians, Wesleyans, Jews, Turks, infidels, heathen, and Coolies shared none of it. No more admirable parochial person could have been devised for British Guiana. He could be on good terms with the planters without entertaining any ingenuous sympathies with either blacks or Asiatics. The young of the former he utilised in white stoles for the services of the church. He baptized their numerous illegitimate children with exemplary catholicity, and when they were dead he read the burial service over them with the same freedom from affectation as he would have shown over the body of a deceased planter. Within the narrow precincts thus described, however, Mr. Telfer was a tolerable, good-hearted fellow. His clerical clothes seemed too stiff or too thick to let any natural feeling exude through them. Nevertheless when he came to visit Craig, and found him lying in a precarious state, and heard him appealing so frequently to his absent mother, or unconsciously repeating scraps of prayer and verses taught him in childhood, the clergyman's mind opened a little to the pathos of the situation. He often came back to the sick youth, and would read to him in his calmer moments passages of Scripture or try to solace him by reciting a few prayers and collects of the Church. Craig, too feeble to resist any impression, seemed to be grateful for these clerical attentions, and bore them with an evidently not displeased patience.

One person, however, watched these exercitations with singular jealousy. We have said that Lutchmee always remained by the bedside of the sick man. In her simple mind, as day by day she rendered her services with instinctive quickness and propriety, there had been developed a vague yet powerful interest in her patient. She had never so particularly watched an English face; and this strong youth, with his ruffled auburn locks and pallid features, excited in her mind a sort of fascination which it would be hard to define. It was a pleasure – an honest, simple pleasure – to be near him to look at him, to cool his brow and fan his face, to touch him, and sometimes to rest that fever-stricken head on her shoulder as she administered a potion. She was too natural to attempt to define these feelings to herself: she only began to experience a keen and exquisite delight in every act she could perform for the object of her care. Certainly it was nothing like her strong, deep love for Dilloo, – rather was it a strange, half god-worship, than like any mere mortal affection. Had Lutchmee been able to analyze her own feelings, she would have detected danger in the acute jealousy excited in her mind, by the intervention between her and the sick youth of anyone but Missa, for whom she now had a true regard. The clergyman was her special aversion. On his first visit he had looked round carelessly, and said to Drummond, who had brought him in, –

'Who is this person? A Coolie woman! You had better send her away.'

'She is one of my Coolies, and acts as nurse,' replied Drummond. 'If you are going to say anything that may shock her or do her harm, I will get her to wait outside. But she may be wanted. And besides,' added he, maliciously, 'who knows what good she may get from you?'

The other was too self-involved to see the irony of Drummond's remarks.

'I fear it is no use,' said he, naively. 'All I have seen of these people convinces me that attempts to convert them are mere loss of time.'

Drummond was silent, but he could not help reflecting that when he had any business in hand he was wont to exercise more hope and energy in it than was displayed by this minister of the indefatigable Christ.

Lutchmee, for her part, could not comprehend the remarks that had passed, but she divined that the 'missionary' had tried to exclude her from the room, and her feelings towards him took shape accordingly. When he used to come and read, or, opening a book, knelt down and prayed, she scornfully turned away. The moment he was gone, she tried every method her simple ingenuity could invent to divert Craig's thoughts from the minister or his conversation. One day, far on in the illness, she found him in tears after the clergyman's departure. She wiped them away and very prettily scolded the absent visitor for making her massa cry.

'Oh!' said Craig, half to her and half to himself, 'don't say anything against the poor man. He does his best, and I feel the better for it.'

This was the first time that Craig had thoroughly noticed Lutchmee. He had often, since the recovery of his senses, regarded her dreamily and carelessly, as a quiet, useful attendant. The crisis of the fever was now over, and the doctor was beginning to hold out hopes of pulling his patient through in safety.

Craig, this afternoon, somewhat interestedly watched the lissome figure and silent motions of the nurse.

'You're Lutchmee?' said he.

'Iss, massa.'

'Have I been sick long?'

She held up three fingers 'Tree weeks, massa.'

'Oh! I remember; there was a row, wasn't there? Why, I must have been wounded. I can scarcely move. Here, come and help me to sit up.'

'O no, massa: no sittee up dis too long time.' And in a moment, Lutchmee's two little arms were holding down the young giant, and her brown smiling face hung over his as she shook her head.

'You're about right,' said he, looking at her with a sort of half affectionate feeling that any kindly nurse may excite in her helpless patient. 'When *you* can hold *me* down, you little minx, I must be weak indeed.'

She smoothed his hair with her hand, smiling the while, to see him better. This she did with the same fondling simplicity with which a dog would have rubbed his head against his master's hand.

'Massa Telfer make um well,' she said, thinking she might have done the clergyman an injustice.

Craig was lost in thought and did not notice her. He had been ill so many weeks, and, as he now began for the first time to apprehend, very dangerously. The words Telfer had read to him had recalled vividly to his mind his home life, from the influence of which he felt as if a great gulf just then separated him. A sense of extreme loneliness came over him. Here he was with nothing nearer or more affectionate than this simple and ignorant Coolie woman. The repugnance of race, which, spite of their proverbial adaptability to any circumstances, I fancy to be as extreme in Scotchmen as in other people, forbad the budding of any affectionate esteem in his heart, but he felt arising within him a strong sense of gratitude for her attentions; and, deeper and more insidious than that, a sort of pleased admiration of her pretty features, lissome figure, and graceful ways. Was she not a pretty animal? Then, in a flash, his mother's face came before him, a homely yet a noble countenance, and, almost to his own surprise, happy as was the vision, it threw a curious, unpleasant light back upon his previous thoughts. Yet he could not recall to his mind one idea that his conscience could reprehend as improper. The difference between the two beings, that absent mother and the present slave, was too great to suggest any comparison of his feelings about them. His analysis was neither deep enough nor acute enough to inform him that probably the revulsion caused by the remembrance at this moment of his purest ideal and real in life must be rather from some hidden and unconscious tendency of his previous thoughts than from any inherent evil in the thoughts themselves.

So subtle are the beginnings within a man's soul of the conflict between the spirits of Good and Evil.

CHAPTER XX

SARCOPHAGUS

ONE person had, throughout Craig's illness, shown a remarkable interest in his welfare. Isabel Marston, living a half-solitary life, in a climate and amongst associations, the very idea of which would be enough to depress a girl who knew anything of the versatile charms of civilized societies, found in this tragic incident something more exciting than any of the fictional hazards in the novels with which she was wont to relieve her *ennui*. A young, brave, not unhandsome fellow, gentle-minded though rough-limbed, whom she had always regarded as a more than agreeable acquaintance, and about whom her idle fancy again and again built airy fabrics of hope and pleasure, suddenly brought to the verge of death, and so situated that she might not with any propriety offer to give him those attentions to which her heart impelled her, – this, to a young girl in her circumstances, was a bit of romance, very perilous to her peace of mind. Mr. Marston, with all his affection for his daughter, was by nature so occupied with himself, and had so little idea of any romance in conditions he used to feel to be the reverse of romantic, that he had no suspicion of the state of his daughter's feelings towards Craig. With herself, even, they had hitherto been rather vague symptoms of love than the real phenomena of passion; the less real, no doubt, because Craig, in his occasional intercourse, had never shown (and we, behind the scenes, may say had never felt) anything but the pleasurable esteem of a youth for a beautiful and unattainable object. The best evidence of the coolness of his mind in relation to Isabel Marston was the fact that during the whole period of his delirium her name had not passed his lips. He was very young, very shy, very pure in his thoughts and in his life, and curiously unsusceptible of passionate emotions. Nothing so possessed him as the calm, sweet reverence he felt towards his mother; after which, strongest of his feelings, were his love of practical engagements and his ambition for success. Such a nature may have in it great depths of quiet and pellucid passion, which, however, can be stirred up only by extraordinary storms or unusual perturbations of the elements of the soul.

Poor Isabel Marston was obliged – in that equatorial atmosphere – to fume over Craig's illness in secret. Her father, she well knew, would never have listened to any suggestion of an intimacy with the Scotch overseer. Mr. Marston's innocent unsuspicion of such an unnatural conjunction could not have been more clearly testified than by the manner in which he received the hint thrown out by Gonzales, regarding Isabel's sudden illness when she heard of Craig's accident. The last thing he could have attributed to his daughter was a fatuous interest in a farmer's son. Was not her mother only twenty-five removes from a baronet? Had she not from her earliest years been trained to assume the airs, the position, the style of thought of the aristocracy, and were not all her acquaintanceships in Demerara, except with the Governor's family, and the military, and the judges, well understood to be on the footing of condescension to the exigencies of the magistrate's official position? He never took the trouble even to let these thoughts pass through his mind. They were taken for granted – they were the postulates of his rank.

I know nothing more discountenancing to the interest of a romance of love than the elementary deficiency arising from the fact that one of the two parties essential to the evolution of the plot is not only careless, but unconscious of the flames which are consuming the other. The man who is sleeping next door to a burning house – the person who is sitting over a powder-magazine towards which the fire is rapidly hissing and sparkling its way along the fuse – may evoke an excited interest, and set our sympathies in lively action. But when you have a soul that is at once unconscious of the fire which is burning away another's heart and indifferent to the results – a soul the emotion of which bears no relation whatever to the other's flames, or perils or fate – here you have a situation cold and absurd in the extreme. The romance is one-sided, the play is scarcely worth the candle.

Nevertheless, such is the unhappy state of things which it falls to my lot to narrate. Craig was as cold as an iceberg, and quite as insensible to the furnace that was glowing and fuming within a few miles of him. It is a grotesque irony of fortune, and of fiction too, that a fair, elegant, well-bred girl should have been consuming with passion for the cold, unsophisticated, matter-of-fact son of an Ayrshire farmer. The subject is so painful that I cannot dwell upon it.

However, the state of Craig's mind had for the present little to do with Isabel Marston's interest in him. It is fortunate, for no small portion of the human race, that love may, like a candle, burn at one end. Perhaps all of us who suffer, equally benefit, from unrequited affections. One often picks up unexpected blessings thrown in one's way by unknown lovers or friends. It is well if we ourselves sometimes repay our debts to humanity by distributing similarly gratuitous benefactions. The magistrate's daughter sent a message every day over to Belle Susanne in the name of her father to inquire how the 'young gentleman' was. Her messenger was known in Mr. Marston's family as Sarcophagus, so dubbed by his master from a fancied resemblance in colour and otherwise to some Egyptian stone coffins in the British Museum, and perhaps, for the further reason, that there seemed to be nothing in him. The mind of Sarcophagus is not worth an elaborate analysis. It was a *tabula rasa* with a witness. It was always wiped off clean as a new slate. It took its impressions from moment to moment. It was deficient in memory, in logical or any sequence but that of time or expression: and it seemed to know as little of the characters that were written upon it, and to be as incapable of deciphering them as the Rosetta stone itself. His language, picked up mostly from the pulpit exercitations of Baptist or Wesleyan preachers, some of whom are as lamentably awkward in preaching to Negroes as they are incapable of evangelizing the rural clods in England, in a simple, comprehensible way, was strongly interlarded with words of many syllables, of which the meaning and fitness were mere matters of chance to him. I am not sure that his notion of the meanings of words were not formed on some rough principle of onomatopœia. It would be impossible to report him at length to the reader's apprehension, for one needed to hear him and to be immediately *au fait* with the relations of his discourse to be able to assign any particular idea to some of his phrases. The best instinct of Sarcophagus was a dumb one. You could explain more to him by signs than by words. If you tossed him a bundle of words, he used them as a gorilla would use a bundle of sticks. He unaccountably mixed and twisted them up together, he tore them to shreds between his teeth. Some fibres might remain, but they gave dubious testimony of the original form or shape of the communication.

Isabel's first message about Craig was confided to this messenger. His idiosyncrasy would, she knew, be useful in one way, if it were embarrassing in another. You might safely trust him with any secret – he could not disclose it. She concocted a message which she thought she could so impress on his mind that he could carry it accurately. Marston's cook was a good one. She could make many good things. Her jellies, flavoured with guava and coloured with bright juices, were excellent. Though he was supposed to be dying, what to an unsophisticated girl could appear more natural than to send over to the invalid a shape of jelly? A shape was accordingly produced. It was surrounded by ice to prevent it from what the ingenious Miriam termed 'sitting down.' It was enwrapped in a snowy napkin, and Sarcophagus was to bear it to Belle Susanne and deliver this message, –

'Missa Masson sent compliments wid dis jelly for de young gen'leman dat's sick, an want to know how he git along.'

The simplicity and the vernacular ease of this message often repeated to and recited by Sarcophagus, encouraged the hope that it would reach its destination along with the jelly in a compact shape.

Sarcophagus raised a preliminary objection.

'Ow about de ice, missa? Dere ain't no referumshun in de messinge to de ice?'

'No, you stupid, of course not. The ice doesn't matter. It is only to keep the jelly cool. Say what I tell you, and nothing more. Do you hear?'

Off went Sarcophagus with the pail, covered in neatly with the white damask, singing as he went, –

    Yee ha! – yo ha!
      Who see de niggah?
    Yo ha! – yee ha!
      Where go de niggah?
      Singing for Jee – roo – sa – lem,
          Chorus: Singing for Jee – roo –
                Singing for Jee – roo –
                Singing for Jee – roo – sa – lem!

The result was that Sarcophagus sang Miss Marston's message clean out of his head.

When he arrived at the little wooden bridge which lay across the canal to the middle dam of Belle Susanne estate, he took off the remnant of felt, which he called a cap, and scratched his head in the blazing sun, as, with a puzzled expression on his face, he contemplated the pail.

'Dis yer pail,' he said, 'am gwine to Massa – Massa – Massa? – Bress me; Sahcoffingcuss am de on'y name dis niggah nebber discommember. Massa am Massa – Missa am *Missa* – but Massa what? Missa what? Sometime 'members, sometime dismembers. Dere ain't one word ob de ammunition dat hang about de corners ob dis yer cocoa-nut. Golly! Dere's de pail, but where de messinge? . . . . . (scratch) Ha! I got um! "Missa – Missa – Missa" – No, de ideas hab salivated. I'se quite surplushed – "Missa" – yes dat am de fust word – No! Golly! Here's a humdrum.'

He stooped down and removed the napkin. Beneath it sparkled in the sun the broken ice. In the middle of the ice lay in the reversed mould, also glittering in the sun, the pellucid jelly.

'Ha!' said Sarcophagus, struck with an idea at this vision, 'I reciprocrate de sarcomstiances ob de case. Missa say, "Take um ice to – ". I'm observate, "What I say about de jelly?" Missa Bella responsify, "No matter 'bout de jelly, it keep de ice warm." Ha! if de jelly inconsequenshul, den dere ain't no cause why Sahcoffingcuss not take de jelly, keep the ice from dissolushun.'

Forthwith Sarcophagus extracted the shape of jelly, and proceeded, in the absence of a spoon, by processes not to be described, to entomb it very effectually in his capacious interior. He was smacking his lips over the cooling and luscious composition, when a sharp cut of a whip over his half-naked shoulder caused him to leap to his feet with an exclamation of pain. These poor Negroes are only distended babies in brown skins.

'What are you doing, you rascal? Miss Marston never gave you that jelly to eat on my bridge. Where were you going with it?'

It was Drummond, who had been down looking at the 'koker' which regulated the outlet of water to the sea, and who had approached the Negro unperceived.

'I'se goin' to dis 'state, Massa Drummon',' replied Sarcophagus, rubbing his shoulders; 'but you'm disconnected wid de objective purpose ob de messinge, w'en you'm instigate de jelly as gwin wid de rest ob de articles.'

'So I see!' replied Drummond, smiling. 'The jelly now will only accompany 'the articles,' as you call them, if *you* do, and in a disconnected form beyond a doubt. But, if you were coming to my house with that parcel, sir,' he went on more sternly, as he poised his whip in a menacing way, 'will you tell me what message you had to deliver, and why you dared to open the pail and eat the jelly?'

Sarcophagus scratched his head again.

'Dis niggah quite conflustricated, Massa Drummon'. Missa ober dere gib me dis pail and dis ice, wid strict injections to take 'tickler keer ob de ice. I'se 'tickler keerful ob de ice, and wen I cum to dis bridge, 'xaminated de contents to see how de ice a gettin' on. Den I see it resolving away in consequens ob de heat ob dis yer jelly,' holding up the tin mould he had emptied.

'Jelly! you infernal scamp; there isn't a glimpse of jelly left. Mr. Marston will send you to gaol for this as sure as your name's Sarcophagus.'

'Massa Drummon', de young lady mos' 'tickerlerly stated to me de jelly not any matter – de ice was de subjec' ob de messinge.'

'Well, what *is* the message?'

Sarcophagus was absolutely nonplussed by this question direct. He looked ruefully at the pail – at the mould – at Mr. Drummond – at the sky – for an answer to the conundrum. It did not come. He made a bold dash.

'Missa order me discompliment Massa Craig wid de ice, and gib her bequest if Massa want to know 'ow she goin' on.'

The face of Sarcophagus expressed as sense of triumphant relief when he had delivered himself of these anxiously gathering fragments of his message.

'Look here,' said Drummond, whose sharp mind began to see something of the real state of the case. 'Miss Isabel never gave you such a message as that to knock about the estates with. She gave you this pail, did she?'

The Negro nodded.

'And this napkin?'

Nod again.

'And this ice?'

'Iss, massa, de ice 'tickerlerly.'

'Confound you, shut up! And this mould full of jelly?'

Sarcophagus nodded hesitatingly.

'She told you to bring it to my house, eh?'

''Ceptin' de jelly, massa; dat jelly was expensively expected from de messinge.'

'Be quiet, I tell you. She sent it to the young gentleman who is sick?'

Sarcophagus began to see light, and nodded. 'Ha! dat's de objec' ob de messinge.'

'She told you to give her compliments, or her love?'

Drummond liked his joke.

'Complimen's, massa, dat's de 'spression,' replied the Negro with dignity.

'And to say this was for him?'

'Massa, you'm oberhearn ebery word ob dat dere messinge; all 'cept de remarkation 'bout de jelly.'

'Now I'll tell you what,' said Drummond, 'you're either the biggest fool or the biggest knave in Demerara, I don't know which. But if you don't want me to cowhide you on the spot, and to get your master to punish you after, come up to the house with me. Take back the note I shall give you, and hark you, don't you dare to say a word to Miss Isabel or anyone else about what you have done with the jelly. You're not so great a fool I expect as to do that, but if you do I'll have you sent to Georgetown gaol for three months.'

Sarcophagus looked the picture of innocence as he took up the pail and followed Drummond to his house. There the latter quietly relieved the pail of the ice, and told Missa to put the empty mould away for a day or two. Then he indited this note, –

'Mr. Drummond presents his compliments to Miss Marston, and begs to acknowledge on behalf of young Craig, who is lying very ill, the receipt of her very humane and thoughtful present of jelly for the patient. The latter is at present unable to enjoy anything of the sort, and cannot even be made conscious of the honour done to him by Miss Marston's kind attention.

'Mr. Drummond would take the liberty to advise that any message sent by Sarcophagus should be in writing, as very great difficulty has been experienced in getting from him any message that could be understood, and that he should hereafter in carrying any articles of the same sort for Miss Marston be particularly enjoined to take great care of the *ice*, which he carried so carelessly as to allow a good deal of it to slip out of the pail, thus endangering the jelly.'

On his way home, the mind of Sarcophagus underwent a revulsion. Being charged with his carelessness about the ice, he reminded Miss Marston that she had herself told him it was not intended to be part of her present, and did not matter. Hence she did not suspect the truth. But, warned by Drummond's note, she took care to go over next day and see Missa Nina, and to arrange with her that in future, whenever Sarcophagus turned up at Belle Susanne, with or without any message, or fragment of a message, he was to receive a slip of paper containing, in a word or two, an account of the patient's progress.

Craig knew nothing of the kind inquiries that were being daily made and answered on his behalf. Isabel very discreetly kept herself in the background throughout. The little delicacies that went from Mr. Marston's house to the sick room were sent in his name. Whatever Nina's ideas of the matter may have been, she did not take the trouble to express them. Drummond was too shrewd not to see that all this interest in his young overseer was not pure benevolence; or to believe that Mr. Marston, whom he knew as a good-natured, but selfish, and as he thought overproud person, would of his own motion take all this trouble. As to the magistrate, he had some inkling of the kindly uses to which his kitchen was being devoted, but was too self-complacent to look upon this as anything but a piece of patronising charity, very proper to emanate from his house to any distressed white person in his neighbourhood. When Craig was able to bear it, Mr. Marston even rode over to see him, and to express his congratulations on the young man's recovery. At dinner the same evening he gave an account of his visit to ears that tingled at the recital; and then he astonished Isabel by adding, –

'The young fellow is pretty well bred, and talks very sensibly. He has no one to wait on him but that girl Nina, who does Drummond's housekeeping, and a Coolie woman, a funny little thing, who looks as innocent as a baby. A pretty woman too.'

O, Isabel, Isabel, what concord hath love with the devil, that this very guileless hint of a guileless presence near the sick couch of the poor Scotch boy should set thy whole being aglow with jealous indignation, and raise within thee sharp shoots of evil feeling towards one so infinitely beneath thee in all the graces and attractions of humanity?

'Is he allowed to read, papa?'

'No. Mr. Telfer goes over, and reads to him occasionally. By the way, you often complain of *ennui*. Here is an opportunity for doing good. He is well enough now to sit up. You should take Miriam with you, or Sarcophagus, and go over and read to him sometimes. It would be quite a charity.'

'Do you think I might do so without remark?' said Isabel slyly, her heart meantime almost ceasing its action in the suspense with which she awaited the answer.

'God bless my soul, Bell, what do you mean? Do you think any one would associate your name with that of a Scotch overseer lad, because you went over to do an act of kindness to him? Every one perfectly understands the footing on which all these people are permitted to hold intercourse with us, and your suggestion is, in the circumstances, ridiculous. Surely you would not allow such an idle consideration to interfere with what may be looked upon as a duty, however disagreeable?'

'Oh, no, papa!' returned his delighted daughter, smiling at his indignation. 'You see I am timid, because I have no mamma to tell me better.'

The magistrate blinked his eyes rather shyly, and Isabel, conscious that there was a duplicity in all this arrangement which seemed rather to be the result of circumstances than to be in any way chargeable to her yet felt a little ashamed that her father should in reality be deceived. It was one of those critical positions which very often occur in human experience, in which absolute truth and candour lie in a balance with qualified truth and selfish inclination; and the poise, at the, moment, appears to the soul so equal that it is easy to persuade oneself that either is right; or even that the wrong one is better. Was it to be expected that Isabel should frankly explain to her father a state of heart she had never clearly acknowledged to herself ? Had he not fallen into the trap which might prove so dangerous both to her peace and to his? Had she not honourably met the temptation with a deprecating caution? She held her conscience acquitted by the warning she had given her father, and we cannot any of us throw a stone at her. The exigencies of truth and honour are sometimes too great for humanity to meet, and I don't know that even angels can at all times balance righteous duty and inclination on needlepoints or razor-edges.

CHAPTER XXI

AN UNGRATEFUL SLAVE

WHILE Craig lay on his sick bed, and Lutchmee was engrossed in her wearisome, but daily more pleasurable cares, the fortunes of some of our other characters were undergoing a critical change. Drummond's sharp eye detected that the Coolies, not only on Belle Susanne, but on adjacent estates, were uneasy. An overseer on Hofman's Lust had been beaten and left for dead. It was clear that a strong undercurrent of excitement was moving through the whole Indian and Chinese population of the country. At the Georgetown Club, the rendezvous of Demerara gossip and scandal, Drummond found that his apprehensions were shared by other planters. He was a keen and cautious man, and resolved to anticipate the worst. His first care was to revise the organisation of his estate. Two drivers, who had taken part in the recent *mêlée*, were degraded; the explanation of this breach of faith with the rioters in regard to the promise he had made to let them all off if they returned to work, being, that it did not apply to officials of the estate, whose default could not be passed over without punishment. The sharp-witted Coolies took notice of this circumstance, and, slight and defensible as the act may seem to outsiders, it had an important bearing on the subsequent relations of Drummond to his labourers. The full gravity of such incidents can scarcely be appreciated by any but those who have been intimately concerned in the management of the estates, or in the Government offices, of a Coolie-worked colony.

One of the places left vacant by the removal of the driver was given to Hunoomaun, who the same week received the crowning reward of his strategy in taking home Ramdoolah as his wife. Drummond had thoughts of offering the other post to Dilloo; but, on consideration, changed his mind.

'This fellow Dilloo,' he said, 'is an honest dog enough, and I shouldn't wonder if Pete deserved all he got from him. But the man is a deal too honest and too clever: he has too much influence; and he's like that boy Craig, with sentimental notions of right and wrong, utterly inapplicable in our circumstances here. I mean to do him a good turn in some other way; but that nigger, Johnson, is a big, able fellow: I'll make him the driver.'

Drummond sent for Dilloo, and complimented him very highly on his brave conduct. He gave him then and there a certificate of free pasturage for all his cows on one of the squares of estate grass, and he promised him a silver medal to be worn in commemoration of his bravery and faithfulness.

To the manager's surprise, Dilloo very quietly declined the offer. He had heard of Hunoomaun's appointment to a post which he deemed to be due to *him;* he was annoyed at the manager's breach of faith in creating the vacancies; moreover, he was alarmed by Hunoomaun's promotion to a position in which he knew that that wily enemy would manage to make him feel his power: of this, however, he said nothing to the manager, who was naturally ignorant of the causes of enmity that were at work between the two men.

'Massa, me no take dis. Dilloo plenty money, plenty grass. No wanty money 'cos beat Coolie for massa.'

'What: no take grass for nossing? Don't be a fool!'

'No: no take grass.'

'Well,' cried Drummond, in high dudgeon, 'you Indians are the most difficult animals to manage I ever knew! (*sotto voce*) There's something behind this, I'm sure. Why not take it, Dilloo?'

The Hindoo shrugged his shoulders.

'Massa cheat um Coolie. Tell Dilloo, tell Coolie, no punis for row: den punis Rambux, punis Dos Mahommed. All Coolie no like dat. "Dilloo," say Coolie, "Manahee ebery time talkee true, dis time tell lie."'

Drummond forthwith worked himself into a passion. He told Dilloo, very distinctly, that he thought him a cantankerous rascal, that he had not intended to let off mutinous drivers, and that, if he didn't look out himself, he would be sent to Massaruni. And so poor Dilloo went away to his house in disgrace.

Chester the overseer was present at this interview, and took notice of its result. He was a fellow who could nurse his revenge very closely. Dilloo's dark eye gleamed fiercely on him a moment before he departed, and the overseer had been unable to check the rush of blood to his cheeks.

'That man, sir,' said he to Drummond, as soon as Dilloo was quite out of hearing, 'will always give us trouble: he needs disciplining. The Coolies think too much of him, and he thinks too much of himself. It would not be a bad idea to take an opportunity to put him under that big fellow Hunoomaun, who was a peon, or watchman, or something of the sort in his own country, and, I believe, came from the same village as this man.'

'Oh!' said Drummond, quickly, 'that's it, is it? You may depend upon it, then, Dilloo is jealous of the other's promotion. Just like those cursed Asiatics! And that's the reason of this hoity-toity, no doubt. Yes, you're right: the best way of taking him down will be to put him under Hunoomaun, and give him a few weeks of bush-cutting. I'm sorry he won't let me be kind to him: and his wife there is as big a fool as he is.'

Chester was delighted. He had charge of the back gangs of which Hunoomaun's was one. Dilloo was in a fair way to get some recompense at last for the overseer's broken skin and wounded dignity. The very next week Dilloo was removed from trench-digging, his favourite work, and ordered to join Hunoomaun's gang at the back, to cut the year's growth of weed and brush (a very formidable vegetable indeed in that climate and soil), on some of the fallow fields of the estate. The price paid for this work enabled the labourer to make only two-thirds of the weekly profit he could have secured at trench-digging. It can easily be imagined what a volcano raged in the Indian's bosom, when he found himself degraded in the eyes of his countrymen, subjected to the surveillance and orders of a man whom he not only hated but despised, and obliged to walk nearly seven miles a day to and from his work.

For such methods of punishment and actual injustice as these no law does or can provide a remedy. It is necessarily inherent in any system of bond-service that the sole discretion as to the nature of the work to be done by his servants must be vested in the master. The only check upon him will be the interest he has in the value of the men's labour. Even though a Coolie may be capable of doing the highest class of work, he must, – unlike the free Negro, who has his option, and very decidedly exercises it, – be liable at the whim of his master, or even through the ill-will of an overseer or driver, to be sent to the hardest, least remunerative, and most distant labour on the estate. In the prosecution of revengeful feeling, or of illicit ends, or even in the otherwise legitimate discipline of an estate, such a power, vested as it is in irresponsible hands, must always be dangerous to the peace of the community, as well as to justice and freedom.

For the time, the lesson in self-control Dilloo had recently learned stood him in good stead. He did his work stolidly, but effectively. On the other hand, Hunoomaun was too cunning to take immediate advantage of his triumph. He was unwilling to raise a sleeping demon; and besides, he had, through his wily wife, acquired some hints of matters which might give him yet more importance with Drummond, and assure him of a more complete victory over his rival.

CHAPTER XXII

THE CONSPIRATORS

DILLOO, having done his day's work, was one evening sitting at the door of his hut, mending a drag-net, of the sort used by the immigrants to drag the canals, whereof every nook and outlet swarms with fish. It was past seven o'clock. There was just light enough to enable him to see his work. He was thinking that it was time for Lutchmee to come home to him. He was free to visit her when he pleased, but his native jealousy had been rather roused at seeing the attention paid by her to the young overseer. He had full faith in Lutchmee's honour; though experience had given him little in that of any white man. Craig was a favourite among the Coolies. He never gave them a harsh word, and had been true to them at the magistrate's court, in giving his evidence, – a trait that was as ill-appreciated by the manager as it was valued by the people. Yet Dilloo, ruminating on all that had happened, feeling he no longer owed any special kindness to the estate authorities, and that his wife might not now be safe from molestation, resolved that he would endeavour to get her away from the manager's house. As these things were passing through his mind he suddenly became aware of a figure within a few feet of him, and, looking up, he saw Akaloo, who had approached with the silent and gentle tread of his race.

'Salaam, Akaloo!' said the netter, briskly.

'Salaam, Dilloo!' replied the other almost in a whisper; 'don't utter my name again. I do not want to be known. I have come to see you privately, on the great business. Step into your house and I will follow.'

Dilloo noticed that Akaloo's face was partially concealed by a light cotton scarf, which he had pulled over his head. This, as soon as he had drawn back to a corner of the interior where at that time it was almost dark, he removed.

'Can anyone overhear us?' said he.

'No fear,' replied Dilloo. 'This is outside the village, and I do not think anyone would be prying about my house. Lutchmee is not at home.'

But noticing that his visitor was still slightly reserved, Dilloo rose and carefully scanned the neighbourhood of his hut. Then he returned and sat down between the other and the door.

'There is no one about. The village is quiet. They are killing a kid tonight. What news have you?'

'Much,' replied the pedler. 'I have just returned from a journey up as far as the Arabian coast. I have been to Waakenham, to the West Coast. Everywhere the Coolies are discontented and ready for anything. They are joining the league in large numbers. They complain of everything. First, they are forced out of their beds to work in the morning.'

'Many of them need it,' said Dilloo, grimly. 'Half of the men on the estates do the work for the other half. Why, you have only to look at them. They are good for nothing – the scum of India.'

'True,' said Akaloo. 'But that is not their fault. It is the fault of these greedy Inglees themselves. They want to get their work done cheap, and so they collect for their service the vilest and worst of our country people. Yet when they have brought them here they have no right to treat them badly.'

'Well, I admit it's often very hard for masters to work with the sort of fellows you get here,' replied Dilloo.

'Then, again,' said the other, not noticing this remark, 'they say the overseers and drivers cheat them in taking down their work, and get up disputes at the pay-table on Saturday about the way in which the work was done, when of course it is too late to have it examined. On some estates there are fines and stoppages of money every week, though that is against the law. If they go to Goody office° to complain, they are arrested on the way by the police, and sometimes punished as deserters; at all events are locked up in one of those filthy police stations till the magistrate comes round. Even if they do get to Goody office, and Massa

°The office of the Immigration Agent-General, Mr. Goodeve.

Goody makes inquiry, the sub-agents will believe the manager and overseers before the Indians. The managers pocket the money they cheat the people out of, and they do not give half the hospital supplies. Medicines, food, sheets, beds, they cheat in everything. Two men went out of Porto-Bello Hospital the other day, and hanged themselves. They were Chinese, and I was told by one of their matties that, though they were suffering from terrible ulcers, they were given nothing to eat but rice and a little bad biscuit.'

Dilloo shrugged his shoulders.

'Many of these fellows who complain of the hospitals live like dogs at home,' he said. 'They get very particular when they come here.'

'So they ought to be,' said Akaloo. 'They are promised everything better here, and how bitterly they are disappointed!'

'We have a good hospital on this estate,' Dilloo replied; 'but I do not believe they ever give us what the doctor orders. I should like to see Missa Nina send fowls to a sick woman without special orders from Massa Drummon', and he only gives those when the patient is so ill his case is hopeless. On the next estate they treat the poor people abominably. The sick people rose and thrashed the nurse there last week, and they will be taken before the magistrate to-morrow. Every one knows *the list** is simply a cheat everywhere.'

'Well,' said Akaloo, 'I have seen Massa Gonzales, the Portugee. He has great sympathy with us.'

'I do not trust those men,' interrupted the other. 'They make a good deal of money out of our people.'

---

*The diet list of the hospitals, prescribed by law, and which is hung up in English and Hindustani, for the professed purpose of enabling the people (who cannot read) to check the diet. The doctor is obliged to chalk on a black board over each patient's bed the prescription he orders him, and the diet, according to the Government list. The menu is altogether too good to be believed in, or ever supplied. It however serves, or did serve, the purpose of deluding the Home and the Indian Governments, and of supplying arguments in the English newspapers against busybody philanthropists. How can any employer be accused of cruelty when curried fowl and the best boiled rice are daily dainties of the sick room?

'Perhaps I should not trust him either,' replied Akaloo; 'but he has a spite against the Government. They have put his liquor licences so high he can scarcely make any money. Besides, he seems a kind-hearted man. I know several good things he has done to our countrymen. The planters all hate him very thoroughly. He has had a petition secretly drawn up by a trustworthy person, a lawyer, Mr. Williams. It cost twenty dollars. See, it has the marks of nearly nine hundred Coolies.'

The Madrassee unrolled a long paper, which had been concealed in his bosom, but it was too dark to distinguish anything.

'You must keep this paper, which contains the petition, separate from the signatures, in case of accident or treachery. It can be attached afterwards. All those people who have signed are members of our association. I have brought you, also, some paper for more signatures or marks. Dalhoo is a good scholar, and he is one of your safest men. Get him to put down the Indian names, and Kung-a-lee, the Chinese doctor, will circulate it among his people. He is one of our principal friends, you know.'

Dilloo nodded. He rolled up the scrolls separately, and hid them in different parts of the hut. The petition itself was placed where, as we have seen before, he kept his sharpened cutlass.

'You may leave it to me,' he said, 'to manage matters in this neighbourhood. Did you hear of the riot at this place the other day?'

The other nodded assent.

'I helped the manager that time, because our people were in the wrong. That scoundrel, Chin-a-foo the gambler, was not worth fighting for, and he has ruined some of our best men.'

'Ah, poor Achattu!' said Akaloo, 'he was at one time the richest Coolie in the country.'

'Yes, until you took his place,' replied Dilloo, with a touch of satirical bitterness. 'You live out of our skins.'

'I don't get much out of yours,' retorted the adroit Madrassee, good-humouredly. He never quarrelled with anybody. 'If they were all like you, I should have to work instead of lending money. As it is, I wish to do all I can for my countrymen.'

'You are a good man, Akaloo. You must take care the planters do not catch you. Trust only a very few persons. But I was going to tell

you something which has happened. There is a villain named
Hunoomaun, a chokedar from my village – a coward, a rascal, a
beast, a reptile, a snake, a carrion-crow, a————'

'Hold, Dilloo, what a rage you are in!' cried the other, laughing.

'Ah ! I wish I had him here,' said the other excitedly. 'I would
choke him – I would chuck him – I would chop him –' and the nervous movement of his body convinced Akaloo, who could not see
his face, that he was in earnest.

'Why, what has he done to you? You should not quarrel among
yourselves. I heard only to-day that he has been made a sirdar.'

'Cursed be his head, cursed be his feet————'

'And his nose, and his eyes, and his mouth, and his tongue, his
father and his mother, and so on,' cried Akaloo, interrupting. 'Let
us take everything for granted, what then?'

Dilloo gave a rapid and vehement account of all his relations
with Hunoomaun, and of the latter's wickedness to his wife.

'Plague on the coward! He pretended to help us at the last
moment, though I admit he fought well when he did begin. And
the manager has made him a sirdar, and, would you believe it,
not only am I not made a sirdar, but I have been degraded, and
am sent out to the back with the brush-cutting gang, under that
filthy————'

At this instant the little light that was left of the evening was
completely intercepted by a large body which presented itself in
the doorway. Akaloo drew the scarf over his face, though in the
dusk it would have been impossible to distinguish him.

A gruff voice called 'Dilloo!' It was the voice of Hunoomaun.

'What, in the name of all demons, do you want here?' cried
Dilloo, fiercely leaping to his feet and pushing the sirdar several
feet from the door.

'I came,' said the other, as soon as he had recovered from this
vehement reception, 'by order of Massa Chesta to tell you to be up
to-morrow morning at four, as the back-dam has given way, and
my gang is to go in and mend it. I'll pay you for this blow, my good
fellow, some other time. I have a long score against you.'

'Very well. Get out of my doorway, and don't come here eavesdropping.'

'Oho! have you got someone inside, and it is not Lutchmee?'

'Get away, I tell you!'

And Dilloo made a bound towards the chokedar, who fairly turned heel and ran away. He was not going to try a fall with his antagonist on equal terms.

Akaloo shook his head.

'This is bad work,' said he. 'That man, if he gets wind of our undertaking, will ruin us on your account. I doubt not he is a clever fellow. I must be off before he turns round to watch whom you have with you.'

'Stay,' said Dilloo, hastily unfastening a bamboo slot in the roof, and pushing out a square of the thatch, which he had ingeniously constructed as a secret trap out of the back of his house. 'You can get out by the third turning to the dam on Hofman's Lust, and then you are safe.'

As soon as his friend had gone, and he had refastened the trap, Dilloo walked out of the door of his house, in the direction taken by Hunoomaun, and, keeping a sharp look-out, he soon observed a figure hovering about a house a couple of hundred yards from his own. Dilloo made sure this was the peon, and, dashing rather noisily into the canal, he gained the other side, and made up a side dam. His *ruse* was successful. Hunoomaun took this to be the stranger who had been visiting Dilloo, and he was determined to discover who he or she was. But Dilloo was too quick, and better acquainted with the estate than his pursuer. He took a good round outside the fields of growing canes, and then, seeing Hunoomaun still followed, he splashed into the canal again a long way up, as if to cross it. In fact, however, he quietly swam down under the water, for some distance, and while Hunoomaun passed through and continued the pursuit on the other side towards the next estate, Dilloo, slipping out of the canal, reached his home unobserved.

CHAPTER XXIII

QUAINT RIVALRY

ISABEL MARSTON had no sooner attained, with a favouring fortune quite exceptional in love affairs, to the possibility of realizing her wishes, than she began to feel the embarrassment of success. Her father was equally unimaginative and unpractical. No man either of sense or of sensibility would have thought of exposing his daughter to an association which might be perilous to her affections in a way directly inconsistent with his wishes. She, when she came to reflect upon the astonishing proposal which had at the moment so delighted her, could not help feeling a doubt about the propriety of taking advantage of it. It was impossible any longer to blind herself to the fact that, whether from the sheer emptiness of her own heart, or from the essential worthiness of the object, she was quite, perhaps irretrievably, in love with the young Scotchman. If parents will not provide other funds of amusement or occupation for their daughters, they must expect them to take the slightest opportunities of investing their affections, even upon a liability that is limited. For the young girl, there was at the time, probably, among the two thousand Europeans in the colony, no other person upon whom she might with equal propriety have settled her thoughts in trying to relieve the monotony of her life.

The critical word 'duty,' which the magistrate had unadvisedly employed in relation to his proposal, that she should undertake a charitable service for the sick youth, finally removed Isabel's scruples. A man will commit a murder if you can convince him it is his duty to do so. A woman in the name of duty will risk her good name. The casuistry which depends upon terms, with too little regard to their applicability, is often more perilous than any other of the subtle perversities of conscience!

So, two days after the conversation with her father, Isabel, dressing herself with more care than was necessary for a charitable visit to an indifferent Scotch person, ordered Sarcophagus to accompany her in the buggy to Belle Susanne. He was compelled to forego his favourite ragged shirt for a clean one, and to don an old white jacket of his master's, kept for special occasions. He carried in his hand some more of the jelly, which the patient was now better able to appreciate. Two messages of thanks for previous favours had reached Isabel through Nina, direct from the sick-room.

Missa Nina received the charming girl very kindly. The Creole loved to look on the clear sweet face of the magistrate's daughter, and, too simple to think of the proprieties, or of mistakes in love affairs, she was ready enough to take her humble part in bringing together a pair of such nice young persons as the overseer and Isabel.

She plumped into the gallery, where Craig was sitting propped up by the pillows Lutchmee had ingeniously arranged about him, while the latter was fanning him gently with a big palm leaf, and said, –

'Mister Craig, there's a young lady come to see you, and bring you some more jelly.'

Craig had been day-dreaming under the influence of the soft gales kept up by his faithful nurse, and this interruption to a very gentle flow of thought came rather abruptly.

'Miss Marston!' he exclaimed, with some surprise. 'Come to see *me*, Nina? Surely there must be some mistake. Mr. Marston was here only two days ago.'

'Yes: no mistake. She's here, Mister Craig, looking most beautiful, dressed all in white with bows of pink, hat trim———'

'Confound her hat!' said Craig, quite unconscious that every word of this conversation was distinctly audible by the subject of it, who was in the dining-room. 'I'm not fit to see a young lady just now, Nina. What's to be done? Look here, Lutchmee, collar! – necktie! – get a brush and comb, Nina. Oh, bother, everything's out of order!'

'I beg pardon, Mr. Craig,' said a heavenly vision, suddenly placing itself before him. 'Don't distress yourself about your appearance. You are on a sick bed, you know, and your hair can't always be kept smooth. I came over to ask how you are after your

dreadful illness; and papa said he thought – I might – perhaps – be
of some use in reading to you – and – and———'

She had stretched out her hand to Craig, who, looking with
dazed eyes, and in a half-stupefied state, upon the lovely face
before him, mechanically put out his thin white fingers towards
his visitor. Before their hands could meet, Lutchmee, who had
been watching the scene with a quick, instinctive distrust, rushed
forward, and taking Craig's hand in hers held it to her bosom,
which panted with excitement as she turned her glowing and
angry eyes towards Isabel.

'Lutchmee!' said Nina, pushing her aside, 'what are you doing?
Go away! Miss Bella, she's very rude, – don't mind her.'

Craig's face flushed with mingled surprise and resentment at
this incident, and Miss Marston's grew red with feelings not
difficult for us to analyse. Lutchmee sulkily withdrew from the
verandah, and for a minute there was an awkward pause. The
Scotchman partially recovered himself.

'You must not mind the poor Indian woman, Miss Marston.'
('That's all very well,' thought the poor girl.) 'She has been at my
bedside all through my illness. It is very kind of you to do me the
honour to come and inquire after me. I have also to thank you for
several very pleasant dainties which have made my illness more
bearable – though Nina is very good, and gives me many nice
things,' he added, glancing at the Creole, who was evidently
listening to the conversation with both her ears. 'Hallo,
Sarcophagus, are you there?'

The grinning Negro came forward and made a deep bow.

'Mos' delectable to see Massa co-alessin' so fav'rable. I'se
'company Missa Bella on her mission ob affection: carry de jelly
for Massa Craig.'

With that Sarcophagus deposited the mould on a table, and
retired upon a very decisive sign from his mistress, whose face was
red with a heat that was strongly reflected in the countenance of
the young overseer.

Craig was so disquieted by these untoward incidents of the
visit, and Isabel was on her part so annoyed, that they found it
difficult to get up any conversation. Missa Nina good-naturedly

tried to draw out a few phrases, but the results were unimportant. Isabel mentioned her willingness to read for the young man, and asked him what book she should bring to begin upon; but she did it rather constrainedly, and he was too *distrait* to reply. So, after a very awkward interview, the close of which Lutchmee came back to watch, Isabel rose and took her leave. Her farewells were very abrupt, both to the patient and to Missa Nina, and the pace at which she made the horse tear along in the buggy caused Sarcophagus to distend his eyes to an enormous degree.

'The young gen'leman am berry much dislocated, Missa Bella,' he remarked unadvisedly. 'You'm require to visitate dat young man berry frequen' 'fore he ressimprocate your attenshins wid de right impropriety.'

'If you don't hold your saucy tongue, sir, I'll give you the whip,' she cried, vehemently.

And, indeed, it would have been a relief to Isabel if she could have vented her feelings on some one in an energetic way.

Craig's reflections upon this visit were decidedly uncomfortable. Simple-hearted as he was, the peculiarity of the incidents, and the broad hint of Sarcophagus, forced him to think again and again over every little detail of the interview, and to recall the bright, though confusing presence, of the fair Isabel to his mind. It was a pretty picture, spite of the background of stupid circumstances, and in the idleness of convalescence he naturally dwelt upon it. There was something flattering to his vanity as well as pleasant to his sense, in the interest she had shown for him. On the other hand, there was a counteracting influence. When the white girl had departed, Lutchmee returned to his side with tears in her eyes. He scarcely knew how to treat this manifestation of feeling. Her singular interruption during the interview with Isabel had suddenly revealed to him something unsuspected and unthought of – or, perhaps, something which he had been half-consciously concealing from himself up to that moment, and which he would much rather have allowed to remain unexpressed.

As he had become convalescent, he had amused himself with Lutchmee's artless, pretty ways. She showed her delight at his recovery by twining her hair in the most becoming wreaths, and dressing in her gayest calicoes. She used now and then to go to her husband's house, and Dilloo would watch with pride her light springy form as she walked 'with the dignified ease of the phenicopteros' from his house to that of the manager. He had several times been to the sick-room, when Craig heartily thanked him for his wife's assistance, but this was unwittingly done in a way to excite the Coolie's suspicion. Craig put his arm affectionately on her shoulder. She was a coloured woman, and he meant nothing by the simple action. But to the other it had an unpleasant and natural significance. Something that Dilloo's quick glance detected, of the subtle understanding almost inevitably created by sick-room intercourse between any two human beings who are ordinarily agreeable and of opposite sexes, sent a pang of jealousy through his heart of which he was immediately ashamed. Did not Lutchmee, when he went away, accompany him to the garden gate, and did she not stand there looking admiringly after the fine form of her husband, as he walked off proudly, clad in his whitest muslins? Yet, as we have seen, Dilloo could not any longer suppress the wish that his wife should return to his house, and, on the first opportunity after the scene described in the previous chapter he had told her his desire.

That little intimation was a critical point in Lutchmee's experience. It had come the day before Miss Marston's visit. The Coolie had hitherto been giving herself up to her genial toil, with a devotion which by degrees grew to an enthusiasm, as her intimacy with the manly young Briton increased. As he grew better he talked freely with her, and she prattled to him. The life was new. It brought into her life fresh human elements, feelings she had never experienced before: ideas – novel, sweet, piquant. Very pure, very simple, even very holy seemed this time to her – and yet, to the least worldly observer, how charged with peril was the atmosphere of these halcyon days! Dilloo's sudden hint to her to prepare for her return home struck in harshly upon this contented, delightful peace. It woke her up to the fact that the agreeable season must soon close – it brought her back to common life and to her wifely duties – and, though she could not analyse the meaning of the feeling, Dilloo's request disquieted her with a conscious unpleasantness. She would rather not have been reminded by him that he had a claim on her superior to the charming engagements of her recent life. The immediate feeling passed away, but, for the first time in her experience, there had crossed her mind an idea like a shadow of regret or of resistance towards the supremacy of her husband in her heart.

Craig's generosity was rather touched by the awkward exhibition of jealousy which had marred the interview with the magistrate's daughter. He said nothing to Lutchmee about it, but he could not help recurring to it as an evidence of her liking for him. He patted her kindly on the shoulder, and told her not to cry, and in a very short time she recovered her liveliness, and things went on as before. But from that moment the poor Indian woman was conscious that he was more tender to her. Would he not have been gentler to his dog had it received a blow?

A few days after this Dilloo went to Drummond, and insisted that his wife should be sent home. The manager made no objection. He once more looked upon Dilloo as a dangerous malcontent, a feeling Chester took care to encourage, and he did not care to cross the Coolie until he could gain a decisive advantage by it. Craig was now nearly well enough to undertake a journey to Barbadoes, to perfect his convalescence, and Lutchmee could be the more easily spared.

When she went away, Craig shook the little Indian woman warmly by the hand, while with look and voice he cordially thanked her for all her care. The act was done in a frank and manly way, and as he looked into her brimming eyes and pressed her small hand, no thought but that of honest gratitude filled his heart. But it was the moment in Craig's inward experience when the antipathy of race finally died within him; and as they stood there hand in hand, this woman, without reference to colour or features, became to him as a fellow-being of one blood and one humanity with himself. If there be something true and noble in such a revelation to a man, may it not also bring to him new and unforeseen dangers?

CHAPTER XXIV

SHORT AND SAD

ISABEL MARSTON, as we have seen, returned home from her first and last venture for Craig's entertainment in no amiable mood. Her anger was set on fire by the innocent but suspicious act of the Indian woman. It burned the more that Craig's treatment of the affair rather tended in Isabel's eyes to convict him of at least folly in his intercourse with the Hindoo. Why did he not shake her off as any gentleman ought to have done? Why should he permit her, a Coolie woman, not only to be so familiar, but so demonstrative – and absolutely to seem to be *jealous!* – jealous of her, Isabel Marston, the white belle of Demerara! Each time this thought recurred to her mind, Isabel's heat increased, and it was dangerous for Miriam or Sarcophagus to be in the neighbourhood. Her anger was very tropical in its intensity as well as in its manifestations. Then there was that coarse and candid remark of the idiot Sarcophagus – what could have been more exasperating? To a refined girl, conscious that her heart had run away with her, how intolerably humiliating was that premature presentation of the matter in a concrete form. The walking representative of stone coffins suffered for many a day for that single misfeasance of his too ready tongue.

'Isabel,' said Mr. Marston one evening, – he with his cigar, lounging after dinner in his cane chair, she lolling gracefully in the hammock, which she kept in gentle motion, – 'how about young Craig? Have you been over to read to him yet?'

ISABEL (*shifting uneasily in the hammock*). No: I have been over, you know, but not to read.

MR. MARSTON. Did you see him?

ISABEL. Yes. (*Another shudder of the hammock.*)

MR. MARSTON. Well?

ISABEL. O nothing, papa. He's getting better.

MR. MARSTON. Did you offer to go occasionally and amuse him?

ISABEL. I don't know, I'm sure. He seemed so taken up with Nina and the Coolie woman, I don't think he cared much about my visit.

MR. MARSTON. Confound his impudence! Those Scotchmen are the coolest people in the world. Did he not even condescend to thank you for the kindness of your offer?

ISABEL (*having vented her spite in the last sentence, and taking alarm at her father's tone*). O yes! I only hinted at it, you know; and I think perhaps he felt a little shy.

MR. MARSTON. Is that all? Well, very proper for a boy in his position.

ISABEL. Yes.

MR. MARSTON. Mr. Drummond tells me he is going away.

ISABEL (*with a slight start*). Where to?

MR. MARSTON. (*After a long puff, which tests the young lady's patience extremely.*) Bar-ba-does.

ISABEL (*carelessly*). To recruit his health, I suppose?

MR. MARSTON. I don't know. I have an idea Drummond thinks him too much of a codling. Drummond likes men of strong will, and not too squeamish; who will be faithful to the estate before all things. This young man is unlike any of the overseers, or else I should never have allowed him to come here. He is honourable, and in some respects gentlemanly, and I have noticed that in court he is very particular about the truth. In that assault case he behaved nobly, and I felt bound to congratulate him, though it made Drummond tremendously testy.

ISABEL. Then he is going to Barbadoes for good?

MR. MARSTON. Oh, I don't know anything about it; nor do I care! But I should think it likely. Why don't they bring the coffee? Do go and wake them up.

Now Isabel had been convincing herself that she did not care 'one bit' for Mr. Craig, and that gentleman might go, or act, or think, or refrain from going, or acting, or thinking, whither or how, or what he pleased, for all it mattered to her. But, in truth, when she jumped out of the hammock to hunt up the lazy Sarcophagus, her heart was going pit-a-pat in a way the reverse of indifferent. She could not define the reason why, nor did she attempt to do so; but a great shadow of disappointment and apprehension had suddenly come over her. In fact, she did not immediately return to the verandah, but went up to her room with a bursting heart; – and – yes, miss, it must be told – threw herself down on the bed and cried very heartily.

CHAPTER XXV

PLOTTING

WHEN Craig had gone, and could not even be inquired after, Lutchmee for a short time felt very keenly the change of life from the sick-room to her own home. But her real love for Dilloo, and his delight at her return, his grave but more marked fondness, soon restored her to her old contentment. She was able to do much for her husband in preparing his meals, or in assisting to tend the cows. As Dilloo found himself becoming more deeply involved in the plot which Akaloo was hatching, and at the same time was daily more sensitive to the intolerable supremacy of Hunoomaun, his heart turned with greater passion towards the only being whom he loved and trusted, and his jealous watchfulness over her grew proportionately more strict.

It was now necessary that the Indian wife should take her part in the labour which she was indentured to perform on the estate. Drummond would have scorned to exhibit towards her any direct ill-will, but he did not put himself to the trouble he was wont to take for his favourites, to look after her destination as a labourer. His misunderstanding of Dilloo's character led him to look upon the Coolie with increased suspicion.

It is inevitable that in the anomalous artificial relations created under the labour laws of Coolie colonies, a labourer's cleverness or independence should excite suspicion oftener than confidence in the mind of his master. What would be your disquietude were one of your horses to begin to display an intelligent apprehension of his rights and wrongs? To the employer the ideally perfect conditions of such systems of labour must be absolute subservience and narrow intelligence on the part of the employed. The complaint that education or ability may make a man too clever for his work, comes not only from English farmers or from noble

Marquises in a House of Peers, it has its special grounds wherever slavery, or any modification of slavery, is the order of labour. Equality of rights or of ability in a bond-servant is as irrecognisable as equality of position. In judging of the system this should never be forgotten; it is the key to many of its delicate and most difficult problems. Such a system can only be endured by any right-minded man as an interval of pupilage for better things, and can only avoid condemnation in proportion as it proves itself to serve that end. In that view it may be made, with wisdom, forbearance, and the most rigid oversight conscientiously enforced by a strong Government, a means of incalculable good; but only the most ignoble avarice would desire it to be protracted beyond the shortest possible period of duration. Hence the question for the present and the future is, how to secure for the Coolie the maximum of the benefits of the system by which alone he can be brought to the possibility of better prospects and advantages; meanwhile reducing to the very least the necessary restraints or inevitable disabilities of his half-bondaged state. This is the state which it is the natural interest of the planters to prolong, – the policy of humanity and statesmanship to shorten.

Drummond then, finding both his servants to be too-clever-by-half, took no pains about either Dilloo or Lutchmee. He left it to the overseers to assign them their tasks. It is a horrible fact, which we would not again unnecessarily refer to, that the Hindoo wife was exposed to the rival advances of two or three overseers, and that her simple and determined virtue subjected her to the animosity which they were, without fear of censure or discovery, free to carry into action against both her and her husband. Martinho, the Portuguese, was the most resentful of these libertines. He had an inkling from Ramdoolah of the state of affairs between Hunoomaun and the too independent pair. Lutchmee was, by his direction, on the ground of laziness in the megass-yard, – a laziness due to a cause which ought to have appealed to any manly sympathy, – sent out with the weeding-gang to the back of the plantation. She patiently bore up against the additional strain thus put upon her. It was work she had never done, and in her condition especially painful; but her husband was working not far from her. She walked by his side the long distance to and from their tasks, and sometimes of an afternoon, when the day's labour was finished, they would lounge under the bamboos at the back-dam, or she would rest in the shade while he penetrated the jungle in search of birds or iguanas.

Lutchmee's quick apprehension discerned that her husband was daily growing more reserved and gloomy. He showed her no unkindness, – nay, he seemed more tender in his treatment of her, but he talked little, and frequently absented himself without giving her any information of the object. She noticed that at the back-dam he often wandered away over the bounds of the adjacent estates; and two or three times she saw that men from those estates, who seemed to have met him casually, engaged with him in long and earnest conversations. It was unusual for so many persons to frequent the back-dams, and Lutchmee began to have a suspicion that Dilloo was engaged in some perilous plot. She asked him about it.

'Dilloo, why do so many people come and talk to you out here?' she said one evening to him. 'That was Akaloo who was with you just now under the bamboos.'

'Hush!' said Dilloo, looking round, cautiously. 'Don't mention any names in talking out here. We are never safe.'

'Why not, dear Dilloo?' said Lutchmee, putting her soft hand on his shoulder. 'Surely there can be no harm in mentioning the names of our acquaintances. Why should you have any fear?'

'Oh, I don't mean everybody! I mean – the one you mentioned. Don't speak of any one you ever recognise out here!'

'What can be going on? I am certain you are doing something with these men which is secret, perhaps dangerous. Why do you not tell me about it? You can trust me, – you used to trust me.'

'Lutchmee, darling,' said the man, 'you are young and a woman. I trust you as ever with all my own secrets, but this is not my own, it belongs to hundreds of people – to all Coolies.'

'Then it belongs to me!' interrupted his wife.

'Yes, some of it does. But it would have been better had you never suspected or known anything of it. I wanted to keep you safe, whatever might happen to me.'

'Oh, Dilloo, are you in any danger?'

'We are engaged in a great plot. Coolies on every estate are pledged to it. At first we are going to act peaceably and demand justice from the great Sahib, the Governor. If he will not give it to us, then——' he stopped, and significantly made a grimace. 'Anything is better than this. Everyday Hunoomaun is more ferocious to me. He cheats me every week in setting down my work. And you, my poor Lutchmee, in your present state you cannot long endure the stooping labour you have to do. This shall stop – *this shall stop!*'—— and leaping to his feet he fiercely stretched out his arms and cursed the Government, the officials, and the people who had brought them to their present position. In the act a piece of blue paper dropped out of his babba.

Lutchmee picked it up. It was foolscap, and contained both printing and writing. She, of course, could not read it: it was in English.

'What is this?' she said.

'That? Oh, I did not want to trouble you about it! It is a summons to the Mahitee's court for to-morrow.'

'What for?'

'For absenting myself from work Friday last.'

'Why I thought you were at work all day.'

'No. I had to go a long distance to another estate on an important matter.'

'That you have been speaking of?'

He nodded.

'Will they fine you?'

'No. I had done five tasks, and Akaloo says I am not bound by the law to work five days if I do five tasks. But the overseer says I am bound to perform my tasks on five succeeding days. He knows I work fast, and wants to get more out of me.'

'I hope the Mahitee will not send you to prison?'

'No fear. He will fine me if he punishes me at all. Am I not the best workman on the estate?'

'They have a spite against you. They will do all they can to hurt you. I will go with you to Mahitee's court to-morrow.'

'Oh, you must not do that. You have not done five tasks this week, and they may summon *you*.'

'Well, I shall run the risk.'

They went to the canal, where there was floating a raft of brushwood which Dilloo had recently made for his wife, now within a few months of her confinement. As a rule, women in that condition were very kindly treated on Drummond's estate. They were allowed to rest from work, and to lounge and feed, if they pleased, in the hospital. But Lutchmee and her husband had forfeited the manager's regard, and he left them to the overseers, who of course might or might not carry out the usual practice of the estate. Ramdoolah had been brought into requisition by Hunoomaun, and she assured Chester, who was willing enough to believe it, that there was nothing the matter with Lutchmee, and that her indisposition was a pretence. It is so common a thing for a Coolie woman to malinger, that Chester was able the more safely to disregard his own convictions in favour of Ramdoolah's theory.

Lutchmee sat on the raft, and Dilloo seizing a withe of grass which he attached to it, plunged into the canal, and, walking down its centre up to his shoulders, gently drew his wife the whole distance home. She laughed and clapt her hands as she watched his shining limbs, smoothly dividing the brown bush-water.

CHAPTER XXVI

DIDACTIC

IT is necessary, before unfolding any farther the events which befell at Belle Susanne, to refer in a rather matter-of-fact way to the condition of the Coolie labourers in British Guiana at the time which our story describes; and to the various circumstances of injustice which had given rise among the whole Coolie population to a dangerous feeling of discontent.

The reader will already have gathered that the root of the injustice had been struck in India in the exaggerated representations made by the native recruiters to induce the Indians to emigrate. These were bad enough, and may be found to be unavoidable in circumstances where so much is left to depend on the statements of irresponsible and unconscientious Hindoos. The Indian magistrates, who were bound by law to make a personal examination of the intending emigrants, and might by conversation have informed the applicants what were the real terms and meaning of their contracts, sometimes did not see the people except in the distance and as a body, or if they did, were unable to give the time necessary for a proper examination. At the Hooghly depôt, the emigrants were treated very much like a flock of sheep, being looked at, verified, and counted, it is true, but without proper regard to the question whether or no they distinctly understood the terms of their undertaking. Hence it was not until he landed in Demerara, and came in contact with the Immigration Agent-General, that the Coolie began to surmise what were his engagements in the estimation of his employers; and never until he was fairly upon the estate, and in communication with older immigrants, did he discover that he was the subject of penal laws of a peculiarly harsh and stringent character. The inequality and injustice of the 'Masters and Servants Act' in England was reproduced with aggravated incidents in the case of men who in no circumstances were free to change their masters for five years at a stretch. While the Coolie, for any breach of his contract (e.g., not performing five tasks a week, or for damages not wilful), was liable to either fine, or imprisonment in the discretion of the magistrate, there was no breach of the labour law, however gross – such for instance as the non-payment of the wages on which the men's living depended, or such neglect of a doctor's orders in hospital as might affect a patient's health for life – which subjected the master to imprisonment. This was the more glaring because there was open an alternative and quite sufficient mode of punishment, which was actually made a supplementary one; for not only was a Coolie punished by imprisonment, but he was liable in addition to have the period of that imprisonment added to his five years at the end of his identure, and was thus practically obliged to suffer twice over for the same offence. Had the magistrates in inflicting their penalties duly considered this, it would not have mattered. But the punishments they imposed were often intolerably heavy.

It is right also to mention, as another instance of the normal state of conscience of legislators and administrators in such colonies, that the law was so worded as to afford an excuse for a gross injustice. Though the law was clearly intended to permit an emigrant to perform, in succession, the whole of the maximum number of tasks of labour that could be exacted in a week, and then for the remaining days to be at liberty to dispose of his time as he pleased, the magistrates held that he was bound to perform a certain number of tasks on a certain number of succeeding days in the week; and hence a man, who had by the Wednesday really performed his legal week's work, was, if he absented himself on the Thursday, brought up and punished with imprisonment.

Again, there were on the part of many managers those other wrongs which were specified by the Portuguese, and by Akaloo in his conversation with Dilloo. Stoppages at the Saturday pay-table for alleged neglect in tasks that had been finished days before, and without notice to the supposed defaulter at the time of his default, preferred too late for any reference to arbitration, were subjects of rancorous discontent on several estates. On others, illegal fines were levied; and on almost every estate such instances of personal wrong inflicted by managers or overseers or drivers, as have been disclosed by the incidents of this tale, gave rise to the indignant sympathy of the little immigrant communities, and aroused very serious disaffection.

Not only did a Coolie suffer such petty injustices while actually indentured, but at the termination of his service, when he was discharged from his engagement, he found that the law had ingeniously surrounded him with conditions invented to drive him to reindenture himself for another five years. There was no provision for a shorter term of service. He was tempted by the offer of the fifty dollars bounty-money in cash. The law obliged him, if he wished to be free, to take out a certificate, for which he paid a couple of months' wages, and to carry about this certificate always on his person. It was taken for granted that every immigrant who was found on the roads walking about free was a deserter, unless he could produce this certificate of his discharge. If he had perchance left it at home, he was liable to be locked up at the police-station until he could prove himself a freeman. In one Coolie colony, that of Mauritius, where the immense number of immigrants renders it the more difficult to identify them, an ordinance was passed ordering that a photograph of the free Coolie should be attached to his certificate, for which he was charged the value of a month's labour! It was alleged that the photographer who succeeded to the benefit of this infamous piece of jobbery realized by it a large sum of money. Spite even of this precaution, constant instances of illegal detention, under the vicious activity of the police, made the lives of freemen so miserable that indenture-ship became a preferable resource to freedom – a consummation devoutly to be forwarded in the interest of the planters. Did a man, although carrying the certificate, go from one district to another without previously obtaining a *visé* from the magistrate, he was subject to arrest and to detention in horrible dens.

In addition to these, there were other subjects of complaint, arising out of the difficulty of fixing a standard of wages satisfactory to the Coolies. They were, according to the law, to be paid at the same rate as the free Negroes in their own neighbourhood, a standard which clever managers by the nature of their arrangements with the Negroes could easily render inapplicable, and which in the case of a large number of estates in islands or sequestered places could never be applied, because there were no Negroes employed in the vicinity.

No one can be surprised that these things had excited to a high pitch the ill-feeling of the whole immigrant community. At the same time Blacks and Portuguese were dissatisfied with the incidence of taxation; so that altogether British Guiana was not for its Governor a bed of roses, though he received a salary and perquisites of more than six thousand pounds sterling a year.

Dilloo had, on his first arrival at Belle Susanne, behaved with great discretion, although his quick mind soon appreciated the evils and the wrongs of the system of which he was a victim. He saw that many of his countrymen were good-for-nothing people; while, on the other hand, not a few had, by application and thrift, been able to amass respectable sums of money. He invested his own bounty-money in a cow, and worked with assiduity to earn as much wages as any of his fellows. But his sympathy was aroused by the wrongs of which he was a constant witness, and was still more keen when he found that the magistrate's court did not afford redress for them. The stipendiaries seemed to the Coolies to think that it was their duty to administer the law in the interest of the planters: they disbelieved Coolie evidence, and placed undue reliance on that of the employers. In fact, they so far encouraged the notion that to bring an immigrant before them was to convict him, that in one instance a manager was extremely indignant with a magistrate who remonstrated on finding that an overseer had been deliberately sent to testify in a case knowing nothing whatever of the subject of inquiry! In Dilloo's mind the sight of these wrongs inflicted on his weaker countrymen aroused as much indignation as did his own disappointment. The Indian's ideas of ethics were, no doubt, vague and distorted; but he had much nobility of character, his sentiments were usually generous, and, with all his native education in cunning and deceit, he was inclined to the side of truth and honour. When his ability forced him to a leading place among the immigrants of his estate, he candidly manifested his feelings, much, as we have seen, to the injury of his good-standing with his superiors.

He again and again acted as spokesman for his brethren when they had complaints to make to Drummond; and this gave the manager the impression that the Hindoo was a firebrand. His evil character culminated in the event which led to his imprisonment.

The incident arose in this way. A man, named 'Rambux No. 2,' had been appointed stable-boy to Simon Pety. Rambux No. 2 was a weakly fellow from the streets of Calcutta, quite equal, however, to the amount of light work involved in his appointment. He spent most of the day lounging about the stables, which sheltered from the night-air and the vampire bats the horses of the manager and the mules of the overseers. The saddles and bridles of the latter rarely received any other attention than that of the cobbler at Guineatown; and, with the exception of Mr. Drummond's harness and buggy, the general plant of these stables was of a primitive sort. However, Simon Pety naturally wanted to put the maximum of work on the shoulders of Rambux No. 2, and Rambux No. 2 reciprocated by desiring to do the minimum of work for Simon Pety, – a diversity of operations which brought about anything but one spirit.

Another thing led to discrepancies of opinion. Rambux No. 2, a dark, hill Koord, was a hideous idolater. He had a baked clay idol in his house. When a kid was killed, he performed curious rites with its blood. He had weird and terrible notions about the devil.

Simon Pety would talk to a cocoa-nut tree, or to himself, in the absence of an intelligent audience, in direct controversion of the Duchess of Newcastle's aphorism, that 'conversation requires witty opposites.' Any answer or no answer would satisfy Simon Pety. Rambux No. 2 was one of his butts. He took it into his head that he ought to try to convert Rambux No. 2 to Christianity – that is, to his own ideas of it.

'You heathen, Rambux,' he said one day. 'Sabby you go to hell, sure as you'm born.'

'Iss,' replied Rambux No. 2, showing his black teeth, and test-ifying a thorough enjoyment of the prospect: 'me sabby – all right.'

'Debbil take you – eat you – scrunch you so,' persisted Simon Pety, illustrating his metaphor by biting a piece of sugar-cane and grinding it between his teeth.

'Iss, iss. Oh good – debbil!' replied the other, with a delighted face. 'Pray, debbil, eat um so.'

'You'm great sinna! No pray debbil! pray God – God lub 'im – Christ, too, lub 'im – die for 'im – save 'im soul from debbil! Rambux no lub Christ?'

'No: Rambux no sabby 'im – lub debbil. O too much lub debbil!'

The Indian took a small, dirty, rather crudely-formed image from the string round his neck, and, placing it on the ground, made a profound salaam – went on his knees, and finally on his face, flat before the piece of clay. Simon Pety did not conceal his disgust and horror. He expressed it in an energetic way – the spirit of the old Reformers was in his heart. Taking down a rawhide used for the mules, he gave Rambux No. 2 a cut, full of sanctified zeal, over his naked thighs, that made him start and howl to his god in a most appropriate spirit.

'Get you up, Satan! Get away, you 'bandoned sinna! Dat am committin' de sin 'gainst de Holy Ghos'. You'm sartin to be damned.'

Simon Pety seized upon the idol and flung it a hundred feet away. It was well for the audacious iconoclast and missionary that his would-be convert was no match for him; otherwise the wrath that blazed in the other's face would have proceeded to a very infernal manifestation of zeal on behalf of his Satanic majesty. As it was, the Koord made a rush at his instructor, and the latter gave him another cut with the whip. Forthwith Rambux No. 2 raising a great outcry, again rushed at the Negro, who knocked him down, and proceeded to lay the cowhide over the man with furious enthusiasm. Several Coolies ran to the scene, among them Dilloo. Before Master Pety could turn round, or call for assistance, he was thrown on the ground. Fortunately for him Dilloo was not carrying his favourite lattey; but one or two others were better provided, and they belaboured the evangelist very thoroughly, while Dilloo supplemented their exertions with the whip which he wrested from Pety's hand. The row brought to the spot Martinho and Craig, who seized on Dilloo and rescued Pety from an ugly fate. The whole of the Coolies were arrested.

When the case was brought before the magistrate, Pety swore, that the man, Rambux No. 2, had disobeyed his orders, and, on being 'demonstrated wid very quietly,' had deliberately gone for a band of Coolies, who, headed by Dilloo, came into the yard and assaulted him. This was of course denied by Rambux No. 2 and the other Indians present. Rambux gave his version of the tale to the interpreter, who discreetly suppressed it. The practical rule of some magistrates in British Guiana, the result of sad experience, is that one Negro or white man is to be believed before twenty Coolies; and although Craig deposed, in the teeth of Martinho's evidence, that when he arrived on the scene Rambux No. 2 was lying on the ground exhausted, and – as was evident even now – much cut with a whip, Mr. Marston thought that he should hit the mean of justice by sentencing Dilloo to three months' imprisonment, and discharging the rest with a caution.

Craig's conduct in this case met with a severe reprimand from the head overseer.

'There is no use,' he said, 'in letting out too much to the magistrate. But for you, that fellow, Dilloo, would have been sent to Massaruni, and a good job for the estate.'

Craig indignantly replied that he should not hold himself bound to swear in accordance with the views of any master or overseer; and, moreover, that, in his opinion, the immigrants were entitled to all that could be advanced in their favour.

'You will never do for Demerara, my fine fellow,' said the planter. 'These niggers are brought here to work, and you must make them do it by hook or by crook. With your squeamish views, they would soon get the whip-hand of us; and we might as well shut up shop altogether.'

Drummond was very much annoyed at this circumstance, since Marston, with a capricious touch of good feeling, had spoken in high terms of the young man's honesty, and had reflected unpleasantly on Mr. Martinho. Drummond instructed the head overseer never to call for Craig's evidence again, unless it was absolutely necessary.

'He's too particular for his place,' said the manager; 'but he's a shrewd, hard-working fellow. As he grows older and gets used to these people, he will see that you cannot meet their lying and cheating on fair ground, and that it is a mistake to yield them a single inch.'

By such reasoning Drummond satisfied his own conscience. He chose to erect within himself a court of justice regulated by principles and administering conclusions of its own. It struck a rough balance, which might or might not be a just one, between the known chicane of the Indians on the one hand and a reserve or perversion of truth in order to outwit that chicane on the other. Most planters are like him, and might defend themselves with considerable ingenuity in those curious tribunals set up by men called 'practical,' wherein actual benefits are held to be superior to abstract principles.

CHAPTER XXVII

JUSTICE

THE Guineatown court-house was a wooden building, surpassing the other barn-like buildings of British Guiana only in the height and thinness of the poles whereon it was supported. It lay inside a broken fence surrounding a rough grass-grown piece of ground. A very long flight of steps led to the court-room. Under these were the police-barracks and lock-ups for prisoners, places which could not be described without considerable expense to one's feelings. Round this building, at ten o'clock in the morning of a court-day were to be seen signs of animation. A body of the black police of the colony, under the direction of an inspector and serjeant, disposed itself about and in the court. Numbers of idle blacks slouched lazily towards the place, and hung about the yard, or, as soon as they could gain admission, filled up the spaces allotted to the public. A few Coolies, also, found their way to these spaces; but the larger number of them congregated in the yard and outside the palings, upon the dam, where they could be seen squatting in groups, men and women chatting earnestly together, many of them dressed in their bright holiday calicoes; or sometimes eight or ten were collected in a body, soil-stained fellows, with discoloured babbas, who had all been summoned from the same estate for some breach of the labour laws. Such groups looked moody and depressed. They were the poor and helpless ones of the flock. Frequent fines and imprisonments had made them careless of the fate that might befall them. Here and there might be seen a new Coolie, summoned for the first time, loudly and excitedly haranguing in his own behoof any who would listen to him. Now and then an overseer on mule or horseback rode up into the inclosure, where he tethered his beast, or gave it in charge to some lounging black, and joined a group of his fellows, who were discussing the cases for the day.

Martinho and Chester were in the group. By-and-by Hunoomaun, in a full suit of calico, which gave his big form a really fine appearance, came along the dam, accompanied by Ramdoolah, who walked resplendent in her best finery. There, also, approaching with slow paces, were Dilloo and Lutchmee, both handsome and well dressed, the wife meekly following her husband. As they drew near the courthouse, a light-coloured Indian stepped out from a group to which he had been talking in low tones, and accosted the Bengalee.

'Salaam, Dilloo! The lawyer cannot come to-day. I offered him the forty dollars. He has a case in the Big Court.'

Dilloo looked disappointed.

'That is bad,' said he. 'Did you ask him what the law was?'

'Yes. He charged me ten dollars for telling me, though. He says if you had done five tasks before Thursday you were entitled to go free for the rest of the week.'

'Who will tell that to the Sahib?'

'You must run your chance of that,' said Akaloo. 'You cannot speak Inglees well. You must get the interpreter to do it for you. I have seen him; I gave him a dollar to interpret truly. I am watching to see that he does not take anything from the other side. See, there he is lying in the corner.'

While they were speaking Chester sauntered up to the interpreter, and the trio closely observed the interview. They could not hear what passed, but we can supply the report:—

CHESTER. You interpret to-day?

INTERPRETER. Yes, massa.

CHESTER. You know a man called Dilloo, at Belle Susanne ?

INTERPRETER. Yes, massa.

CHESTER. I have a case against him. Does he know Inglees well?

INTERPRETER. No, massa. A little only.

CHESTER. Well, see that you do not interpret for him. Do you understand?

INTERPRETER. Yes, massa. No speak Dilloo's words to Mahitee; no speak Mahitee's words to Dilloo.

CHESTER. Exactly. Nor anything his witnesses may say. I'll give you two dollars after the court is over.

He sauntered back again. Before he had reached the group of overseers from which he had emerged, Akaloo was by the side of the interpreter, and addressed him in his own language.

'The overseer has been speaking to you?'

'No: no one has spoken to me since you did.'

'Yes, he has spoken to you: I saw him. He just left you.'

'He spoke to another man.'

'No: he spoke to you. I tell you I saw him.'

'Yes: well, – he *did*.'

'What did he say?' said Akaloo.

'He only told me there were not many cases to-day,' replied the man, who was so in the habit of swearing that he would tell the truth that he rarely thought about doing it.

'Did he tell you about Dilloo's case?'

'No, not a word.'

'Will you take five dollars to tell me what he said; true, – true?'

'Yes.'

'Well, tell me.'

'Give me the money first.'

Akaloo was not so confiding.

'Everyone can see us here,' he said. 'You can trust me; you know me well. Tell me the truth and I will give you the money.'

The man told him what had passed. Akaloo's face testified neither surprise nor disgust at the interpreter's dishonesty; the truth was he did not feel either. His business was to outwit the other side.

'Now,' he said, 'listen. I will give you in all ten dollars. You must tell Mahitee so and so when Dilloo tells you. I shall be in court and can understand you, and if you do not speak as I wish,' said the Madrassee, his eyes glowing darkly as he looked the interpreter in the face, 'you will be very sorry for it before three days are over.'

The scoundrel was a coward, and if the truth were put in the balance with his life, as he well knew the other meant him to understand, there was not much doubt about his choice. There are any number of Christians who in similar circumstances would be equally conscientious.

When Akaloo acquainted Dilloo with the nature of the interview between Chester and the interpreter he was much incensed,
though he had testified no anger when Akaloo told him of the
negotiations on his own behalf.

These preliminaries of justice had been duly performed, and
everyone was patiently waiting the arrival of the magistrate.
Mr. Marston considered it more dignified to be late than punctual
at his courts, and arrived half an hour after his time. He had been
breakfasting with Drummond, who accompanied him in his
buggy, as it was driven in among the Coolies, many of whom were
summoned from Belle Susanne. It could scarcely fail to give them
all the impression that the 'Mahitee' and 'Manahee' thoroughly
understood one another. And as a matter of fact, Drummond, who
was much interested in Dilloo's case, had been entertaining
Mr. Marston at breakfast with an account of Dilloo, and with his
views of the immigrant's conduct. He had judiciously mingled
hints of the Hindoo's ability and craft, and of the danger such a
man was likely to cause to the peace of an estate. What is the
advantage of his position if it does not secure a man 'justice'?

The magistrate and the manager went up the long flight of steps
together, and the latter, as a justice of the peace, took his seat on the
bench near the former. Here the analogy to English county justice
was exact, where landlords and employers of labour may occupy
seats upon the bench which is adjudicating on cases in which they
are deeply interested, though they are not taking part in them. But
Englishmen can understand that the arrangement tends to no prejudice of right, while to Coolies, not understanding the language of
the court and full of the suspicions of Asiatics, it is inexplicable.

After the prisoners' cases had been adjudicated on, the summonses were called. A policeman shouted from the head of the
steps the names and estates of the defendants as they were required. Akaloo had succeeded in getting Lutchmee a place inside
the court beside himself, and they sat there watching intently the
process in every case. After a number of summonses had been disposed of, the name of Dilloo was called.

The court was not a large one. Its aspect was primitive
enough, but in it was administered justice according to English

forms and precedents. The panelling and appointments were all of unpainted deal. About one-third of the room was occupied by the low platform, fenced in by wooden palings, constituting the bench, in the middle of which, at a plain table, sat the Justice. The chairs near him were occupied by Mr. Drummond and the managers of Hofman's Lust and New Holland. They took no part in the examinations, but in one of the previous cases one of these gentlemen had given evidence from the bench against a defendant. Immediately in front of the magistrate's table was a wooden pen or dock, beside which was the stand for the interpreter and witness. Behind this a space was kept clear by the police for prisoners, defendants, and witnesses. On either side, with the exception of a few seats assigned to any legal attendants at the court, or to overseers and reporters, were banks of seats crowded with representatives of the mixed population of British Guiana.

When Dilloo's name was called, all eyes looked anxiously towards the entrance. Many of the spectators knew that this was the man who had beaten Simon Pety. Pety himself had slipped upstairs, with the Christian desire to see punishment inflicted upon one against whom he had a grudge. Hunoomaun was waiting among the witnesses, and Ramdoolah's black teeth grinned maliciously at Lutchmee, who, overcome by the heat and thrilling with apprehension, could scarcely keep her seat.

As the noble-looking Hindoo passed noiselessly into the court, and firmly walked forward to the box, he touched elbows with Hunoomaun. The chokedar tried to look firmly in the other's face, but his glance quailed before the fiery passion that glowed in Dilloo's eye. He drew aside, and Dilloo, stepping lightly into the box, saluted the magistrate.

Mr. Marston looked at the face and figure and dress of the Hindoo with some admiration. He had an Englishman's love for a fine man; and here was one, tinted coffee colour.

'It's a pity you should bring up such a fine-looking fellow, Drummond,' he whispered to the manager.

'Ah! He's a regular devil, though,' replied the other. 'I told you he was the same man who nearly killed my groom.'

'Yes, the sanctimonious scoundrel! I never felt easy about that case, you know,' said the magistrate, smiling.

The other smiled also, as Mr. Marston turned to his duty.

Dilloo had watched the conversation keenly. His imagination filled it with meaning.

'Where is the summons?' said the magistrate.

He looked at it.

'It is "for absenting himself from work." That will be under section 7 of the Ordinance 9, of 1868? Who appears to prosecute?'

'I do,' said Chester, standing with his arm on the paling that environed the Justice. 'The defendant absented himself on Thursday. I was the overseer. I produce my book.'

'Tell the defendant the charge,' said Marston to the interpreter.

The latter uttered a few words, Dilloo nodded.

'He understands it, sir.'

The overseer was then sworn, and deposed to the defendant's absence on Thursday. Hunoomaun, having been duly sworn on a glass of water, also deposed to Dilloo's truancy.

'Have you explained to the defendant what the witnesses said?' asked the magistrate of the interpreter.

'Yes, sah.'

'Does he wish to ask them any questions?'

'Yes, sah. Ask Hunoomaun whether this man have not done five tasks by the night before?'

'What has that to do with it? The summons is for 'absence from work,' not for non-performance of five tasks. Explain that to him.'

A long and confused colloquy ensued between the interpreter and the defendant. As the former did not comprehend the point put by the magistrate, it is no wonder that the latter never had an inkling of it.

'Have you explained it to him?'

'Yes, sah!'

'Well?'

'He says nothing.'

Mr. Marston looked at the section again.

'As a matter of fact,' said he, to the overseer, 'had the man done five tasks by Wednesday night?, Because, if he had it would be rather hard to punish him.'

Drummond made a gesture of impatience. It was seen by the magistrate, also by the defendant and by Akaloo and Lutchmee.

'Not,' replied Chester, steadily, 'according to my book. I see my book only has him down for three tasks. Ask the driver, sir.' Chester had provided against this defence.

Hunoomaun, with well-feigned reluctance swore, through the interpreter, that Dilloo had only performed three tasks that week.

'I don't mean to say that it is of any consequence to the legal bearing of the case,' said Marston, apologetically, 'but it might have affected the penalty. Well, the case seems to be proved. Ask him if he has any witnesses.'

INTERPRETER. He says he has no witnesses. He says he did five shillings' work by Wednesday night.

The interpreter was keeping faith with Akaloo.

A Coolie summoned for breach of contract under the labour laws was, and while I write (two years after) still is – spite of the recommendation of a Royal Commission – treated like a criminal in England, and not suffered to give evidence in his own case. Dilloo had not expected the denial of so plain a fact as his perfor-mance of five tasks, and had brought no witnesses to prove it. Akaloo understood the position.

'Dilloo !' he called out in his own, language, 'ask the Mahitee to put off the case to another day, to allow you to call witnesses to prove you had done five tasks.'

'Silence!' cried the Judge and two black policemen, and all the justices in chorus.

Dilloo took the hint. He accordingly instructed the interpreter, who asked for an adjournment. Drummond whispered to the magistrate:

'It's only a *ruse*.'

'Oh, nonsense!' said Mr. Marston aloud to the audience. 'There's no use in encouraging the defendant to bring a lot of Coolies here to commit perjury. At all events, I am of opinion that, looking at the section, the point has nothing practically to do with the case. Ask him whether he was absent from work on Thursday.'

'He says "Yes," sah!'

'Well, then, there's nothing more to be said. The case is quite clear. I fine you ten dollars, or one month's imprisonment. Will he pay the money?'

Dilloo shook his head, and gave a decided negative when he understood the question.

'He says "No," sah! You not give him justice.'

'Then remove him. Who comes next?'

CHAPTER XXVIII

A TREACHEROUS WOMAN

BEFORE Dilloo had had time fully to apprehend the result of his trial, he was pulled out of the dock and hurried from the court. For the second time, in his case, British justice, drawing a bow somewhat at a venture, had made a bad shot. Lutchmee, following him down the steps, silently wept and wrung her hands. By her side went Akaloo, whose natively yellow face looked a mortified blue, though he fought with his feelings bravely. The three were allowed to remain and converse together in the yard until the court broke up. The Indian woman sat down and rocked her body to and fro, moaning to herself, while Akaloo and Dilloo conversed in undertones.

'I shall go and complain to Massa Goody about this,' said the Madrassee.

'What use?' cried Dilloo, fiercely. 'Why need we bear this any longer? You see they are all alike. The Mahitee and the Manahee pull together. They pretend to give us justice in their courts, and go through the form, but never give us the reality. Massa Goody is very kind, and tries to help us, but Governor-Sahib won't let him. Do not trouble yourself any longer about the petition,' he added, with clenched teeth and frowning brow. 'Wait until I get out: tell the Coolies to be all ready, and then let Massa Drummond and Massa Marston look out for their houses!'

'Stay, stay; not so fast,' replied his more sagacious friend. 'You must remember the British Queen is strong, and her arm is long. If we *could* kill all the Inglees in Guiana, she would be sure to find us out and punish us. We must put ourselves in the right, and try every fair means before we take to fighting.'

'For my part, I wish to fight – and die!' said Dilloo.

Lutchmee was alarmed by his vehemence.

'Calm yourself, my man,' she said softly, with a caressing gesture: 'we will talk of this when you are free. But, O Dilloo, tell me, what shall I do with myself while you are away?'

He looked at her tenderly, and his thoughts all gathered in his eyes in a dense cloud. A lonely woman – in the hands of Drummond and his overseers – at the mercy, possibly, of Hunoomaun and Ramdoolah, with no strong arm near to protect her, and by the conditions of her indenture restrained from seeking shelter elsewhere: no one will think the less of his manliness if her husband's realizing glance at her situation overpowered him with anxiety.

'Poor Lutchmee!' he said; 'you will be alone, and so soon you must "sit down."[*] You ought not to do any more work. How is she to get on, Akaloo?'

'She must go to the doctor and get an order to stop working.'

'Very well. Go, Lutchmee, to the hospital, and if you can, get them to allow you to stay there. You will be safer than you would be alone in the house.'

'Now,' said Akaloo gently, ' I think the court is rising. One word more in your ear. The petitions must be presented at once. There are many signatures. Mr. Williams will send them to the Governor-Sahib on behalf of the Coolies. You have some of the papers at your house.'

'Yes,' replied the Bengalee; 'you know where they are hidden. Go now with Lutchmee, and get them. But I tell you it is of no use. These rascals need to be waked up with knives and latties. You are obliged always to kill a few people to make the great Inglees-Sahibs listen to any complaint.'

'That may be true,' replied the other with a shrug; 'but,' tapping his friend on the shoulder with his finger, 'though it may bring about an inquiry and win better things for the Coolies, remember this – *the men who do it will be hung!* The Inglees take blood for blood, before they ask who was wrong and who was right.'

Being a great people, cannot we English afford to overlook the caustic insolence of Master Akaloo?

[*]This is the delicate way in which the Coolies are wont to describe the approaching perils of maternity.

'So be it!' replied the other grimly – the ferocity as well as the fatalism of his nature speaking plainly in the set lines of his face. At the same moment, his glance rested upon Lutchmee, who, appalled by her husband's aspect, regarded him with eyes wide open and quivering lips. His features relaxed. Then he said softly –

'If we die, Lutchmee, we shall die together. Neither you nor I need fear death, and the Hereafter will be the same joy or sorrow to us. If we sink into Nothing we can at least know no trouble. Were it not for you I should not care to live in this cursed world any longer. Meantime, do not fear. I shall never forget I have my Lutchmee to protect. You must now go. We shall meet in a month. Farewell, my Flower!'

As they were taking leave of each other, they became conscious of the fact that two pairs of eyes were intently watching them from about half-way down the ladder of steps. Looking up, they saw Hunoomaun and Ramdoolah, who could not conceal a malicious expression of pleasure at the painful scene.

'Carrion!' screamed Dilloo, in a rage. 'Go your way. Do not stand up there and cast your foul shadows on purer and better people.'

'Son of Satan,' replied Hunoomaun, 'save your breath. He that triumphs can afford to laugh at the beaten hound. Get to thy prison, coward, thief, beggar, imp of hell! Thou shalt often go there again, – ay, and that baggage, thy wife, with thee!'

'Peace, traitor and womanly reviler!' exclaimed the moneylender. 'It is unnatural for thee to be the tool and the accomplice of the injurer of thy countrymen. The curse of heaven rest for ever on thee, O traitor and dog!'

'Ha!' screamed Hunoomaun in a voice that brought the police to the spot, and created immediate excitement among the loiterers in the yard. 'Beware, you yellow snake! I know more than you think, and will yet be your ruin!'

His mouth was shut by the sable constables, and he was pushed off the steps, while Akaloo and Lutchmee made what speed they could to get to Belle Susanne.

As soon as Hunoomaun had shaken himself and recovered a little from the tempest of his wrath, he turned and threw a glance at the retreating pair. The court had risen, and the police were arranging the prisoners, among whom was Dilloo, for their walk to the gaol.

'Do you see that?' said Hunoomaun to Ramdoolah, and pointing to Lutchmee and her companion. 'They are going off together. Your suspicion, my most cunning Ramdoolah, is correct. There is something in the wind. What brings Akaloo down here to-day, and why does he mix himself up so much in Dilloo's affairs? Did you hear him in the court call out to Dilloo what to say? He is a serpent.'

'He is very rich,' replied the woman; 'still I do not believe he can buy Dilloo's wife. Dilloo is too rich himself to want to borrow money of Akaloo. And yet I'll swear I saw him last week going towards Dilloo's house in the dusk, and here he is again to-day. Lootah told me, too, that one day she saw him walking from the back dam to New Holland, and soon Dilloo went after him. There is some plot going on, I am sure.'

'I think so, too,' replied the sirdar. 'You know there was a stranger in Dilloo's house the night I went there. It was not Lutchmee. She was away at the manager's house. I am certain the men in my gang have some secret understanding with Dilloo. He has set them against me. They are as sullen as they can be.'

'Look out, then, and punish them well,' said the woman. 'Summon one or two to every court, and take off part of their money at every pay-table. The manager will like you the better for being sharp and strict.'

Ramdoolah was rather overreaching herself here. Drummond, like every good manager, was in the habit of judging of a driver's capacity, not by the number of men he punished, but by the work he got out of them. Hunoomaun's cunning, however, was in this instance as much at fault as that of his Delilah. He resolved to pursue a policy of combat.

'See! They still go on together,' said he. 'Follow them, my Ramdoolah, and watch what they do. If they notice you, pretend that you have something to say to Lutchmee. Ask the price of that cow which is so handsome. Ah, what a cow! I wish we had it. We must either have it or poison it. It is the best cow on the place.'

Ramdoolah parted from the sirdar, and slyly followed the Madrassee and Lutchmee. She saw them pass round the Negro-

yard and enter Dilloo's house. Then she quickened her steps.
When she arrived at the side of the hut and had stopped and
listened a moment, she held up her hands in horror or amazement
admirably feigned, and none the less histrionic that there was
nobody there to witness it. The door was closed. She could hear
the low voices inside, but could not distinguish the words. It was
clear that the two had gone behind the screen which divided the
house into two compartments. She slipped round to the other
side. Through the wattled wall she could now easily hear what the
inmates were saying.

'Are these all the papers?' asked Akaloo.

'There are only two hiding-places that I know of,' replied
Lutchmee, 'and I have searched them both. There is nothing left
but a cutlass.'

'Good; I will take these with me.'

'Stay, Akaloo,' said Lutchmee. 'Tell me what all this is about?
What are you and Dilloo doing, and why does he talk secretly with
many people? What takes him to the back of the estate so often? I
saw him meet you there one day.'

'Has he told you nothing?'

'No.'

'It is the husband's right to keep his own secrets. A wife may not
be foolishly curious. That which Dilloo telleth thee is his and
thine; that which he hideth from thee is his only.'

'Ah! yes. But, Akaloo, Akaloo! my heart is breaking! I cannot tell
what it is, but something in my bosom tells me there is danger floating in the air, and breathing in the wind, for Dilloo and for me! O
Akaloo, if thou knowest anything that can calm my trembling heart,
tell it to me, for I can scarcely carry this load of fear and sorrow.'

Ramdoolah's face on the other side of the wattle was a picture
of malignant triumph.

'Aha ! my fine-faced beauty!' she said to herself, 'your pride is
coming down, I think. You have to confess it at last.'

Forgetting herself in the enjoyment of her satisfaction, her
head rustled against the dry leafy partition.

'What's that?' cried Lutchmee and Akaloo together.
Ramdoolah gathered up her robe and ran as fast as her mature

figure would permit her to go. The Madrassee and Lutchmee rushed out of the hut.

'Who is it?' said he, pointing to the retreating form.

'Ramdoolah,' cried Lutchmee. 'O Akaloo, if she heard us we are lost!'

'No,' replied the other coolly. 'Everything which concerns the subject of our conversation will be known all over the country in a day or two. But in any case I do not think she could have heard us.'

'See,' said Lutchmee, pointing to the prints of two naked feet in the soft clay, close by the wall on the side of the hut. 'She has been here.'

'So she has,' said the other. 'And that is just near the spot where you and I were talking. She is truly a she-dog! If you have anything valuable about there, bury it somewhere else. She is a thief as well as an eavesdropper.'

Akaloo had by this time concealed the papers in his bosom, and now, bidding farewell to the young wife, he walked off in the direction of New Holland estate, where one Nobbeebuckus had a second batch of papers ready for him.

CHAPTER XXIX

BROWN AND WHITE

As soon as the Madrassee, Akaloo, was out of sight, Lutchmee entered her house, closed the light door, and sat down. She drew her scarf over her head, and placing her two hands above it, remained in that attitude moaning softly to herself. She was weary, heart-sick, widowed for a while; her husband had been wronged and sent to humiliating punishment; and she, lonely, in a land not merely of strangers, but as she believed of oppressors, was left to the mercies of men to whose power and license there was apparently no restraint.

Thus it seemed to her, sitting there and thinking in her simple way in the darkened house. That which commonplace orators like to define as the 'ægis' of British protection was as certainly over her as it is over any agricultural labourer in an English county, and perhaps quite as effectually. There was no wrong she could suffer for which English law and a parental, nay a grandmotherly Colonial office, did not theoretically provide a remedy. Unhappily to her at that moment – and few will be surprised to find her so unreasonable – the remedy and the application of it looked equally up in the clouds.

Thus she sat mourning for Dilloo and bewailing her own misery. She had been in this posture for some time, when she was startled by half a dozen short, peremptory taps on the door, given by a switch or cane, and by the sniffing of some animal at the cracks in the walls. She knew the latter could not be one of the manager's dogs. They always had a warm reception in the village. Though alarmed, she did not move.

Again the rapping came rather more briskly than before. No answer being returned, the door was pushed open by an impatient hand. Lutchmee removed her chudder sufficiently to uncover her large eyes which she turned to the doorway, and there stood, looking at her from under a light-brown umbrella, what seemed in the lustrous tropical afternoon to be a spirit in white. The large eyes of the pale-faced beauty looked into the large eyes of the handsome Hindoo, and they recognised each other in a moment. They had last met at Craig's bedside.

The Indian woman dropped her eyelashes, and quietly restoring the scarf to its place, went on moaning as before.

Miss Marston looked curiously round the hut. It was close and hot, and the odour of the cocoa-nut oil, with which the inmates loved to anoint themselves, came out strong and heavy. But the little place looked neat. The floor and the earthen base of the walls were daubed with chunam. On the walls were pinned three pictures, one an old coloured page of the *Illustrated London News*, representing a Christmas time at an English country place. The Elizabethan gables of a house could be seen in the distance. In the foreground was a group of children laden with sprigs of holly and misletoe; an old man had taken off his hat, in which they were dropping some coins, supplied, no doubt, by the comfortable-looking pair who smiled so kindly on this infants' rehearsal of charity. Behind the old man a red-cheeked girl curtseyed her thanks and Christmas greetings. The ground was white, and in the white were footprints. The great trees overhead had lost their leaves. Lutchmee had often studied with curious eyes this wonderful scene. To her it was a real fairyland. The snow, the death of vegetation, were as strange as the history and meaning of the time which gave its point to the picture. It would have been difficult for her to associate in any way with religion the scene thus pourtrayed. This scrap of paper, which had survived a voyage of six thousand miles and numerous perils of a vagrant life, thus to find a resting-place on the wall of a South American hut, is a type of the many minute items of very potent influence which a high civilization scatters as seeds to the four winds of heaven, knowing not where they may fall – unable to trace their far-off fruition.

The two other pictures were small and very common prints of the Queen and Prince Albert, pasted on the wattle. A few pots neatly arranged, and a stool with bamboo legs, completed the furniture of the house so far as it could be seen from the outside.

As Lutchmee drew the calico over her face, Miss Marston's dog, one of the smaller Orinoco hounds, ran in and licked the Indian woman's naked arm. She started up with a shriek of fear, which sent the dog quickly out of the hut, and, uncovering her face, looked angrily at Isabel, who was laughing heartily at the incident.

'What Missa look for? Why bring dog to Indian house?'

'Oh, I'm very sorry,' cried Isabel, becoming instantly serious. 'The dog is quiet and meant no harm to you. Why, Lutchmee, what is the matter with you? What makes you so sad and angry? I want to speak to you: may I come in?'

Without waiting for a reply she closed her umbrella, and entering, sat down on the bamboo stool.

Lutchmee stood gazing at her less fiercely, but still with a sulky aspect. This was the lady to whom Craig had given his hand; who had caused her to be humbled in Craig's presence. Craig was the only white man for whom the Indian woman had ever felt a regard. Her first feeling of sympathy had gradually, as she thought of him, grown more and more into a pure and delicate esteem. Isabel's appearance to-day recalled a scene Lutchmee had often pondered over with indignation. But, what was worse, the young lady's apparition reminded her of Craig's absence from the estate at this critical period of her fortune, and filled up to the brim, if that were needful, the cup of her sorrow.

'Why Missa come?' she said more softly.

' Sit down, Lutchmee, please. Something has happened to you. You have been crying.'

'No. No cry. Nossing.'

'Oh, yes, there *is* something. Please sit down. You are not well.'

And Isabel, rising, put her hand gently on the woman's shoulders. After a moment's resistance Lutchmee sat down on the floor in obedience to the soft pressure, and Isabel resumed her seat.

ISABEL: What are you doing here, Lutchmee, all alone?

LUTCHMEE: Man Dilloo gone prison.

ISABEL: Your husband gone to prison? What for?

LUTCHMEE: No sabby. Mahitee send um prison.

ISABEL: My father? Then he has been doing something wrong, or he would not have been sent to prison.

LUTCHMEE: No, Dilloo good; Mahitee bad, too bad. Dilloo all time good man.

Isabel cared very little about an Indian's opinion of her father. In fact neither he nor she would ever have taken the trouble to find out what estimate was made of their acts by the inferior people around them, or what influence their lives were having on the lives of the hundreds among whom they dwelt. At any other time Miss Marston would have been angry at the imputation cast upon the magistrate, but just now she had come for a purpose; and, besides, the melancholy state in which she found Lutchmee appealed to her sympathies. She said, –

'Why should you say so? Mahitee good, – Mahitee friend to all Coolies.'

'No,' replied Lutchmee. 'Mahitee friend Manahee. Eat um breakfas'. Ride um buggy. Drink um rum.'

Isabel was for the moment half amused, half stung. She had never before concerned herself specially in any way about the justice her father administered or the subjects of it. She used to look at the Coolies on the road with curiosity or aversion, accordingly as they were well or ill dressed in their picturesque costumes. They were creatures made to work for sugar-planters, or, failing that, to be adjudicated on by English justice, English justice being embodied in her father, and no doubt they deserved all they received at his instance. But here, by this poor Hindoo girl, there was suddenly suggested to Isabel's quick mind a view from the other side, and she took in immediately all that Lutchmee meant to imply. It seemed too absurd. She tried to explain to the other the commonplace principle which would be immediately advanced by any English person who took a superficial glance of the subject, and urged by any planter who, not himself taking a superficial glance at it, knows that most outsiders, including Secretaries of State, will do so, – that English justice majestically does its work without regard to friends or friendship. But all Isabel's warmth could not shake the Indian woman's prejudice.

'No, no! Manahee friend Mahitee. Mahitee love Manahee, – no love Coolie.'

Isabel gave it up. She changed the subject, and turned to the real object of her visit.

From the time when, as we have described, she had thrown herself on the bed that afternoon in a paroxysm of grief, she had felt herself hopelessly carried away on a tide of passion. Her feet could no longer touch ground: she was swept along in a powerful current. And this metaphor, commonplace and rude as it may appear, is really the one that best illustrates her condition. She had quite lost her self-control, and was tossed about in a manner that may fairly be described as billowy. Your tropical young lady has tropical passions. The placid sedateness of cooler climes is to her mere indifference. In those hot countries love comes not on zephyr's wings, but sweeps along in hurricanes and monsoons.

In fact Miss Marston was intolerably affected. Sal volatile and red lavender had ceased to have any efficacy for her malady. She passed through all the versatile stages of unanswered and unanswerable passion. There was an action and reaction. Again and again had she dismissed the young overseer from her mind, peremptorily for ever. Again and again had the shade of that gentleman returned to control her imagination with greater vividness and more emphatic ascendency. The unsettled term of Craig's absence made the situation all the more unendurable. Would he ever come back? Was he gone for good and all? In her anxiety to learn the truth she once more essayed to get it from her father. He was as testily indifferent as before. Indeed he coarsely and profanely hinted as an equally acceptable alternative to the poor lad's return, so far as he, Mr. Marston, cared about it, a fate reserved by popular and theological opinion for the wicked. Isabel strove to repress her impatience, but in vain. Each day reproduced and enhanced the longings of the last. Her appetite declined. She became moody and taciturn. She swung in the hammock hour after hour, dreaming illusions. Miriam and Sarcophagus, having put their woolly heads together, came to the decision that she was very ill, and that she must be under the influence of the Obe man. They felt the full effects of her temper. The magistrate even was afforded some uncalled for reaction from the dulness of court work by fierce encounters with his daughter on the most trivial issues.

Miriam averred to Sarcophagus, –

'If dere ain't somefin' de matter dere's goin' to be. De Obe man got hold ob her sure enuf.'

'No, Miriam, not yit; but he will if de Lord don't stop him,' said Sarcophagus, who was always stowing away something in his vault-like interior, and at the moment happened to be consuming a roast plantain which had been well buttered by the cook. 'My 'pinion it ain't Obe. De case is obvious. I see troo it de time ob de jelly. – O golly, wan't it good dat jelly! Hi! Miriam, make some more ! – You see, Miriam, Miss Bella mos' sofistically infected. Donno how, – donno why; but so she be. Look'ee here, Miriam,' pointing to the cook with the fragment of the roast plantain, before he consigned it to final perdition, 'de Obe man in dis case is de young gen'lman oberseer ober dere at Belle Susanne. Ki! dere's where de pison come from, Miss Miriam.'

'Look'ee here, Massa Sarcophagus,' responded the cook, seizing a huge ladle, an action which led the worthy to put himself in safety outside the door, 'you make remarks most disrespectible to my sex, sah. Miss Bella lady ob position, never trow away her confections on obersear chap. You git away, or else I go gib you somefin to swear about, I will.'

This, then, was the state of things in the magistrate's house, and of public opinion below stairs. Isabel was really at her wit's end to know what to do. She shrank from asking Mr. Drummond about his over-seer, knowing how quick the planter was in taking up points. If she went to Nina, that good woman would put this and that together and proclaim her discoveries, if not on the housetops, in the verandahs of British Guiana. So, after many struggles with herself, Isabel had made up her mind to go to Lutchmee and find out whether Craig had, before leaving, given to his gentle nurse some clue to his intentions. The idea was humiliating, but love unfortunately has a habit of forcing people into humiliating situations. Thus Miss Marston was now sitting on the bamboo stool in the Indian's hut.

'Where Massa Craig?' she said at length, blushing scarlet as she uttered the words.

'Gone Barbado,' replied the other, looking curiously at Isabel.

'Massa Craig come back soon, eh?' asked Miss Marston, in as indifferent a tone as she could assume.

'No sabby. Gone dis too long time.'

'Lutchmee want Massa Craig come back?' inquired Isabel.

The Indian woman opened her eyes so wide at this question that Miss Marston could not help laughing. Of course she wished Craig to come back again.

'Massa Craig no time come back,' said Isabel, tentatively.

Lutchmee looked at her earnestly. Had she been a white woman, her face would have been pallid; as it was, it showed intense chagrin.

'Yes, yes, Massa Craig come back. Oh, he not stay all time?' She had crept up and laid hold of Isabel's dress and looked up anxiously into her face for an answer. Just as Isabel was about to reply, a big form darkened the doorway, and the two women glancing up together, their eyes fell on the features of the very person of whom they were speaking. Clear, bright, and hearty, with the air of health breathing out of his smiling lips, and the light of it glancing out of his blue eyes: looking as if the rosy fingers of the sun-god had tinted his cheeks with his glowing favours, looking as if the warm wafting breezes that had borne him home had carried joy and strength upon their wings, Craig had come back again.

CHAPTER XXX

'TO HIT THE MEAN'

MR. MARSTON, after a long, hot and disagreeable day's work, returned home to dinner in no pleasant temper. Court-day was not seldom a day distinguished by a painful disturbance of the magistrate's equanimity. In those long sessions every mental, physical and moral quality was amply tested, in trying to swim to the truth through conflicting billows of evidence; in sitting in a suffocating court, the atmosphere of which was divided between the odour of cocoa-nut oil and of exuding Negroes; and in an effort to preserve an even balance between the sense of duty and the natural liking for a quiet life. But on this particular day it was clear the magistrate's temper was hopelessly off the balance.

Now Isabel's tone was, for a cause we know of, and by a rare accident, precisely the reverse. Every one who has a temper, will own how aggravating it is, when you are out of sorts, to find some one else in the most angelic humour, ready to smile at your anger, to bow to your rage, to strew flowers, as it were, before your irritated footsteps. It would have been some relief to the magistrate to find Isabel in the disposition to take him up pretty sharply, and thus enable him to set off his irritation against her ill-nature. But, lo, to the magistrate's surprise, that contrary and never-to-be-relied-on person met him shining with beauty and good-humour, wreathed in her prettiest robe, bright with her gayest ribbons, and *riante* with her softest laughter.

After giving him a kiss, which he moodily received, she sat down and watched him, her fingers trifling lazily with a bit of tatting, her little foot, with its white gossamer-laced stocking, gently tapping the floor with the wafer sole of a thin French shoe, her head on one side, a slight colour in her cheek, a lustrous pleasure in her eye. Oh, Craig, Craig, what a sad, Scotch, hard-headed unsentimental block you are not to see how absolutely all this combination of sweet life and pretty ornament glows and quivers there for you !

'Why, papa,' cried the young lady at last, after regarding the magistrate with some consternation, as he searched for this and that he did not want, tumbled about his books and papers on the great table, turned in and out of the hammock, and energetically moved about in the steaming air as if the thermometer showed ten degrees below zero, and exercise were indispensable to keep up the circulation, 'what *can* have happened to-day? There, you have made your hair a positive fright, rolling in that hammock! Has the Court reversed another of your decisions, or is Gonzales going to bring an action against you for the money?'

'Oh, no,' said the magistrate, 'nothing of that sort; but I am thoroughly disgusted with this place.'

'But, papa, I think I have heard you make that remark before, and *I* make it very often. It is not a new idea, you know, and it cannot have been the sole cause of all this excitement.'

'What excitement, Bella?' cried the magistrate, ready to join issue on anything. 'I don't know what you mean.'

'Well, you know, Mr. Marston, sir,' said the young lady, jumping up and pulling his whiskers, while he glared into her saucy, happy face, 'for the last quarter of an hour you have been possessed, – "possessed," you know,' she repeated, nodding at his frowning glance. 'See Matthew, Mark, Luke and John, at the right chapter and verse; and I want to know where you picked *him* up.'

'Bella!' said the magistrate, abashed and rather beaten by these novel tactics of the young lady, 'don't be ridiculous. I am very much put out, and have good reason for it, too.'

'Well, papa, then lie still in the hammock. Now here's some Florida water, and here's a comb; and now I'll wet your temples, and now I'll comb the nasty temper away – like this.'

Under the soothing influence, the magistrate's brow relaxed a little, but there was still a rough disturbance within his breast. Miss Marston drew it out.

'Now what has occurred to-day? You seem unusually flustered.'

'Well I may be. It is a miserable existence enough for a "gentle-man – and – and a scholar,"' he said, hesitating to use the well-worn formula, but too indolent to compile another – 'to be obliged, day after day, to investigate the wretched details of disputes between lying immigrants and hardfisted managers. But, confound it! these managers seem to look upon me as if I were their servant, and not the administrator for the district of Guineatown of the Queen's justice! What do you think Drummond did to-day?'

'I should be prepared to hear anything of Mr. Drummond,' replied Miss Marston. 'He is a strong character, the strongest about here – except, perhaps, Craig,' she added to herself. 'I should think if he made up his mind that a murder was necessary for the salvation of society he would do it, though he would not do it for his own direct interest, I fancy.'

'Take care what you say!' said the magistrate, holding up his finger and looking anxiously towards the door through which the Portuguese had so unexpectedly appeared. 'Remember how Gonzales caught us the other day. Drummond is a very good fellow in many ways, though arbitrary by nature, and I don't care to formulate my opinion of him. But what do you think he did to-day? He attacked me coming home about my conduct on the bench, because he thought I had said something which was too favourable to a Coolie who was up for breach of contract from Belle Susanne. I imprisoned the same man some time ago for beating a groom – he's as fine an immigrant as I ever saw, every inch a man. Well, Drummond grumbled at me that time because I chose to deal with the case summarily, and did not send the man up for trial, when they hoped to get him to Massaruni. I suspected that infernal psalm-singing old hypocrite Peter had provoked the attack, and resolved to give the Coolie another chance.'

'Was his name Dilloo?' inquired the young lady casually.

'Yes. How did you know anything about it?'

'Perhaps you remember I told you that when I went over by your directions to read to that young overseer Craig———'

'Humph! You're always bringing up "my directions" to you to go and read to that fellow. One would think you had a fancy for him.'

It was well the magistrate's eyes were turned away from the crimson face above him.

'It's always the way with women,' he went on. 'If a man does do or say something in a moment of weakness or good-nature they never forget it to him. Well, what were you going to say *apropos* of that young overseer?'

'Only that Mr. Craig had a woman in to nurse him, who was this very Dilloo's wife, and to-day I happened to see her, and she is such a nice little woman, and is in great distress about her husband. She says that he has been unjustly dealt with.'

'Of course she does!' cried the magistrate, uneasily turning his head, and consequently getting a twist of one of his harsh locks in Miss Isabel's comb, which made him howl again. 'You can never get a Coolie to own to the justice of any magistrate's decision. They lump us up with the planters, and think the whole white population is banded together against them.'

'Do you suppose it is because they think you are too friendly with the managers?'

'To be sure it is. They often say that, I am told. They seem to think one cannot be a friend out of court, and an honest man in court.'

'It was something like that which I heard from the woman to-day.'

'Never mind the woman. Let me finish my story. The same defendant, Dilloo, was up to-day for absence from work – one of Drummond's best hands, as he owned to me at breakfast. His defence was that he had done five tasks in three days, and was therefore free for the rest of the week. Well, though I thought and still think that is not technically an answer, as I read the ordinance, I should deem it my duty to consider it in mitigation of punishment, because even you can see——'

'Thank you very much, papa.'

'That it shows the fellow had to some extent acted up to the spirit, if not to the letter, of the law. And – would you believe it? – Drummond, and Fluyschutz, and Langton were perfectly savage with me for suggesting such a thing! They said the Coolies were hard enough to manage already without having ideas put into their heads by the magistrates, and that, if we side with them on one single point, they are so cunning they will take the utmost advantage of it. The old story! By———, if it were not impossible for you and me to live in this dreadful hole without some one to talk to, I would break with every one of them, and do my duty straight through!'

'But, papa,' said Miss Marston, dropping the comb, and coming round to the front of the magistrate, and speaking with gentle animation, '*don't* you do your duty straight through?'

'Why – well – of course I do – or at least I think – I try to!' exclaimed the magistrate, forced to face his own words in a very disagreeable manner.

It was very curious that, with those very words on his lips or in his thoughts again and again, he had never put them directly to himself in the plain way in which his daughter had just presented them. They involved nothing more than the doubt he had only the moment before confessed, and yet his self-love did not like to own the whole truth to himself.

'You shouldn't put it so offensively, Bella,' he went on, hardly knowing what to say. 'I do try to do my duty; but nevertheless, there is a sense of restraint which I don't like, and which – and which, you know, seems to affect my – my – I mean, interferes with the facility of – my———'

'You really mean, papa, that it warps your judgment?'

'Well, no, my dear; not quite so strong as that,' said the magistrate, wishing the truth to be expressed to the outward ear in a more complimentary sense than that entertained by the inner man. But Miss Marston, being by nature a direct and frank young lady, was aiming at the exact representation in words of the poor magistrate's conscientious feelings. She was getting quite an insight into matters that had never occupied her thoughts. It would seem that, after all, Lutchmee and the other Coolies had some ground for their suspicions.

'Now, papa, that *is* what you mean. And do you know what I would do? *I would do my duty straight through, and take the consequences.* You need not think of me. I can do without Mr. Drummond's company, or Mrs. Leech's, or those pale brown

Misses Kit Kats, and the whole round of planters' friends. You don't care about these people really in your heart – only you don't like to be on bad terms with any one; but just think how shocking it would be if even the smallest mistake of yours should result in an injustice to one of those Coolies.'

'My dear,' interrupted the magistrate, 'you need not waste your sympathies on them. They are a cunning, weak, treacherous lot.'

'Then why do you trouble yourself about what happens to them, Mr. Marston?' said Bella, triumphantly. 'Why are you out of sorts now at what Drummond said to you ? If Mr. Drummond or Mr. Fluyschutz said anything of that sort to me, I would soon let them know my opinion.'

'Then I beg you will not, Miss Marston,' replied the magistrate with some severity. 'I have quite enough to do to steer my course without having it complicated by your interference.'

'Dinner, Missa Bella!' said Sarcophagus, appearing at this juncture, to the magistrate's relief; and rising from the hammock, he gave his arm to his daughter.

It is unfair perhaps to take Mr. Marston behind the scenes in this way, half dressed and not in his character. He did try to do his duty, taking his ground in little matters as he had done that day; and not seldom had he been assailed with resentful strictures by members of the planting community. It would be impossible for an English gentleman in his position to get off with any other experience. A magistrate in a colony where Coolies are employed is watched with hawks' eyes. Every indication of mercy or even of impartiality to the coloured parties to a suit is stamped as a reflection upon the character of the planter suitor on the other side, or a concession dangerous to discipline, and therefore impolitic. As if the justice the magistrate is put there to administer can ever be impolitic! The same spirit and feeling is now being exhibited by Indian civilians, and an attempt has been made to embody and enforce it in law.

To allow East Indians to think that it is possible that the courts may err is deemed unwise, by men who, like the late Lieutenant-Governor of Bengal, affirm that as India must be despotically governed, the more absolute you make the despotism the better.

But we, the English people, can never consent to hold an empire, or any scrap of empire, on terms repugnant to all our ideas of natural right, of civil liberty, and of human justice. We know too well whither the despotic feeling once engendered, once permitted to grow and gain strength, will lead even our English people, trained in the principles and accustomed to the habits of freedom at home. The civilian and the planter must alike learn that we will not withdraw from our fellow-subjects of any colour the right to challenge the mode or the effects of the administration of justice in inferior courts, and more particularly when life and liberty as well as property are at stake.

To return to the planting communities. Instances of magisterial lenity are canvassed at the Georgetown Club and in every estate verandah throughout the colony. If the magistrate is not openly insulted in some such case he is fortunate beyond his expectations. Hence he may, like Mr. Marston, sit in his court conscientiously anxious, as well as resolved to do justice, but restrained in the operations of his judgment by the powerful influences which surround and oppress him.

In the case of Dilloo Mr. Marston had given a decision which in a later instance, before another magistrate, when the Coolie who defended it had been fortunate enough to secure a barrister to insist on the point, was proved to have been incorrect; and indeed a careful reading of the section of the ordinance by any sensible man would have been sufficient to show it. But the magistrate was not aware of the injustice he had done. He had looked at the letter of the law, and at that even not very particularly – it was not his nature to be precise and cautious. His mind had been prejudiced against the defendant. He thought he had given the latter every opportunity of defending himself. He had run the risk of a quarrel with Drummond by a Quixotic leaning toward mercy. On the single point disputed by Dilloo, two witnesses, one a white man, had sworn that the defendant's answer was untrue in fact. There had been no counsel present to advocate the point of law urged by the Coolie – namely, that when he had done five tasks he was entitled to a week's discharge. Still less had there been anyone competent to press the equity of Dilloo's plea. Thus an innocent man had been swept into the sewer of justice – the victim of an unintentional, insensible partiality, resulting from a variety of complicated and protracted influences, and of habits of judicial administration which left no margin for equity and little room for mercy. The only person who could have seen that justice was done and who would have ensured the proper presentation of the Coolie's case to the magistrate – namely, the Immigration Agent-General – was forbidden to appear in court without the permission of the Governor, and was kept carefully deficient of funds wherewith to employ a counsel.

One needs to study minutely, and on the scene, either slave or Coolie system, legislation, and administration, to appreciate the cunning ingenuity with which it is possible to create – to conceal from the outside world – to surround with delusive aspects of equity, and benevolence, and benefit – conditions of life which are intolerable to thousands and tens of thousands of our fellow-creatures.

CHAPTER XXXI

'UNCERTAIN, COY, AND HARD TO PLEASE'

IF Miss Marston, on the evening of which we have spoken, displayed a temper so angelic as to disappoint her father of his wonted tonic anti-irritant, it would seem to have arisen more out of the natural perversity of womankind than from any pleasurable cause.

As the two women – Bella and Lutchmee – looked up at the manly figure which darkened the door of Dilloo's hut, each uttered an exclamation. Craig himself was not less surprised at the fortuitous meeting than they, but his self-possession was greater, as his nature was more slow.

'You here, Miss Marston!' he said, his eye wandering first to the superior beauty. 'Have you been paying my nurse a visit?'

While he was speaking Lutchmee got up and approached him, and, gently taking up his hand, kissed it. Though she felt angry with herself at the absurdity of the emotion, Bella's face flushed at this simple act of courtesy. On his part, the cool young gentleman, scarcely heeding Lutchmee's act, stretched out the very hand she had kissed and shook Miss Marston's white fingers with true overseer's vigour.

'I am so glad to see some face I know,' he said quite unaffectedly. 'I hope you father is well?'

A change had suddenly come over Miss Marston. Five minutes before she was panting for just such an interview as this. But now that Mr. Craig stood before her, hale and hearty, addressing her with his quiet deliberate voice and manner, all her passion ran back into her silly little heart again, and left her to all outward appearance constrained, indifferent – almost chill.

'He is very well, I thank you,' she said stiffly. 'How long have you been away?'

'Three months, Miss Marston. You must have been very agree-ably occupied in the meantime?'

'Why?' she inquired, with a slight tinge of vexation in her tone, because she knew what was coming.

'To forget so easily how the time was flying.'

'Oh, no!' she said, recovering herself with feminine celerity and equally feminine vindictiveness. 'There really was nothing to occupy me, but I had not thought upon the subject.'

I cannot believe that any recording angel dropped a tear upon that lie, or ought to have done so. When all these matters come to be settled one shudders to think of the strange little delicate casu-istical issues that will have to be adjudicated on in the experience of many love-torn damsels.

Craig felt the situation to be getting awkward. The foolish fellow was looking about him, instead of straight into the eyes of the perverse angel before him, or perhaps even he might have detected the tell-tale pleasure that glowed in them, deep behind the assumed coldness of the moment. He turned to Lutchmee: but here he had to deal with another woman. Abashed and angered by his disregard of her greeting, she had stood glancing from one to the other with her dark eyes, over which a sullen cloud was beginning to brood. When he turned to her he held out his hand, but she did not move.

'What is the matter, Lutchmee? Are you not glad to see me?' He took her hand perforce and shut it up tightly in his huge grasp.

Lutchmee looked and felt inclined to draw it away, but forebore.

'Massa talk lady, talk Coolie woman noder time,' she said, with a lowering glance at Bella, whose face, now that Craig had turned away, was glowing in a joyous sunlight.

'No, no!' said Craig, touching her brown cheek with his other hand. 'Glad to see you, Lutchmee. It was you I came to see, you know.'

O stupid Caledonian! thick-headed, slow-blooded youth! Why blurt out in words so plain a fact, so uncongenial, at the very moment when angelic fortune smiled upon you, bright and fostering?

'I am afraid,' said a clear, cold voice behind him, 'I am in the way. I must be going home. Good-bye, Lutchmee! Good-day to

you, Mister Craig! Here, Carlo!' And the young lady swept out of
the hut like a swift bright cloud in a gale, before Craig could bring
his deliberate forces into action either by speech or gesture. He
did not understand Lutchmee's triumphant look, this field of
woman's character being new to him. Had he done so he might
have escaped dangers which quicker, though less noble, natures
would have easily foreseen.

He remained at the hut some time listening to Lutchmee's story,
in her broken English, and with its simple, native candour of statement. As he listened, his mind gradually opened to the difficulties
which surrounded her, and thence, as a natural corollary, threatened to involve him, for he was too grateful to her not to feel that it
would be his duty to become her protector. He was naturally too
just, even had he owed her nothing, to permit wrongs to occur
under his observation without at least a protest. And the more the
position was developed to his view, the graver it appeared.

When he bid Lutchmee adieu, she looked up to him with a half-
caressing and entreating air of confidence, which touched him
deeply. He took both her hands, and looked down upon her com-
passionately. She was to him a mere child.

'I will see Massa Drummond, Lutchmee, and get you into the
hospital. You must take care what you say. Do not put yourself in
the way of Massa Chester. See the doctor every time he comes,
and if you want anything, or are in trouble, send for me.'

She kissed his hand again, and watched his tall figure as he
walked away until he was out of sight. Before then, however, she
was witness of an encounter in the distance and out of hearing.
Master Martinho met and greeted Craig. Then he went on to say, –

'Ha! ha! Mr. Craig. Coming from the pretty Coolie's already?' etc.

Craig looked at the fellow darkly. His hateful words and suspicions roused a deep and terrible anger in the young overseer's
breast. He subdued it, however, by a violent effort, and bidding
the man 'Good-day,' walked on moodily. It did not strike him at
the time that this gross suspicion of him in the minds of the other
overseers, coupled with his proper obligations to Lutchmee,
might drive him into a dubious position, and be one of a chain of
influences leading him to some perilous conclusion.

In the evening he met Drummond, who had been away all day at Georgetown. He was greeted by the manager with great cordiality. Naturally generous, the great planter had felt a real sympathy with the promising young overseer, who had undergone such danger in his service. But there was a cloud on Drummond's brow. The private news among the leading men in the metropolis of the colony was of a disquieting nature. The sullenness of the Coolies in every part of the country alarmed their employers, and not a few of the latter suspected that they were on the eve of an important crisis. The number of cases brought before the magistrates were alarmingly increasing. On a distant estate on the West Coast an overseer had been beaten. The Inspector of Police received orders to be on the alert, and the Governor had been advised by some of the prominent agents to ask the General, commanding at Barbadoes, to hold troops in readiness to increase the force quartered at Eveleery.

Our young Scotchman, knowing nothing of these things, hit upon a rather unfortunate topic.

'I find, sir,' he said to Drummond, 'that Dilloo, the man who helped us in the scrimmage here, has been sent to jail.'

'Yes,' replied the manager, with a frown, 'and serve him right, – a cantankerous rascal. Hunoomaun declares he is getting up a conspiracy, but I cannot get any trustworthy evidence of it. These fellows are intolerable liars.'

'I have been to see Dilloo's wife, who was my nurse,' said Craig simply, 'and I find she needs to go to the hospital. She is not well.'

'Oho!' said the manager. 'Take care what you do with that young woman.'

'I shall do nothing, sir, that is not strictly honourable,' replied the overseer, colouring.

'I dare say not, Craig; but Dilloo will not be inclined to believe that if you take too keen an interest in her. Chester thinks she is shamming.'*

* In justice to Mr. Drummond it should be mentioned that it is not an infrequent case for women to sham illness to avoid the estate work.

'Well, sir, I naturally feel grateful to her for her attentions to me, and should like to befriend her. At least she might go to the hospital, and you could get Dr. Arden's report.'

'Very well, Craig: but I want to say something to you. Anything you do for these people is sure to be misunderstood. I can see plainly enough that we are going to have a critical time. We must act cautiously and firmly. If any overseer like yourself shows any partiality or extra kindness, it will be injurious to discipline. You had better leave Dilloo and his wife to be dealt with by the ordinary estate rules; otherwise you and I may have a misunderstanding. For this time let her have the benefit of your good word, but don't take advantage of me again.'

CHAPTER XXXII

CHARITY SEEKING NOT HER OWN

THE day after Dilloo's conviction brought to the magistrate's house, in a light covered American waggon, drawn by a gay and handsome little horse, an important-looking gentleman, from whose appearance it would seem that he and the climate were on friendly terms.

As he emerged with some difficulty from the creaking vehicle, the lazy springs of which yielded in a very marked manner under his weight, he caught the eye of the magistrate, who hearing the sound of wheels, had come down to welcome him, and seemed to be regarding him with some amusement.

'Begad, Marston!' he exclaimed. 'How are you and the divine Miss Bella? I'm thinking that getting out and into these crazy Yankee traps is the last thing they're made for. And when you are in,' he added in an undertone, rubbing himself in one or two places, 'it's like riding on a rail, without the tar and feathers, begad!'

'Trying enough, Major, to a man of your weight and dignity. But, good heavens, man, what have you been doing with your face?'

'Mosquitoes. Faith, I'm half killed with them, if not entirely! It's all owing to me good blood. They're so thick along the shore road, I could scarcely see to drive. They shut out the sun completely, every ray of it. Whisper now, and I'll tell you a fact,' he added, with his eyes twinkling: 'a rale fact this time, mind ye. I dropped me whip opposite Colman's, and, begad, sir, I was getting out of this machine to pick it up, when me foot slipped on that little scraper of a step there, and, on me word and honour, Marston, as an officer and a gentleman, if it hadn't been for the millions of mosquitoes, as thick as porridge, sir, that held me up, by George, sir, I should have fallen to the ground!'

'Good,' said Marston, laughing. 'That is extracting sweet from torments! Such a fact deserves to be recorded. Come along, and tell the story to Bella. She professes to be something of an entomologist. So thick that even *you* were borne up by their wings: fifteen-stone ten, at least; say sixteen, in round numbers. Admirable!'

The magistrate led the way, followed by his guest, who maintained the deepest gravity, while he mopped his reeking features and bald head with an immense bandanna. Miss Marston, who had made some preparations of the toilette in honour of the visitor, received them in the verandah.

'Ah, Miss Marston!' cried the Major, after the usual salutations had been exchanged. 'Here I am, more dead than alive. It's life to see you, lovely and blooming as ever. "Ah! believe me, if all those endearing young charms –"' he stopped with a gesture.

'Yes, Major! Go on, please, if there's any more,' replied the young lady.

'I can't, miss. Me feelings won't let me. Faith, do ye see me face? I've been eaten up by millions of mosquitoes.'

'I was not aware that the feelings you speak of settled in the face, Major. Come and let me give you some nectar to soothe your irritation.'

'From such a Hebe, fair and sweet, who would not a poison take?' cried the Major, striking an attitude and taking the glass.

While the Major is trying to cool his heated frame with an iced punch and bitters, and repeating his remarkable experience to the scornful Miss Bella, we must put him on the stage in his proper dress and character.

Major O'Loughlin, one of the numberless tribe of the O'Loughlins of O'Loughlin in County Kerry, a district which in its situation is suggestive of extremes, was Intendant-General of British Guiana. There, and in other Crown colonies where no public opinion exists to extinguish useless bureaus, there are many officials; and every official is something-or-other-General. The Major, a half-pay officer, had been more lucky than such *enfants perdus* of the army usually are, and it was perhaps for the very reason that he was not a fighting man; for soon after he had

retired from his post in the old commissariat, a military friend –
who, to his own surprise, had received from *his* friend, a Colonial
Secretary, an appointment as Governor of Demerara – bethought
him of the Major, and procured him the Intendant-Generalship,
an office he had filled for twenty years. This had made him an *ex-officio* member of the Court of Policy, as the Legislature is called,
and endowed him as well with a very respectable salary. It would
be cruel to inquire too closely into the value of the service which
the Major rendered to the public of the colony in return for the
money. That were, in the West Indies, an impertinent and invidi-
ous examination. He was supposed to regulate the internal economy of British Guiana, – to be, one may say, a Minister of the
Interior. And although the Interior is almost uninhabited, yet the
position might have been made, by an intelligent and conscientious officer, both an interesting and a useful one, for it included
the management of the public lands and forests, the charge of the
Indians who roamed therein, and a fatherly superintendence of
the Negroes and Portuguese who form the real 'people' of the
colony. If it were not made by the Major as interesting and useful
as it might have been, no one should conclude that he was not
potentially intelligent and conscientious.* In tropical climates
those qualities are apt to become torpid, motive being not infrequently necessary to their development in some natures, and
what motive can there be for steady labour in these wretched little
colonies?

– I have known a man, a young one, born out of England, yet endowed with all the noblest characteristics of an Englishman,
brave, bold, energetic, steady, thoughtful, possessed with a chival-
rous sense of duty, who, exiled as an official to the murderous climate of Western Africa, and placed in a situation where there
were no European eyes to cheer or to watch him, pursued with a
strong, self-reliant love of work and of duty, the advantage of the
Queen he served, the sowing in that wild ground of the seeds of
civilization, the protection of the petty interests committed to his

* There is no office of this title in British Guiana. To avoid even the suspicion
of making a personal attack I have created a characteristic bureau.

care. But to him no interest of his nation or his fellowman was petty. The sincere devotion to right made of him a hero, unchronicled and unknown. And he, who had never wielded sword, called out to save the wretched subjects of his administration from the inroads of the slave-catcher, gathered a few dusky police, and led them through the terrible country to the lair of the enemy, and charging sword in hand at the head of his handful of men, received a load of slugs in his body which he will carry to his dying day. With a maimed hand and scarred breast, he lives still with unwounded conscience and unblemished honour, a specimen of the Englishman whom we love in poetry to worship, but so often fail in prose to reward. –

A red-faced, jovial, loud, kindly Kerryboy was the Major, with as varied, and, by his own account, as unique an experience of travel as Ulysses himself, but with less precision in his reminiscences. One thing was certain. He could stand any climate, and assimilate any quantity of edibles and drinkables.

'Begad,' he used to say, 'nothing surprises me more than the easy way I see men die off in the tropics! Ay, and knowing that they're to be buried, by Jove, within ten or twelve hours of their decease, before the corpse has had time to cool off! I've heard men meself argue, "'Twas the brandy that slew so many." Why, look at me, will ye! I've been drinking brandy these forty years in every climate from Indus to the Pole. It's true I was like St. Paul, ye know: "me moderation was known unto all men." – What! Ye're laughing, are ye? Begad, sir, I never took more than I could carry, and I'd like to see you take yer oath of that same! It's you young men that bring the tropics into bad odour with yer excesses. There was me own predecessor, I'm told 'twas of swizzles he died. How could a man die of a healthy beverage like that, I'd like to know? What's a swizzle? It's composed of good chemical elements entirely. There's nothing in it but good Hollands, and good Angostura (an anti-febrile mixture, – sure ye know it says so in four languages on the bottle!), and good sugar and ice to cool it. Faith I could live on it easily for forty years. Who was it the yellow fever took off last, I'd like to know? Wasn't it Captain Sweeny, and he a teetotaler, poor foolish young man, in a climate that strains all yer mental and bodily powers in the way this does! Begad! sir, it's me own opinion that more people die of starvation than of eating and drinking.'

The Intendant-General steadily stuck to his principles (though most people believed he was what he was, in spite of those principles), and exhibited the result in a portly form and a jolly rubicund visage. From the pink blushing apex of his benevolent head the colours improved in tone, until they reached perfection in the deep flush tints of his nose and double-chin. His small, light blue eyes were always dancing merrily, belying his most serious protestations or affirmations by a twinkle unknown to any eye but that of an Irishman. A sprinkling of grey whisker on either cheek, and two tufts of rapidly-whitening hair over his ears, both of which he treated with a careful coquetry quite out of proportion to their importance in relation to his face, adorned the Major's countenance, over which there played the sunshine of a perpetual smile and the rain of a chronic perspiration. Hence his brightly-coloured dewy face suggested to one the idea of a stray bit of rainbow.

He was a bachelor; a fact to which he always referred with a tragic sigh, as if to indicate that there were reasons he could divulge to account for it which must forever remain a mystery; but, to use a lawyer's term, that it was not by his own *laches*.

In default of natural subjects or objects of affection (for a wife and children may be one or the other), the Major, who had saved some money, looked about him for wards of a less selfish philanthropy. He had some difficulty, however, in determining the channel in which his benevolence should run. There were hospitals on every estate, besides a large one in Georgetown. The fearful creatures, who at one time made the streets and highways of the colony hideous with their leprous deformities, had been gradually removed to the asylum on the Essequibo. The Major's mind was not genial to religion, and he was quite indisposed to endow either church or chapel. By a quaint yet touching fancy, his heart yearned after some solace to his childlessness, and he resolved to found an orphan-asylum.

'Faith, sir,' he said to a friend, in an exquisitely innocent equivoque, 'I'll have a family of me own, and me a bachelor!'

Accordingly an orphan-asylum was built, of considerable size, with accommodation for fifty orphans and the necessary staff. This he surrounded with a pretty playground and garden, and established as managers a coloured-gentleman and his wife from St. Vincent. And then for the first time he began to turn his attention to the question, where the orphans were to come from? The Major and everyone else had taken it for granted that the supply of fatherless and motherless children in a populous community like that of British Guiana was practically unlimited. But when the building had been finished, and the Governor and the Bishop had opened it with great *éclat*, and it was duly advertised in the newspapers that applications would be received for the admission of the orphan children of married persons deceased, the only *bona fide* application that came in was one on behalf of a poor little cripple who had been born with a crooked back, and walked about like a deformed Manxman on two legs and an arm. The poor Major, who had pictured to himself a house crowded with brown-skinned infants who should learn to look up to him as their benefactor, and, as they became ornaments in coloured society, would recall the name of the good Intendant-General who had made them what they were, was terribly dejected by his ill-success. He thought that either the orphans' friends would not give them up, or the orphans of elder years were indisposed to barter their liberty for his charity. The Bishop, however, a shrewd man, knowing his diocese well, and its coloured laity particularly, hinted to the Major that, by restricting his beneficence to children of married persons, he was not only raising very delicate questions, but reducing his field of operations to very small dimensions. He had therefore resolved to throw open the blessings of his charity to children whose fathers and mothers were dead. But here again obstacles arose out of the anomalous moral condition of Negro society, from the difficulty of ascertaining who the male parents were, a necessary preliminary to the inquiry whether they were dead. The good Intendant-General was at his wits' end. There was the orphanage and never an orphan. Besides, the missionaries of the Baptist, and Methodist, and Papal persuasions earnestly

dissuaded their people from having anything to do with an insti-
tute of which the Major was the head and the Bishop a patron.

'O'Loughlin's orphans' were the joke of the community. He was
never met by a friend who did not ask him with emphatic interest,
'Well, O'Loughlin, how many have you got?' – just as aggravating
friends cross-examine a luckless fisherman or sportsman as to the
contents of his creel or bag with exaggerated inquisitiveness. The
Major, however, disarmed everyone by his good-nature.

'Faith,' he would reply in a confidential whisper, 'don't mention
it to a soul, but never a one. Its d——— hard a man can't do all the
good he wishes to do. But, listen, I've heard of one on the West
Coast I'm in hopes of catching.'

And so the worthy philanthropist went about not exactly
searching the highways and hedges, but the dams and bushes of
British Guiana, his pockets filled with sweetmeats as bait for the
young ones, and with money for the elders, should they prove to
be open to such solicitations. His visit to the magistrate's house
was connected with this pursuit of charity. He wished to rummage
Guineatown for orphan candidates.

'Do ye happen to know, Miss Bella, of ever an orphan or a
deserted baby in the neighbourhood?' cried the Major, with an extra
twinkle in his jocular eye. 'There's a beautiful place lying empty for
want of them, and all me money spent to no use. Can't ye hang a few
parents for me now, Marston, and give me benevolence an object?'

'Well,' replied Marston laughing, 'you should go to the Chief-
Justice for that, you know; it's beyond a magistrate's power. There
are some fellows who deserve hanging well enough at
Guineatown, but that is most likely the very reason they won't get
it. I'll tell you how you can get a shoal of orphans on one side at one
blow, – that is, by killing off Drummond's driver, Pete.'

'Ye don't say so!' cried the Major, dropping his knife and fork;
'I'll have that monster watched till he dies. Could ye give me the
address of his children?'

'No, nor any one else,' said the magistrate, anxious to change the
subject. 'Go over to Guineatown yourself, to-morrow morning.
I know little about the place, but there must be dozens of loose
children to be picked up there for a glass or two of rum.'

The Major, always sanguine, pricked up his ears at the hopeful prospect.

'Bedad, then I'll go and see. Will ye oblige me with the assistance of an angel, Miss Bella, and help me to persuade these stiff-necked fools to give up their babies? Faith, if ye'd only give me your countenance now, the place would be filled in a jiffy, sure.'

'I'm afraid I can hardly do that,' said Miss Marston, glancing slyly at the rubicund visage of the Major. 'But, I can at least accompany you and see the fun. It is quite a new idea to go fishing for orphans. I hope you have brought hooks and lines?'

'Now ye're joking me!' cried the Intendant-General. 'But it's getting beyond a joke. Faith if I don't get the creel filled very soon, it's not fishing, but shooting, I'll go in for. If there is no other way of catching orphans, I'll make them, begad! I'll not be baulked of me charity.'

The Major said this in so terrible a voice, and with so truculent an air, as he twisted his grey moustachios, that any one who had not looked into the depths of his blue eyes, would have thought him capable of doing what he threatened.

CHAPTER XXXIII

THE PURSUIT OF CHARITY

THE magistrate's household was generally astir at five o'clock; and at that hour next morning Sarcophagus roused the gentlemen from beneath their mosquito nets, and served them with fragrant cups of coffee, while Miriam performed the same office for Miss Marston. By six o'clock she and the gallant Major were wending their way along the dam towards Guineatown, to enjoy the novel sport of infant hunting.

Guineatown was a sprawling mischance of wooden houses, huts, and shanties, swarming with Negroes, and unlike any village familiar to English eyes. No quaintly-gabled inn, no thatched and rose-embowered cottages, no lazy stream purling along under the bowing arches of an ancient bridge uniting the ends of a picturesque and straggling street, no ivy-covered church peeping from among the paternal trees; nothing but a treeless waste; in wet weather a swamp, in dry weather baked and cracked with torrid heat; intersected by mud causeways, which constituted its streets, all jagged and broken away in many places by draining floods, or the misapplied energy of mischievous children.

Alongside these ragged roads there stalked, in a sort of irregular skirmishing line, the long-legged hovels of the inhabitants. Here and there, amid the box-like rudeness of these residences, there stood out conspicuous a few decent-looking shops, with their dazzling white clapboards and green jalousies, belonging to well-to-do Creole or Portuguese traders. Except in these rare instances, the village exhibited all the signs of indolent decay and good-for-nothingness, too familiar to him who visits the Negro at home in the West Indies, and especially in Demerara, where the natural characteristics of the climate and soil are so congenial to the cultivation of laziness. Already, as the visitors picked their way along the broken dam which looked like the glacis of a fort after a bombardment, they could see lazy Negroes lying prone on their faces in the sun, or on their backs, idly kicking their heels into the air. To these, now and then, women could be seen carrying roasted plantains. Over the road, and in and out among the shaky props of the hovels, ran numbers of naked or half-naked youngsters of both sexes, at sight of whom the Major's eyes twinkled.

'Do ye think now, Miss Marston, if I had an omnibus here, I couldn't run off with a dozen or two of these children? Faith, one's so like another, I don't see how their own fathers and mothers, if they have any, and God only knows whether they have or not, would recognise them dressed in the livery of the Kerry Orphanage. Look here now!' stopping at a group of six or seven, whose plump black bodies and limbs shone with health, save where the cleaving mud had left the evidence of their loving caresses of mother earth, 'is there any one of ye an orphan? If there is, hold up yer hand.'

The children, all about six or seven years old, stood in a group close together, leaning their brown shoulders against each other, with their fingers in their mouths, their curly hair standing stiff and crisp above their ample foreheads, – rather a pose for a phrenologist who should examine those large craniums for any striking qualities! – their bright black eyes and all their dental ivories glistening, as the Major took a bag out of his pocket and disclosed some of that brilliant and resistless bait to infancy, called 'bull's-eyes'.

'Now, quick: who's an orphan?' cried the Major, holding out between his finger and thumb a tremendous lump of saccharine brilliancy.

The shoulders rubbed together, the little bodies quivered with supple ecstasy, the bright eyes danced black and white; but not a child spoke or came forward.

'Here's another!' cried the Major, getting excited. 'Now then, – who's an orphan?'

The children gazed wistfully at the bait, but made no attempt to take it. Miss Marston took one of the seductive lumps into her fingers, and held it up, saying, 'Come to me.'

In an instant the whole party charged at the daring young lady like a troop of wild colts; and before she could prevent it, the tallest urchin jumped up, snatched the dainty from her hand, and, rolling down the slope of the dam, made off to the maternal nest, with one side of his face enlarged to a monstrosity. The Major, however, by a rapid flank movement, got into the rear of the remainder, and called on the enemy to surrender.

'Now, me dear children,' he said, holding up a handful of the great peppermint balls, 'here ye are, if ye'll tell me where I'll find an orphan.'

He looked so greedily at them all the while, and with so benevolent an earnestness, that Bella, catching a glimpse of his face, laughed out loud. The children instantly set up a sympathetic roar.

'Oh, my dear Major!' she cried, 'forgive me. But you look as if you were going to eat them.'

'So I am,' growled the Major, 'if they don't capitulate. Do ye hear?' in a terrible voice. 'Will you go home with me?'

The children scattered like a group of flies, shouting 'No, massa!' and were soon safe from pursuit.

O'Loughlin took off his hat and wiped his forehead with vexation: the sun was growing hot. This act was received with a burst of laughter from the piccaninnies. 'Hi: see de white gen'leman's head! Got no wool on: hi, hi!'

That ancient African 'Uncle Ned,' whose capital and capillary defects have so long been a subject of musical ridicule among us, was amply avenged on the outraged dignity of the Major, who, blushing a deeper red than ever, rapidly donned his hat, and threw an angry glance at his tormentors. But Miss Bella walked gently towards them; and beckoning to one, a girl, a little bolder than the rest, asked her if she knew what an orphan was? To which the reply was, 'No, sabby.'

'Have you all got fathers and mothers?'

'Me hab fader and moder. Sally, Tom, Zeke,' pointing to some companions. 'Sam, he fader dead.'

On which, Sam rammed his knuckles into his eyes, and set up such a howl as a sucking jackal might vent at the loss of its dam.

The Major pricked up his ears; and, taking a mean advantage of Sam's absorbing grief, pounced down upon him in military style, and captured him alive, but without dress or accoutrements.

'Ha!' said the Major, out of breath, holding on with needless and I dare say somewhat painful tightness of grasp, while the child wriggled and roared most lustily. 'Hurrah, Miss Bella! Here's a prize. Ask them, please, where his mother lives?'

But meantime the rest of the children, alarmed by this hostile movement, had scampered off, leaving the child too full of his grief to give any information. The Major crammed a huge bolus of sugar into his mouth, and thus effectually gagged him. But his roars had reached maternal ears; and as the gallant victor was proceeding to lead his captive in triumph towards the village to make inquiries, a slovenly black woman rushed out of the nearest hut and encountered him.

'What you do my chile, you fellah? Let um go!'

'My good woman,' cried the Major, gently repulsing her as she tried to seize the boy's unoccupied arm, the urchin seconding her aim with all his force, 'permit me one moment. My dear good woman, stay a moment! I wish to do him a kindness – Oh, confound the little rascal!' shouted he in a rage, suddenly letting his captive go; for that precious infant had succeeded in getting his head round to the Major's hand, and had taken a large grip of the back of it fairly between his teeth, leaving a very plain record of their visit in blue and red. 'Take him away, you wretched woman! I meant to make his fortune, but he is as good-for-nothing as yourself. I'll have nothing to do with him.'

The Major was well nigh getting into trouble by his angry exclamations, for several villagers of both sexes had come up, and the woman was furious; but Bella again came to his assistance and soothed the virago's anger. Miss Marston was well known by sight as the magistrate's daughter; but none of the people recognised the Major, either personally or officially, and his present proceedings were looked upon with no little indignation.

'What for you go steal dis young lady's chile, sir?' said a gallant Negro, who had turned up off his back, and who displayed a capacity of sinew which an Englishman might envy, through a fringe of rags of which an Italian would be ashamed.

'My good people,' said the Major, 'look here! I'm Major O'Loughlin, Intendant-General. You all know me. I have come

down here on an errand of kindness. I have built an asylum for orphan children, and if any of you know where there are any children who have no father or mother, I will take them, dress them,
feed and educate them free. Do you hear? all free, – for nothing.
Now can any of you take me where there are any children about
here who have no one to take care of them? or whose mothers
would be willing to let me take care of them?'

They shook their heads. One ancient hag however, – grey,
wrinkled and toothless, smiling a malicious smile, replied, –

'Dere's Susan Sankey, she hab piccaninny. No fader, I guess; –
least de fader don't live about dis town, reckon, –'

'Tell me, please, where she lives?' interposed Miss Marston;
who seeing the group were receiving new accessions every
moment, and in every state of dress and undress, was anxious to
change the scene.

'Ober dere,' was the reply, emphasized by many dusky digits;
and in the direction indicated marched the Major and Miss
Marston, with great gravity, the crowd attending them at a
respectful distance with many a giggle and whisper.

'What Susan Sankey say? Yah, yah!' laughed a grotesque fellow,
in a shirt and demi-pantaloons airy with holes, with a mouth so full
of teeth you wondered he ever got it shut. 'Yah, yah !' softly
murmured the chorus.

'White folks come take away Susan Sankey's baby,' cried two or
three to the new comers, who were continually increasing the
crowd. 'Piccaninny hab no fader. Officer goin' take um, I guess.'

Now Susan Sankey, quite unconscious of the movement in the
village and the designs on her unworthy offspring, was making a
fire under her house to cook a breakfast for herself and her
piccaninny. The latter was propped up in a box which stood upon
the landing of the steps by which her rooms were reached. Being
in complete dishabille, – in truth, having on only the garment in
which she had slept, – she was unprepared for visitors, and we
must fairly say had no good reason to expect them at that early
hour of the morning. Great indeed was her astonishment on rising
from the fire, which she had been aiding with a vigorous exhala-
tion, when she heard the murmur of an approaching mob, and

discerned the Major and Miss Bella Marston close upon her with their undesired attendants. In an instant, drawing her calico garment about her form as closely as possible, she darted up the stairs: a movement which delighted the crowd, some of whom shouted after her, –

'Hi, Miss Sankey, take care piccaninny: officer come, take um away.'

The Major stamped his foot and turned upon the crowd.

'Get out of the way, ye fools: d'ye hear! I don't mean to do any harm to the woman, or the baby either. Do, my dear Miss Marston, go up and speak to her, while I manage these people. Good heavens,' cried the Major, desolately, 'what one has to endure to do a good deed! By heaven, if ever I undertake to do another, may I be shot!'

Miss Marston, ascending the stairs and disappearing into the room, would have been followed instantly by a dozen lithe youths of both sexes, but for the Major, who, flourishing his stick, threatened the bastinado if they did not desist. But Susan Sankey, who had caught up her child, had retreated to her bedroom, and barred the door; through which she shrieked her fears and maledictions in a manner so hysterical, that poor Miss Marston could get no entrance for her own quiet and dulcet accents. On hearing this, the Major, who, like a gallant man, was extremely vexed at the awkwardness of the position for his companion, resolved to beat a retreat; and with that view mounting the steps, delivered a second address, assuring the crowd that he had none but a benevolent object, begging them to send him from the village candidates for the benefits of his charity; and he ended by throwing his bag of sweetmeats and a handful of small silver into the throng. This last motion was received with yells of delight, followed by a general skirmish, and shrieks of laughter and pain from the struggling mass. Taking advantage of the diversion, the unsuccessful infant-hunters retired in unbroken order, but with a haste not altogether dignified.

The Major was sadly depressed by the incidents of the morning, and their bad success: and only recovered himself after a hearty breakfast.

'Miss Marston, dear,' said he, over his cigar in the verandah, while a suspicion of moisture dimmed his eyes, 'except in love, now, where all yer sex are so cruel, did ye ever hear of a man being so disappointed in looking for a chance to be kind? Faith, but I was a fool not to send the money home to me native county, where, I'll warrant ye, the number of orphans they'd make for the purpose, if it was necessary, would fill it twice over; though begad, I believe a supply would be the last difficulty they would have. Only, ye see, in the old country, they're mighty fond of scrimmaging over charity funds, and the Protestants and Roman Catholics might find out some way of wasting the money in litigation. So after all, may be, I'm better with it here, where I can see it, and look after it. But, see, now, I tell you, as sure as my name's O'Loughlin, if I don't get these Negurs to supply me place with inmates, faith, I'll just take the gun and go shooting Indians up beyond the settlement, and bring down their children and make Christians of them in spite of themselves. Sure, Providence never meant a place like that to be built and kept empty.'

CHAPTER XXXIV

COLONIAL GOVERNORS AND THE LOCAL ARISTOCRACY

INTENSE was the excitement, and extreme the heat of feeling in the naturally tropical atmosphere of the capital of Raleigh's famous Guiana. The heart of the capital, that is its club, – morning house-of-call for tonic 'swizzles,' afternoon lounge for whist and billiards, – not untempered by draughts of the aforesaid tonics, or of sparkling mixtures of iced soda and sterner liquors, – was violently palpitating. Very rarely were its latticed verandah and wide rooms so crowded with members, and so filled with a lively roar of conversation. Merchants from Water Street, estate attorneys, government officials, plantation managers – the latter receiving new and warm additions, as men hastily rode or drove up to the hotel opposite – all were loud, animated, effervescent. Never had the resources of the intelligent Creole who mixed the amber and mahogany-coloured fluids into cool, though not cooling elixirs, been so heavily taxed. For the matter in hand required all the force, if not the clearness, which stimulants could give it.

What was the matter? A day or two before, Mr. Williams, one of three or four barristers who earned a precarious subsistence by picking up the legal crumbs which fell from the tables of an Attorney and Solicitor-General, – for these little Crown colonies are not considered to be fully shotted in a legal sense without being loaded with a brace of law officers, – had presented to his Excellency Mr. Thomas Walsingham, a memorial, purporting to be signed or marked by some twenty thousand Indians, and several hundred Chinese. This bold document set forth in simple but decided terms a list of grievances of which the petitioners, for the memorial assumed the form of a petition, complained, and which they prayed the Governor to examine, and in Her Majesty's stead to have redressed.

Some of these grievances no doubt would seem very small to the official eyes in Downing Street, or to that portion of the English people to whom grievances have become a nuisance, being so various and so frequent, and so persistently presented to public view by energetic societies. What is the retention of a few small coins from the dregs of the Indian population of a West India colony, to a people engaged in the government of world-wide Empire, sympathizing with suffering populations in Europe, spending hundreds of thousands in suppressing the African slave trade? What if men and women are occasionally imprisoned by mistake, or wronged by careless magistracy and bad interpreters, or deprived of rights and privileges which have been assured them by contract? Is there not the contract? Are there not laws? Are these laws not administered by Englishmen? Is there not an English executive? Above all, is not sugar (a valuable commodity much used in this world, and helping to sweeten it), produced by this system at a cost which makes some Englishmen, who are high in position, and conspicuous for their influence, rich? Are you to jeopardise this splendid trade? This is not a good working griev- ance. There is not enough blood and outrage about it, – though neither are absolutely wanting if you did but examine and see, – it is altogether too small a matter to challenge public attention, and excite great popular demonstrations, and stir up public enthusiasm.

When Mr. Williams, who did not lack the quality of forwardness, presented himself in the little room appropriated to the really hard work of Governor Walsingham, followed by a Negro clerk carrying a prodigious cylindrical parcel, his Excellency was taken aback.

'Good morning, Mr. Williams,' said the Governor, who had some inkling of what was coming. 'What is this you have brought in with you? You might have left it outside with my secretary.'

'I have explained to him already, your Excellency, what it is, and I bring it in with his permission, as it is for personal presentation. It is a petition, your Excellency,' here Mr. Williams drew himself up and began to speak in a solemn oratorical tone, 'from twenty thousand Coolies and———'

'O stop! Mr. Williams,' cried his Excellency, rising for the first time and looking at the roll of paper as if it were a parcel of dynamite. 'A petition from Coolies, Mr. Williams? Really, this is very irregular and awkward. How did it get in here, eh? I must consider what I ought to do about this, you know. In fact the law officers must be consulted about it. It is a very serious business, Mr. Williams, quite unprecedented indeed!'

'Undoubtedly, your Excellency,' replied the barrister. 'And for that reason I trust your Excellency will consider it a matter worth your attention. Ahem!' starting off again in the sonorous tones of his professional practice. 'This, your Excellency, is a petition to you, as Her Majesty's representative, and presented in the exercise of an undoubted constitutional right, setting forth the grievances————'

'Stop, Mr. Williams, if you please. I cannot allow you to get the petition presented in that way: take it away until I can consult the Attorney-General.'

'Surely, sir,' replied Mr. Williams, who was as Welsh as his name, and pertinacious as any Celt: 'Surely your Excellency cannot consider it necessary to consult the law officers of the Crown whether a petition is to be received or not?'

'Pardon me, Mr. Williams,' said his Excellency, flushing up, 'I cannot allow you, sir, to question me as to what I will or will not consider necessary. You see I am not Her Majesty, and only her representative, and I am not quite clear that the same rules would apply to me that apply to her! You should send it to London, Mr. Williams, or to Windsor, or Balmoral, or Osborne, or – wherever it ought to go, Mr. Williams,' said the Governor, after pausing as if he were about to suggest 'Jericho,' or some less agreeable place; 'but you see I may compromise myself by accepting such a petition. You see I don't even know what is in it, Mr. Williams.'

The Governor walked about the room in great agitation.

'Your Excellency can only ascertain what is in it, I respectfully submit,' replied Mr. Williams, 'by perusing the petition. I will just unroll it.'

'Oh, for God's sake! Mr. Williams. No, sir, – certainly not!' cried the Governor. 'I say *stop*, sir!' I insist on your not unrolling it!' for the daring advocate was in the act of untying the obnoxious roll. 'Take it away, sir,' shouted the Governor in a rage to the black clerk, while he violently rang the secretary's bell. The clerk and the dangerous parcel disappeared and the secretary entered.

'Mr. Coulthurst,' quoth the Governor, 'I am surprised that you should have permitted an important interview of this kind to take place without a previous arrangement. Here is Mr. Williams, who brings in a large, – ah, – roll of paper, which he states is a memorial, or petition, or whatever you like to call it, from twenty thousand Coolies, sir, and you show him into my room as if he had come for a morning call!'

'I beg your pardon, sir; I thought it would be received as a matter of course.'

'And what right had you to suppose anything of the kind, sir?' roared the Governor. 'It may – I say it *may* – contain statements of a libellous character; it may contain charges against the Government———'

'It does,' interrupted Mr. Williams, sententiously.

'Pray don't interrupt me, sir! I was going to add it may even implicate ME in those charges; and are you not aware, sir, after all your experience, that if it is once received by me it becomes a State paper and, may be called for by the Home authorities, and printed in a blue book?'

The secretary stood mute, while the irrepressible Mr. Williams unfeelingly interposed once more, –

'Excuse me, your Excellency, that is precisely what we desire.'

'Exactly, sir,' exclaimed the Governor in a fury. 'And who – and who the deuce are "*we*," sir, I should like to know? Eh? A parcel of poor immigrants and a beggarly barrister, making money no doubt out of hatched discontent!'

'Pardon me, your Excellency,' replied Mr. Williams, with dignity: 'I cannot remain here to listen to such language even from your lips. In the discharge of my duty to my clients I have simply to ask you once more whether you will receive the petition I have tendered to you?'

'No: I will not!' said his Excellency, sitting down with an emphatic bounce in his chair. 'And I wish you good morning, sir.'

Mr. Williams bowed and retired. He had often before shown in that fiery colony a dangerous command of himself. Moreover he knew his man, and was resolved to await his opportunity. The effect of red pepper is rarely lasting.

And in truth as the Governor's temper cooled, wiser thoughts supervened. He knew Mr. Williams to be both a determined and a fearless person, possessing indeed those qualities which easy-going persons of a malicious and envious turn call 'cantankerous.' Every Governor is possessed with a wholesome dislike of a hostile reference to the Colonial Minister. The power which that great official has over the destinies of millions, through his power over Her Majesty's viceroys in our world-wide empire, is but little apprehended by the British public, and would rather astonish it were it to take the trouble to investigate the matter. Governor Walsingham, however, knew it by experience, and therefore he consulted the Attorney and Solicitor-General. Neither of these gentlemen, – without any impeachment of their honesty, be it said, – dared to give other counsel than that he gave, namely, that such a petition, since it was in their opinion in its very nature an act calculated to provoke a breach of the peace, and dangerously excite popular discontent, ought not to be received. They lived on and out of the planting community, and their thoughts were as planters' thoughts, and their ways as planters' ways.

Furthermore, the Council was called together to consider the matter, as information came in from all quarters that the Coolies – among whom news runs with almost electric speed – were manifesting a turbulent and refractory spirit: I use the Governor's own words. The Council consisted of official members and planter representatives in equal proportions; some of the officials, by the way, being themselves planters or relatives of planters. These also advised the Governor not to receive the petition. In the meantime, it may be observed, no one of them knew what the petition contained.

But Mr. Williams was not by any means to be check-mated by his legal superiors or defeated by resolutions of the Council. He executed a sharp strategic movement. He addressed a strong letter to the Colonial Minister in London; giving a graphic account of the interview between the Governor and himself, and enclosing a copy of the petition. This he sent to his Excellency under cover with a letter, in which he requested the Governor in the usual way to forward the communication to the Secretary of State for the Colonies. This obliged the Governor to act on his own responsibility. He knew that if he declined to forward the documents, they would be sent to the Colonial Office, and explanations would be demanded. It is very awkward for an official to be asked for explanations upon information which he himself has not conveyed. It is impossible to avoid the feeling in such a case that a man is on his defence, and in that very feeling the assailant gets an advantage. So after spending a sleepless night, in which his pride and his caution had a severe struggle, his poor Excellency arrived at the decision that it was the better policy in his own interest to accept and forward the memorial, accompanied by his own remarks, which would then reach the Minister at least as soon as the charges.

Mr. Williams was not surprised when the Vice-regal Secretary entered his office and begged him to withdraw his letters and wait upon the Governor with the dynamite parcel.

Thus at the instance of a game little Welshman, whose life, and wife, and home were at the time by no means as secure as one would have been proud to assert of them in an English colony, *one* was scored, to begin, for the Indians, – a success, however, that might only be a precursor of sorrows. For the rage of the planters knew no bounds; and here it was, puffing and exploding viciously in the Georgetown Club, and intensified by repeated stimulants of exciting spirits. Fists were shaken with a vigour singularly inconsistent with the relaxing character of the climate ; oaths and exclamations, being most emphatic, rose above the general din. No one regarded the billiard tables, round which the crowd surged. In the wide verandah, in the middle of a group of the principal men, stood Drummond, dealing with His Excellency in no measured terms. 'Old woman' was the least derogatory of the expressions freely used in describing Her Majesty's representative; but the reader may be spared the vocabulary of West Indian rage.

'We must have him out of this, I say, as soon as possible, the chicken-hearted idiot! What call had he to go and accept a heap of dirty foolscap, libelling every gentleman in the community?'

'Hear, hear!' cried a ruffianly-looking manager from the Arabian Coast, whose name was Harris, and who meant what he said.

'The whole thing has been concocted between that rascally little Portugee and that sneaking attorney. If their houses are not burned down by to-morrow night, it won't be because they don't deserve it.'

'Hear, hear!' cried the chorus.

If Drummond, generally a cool-headed and steady-tongued man, respected in the colony for his judgment, was so overcome by his anger, what must have been the state of mind of others more fiery by nature and injudicious in practice? A new voice, however, was raised by an exceedingly prim and smooth-spoken gentleman, Mr. Ingledew, one of the wealthiest and ablest agents in the colony. In such communities these calm, cold-blooded persons soon acquire a singular and dangerous mastery. Cautious never to be guilty themselves of any excess, they secretly encourage it in others, and no Commission is sharp or shrewd enough to convict them of folly or error.

'Gentlemen,' he said, after clearing his throat in a careful and precise manner which commanded attention, 'let us proceed to discuss this question in a manner becoming its gravity. The subject naturally divides itself under three heads. There is, first, the treacherous combination – I think I may, without exaggeration, term it a conspiracy (hear) – between Gonzales, Williams, and certain other persons unknown, to inflame the animosity of the Coolies against those whom I and you and every one conversant with the subject know to be their best friends. It will become the imperative duty of every manager to ascertain what individuals among the Coolies have been specially prominent in this criminal incitement of the labourers. Then there is, secondly, the question of the course which it is our duty to pursue with regard to the unpatriotic, unnatural, and revolutionary conduct of – I blush while I allude to his origin – that *white man* Williams (loud murmurs). Gentlemen, I beseech you, endeavour to repress your feelings. It may be true, it *is* true, that no punishment, however vindictive, could sufficiently repay the scoundrel who lends his miserable abilities in a mercenary manner to encourage in the minds of poor ignorant labourers ideas and aims which are so utterly impracticable (loud applause, testified in every possible manner), and I may add, which, if once they are permitted to gain possession of the Coolie mind, will render it impossible for your agriculture, your commerce, your trade to continue to maintain even the qualified success which it now experiences. Lastly, gentlemen, there is the deplorable feebleness and vacillation of – hem! – the Executive.'

The uproar of groans might almost have reached His Excellency's ear through the open windows of Government House.

'Hem, gentlemen!' continued Mr. Ingledew, raising his voice to reach the enlarging circle of his auditors, 'with regard to the Executive, I fear nothing is at present to be done. Unhappily we cannot depose him: we are not an independent people. He has resolved to forward the scurrilous document, which is a libel and an insult upon everyone connected with the planting interest, to the Colonial Minister. We must leave the Executive, gentlemen, to be dealt with by our friends, the "Sugar-growers Committee," in London. But the immediate question before us is, how are we to meet the danger with which we are menaced, – of robbery, of assassination? – Ah!'

The speaker's word proved to be far nearer the fact than he intended or imagined; for at the moment a revolver, incautiously waved by an inspirited manager, went off with a loud report, and the ball whistled close to the orator's head.

'Ahem, gentlemen!' continued Mr. Ingledew, after the excitement caused by this incident had subsided, and as he wiped away the dew of fright which had gathered on his brow, 'the most important consideration of the moment is one of life and death. We are few in number, scattered through a large population of labourers whom these conspirators have hounded on to seek our destruction.'

The audience grew fearfully agitated. He had touched the sore point with them all. They trembled, as well they might, at any manifestation of a sense of right or wrong by the poor people whom they professed to be treating with romantic kindness!

'Gentlemen, we must take instant measures for the preservation of our lives and property. Williams at least must be arrested and the Portuguese Gonzales. The police force must be increased, and all the whites sworn in as special constables. I should further recommend the proclamation of martial law, and that a schooner be sent to Barbadoes with a requisition for more troops,' etc., etc.

Thus Mr. Ingledew. His speech was cunningly conceived to hit the popular feeling and animate the general apprehensions. His hint was at once taken. Drummond was called to the chair, – that is, he sat upon the edge of a billiard-table, while resolutions were rapidly passed, demanding the arrest of Williams for aiding Coolies, – who are, after all, English subjects, – in exercising a right confirmed to Englishmen by Magna Charta. A Committee immediately went to wait upon the Governor. He received them civilly, but recoiled without any hesitation from taking the responsible steps on which they insisted.

When the deputation, failing in their aim, returned unsuccessful from Government House, the agitation in the club became terrific. It is almost impossible to convey to home readers an idea of the state of mind into which British gentlemen can work themselves when they constitute, as in the Mauritius or in Barbadoes, an alarmed minority in the midst of a great community of natives and imported servants, whom they will protest to you and the rest of the world they govern with even undue generosity. The outer public (I should say to these self-satisfied Pharisees) cannot help sometimes suspecting that when you know that those of another colour are one or two hundred to one, and that they have not received perfect justice, or have actually received gross injustice at your hands, your equanimity cannot bear the test of the discovery that the majority have awakened to their wrongs, and mean in one way or another to have them remedied. And if the remedy is likely to touch your pockets your anger will doubtless be proportionately increased.

But now a new and startling incident drew the attention of the whole company to the verandah of the club.

One of the members, looking down the street through the jalousies, had detected Gonzales, who, fresh from an interview with Akaloo, was really at the moment on his way to see Mr. Williams, and was approaching the club. Unluckily for him he did not observe, until he was too near to retreat, the flashing eyes that glared upon him from the jalousies, or hear the mutterings of the coming storm. The rude-looking manager from the Arabian Coast, before mentioned, Mr. Harris, stood among the planters, whipping his powerful leg with a coarse 'raw-hide.' As the Portuguese advanced, this gentleman slowly descended the steps leading from the verandah of the club, and in a few strides had come up face to face with Gonzales and seized him by the collar. The Portuguese paled and winced for a moment, and heartily wished he had had in his hand the long-bladed knife which lay in its sheath in a cupboard not far from his bed. He recovered himself in a moment, and said quietly:

'Will you be so good as to let me pass, sir?'

'Let you pass! you d– thief!' roared the other. 'I suppose you are on your way to Williams'. Eh? Eh?' he said, imitating the well-known manner of the Portuguese. 'What are you doing with the Coolies?'

'I am doing nothing, sir, but what is perfectly legal, sir! Let me pass, sir, I pray you. Otherwise I shall be obliged to charge you with this assault.'

'Oh!' cried the other. 'I'll give you something, you Portuguese hound, to charge me with. Take *that!*'

A fierce, wicked cut went across the smooth face of the Portuguese, and left its mark in a red and blue pattern, a mark that the resentful skin would never lose. Hard again and cruel was the second blow that came down over the now uncovered head. Heavy and cruel yet upon the sinking form, the rain of blows which began to draw their bloody lines through the thin white clothes. It was a long and brutal punishment that the furious maniac inflicted on his shrieking victim, until he himself was weary, and the victim had ceased to cry out. And all the while that group of manly Britons in the club, with clenched teeth, and a general aspect as of men who thought a wholesome thing for the State was being done, looked on without an effort to interfere. Among them were several officials, who like Gallio assumed indifference, or else openly approved the act. When Mr. Harris, heated by his exertions, left the unconscious Portuguese, and rejoined the company, he received a perfect ovation.

'Quite right, old fellow. We'll stand to you!'

And they did.

Gonzales lay a long while in the afternoon sun. None of the mixed crowd of Portuguese, Negroes and Coolies, which speedily gathered dared to render him any assistance. At length two women from the Catholic convent came with a litter, and, with the aid of two or three of his friends, conveyed him to their retreat. The Portuguese was well known and respected by his country-men, and never had the few British residents of the colony been in more fearful peril than on that night, – not from their suspected Coolies, but from the incensed and fiery Portuguese who thronged the streets. Had there been a man for the situation, very few letters to Europe would have gone out by the next steamer from the Demerara river.*

---

* An incident similar to that in the text happened at Mauritius, and is related in the Commissioners' Report. — Monsieur de Plevitz, who took an interest in Coolie grievances and presented a memorial on their behalf, was severely beaten with a stick by a cowardly planter, who was afterwards fined for the as-sault. The planters of the Mauritius, who would, I dare say, feel it a deep in-dignity to be called anything but gentlemen, manifested a ruffianly complicity in the dastardly act by subscribing a shilling a-piece to pay the fine. Such an incident never occurred in Georgetown. I speak from a fortu-nate experience when I say that I hope it was practically impossible among the men who used to frequent that institution when I was there. The reader will remember that the developments of the Coolie system in all our colonies are being grouped in one scene for the sake of convenience.

CHAPTER XXXV

A CURE OF SOULS

MISSA SANKEY had been deeply stirred in mind and heart by the awkward incidents attending the Major's visit. Her dignity had suffered extremely. Her pride and vanity had been incurably wounded. She had exhibited herself – involuntarily 'tis true, but the fact was none the less shocking – to a vulgar and uncharitable public, in a garment only a degree removed in its simple and primitive naturalism from the original apron of mother Eve, who, by the way, was, for all we know, of the same hue as Missa Sankey. Merely to recall such a wound to her complacency, sent a thrill of angry shame through her being, which nature however had denied her the privilege of expressing in a way that could be seen – by a blush. Besides, it added an extra sting to her humiliation that her usual attire was most tropically magnificent, both in style and colour. Then there was other ground for serious reflection. Although, being a widow, the fact that she had an infant capable of exciting the Moloch avidity of the generous Major, was in itself no suspicious matter; yet the attempt just made, as she firmly believed, to snatch that jewel from her hands, could not but remind her that his origin was not strictly praiseworthy. The attempt of the hungry philanthropist, she thought, might perhaps be a divine judgment upon her for her sins.

Accordingly long after the white visitors had vanished and the black crowd had dispersed, Susan Sankey sat weeping copiously and in earnest. The closer she reviewed her situation the more uncomfortable she felt. Scraps of vague denunciation, oft uttered in her hearing by honest Baptist and Wesleyan evangelists, came up in memory to terrify her. Powerful illustrations, long forgotten, of the punishment which all sin must incur were now brought back to her imagination with vivid effect. So poor Missa Sankey, alone with her own consciously-wicked self, and having a very lively belief in things supernal and infernal, mingled her sobbing with ejaculations and prayers. How long this seasonable sorrow might have lasted, had it not been for the most substantial cause of it, one cannot tell. But the vexed piccaninny, left to himself and aroused by hunger, suddenly exhibited a precocity of grief which surpassed the maturer sorrows of his mother, and challenged instant attention. It was then that Missa Sankey, restored as it were to practical life, took, as we shall see, a most practical resolution. If repentance was to put her right with heaven, she was determined it should also make matters straight upon earth. Simon Pety should verify, in a literal sense, the maxim that, 'Sins come home to roost.'

Missa Sankey turned over her wardrobe, not a poor or inconsiderable one, and, after prolonged hesitation between one thing and another, at length made choice of a costume which she deemed to be appropriate to her purpose. She endued herself with her most admired finery. The child was also curiously and richly tricked out, after his little brown legs and arms had been polished to a nicety. Then, taking him up, she wended her way to Belle Susanne. By the time when she came in sight of the manager's stable, which was indeed her destination, evening was nigh at hand. Next to the stable was a sort of den, consecrated to the uses of the gallant Pety; and Missa Sankey intended in that den to beard the unfaithful swain.

Before, however, she had reached the yard, the noise of wheels close behind her made her turn and step aside; and the object of her search appeared, seated in a waggon in which he was driving Mr. Drummond home from Georgetown. Simon Pety's muscular heart beat somewhat wildly when he saw Missa Sankey trudging along the road, in a black silk petticoat, with voluminous flounces; a white-and-yellow striped opera cloak, – remnant of some London 'clearance of stock,' exported to the colony by an adventurous firm; and a white tulle and blue silk bonnet, trimmed with violent scarlet flowers; making her altogether look very much like a toucan, a scarlet ibis, and a paroquet rolled into one; while she bore in her arms that inconvenient baby, whose motley was

every whit as remarkable as that of his mother. Drummond, as
they passed her, looked sharply at Susan and then at his driver.
The latter gallantly raised his hat and gave a ghastly grin at the
widow, who however returned to his salute only a staid and
sorrowful acknowledgment. Master Pete's quick Negro temperament went down several degrees, like a barometer when heavy
weather is threatening.

'One of your young ladies, Pete?' said Drummond, maliciously,
as the man whipped on.

'Missa Sankey, sah! I hab de honour ob her acquaintance, sah.
Mos' sartainly fine young lady!'

'Yes: and a fine young baby, Pete. Who is her husband?'

'Widow, sah: mos' respeckable widow. Owns de largest plantain
ground back ob Guineatown.'

'Oh, ay! I know the place: Jabez Sankey's lot. I remember *her*
well. If she's after you, you are a lucky man, Pete. Jabez Sankey
was a thrifty fellow.'

At any other time Pete would have accepted this compliment as
one only due to his superior attractions: at present he had a feeling
that something uncomfortable was to come with his luck. Having
to get down to open a gate, he did not gain much on Missa Sankey,
who reached him just as Drummond was about to walk away, after
giving some directions. Without taking any notice of the master,
Susan went straight up to the man.

'Simon Pety,' she said, in a half-hysterical voice, 'de Lord hab
send me a message.'

'Missa Sankey,' replied Pete, in great embarrassment and glancing sideways at Drummond, who chose not to stir, 'de Lord berry
good. How'd de message arrive? – angel or black gen'leman?'

'Oh, Pete!' said Susey, bursting into tears. 'Heah, take de chile
quick! Ken't hold him no longer.' And, throwing the infant into
Pete's arms, she sank on her knees, and crying, 'O Lord, O Lord,
forgib me!' wept bitterly, down on the black silk flounces.

Pete was a Negro, and to a Negro crying is catching. He really
liked Miss Sankey, as much as his selfish and volatile nature
would let him. This scene in the open air, and the remorse of the
woman, and the pricking of his own conscience, and the baby in

his arms, who laughed at him very prettily, and Mr. Drummond looking on at it all, made Pete unspeakably awkward and embarrassed.

'O Pety!' sobbed the widow, 'O Pety! De Lord say you got to marry me 'cause ob dat chile! What you say, Pete? Nebber shall be happy till you do. O Pete, s'pose you marry me, p'raps de Lord go to forgib us!'

Pete did not look as if Missa Sankey's hope was his own. His ordinary confidence had deserted him. Had there been no spectator by he would very likely have gone on his knees beside the poor woman and have prayed with her as one 'under conviction'; for the sympathetic nature in him would have won its way, and, bad as he was, her grief excited some compunction. But there was another restraining element in his thoughts, and that was a fleshly one – to wit, a certain Miss Rosalind Dallas. So Master Pete said, in a hesitating way, but gently, –

'How you sartin, Susey, de Lord send de message? He allays appear mos' like an angel or a flaming fire.'

'No, no, Pety!' cried Susan Sankey, holding her hands over the opera cloak on her capacious bosom. 'Nebber come to me like dat. I feel it *heah!* Ken't hab no peace widout it, Pety!'

'Dere ain't no peas to de wicked, Susey,' said Pete, recovering slightly, and automatically starting on his favourite career of misquotation. 'Dey all like de green bay tree. Cut it down: why cumber it de ground?'

He would have wandered on, but Drummond could endure no more, and struck in sharply.

'Look here, Pete: is that your child?'

'Hum!' said Pete, looking at the infant in his arms, and then at Missa Sankey.

'Yes!' cried Susan: 'dat's Pete's own chile, Massa Drummond, sure as he lib.'

'Well, then, you scoundrel, why don't you marry the woman? Don't stand there quoting texts at her, you old hypocrite! I tell you you *shall* marry her! Get up, Susan Sankey, and wipe your eyes for a stupid woman, and he shall promise you now, or I'll know why not!'

Missa Sankey rose and took the baby from Pete, who gladly resigned it to her. He hesitated a moment and then spoke.

'Well, Missa Sankey,' he said, 'if de Lord and Massa Drummond both say marry Miss Sankey, dere's on'y one way – to do de Lord's will. De young man afterward repented and went, I guess. Marriage honourable to all, Susan: let no man put it asunder.'

Drummond laughed so loud and heartily that Susan, smiling through her tears, looked like a polished black pot boiling over.

'Now,' said the master, 'look here, Pete; you had better arrange that this little affair should come off as soon as possible; and if Miss Susan will come and live here with you, and you will promise to be true and kind to her, I'll build you a little house, and the piccaninny shall play about the yard. Put her into the waggon and drive her home : she don't look fit to walk.'

It was getting dark as the horse turned out of the estate dam into the Guineatown road. Susan Sankey had been sitting quite quiet, happily dropping tears on her baby's face. She was saying to herself, with very genuine intent, that she would try and do her duty better to the good Lord who had brought her out of the depths and changed her mourning into joy. Mr Pete's reflections were not so bright, though he was not crying. He had been practically *check-mated!* What he was to say to Miss Dallas, a young lady of vigorous character, who would undoubtedly have her remonstrances to offer on this forced arrangement, he was vainly endeavouring to forecast. She might take it on very seriously. She might even go to the Obe Man and get that villanous agency of the devil to cut short Pete's thread of life. He had always looked upon Miss Sankey as a safe and quiet friend who would not break out upon him. But now he had given his word to her, Drummond being witness, and it was impossible to draw back. Such were the thoughts which were gloomily clouding his mind, and, truth to tell, making him feel in any but a frame of bliss, when he felt Susan's soft arm round his neck (she had slipped off the opera cloak, and her dress was low cut, with short sleeves), and received on his undeserving cheek a cordial smack which made him wince.

'Deah Pety!' said Susan Sankey; 'deah ole Pety! we go lub one anoder, as de good book say, and serve de Lord now togedder all our days, Pety! Dis little piccaninny lub you too, Pety. O Pety, say someting, or I'll scream out! I feel so happy.'

The genuine feeling of poor Susan wrought its influence, as genuine feeling almost always does. Pete's heart was a shallow but an open one. The muddy water began to settle. Under the spell of Susan's happy voice and the pressure of her soft arm, the threatening shadow of Rosalind vanished in the distance, and Pete began to entertain the feeling that he was not so badly off with the widow. But Susan's sincere religious impulse was not so much in harmony with that wanton sinner's feelings as were her demonstrations of wifely affection. He was still – if one may say so of a man of his tint – only a whitened sepulchre, and the whitening was on in extremely thin patches.

'Susey,' he said, after driving along a little while, silently submitting to her caresses, 'I go to make you happy, if I ken, sure; I go try be berry good to little piccaninny. We try to eddicate dis chile in de right way. As de good book say, "Train up a child in de way he shall go, and when he get old he bring forth fruit, some sixty-fold and some an hundred-fold."'

'Simon Pety,' said Susan, firmly in his ear, 'Simon, you promise to be good man now; nebber leabe Susan – allus be good to me now – sartain, Pety?'

Pete was stirred far below his skin and ear-drum by Susan's earnest voice and manner. Her real affection and softened feeling penetrated to his heart.

'By de help of de Lord I *will*, Susan Sankey!' cried Pete, hysterically, as the first genuine tears that had glistened in his eye for many a long day burst forth, and he threw his unoccupied arm round Susan's waist and inflicted on her cheek a huge salute, which was better received than the unlucky one erst bestowed on the widow with concomitant mucilage of fou-fou soup!

Now when Pete did this, the strange wild African nature of Missa Sankey waxed uncontrollable. She laughed out boisterously until the thin covering of the waggon shook again. Whereupon Pete must needs laugh too. Then in sheer gladness of heart she

broke into song, irrelevant doubtless, but not without a meaning
for her. It was a revival hymn set to a plantation melody, and both
tune and words were, I imagine, as sweet and as sensible as some
that are in vogue with educated Christians in England when giving vent to their religious feelings in song. Simon Pety caught the
infection of Susan's joy, and their voices stirred up the night which
was now thick about them.

> Come, sinner, will you come along wid me –
> Come, sinner, will you come along wid me –
> Come, sinner, will you come along wid me –
>   Go up to de trone of God ?
> Yes, Christian, come and go to glory!
> Yes, Christian, come and go to glory!
> Yes, Christian, come and go to glory!
>   All de way to de trone of God!
> Now we trabbel on to glory!
> Trabbel up de road dat lead to glory!
> Climb up togedder into glory –
>   Singing Hallelujah!
>   Singing Hallelujah!   Now and ebbermore!
>   Singing Hallelujah!

Shouting this song, Pete and the widow arrived at her house.
He descended and bore the baby into the room so familiar to him,
but which, when Susan struck a light, seemed to wear to his eyes,
and hers also, a new aspect. As he was about to take a tender
farewell, the widow showed that the events of the day were still, for
her, matters not merely of temporal, but spiritual consequence.

'Pety,' said she, in a voice still trembling with emotion, 'pray de
Lord bress you and me and little piccaninny, Pety?'

So he had to go down on his knees and perform a pre-
matrimonial family worship. Pety's prayer that night was not much
more coherent than usual, but it was more sober in its manner and
real in its earnestness. And afterwards, when he had put up his
horse and retired to the room in which he slept, his spirit was
subdued by the infectious penitence of Susan Sankey. His weak
and ignorant nature could only dimly apprehend the meaning of
the spiritual influences which had blown over it that afternoon. He

could simply realize that he had been suddenly aroused to a conviction of a great sin, and that a kindly power had stepped in and shown him a way out of a dark and evil road. The fact that Susan Sankey had been the angel of this deliverance made it none the less sweet or the less promising of permanent good.

CHAPTER XXXVI

SPLICED ROUGHLY

GUINEATOWN was *en fête*. All the living dusky lining of its crowded houses was turned forth upon the day. Old and young of both sexes, in every sort of dress, were ranged along the dams, lounging, chattering, frolicing or singing, with all the light animal zest which came of their wild animal nature. All were keenly watching every chink and cranny in Missa Sankey's house, heartily wishing that its walls were transparent.

Whensoever, in Demerara, it is thought necessary that a Negro should get married or buried, the deed can only be done in a manner befitting a race which estimates values by display. Blacks will often postpone their weddings indefinitely if they are unable to enhance the dignity of the ceremony with such concomitants of splendour and such extravagant festivities as Negro pride has declared to be essential to Negro respectability. To marry or be buried without carriages and a multitudinous following of friends is as great a disgrace with the Blacks as with the Irish. To enter into wedlock or the grave without these were indeed to confess yourself before all the Negro world dishonoured and unknown.

Mr. Simon Peter D'Orsay – who can say whence these blacks obtain their grand names? – and Mrs. Susan Sankey were not of a sort to forego any of the splendours of an aristocratic wedding. Though they were honestly resolved to abjure henceforth 'de world, de flesh, and de debbil,' there was no doubt, as there almost always is after an exodus, a certain hankering after the old Egypt, and they could not reconcile their minds to an absolutely quiet ceremony. Susan had put by a considerable sum in view of such an event, and Master Pete was not without his deposit in the Government Savings Bank, good for the same purpose; so that they could well afford to carry out a programme in the most superlative style of their peculiar circle.

'Susan,' said Pete, with a shy and gallant reference to Miss Sankey's widowhood, as they talked the matter over, 'dese yere sarcumstances nebber come more dan two or tree time, in most folks' lives, 'cept in de case ob de wise King Solomon: he mos' wonderful man; he had a wedding, I guess, most days ob his life, 'cording to Scripshur. Massa Jim Soby, berry wicked black gen'le-man I know ober at Massa Coleman's, demonstrate wid me one time on dat subjeck. He say, "King Solomon pray fur all de wis-dom, and 'cause he too greedy and get too much dat way de Lord take it out ob him anoder way, by super-disposing on him all dat lot o' wives." Poor man, Susey, dunno how he ever fix it so as to git along comf'able wid such a quantity ob ladies!'

'Mister Pete, you begin to git sassy now you goin' to marry me, sah. King Solomon's dat same sort o' man de Reverend Massa Blister gib his discourse about Sunday before last. He say, "Dere's some folks, my brederen, mentioned in de Bible no one ken understand. De're all wonders ob de deep. Dey require de prophets demselves to explain about 'em." I reckon Solomon one ob dose men, sure enuf, – nassy man!'

'Hah!' replied Pete, stroking his beard. 'Be keerful, Susey, be keerful! Don't you go to call any pussin in de Bible bad names. Dey's all ministering sperrits. All Scripture written by aspiration, Susey. Solomon, son of David, must ha' been a good man, I s'pose. But, Susey, my opinion's dis, – dere's only a chance o' good men around in dis world, and all de good women wants to marry dem: dat's how Solomon come to hab so many, I reckon. But, Susey, how about de wedding? De good book say, "Let all tings be done decently and in order. Honour to whom honour – Custom to whom custom"———'

'Well, ain't de good book right, Pete?' interrupted Miss Sankey. 'Dat's why you and me goin' to get married, ain't it? An' now de Lord bless us so much, we go gib all our friends a big wedding, Pete.'

'All right, sartainly, Susey,' cried Pete. 'We go and have a most su-perio-rogatory wedding. Reverend Mister Blister always talk-ing at de meeting 'bout work ob superiororergation: mighty big word, Susey, – dat is most superior kind ob works, I guess. So we

go to have a superiorogatory wedding. Den dere's de bridesmaids.
Dere was ten virgins asked to de wedding in de parable, – how
many you goin' to have?'

And so, after much more talk of this sort, Pete and Susey had
arranged for a wedding on a scale, for Guineatown, almost of
unprecedented splendour. The ceremony was to be performed by
the Baptist minister, the Rev. Joel Amos Daniel Blister – a good
man and true, even though he was more firmly devoted to water
ablution as a spiritual ceremony than as a physical duty. The knot
was to be tied in the meeting-house, and the usual procession of
carriages and of fashionable company was to grace the occasion.
Hence, in Guineatown, public expectation was at a high pitch;
and, in good sooth, the indications were full of promise.

At the earliest hour when it could have been possible for them
to distinguish their dark features in a glass, young ladies and
gentlemen, unable to repress their anxiety to air themselves for
the benefit of their neighbours, began to emerge from their
homes. The ceremony was some hours off, it is true; but these
good people could not postpone their triumph till the time of the
wedding. The gentlemen were dressed in black frock coats and
trousers, and white waistcoats. They had already drawn over their
dusky fingers loose white kid gloves, to which they gave the fullest
effect by holding their fingers straight out and wide apart, like the
wooden hands on which such things are displayed in our glove
shops. Crowned with tall black hats, their ebony faces buried in
collars, which towered majestically over snowy bows and ample
fields of shirt bosom, whereon in some instances shone brave and
startling varieties of flash jewellery, these gentlemen cut a distinguished figure as they marched up and down in solitary dignity,
or stiffly aggregated for a morning interchange of courtesies.

There also appeared a few young ladies who either were unable
to restrain their impatience, or perhaps hoped by striking early in
the day to secure some admiring gallant, to the confusion of the
discreeter damsels who affected a fashionable lateness, or hoped
to win by an artistic surprise. An accurate Court-circular description of the toilettes that glittered in the equatorial sun would
scarcely be credited as true by readers unacquainted with the

people. Most of them blazed in silk of bright hues, well-fitted to
their lithe and handsome figures; or else were wreathed in white
muslin trimmed with ribands. The favourite fashion was the conventional low neck and short sleeves of the ball-room, to display
which, those who possessed the additional glory of a white cloak
or shawl, allowed it to fall gracefully off the shoulders, and to leave
their buxom charms unveiled to all spectators. Upon their woolly
locks, most cunningly coifed, were perched perfect miracles of
incongruous millinery as to colours and materials. With a fan
or parasol the outfit was complete. Their conscious pride and
affected posing gave a delightful and attractive oddity to the
general aspect of the performers, and great was the excitement
created among the uninvited spectators by the appearance of
these birds of plumage, who flitted in and out of their homes with
feverish restlessness, constantly looking out for signs of movement around Missa Sankey's house.

The day wore on, and public interest so-far satiated, somewhat
relaxed under the tropical influences, until, a little before noon,
the hired carriages from Georgetown began to arrive, – large,
two-horsed, covered-in, stuffed, and no doubt to any but Negroes
stifling. No less than eight or nine of these imposing vehicles
drove into the village, some of them containing ample loads of
friends of both parties from the metropolis of the colony. It was an
entertaining sight to see the carriages emptied of their living
contents; to watch the extravagant politeness of the drivers, the
exaggerated courtesies of the gentlemen, the affected elegance of
the ladies, the universal and genial sense of a great occasion
grandly observed, which seemed to inspire all the actors!

These now began in twos and threes to collect in front of Missa
Sankey's house. And at a not quite respectful distance, in a lively
circle, gathered the Guineatown population. Among them a few
Coolies, attracted by the excitement and the display, looked on
amused. The Asiatics are very chary of Negro association, and
these held themselves among the crowd with a certain dignity
which distinguished them from their more volatile neighbours.

While the guests were circling about, and introductions, recog-
nitions, and lively bursts of laughter were the order of the day, a

shout from the observant crowd beyond, called all the performers to order, and they immediately drew up at the foot of Missa Sankey's steps; for there at the top appeared the expectant celebrants, Mr. Simon Peter D'Orsay having succeeded in slipping into the house by the back way unperceived. Never had 'Simon Pety' looked more dignified or more absurd. He had received from Drummond the present of a buff waistcoat, which, as it was made for the body of a man six feet in height, and of corresponding build, resembled, on the inadequately proportioned bulk of Mr. D'Orsay, a loose leaf on an ear of Indian corn. Its ample length encroached on his nether garments down towards his thigh bones. White trousers, which had already become baggy at the knees, and everywhere much wrinkled, a vast pair of glossy boots, a white 'choker,' ample and stiff enough for a clergyman of the old school, with abnormal collar of the antique type, and a large broad-brimmed black hat, set forth the bridegroom. But all eyes were turned to the lady at his side. It was well known that one of the most eminent of the milliners of the Negro quarter in Georgetown had exhausted all her skill in setting out Susan Sankey for this important day; and it was seen at a glance that she had succeeded.

The comely widow, with her deep-tinted regular features, bright eyes, and brilliant teeth, as she stood at the top of the steps, with a half-bashful consciousness of triumph, did, I doubt not, in the eyes of those to whom her tint and physique were natural, look most charming. On her head, above an ornamental, well-oiled mass of wool, which some skilful artist had tried in vain to torture into some imitation of a European *coiffure*, was posed a white silk hat, wreathed with a wreath of the natural flowers of the stephanotis, from beneath which flowed a long veil of white net. So far all was perfect. The veil was parted in front and fell on either side, and through and under it gleamed the dark glossy shoulders and arms of the widow, the latter tipped by white gloved hands. Her bodice was of green satin, relieved by scarlet buttons and trimmings; a mauve skirt, trimmed with bows of tulle and lace, and a pair of white kid boots, which were extensively displayed, completed the widow's toilette, and ravished the eyes of all beholders.

At that sight, with the deepest gravity, and with what the French call *beaucoup d'empressement,* every male guest lifted his hat, a salute responded to by Mr. D'Orsay with an elaborateness worthy of his namesake and predecessor, the great Count. Then, with a certain air of elephantine gaiety, Simon Pety escorted the widow down the steps to the leading carriage, in which he took his place beside her to drive to the chapel; for 'tis a sensible practice of some semi-civilized and of most barbarous people, not to run any risk of the bride's escape. After the happy pair rolled carriages filled veritably to overflowing, for ebony beaux sat on the boxes and hung on behind. In one of the carriages we catch sight of two familiar faces, – no others than those of Miriam and Sarcophagus, who had received the honour of an invitation to this remarkable ceremony.

To describe the condition of Sarcophagus's mind and body would occupy a whole chapter, and need the command of language and the artistic skill of a writer of social articles in a weekly review, or of the special correspondent of a sensational newspaper. The magistrate's factotum was simply glorious in lively incoherency and blundering humour. His whole being seemed to be permeated with a sense of absurdity, and the energetic Miriam was forced to lose her temper in endeavouring to reduce him to a soberness befitting the occasion. His necktie was wriggled to one side, his hat inclined to the other. His shirt, improperly studded, yawned, and displayed a black-walnut substratum, which shocked the delicate young ladies, who were freely exhibiting thrice as much skin of the same colour at the tops of their dresses. He bowed almost to the ground, laughed idiotically, indicated to Miriam in the most candid manner that the day was coming when they together should share the glories of a similar ceremony, while at the same time, to the deep disgust of the magistrate's cook, he regarded other damsels with a broad and unequivocal approbation. Perched at length on the box of one of the carriages, he disturbed the propriety of the march by breaking out now and then into loud 'yah-yahs,' which scandalized the company. His conduct was deeply taken to heart by Mr. John Wesley Darby, a highly respectable black gentleman, butler to the Attorney-General, and

who had his own fancy for Miriam as a thrifty and promising partner for a person of indolent tendencies.

'Mister Roebuck,' he said, addressing Sarcophagus by his correct
name, 'dese presumptions are berry confusing to de ladies, inside
dis carriage, sah, – calculated to excite dere nervousness, sah.'

'Shoo!' exclaimed Sarcophagus, taking off his hat and making a
sweep therewith at the head of the speaker, which had been
projected from the window to administer the rebuke.

Mr. John Wesley Darby retired with more speed than dignity.

'Massa Sarcophagus,' cried the familiar voice of Miriam
through the other window. 'Your conduc, sah, is discomposing all
de ladies and gentlemen. On dis melumcolly occasion you better
behabe more like a gentleman, sah.'

'Miss Mirriam, your most obedient!' said Sarcophagus, kissing
his hand. 'You'm all de time de object of my most despicable
affectation, Miss Miriam.'

Miss Miriam popped in her head, feeling as badly hit as on the
other side had been the namesake of the great Methodist.

The chapel was crowded with an eager congregation which,
utterly unable to restrain its feelings without some counter-
excitement, had been whiling away the time by singing a revival
hymn, beginning thus:

Dere's a feast all ready in de palace ob de Lord,
    All laid for de marriage ob de Son;
And He send out His minister to speak de good word,
    Come and eat and be happy ebery one.
        Come and eat and be merry
    At de marriage ob de Son!
        Come and drink and be merry
    At de marriage ob de Son!
        Dere's plenty for ebery one!

In the midst of a chorus delivered from half a thousand throats,
the bride and bridegroom were seen advancing up the passage. The
song came to a sudden stop, and was followed by an impressive
silence.

The Reverend Mr. Blister was a Lancashire man, with a white
face and black hair, eyebrows and whiskers. The climate and

poverty had acted upon him with effects of form and colour quite contrary to those which it had wrought on the Intendant-General. The worthy minister was pale and careworn. Had you passed him in the street you would hardly have turned to look again upon the ordinary figure in its seedy clothes and wide-awake hat, were it not for the large lustrous eyes, – lustrous, not alone with the inner glow of an earnest soul, but with the dangerous flame of disease. He had worked long and hard in this unpromising field. How little of the sweets even of sacrifice had fallen to his lot! To have been poor, derided, sickly, would have been simply to know the life of primitive and more distinguished apostles. But to labour and see so little fruit; to sow and see such paltry harvest; to garner and thresh, and sift so little wheat; to bleed and sweat over ground so shallow, dry and graceless; – did it not need a faith more than human, and a hope almost supernal to keep this man steadily doing the daily task; – he only a hind in the Master 's field; only a clodhopper among the Master's servants! Too well he knew of what kind were the poor people with whom he had to deal. His views of the remedy for their evil condition may have been, intellectually estimated, narrow, even pitiful; but his limited range in time was compensated by far-sighted glimpses into eternity, and the mind which might have but feebly and irresolutely grasped at things seen, stretched out and up with giant comprehension to realities of things invisible. He could not but believe that for God these half-natures, these seemingly abortive souls, had some tender and loving interest. That nothing should come of such an interest he could not admit. And so he worked on, appearing to sow little but wind, believing that he should some day reap perchance of wheat or some other good grain.

Mr. Blister's extempore prayer was the commencement of the proceedings. It was homely enough, but it brought out Susan's ready tears, and evoked sympathetic sobs from susceptible ladies of various shades in the congregation. He alluded plainly to the fact that Susan was a widow, and most certainly implied by some involved expressions that both she and Mr. D'Orsay were not altogether above the necessity of mediation. That this was no error in judgment was clear from the manner in which those directly concerned accepted this oratorical rebuke. It melted their hearts – which were indeed mere spiritual jellies solvent in very slight heat.

The minister had exhorted the bride and bridegroom, and the ceremony had reached that stage when the gentleman usually fumbles in his pockets for an aureate token of constancy. The happy Pete was in the act of placing on Susan's finger a huge band of yellow metal – not hall-marked, I fear – when a loud shriek from the back of the church thrilled the excited audience to the core, and a powerful-looking young woman, whose hair no doubt would have been dishevelled if it could, strode up the passage or aisle, and snatched the precious symbol from Pete's nerveless grasp. He turned to find himself confronted by an ebonized fury. His lips moved to the words 'Miss Rosalind!' but not a sound came from them.

'What you goin' do?' cried Miss Rosalind Dallas, for it was no other. 'You imposition old hypocriss! Afta say you go marry *me*, den you go and trow y'rself 'way on dis trash!' turning a heightened shoulder, and an extravagantly distorted cheek towards Susan Sankey.

There was a loud 'Hah!' from the congregation. The minister was dumbfounded. Simon Pete, with eyes and mouth wide open, gazed astonished at the untimely apparition. Missa Sankey trembled painfully. Miss Rosalind looked from one to the other with a furious face, and spoke again, her lips almost foaming: –

'Dere! You inconsequenshious bagabones! Dere's de ring!' She threw down the bright hoop and trampled upon it. 'Pick 'im up and put 'im on now, if you please, sah! Miss Sankey, d'you know you goin' to take my leavin's wen you go take dis common plantain of a fellah? Hah! Ladies and genl'men,' facing the audience, and pointing to the abashed bridegroom, 'dis yere man promise me ober and ober again marry ME, Miss Rosalind Dallas: now he go and fix himself to dis woman! Oh, you imposing ole bagabones! oh! oh!'

And the young lady testified her anguish and her muscularity by dancing up and down with a strong pair of legs, and shuddering and screaming in a way that rent everyone's heart. The audience became fearfully and wonderfully excited. They rocked themselves to and fro, ejaculating in the sheer incoherence of emotion, 'Glory!' and 'Amen!'

'Stay, Sister Dallas,' said the minister, meekly. 'My good brethren and sisters – '

But here Miss Sankey took matters in hand, and gave the outward sign of an inward and spiritual grace. Throwing back her veil and dashing the tears from her eyes, she went and threw her arms round the neck of her delirious rival.

'Oh, Miss Dallas!' she cried, in a plaintive voice, 'don't 'ee please go to be angry. You nice young lady! – I show you sartain dis gen'leman bound to marry me. – Oh, Miss Dallas, see heah! De Lord tole me to marry Massa Dorsay: he ole man dese times, not nice young gen'leman fit for handsome young lady like you, Miss Dallas. – Oh let 'im marry me quiet, – 'cause he nebber so wicked to you as he been to me! Oh, Miss Dallas, we bo's been berry wicked, bo's him and me: now we go to make it up!' cried poor Susey, in her desperation letting the cat out of the bag: – 'he fader of my piccaninny!'

And thereupon Susan Sankey fell down in a fit. Pete stood wringing his hands in real anguish. He was getting punished. He thought at the moment, that the Lord was going to take Susey away, and leave him to the tender mercies of a muscular lunatic, whom he had by no means so badly wronged, and his heart told him he deserved the punishment. But the strange, perverse nature of her race and sex was seen in Miss Rosalind at this crisis. When she saw Miss Sankey stretched out on the ground, her comely face o'errun with tears, her eyes rolling, her teeth grinding, and her wedding finery coming to premature grief, while she moaned painfully, – the big rival felt a pang of pity. She stooped down, and picking up Susan's lighter and more flexible form, set her on her feet, at the same time giving her a shake, which brought her to in a moment. Susan thought her end was come. But the discarded damsel gently set to work to rearrange the disordered dress, and then said softly, weeping the while:

'Missa Sankey – all dis not your fault. I'm berry, berry sorry make you feel so bad. – 'Taint no use now, I guess. – Heah! Let me take de dust off dat skirt. – Take de ole man: my heart's broke. –

Simon, you best look out, I say!' And with this threat Miss Dallas rushed out of the chapel.

There was a general consternation. Susan grasped the arm of the trembling Pete in her own, as if she were afraid he would be spirited away.

'Simon Peter D'Orsay,' said the minister, in a quiet and solemn voice, and fixing on the luckless Pete those lustrous eyes, 'do you, having committed a great sin, and being now convicted of it in the sight of God and of the Church assembled in this place, hereby testify your repentance for the same, your desire to be forgiven, your intention henceforth, by God's help, to live a pure, true, and holy life with the woman the partner of your sad and sorrowful backsliding?'

'Oh, Massa Blister, I *do* feel it, dis time, sartain! By de Lord's help I'll try obercome de debbil; by His help desist unto blood. Dear friends and bredren,' cried Pete, not very loudly or confidently, as his wont was, but humbly, – 'dis yere all come ob dat old Adam. When he wax fat he kick. – I been berry wicked. I been like de raging ob de wandering stars – unstable as water, – going about like a roaring lion. Now, I tell you all, I nebber see my sins so clear afore. Here I get put to shame and suffusion of face before all dis people, lest dat I who teach oder people myself come to be a runaway. Missa Sankey and me, now we husband and wife, try to walk in de way ob de Lord. All you go and do likewise!'

'Praise de Lord,' cried the chorus, quite in earnest.

CHAPTER XXXVII

A BAD LOOK OUT

WHEN Dilloo, released from gaol and gaolbirds' company, came back to his wattled hut, it was the darkest and most dangerous moment of his life. For his own part, sullen, resentful, suspicious, – and further excited by what he had heard during his incarceration of the general movement among the Coolies, – almost ready for any desperate design – there awaited him at home a new sorrow, the hissing fuse to a great explosion in a soul too well prepared for it. Through the thin walls of his dwelling he heard moaning and weeping. Lutchmee knew that he was coming, and she had a mournful tale to tell. As he entered she rose quietly and threw her arms about his neck, and cried silently on his breast. Dark and terrible were the thoughts that drove like a whirlwind to and fro within him. He saw that she had been ill; he glanced expectantly round the hut to see if it contained something he had pictured to himself in his prison thoughts, – a pledge of hope and a dear relief to their melancholy life. No! There no coo, no cry, no little baby form.

'Lutchmee! My life, my sweet, my soul! Thy heart and mine are broken with disappointment, as the eggs of birds within a nest where lay the precious hopes of coming life! O Lutchmee! Lutchmee!'

As he sank upon the ground, his strong manly frame unnerved, and his passionate nature for the moment beaten down to a deep despair, she knelt beside him and gazed in anguish on his altered face. What could she say? How blind were her eyes to the sense of Divine o'er-looking, to the long prophetic meaning of sorrows, to the far out-springing visions of greater life, to the glorious wide allurements of an eternal country, to the promised compensations for the dreadful present, in a bright, sweet time to come! To such untutored hearts so limited in range of knowledge and of fancy, what is there in the Beyond, but that vague terror so cunningly expressed? –

> 'To die – to sleep; –
> To sleep! Perchance to dream; ay, there's the rub!
> For in that sleep of death what dreams may come,
> When we have shuffled off this mortal coil ...'

O God! O Heaven! What means this veil which Thou hast drawn over these childlike natures, so crude in idea, so straitened in thought, so weakly cunning in the will of wickedness, so tender, timid, trustful, human, so capable of large and holy love, and yet so little removed from lively and sagacious brutes! Why dost Thou separate these simple ones from spiritual lights and better insights into Thee?

'Dilloo!' cried Lutchmee, nerving herself to try and comfort him, 'Dilloo! Do not mind this. Is it not better that it should be as it is, than to have to bear the evils that will come, knowing that another helpless one must share them?'

She had been thinking over to herself with wifely forethought, what she should say at this painful meeting, and this reference to their hopelessness had struck her as the most skilful way to meet and check his grief.

But Dilloo heaved a great sigh, struggled a moment with his feelings, mastered them, rose from the ground gloomy and stern, and called for a cup of water. His wife went to the corner, and filling the cup at the jar handed it to him. He moistened his lips with it, and then dashed it to pieces against the door-post of the hut.

'I swear,' he said, 'by the life that gave me life, and by my guardian spirits, and by Siva the great Destroyer, and by all the powers of earth, and sea, and sky, that I will live only to revenge myself on those who have done us wrong, on the cursed tyrants who here enslave and torment us; and by day and night, in all seasons, at every time and place, without fear or stay, I, Dilloo, will give myself to work only for their destruction, worry, and death!'

This outburst seemed to relieve him, while Lutchmee listened to it with a heavy heart. Becoming more calm he asked her to relate to him what had passed in his absence. It was nothing very extraordinary. Lutchmee had been sent to the hospital, at Craig's request; but, at Chester's instance, Ramdoolah was called in almost immediately, and before the doctor had paid a visit, to give her opinion in regard to the correctness of the younger woman's excuse to be relieved from work. The verdict was, of course, unfavourable. Lutchmee was ordered to join a bush-cutting gang at the 'back,' and Hunoomaun, although he was not in charge, took pains to secure that she should be forced to work. Craig only found all this out the second day. Having met the doctor and asked him about the woman, he was surprised to find that she had not been one of his patients, and soon discovered the truth. It was too late, however. On the evening of the second day she was taken ill and sent to the hospital, and after passing through great peril, once more looked sadly upon a little form which had never breathed the breath of life.

Craig's deep Scotch nature was roused by this event as it had never been before. When he met the other overseers at supper his silent gloom excited the notice of his mates. But Drummond was there, and Drummond had an interesting narrative to tell, for it was the evening of the very day when the unlucky Portuguese had received the reward of his foolish sympathies.

There is many a philanthropist in England whose head and back are only kept safe by the strong shield of a strong justice. The envious and malicious devilry that would, if it dared, manifest itself in assaults and Circassian forays upon goodness, finds its outlet in brutalities of the pen, in a system of secret literary Obe, and in night attacks of hungry garroters who live by choking, plundering and mauling whatever is more reputable or more worthy than themselves. It is surprising that it should be possible for such birds of prey to thrive among the eagles of higher journalism, to be recognised by them, or to be patroned by any who regard the decencies of life. To change the figure, how much of hateful venom do these poisonous fungi mingle in and among the sweet and healthy growths of our modern newspaper literature! –

'Gentlemen,' said Drummond, after he had narrated the events of the day, animadverted on the conduct of the Governor, and contemptuously wished the Portuguese in Hades, 'there cannot be any doubt that we are all in a position of great danger, and we must be prepared to take our part in suppressing any attempt at a rising if it should happen, which I think is very likely. No one can tell when or where it may begin. Among our own Coolies here there are and have been symptoms of discontent. I should think, from what you tell me, Chester, that that man Dilloo has been concerned in the memorial business.' Drummond here looked somewhat significantly at Craig, who preserved a stern and darkened front. 'Now he will be out of gaol and back here before long, and will require to be carefully watched. He is the smartest man by a long way in our Negro-yard, unless that driver Hunoomaun can beat him.'

'He can beat him, sir, in cunning as well as in strength, I should say,' said Chester.

'I have no doubt about the cunning,' replied Drummond; 'but I trust none of these people. You should keep your eye on every one of them, but especially on Dilloo.'

'Do you think, Mr. Drummond,' said Craig, obtusely, for he ought to have seen that the manager was then in no temper to be argued with on that subject, 'that Dilloo would be really so bad if he were treated with a little more confidence? You remember how well he behaved that time when we arrested Chin-a-foo?'

Drummond looked uneasily at Craig. The reference to the obligation under which Dilloo had laid the manager was more irritating than sedative, yet being an honourable man as the world goes, it touched him for the moment: he instantly recovered.

'Confound it, Craig,' cried the manager, 'is it a time to be soft-hearted when men want to cut your throat? If Dilloo *did* once behave well, have I not tried to pay him for it, and is it not the rascal's own stubbornness and love of mischief which has stood in his way and brought him to grief? Have you heard any of Chester's reports about him? The driver Hunoomaun accuses him of conspiring with a lot of men on this very estate; and, God knows, we may be honey-combed here with secret rebellion.'

'I have not heard anything from Mr. Chester, sir,' replied Craig. 'The man has always seemed to me quietly disposed and ready enough to work.'

'Don't trouble yourself about him,' replied Drummond. 'He may give you reason to be sorry for him as soon as he gets home again.'

'He very likely will,' said Craig, drily. 'The news he will hear of his wife on his return will not tend to soften his heart towards Mr. Chester, or Hunoomaun either; and I admit, if he is at all desperate, he may try to have it out with one of them.'

'What do you mean?' said Chester, pale with mingled fear and anger. 'I had nothing to do with it.'

'Perhaps not,' replied Craig: 'I make no charge. But Dilloo is a Hindoo, and, as I daresay you know, a strong and daring one. (Chester grew scarlet at this chance shot.) I am afraid, when he comes to find out what has happened to his wife, and that it was you who sent her out of hospital, he will draw his own conclusions.'

'D——— you, sir!' cried Mr. Chester, in a rage. 'You will have to explain this——— '

'Stop, gentlemen!' cried Drummond, in a thundering voice. 'I'll have no quarrelling here. Whoever quarrels now, will have to settle with me; and in the present state of things, I'll shoot the first man that offers to fight. Bottle up your rage, Chester: Craig is only a boy. And you, Craig, – why do you mix yourself up with the nonsensical complaints of these wretched people? We must all stick together, man, and well for us if we get off with our lives. There is the *Tadja* coming on. We cannot stop it; and, depend upon it, there will be the devil to pay.'

Drummond went further. He had taken the precaution, before leaving town, to supply himself with revolvers, foreseeing that the rising demand for them would soon completely clear the market; and he distributed to each overseer a six-shooter, and a box of ammunition.

'Don't be showing these things about,' he said. 'Give no cause to the Indians to suspect that we know or fear anything; but keep your eyes open, and report everything to me. And it will be well for two of you to patrol the Negro-yard every night, before you turn in. Crampton, you will arrange for that.'

The manager's anxiety about the approach of the *Tadja* festival was not unfounded. Corresponding to the Mohammedan Feast of the Mohurrun, in India, it is nevertheless but a hybrid and foreign imitation of it. All the Coolies, of whatever denomination, join in celebrating it, as a sort of holiday, or rather of carnival. In the quietest times it awakens the anxiety of the Executive and of the Estate Managers; because on that day feuds that have arisen at former periods between the Coolies of different estates are apt to be fought out, and not infrequently to fatal extremities. In one well-known case, where the Coolies of three estates fought a sort of pitched battle with those of three others, piles of broken bricks were prepared as ammunition; and not content with this, or with their favourite weapons the *hackia* sticks, the death of two persons and wounding of others by gun-shot, proved that the Indians were ready to resort to the direst weapons in these encounters. At the present moment, when the Coolies were so agitated, the opportunities afforded by such a carnival could scarcely be regarded by any one without apprehension.

In Drummond's existing frame of mind, feeling as he did most genuinely that the Colony might be on the brink of a serious rebellion, there was no room for the play either of justice or generosity. The passionate excitement of the white community had overpowered and carried along with it even his usually sober judgment. So long as things go smoothly in such societies as that of Demerara or Mauritius or Barbadoes, and the subject class remains submissive to its fate or fortune (whichever you choose to call it), the masters of the situation can feel that they are working out a providential dispensation, and consider themselves free to be sometimes kindly, perhaps even generous, and now and then to be just. But when the real instability of their relations with the vast majority becomes too manifest, and the quiet assumptions and continued wrongs of years reach a crisis when it looks as if that majority intended to try and balance the long account, the coolest and ablest man finds it impossible to resist the claims of self-preservation or the promptings of avarice. Such men at such times seem to entertain an honest opinion that kindness is weakness, that to deny and resist every demand of the majority is policy, and that any one who is not a thorough partisan is the worst of enemies. The manager of Belle Susanne was a man who took in the whole position with a comprehensive glance, and saw that to save the planting interest from at least a severe fall, there must be no blenching on the part of any individual. One man, known to be of their side, making any admissions of injustice, owning to any just grounds for Coolie discontent, might do incalculable mischief to their cause, especially with that open-eared, open-mouthed British public, with its 'infernal' Anti-slavery and Aborigines Protection Societies, and all the machinery of philanthropic agitation. The astute manager had taken care quietly to impress this upon the leading men in Georgetown. He insisted on the necessity of keeping up an angry excitement among the whites, and of alarming any waverers into silence. That on his own estate an overseer like Craig should subject safety to sentiment, was no more likely to be permitted by Drummond than such folly would be allowed to operate on public opinion in foreign affairs by the practical-minded, rate-paying Briton.

The manager was very angry with Craig. His irritation was the greater because he liked the youth. He would gladly have helped him on, that is in any path consistent with his own ideas. You very rarely see a man who can estimate at its right value a higher walk than his own; but still more rare, if not impossible, is it to find one who would be generous enough to aid another in pursuing aims dictated by higher and purer principles than those of the life he himself leads. Drummond, a man of action and business, looked upon generosity as 'sentiment.' Such men are the blindest and most grovelling of utilitarians. And just now they are threatening to rule the world!

CHAPTER XXXVIII

'TIS LOVE THAT FINDS THE WAY

CRAIG, turning over in his steady Scotch head all the circumstances as he left the manager's house after supper, saw that his
position was becoming uncomfortable, perhaps dangerous.
Drummond's tone, his unwonted excitement, his unusually candid cynicism, aroused unpleasant thoughts in the young overseer's
placid and inexperienced mind. If the manager of Belle Susanne
were losing his self-command, what were the wilder and weaker
spirits to be expected to do? As to Chester, Craig puzzled himself
to think what special motive the half-breed could have had to
injure Lutchmee or Dilloo. Yet he could not shake off the belief
that Chester had intentionally forced Lutchmee out to work,
knowing that she was unfit for it. Dilloo's former collision with the
overseer was of course unknown to the young Scotchman, though
he had inadvertently in the conversation at the supper table struck
Chester so squarely. The gratitude Craig cherished towards
Lutchmee for her kindly nursing made him feel, now that matters
were so evidently coming to a crisis both in the Colony and on the
estate, under the deeper obligation to befriend her. As he thought
over all the circumstances, and considered the probability that
Dilloo would take some dangerous step, and recalled
Drummond's significant warning, his decided mind framed more
definite resolutions. Come what would, he said to himself, he
would not desert the poor woman: she had saved his life, he would
try to be of use to her. Thus she grew into his thoughts; first as a
subject of anxiety, then as an object of sympathy. And so the gradual familiarizing of her *eidolon* in his mind, at that time not over-
occupied or stimulated by other interesting things, insensibly
developed feelings of affectionate interest in her, which, now that
he had passed the Rubicon of race-repugnancy, had in them no

unpleasant or unnatural elements. That she was as yet a mere child to him was, as yet, his safety; but a woman who is a child may become to a simple-hearted man the very devil.

It was not Chester's cue to take up openly with Craig the quarrel begun at the supper-table. The Scotchman for his part was quite indifferent about it; resting simply on his great strength and superior *morale*. The Barbadian resolved to bide his time, and therefore hid his resentment; but this was none the less deep and real. He watched Craig that evening as, after leaving the manager's house, he walked to the hospital to inquire about Lutchmee. 'Look there!' said he to Martinho and Crampton. 'He is going to see about that woman. Poor fellow: do you know I think he is quite infatuated about her! What a pity! For I like Craig; he is a fine young man.'

Your Barbadian or half-negro, when he is bad, is as dangerous and as devilish as Lucifer.

At the same time that he spoke thus he was thinking to himself, 'Aha, you dirty Scotchman: you will soon put yourself in a false position if you go on in this way! If *you* don't, I will do it for you.'

So Chester went to look up Hunoomaun, and primed him to watch, with Ramdoolah's assistance, both Craig and Lutchmee. On his part, Craig, having seen the nurse and made his inquiry, turned back to the manager's house, and slipped up to the large pantry in the back-building, where he found Nina superintending the wash-up after the evening meal. Nina was very partial to the young over-seer, and readily stept out into the garden at his whispered request.

He told her what had happened to Lutchmee, and of the anxiety he felt about her. He had no need to explain how difficult it would be to do anything for the poor young wife, for Nina's quick apprehension and her familiarity with Drummond's humours enabled her instantly to appreciate the situation.

'Take care, Massa Craig,' she said, earnestly. 'He's in a terrible rage, I tell you. He told Mr. Crampton after you went away from tea that you were a fool and an idiot, and that if he found you play-ing into the Coolies' hands he would have you punished. You don't know how these men lose their heads when they feel danger. Then there's Chester: I always watch him. He hates you, and so does Martinho. I heard them saying to one another that you must be got out of the way.'

Craig drew his lips tightly together and could scarcely breathe. Must he face three angry and perhaps desperate men to do a kind deed? Was he not free to be generous or just? Should he be driven away by fear of such people? All his slow strong nature rose against it.

'Nina,' he said, 'were it not for this poor woman I think I would go away. I hate the service. But I am determined not to be bullied out of my gratitude. Then there are other reasons why I do not wish to leave just now' – he stopped.

Nina was smiling in the dark, and he could not see it.

'Pr'aps,' she said, gently, 'if you go over some time and see Miss Marston, she's a very nice young lady, pr'aps she would help you to do something for Lutchmee.'

'Ha! Nina,' cried the overseer, 'well thought of! A woman's wit,' he continued, 'is always the best. She may be able to get her father to do something for the poor woman.'

Craig's simplicity came out here very ostensibly. It was scarcely to be expected that the magistrate would undertake a voluntary interference in the management of Drummond's estate. His position as a justice made that impossible. However, for the moment the idea buoyed up Craig's mind, which was sadly depressed. His straightforward nature was quite embarrassed when he found it necessary, for the sake of the one in whom he was interested, to pursue a cautious and disingenuous policy. Had his own interests alone been in the balance he would have been suicidally open and decided. Men of his character, when they try to carry out a policy of cunning, often come to disaster through their incompetency to go on consistently with the *rôle*. But, in addition to the hopeful gleam which Nina's hint had thrown across his mind, there was another latent pleasure in the idea of seeing the young lady, and of making her a confidante in his present embarrassment. He yearned for sympathy, such sympathy as he had been used to receive from his mother.

Craig could hardly have long remained unsusceptible to Miss Marston's charms, even had he never seen them except on Sunday at church. But it had been managed in some mysterious way that he should be twice asked to the magistrate's house, and twice treated to a most delightful *tête-à-tête* with the young lady. The truth was that Miss Bella had begun to take an interest in the Coolie people, because she had an interest in Craig. She plied Craig with questions about his work and the estate on which he laboured, and being ready to admire anything he said and did, she specially admired the justice and shrewdness of his remarks on the relations between the masters and their servants. These she repeated to her father, who affected to contemn them, though in reality they created a deep impression upon him. Moreover he liked the young overseer the better for separating himself from the low and sordid views which were so evidently entertained by overseers and managers in general. He was, however, too prudent to express any opinion either to his daughter or to the young man, or to Drummond, for he had a suspicion that the feeling among the whites was bringing them to the eve of a period of perilous excitement. Out of this brief intercourse linked on to that which had before taken place, there had grown up in Craig's mind a regard for the young lady, which his practical caution restricted to that stage of feeling, and allowed to rise no higher. He had certainly not as yet received much obvious encouragement to let his feelings run up to blood heat. Bella Marston's fine nature was under admirable control.

The day after the conversation we have detailed happened to be Sunday, and Craig sat in the church watching the handsome face of the magistrate's daughter with a blunt directness which brought a flush to her cheeks. He was, however, so absorbed in his purpose as to be unconscious of his rudeness.

Miss Bella gave him her hand after church with an air of delicate reserve, meant doubtless to be taken as a rebuke, but the pre-occupied young Scotchman coolly overlooked the hint. The magistrate was busy talking with one or two managers about the state of affairs, and a reported rising on the Arabian coast, so that Craig was free to saunter homewards with Miss Bella, a liberty he had never before ventured to take. Certainly it was not resented by the young lady.

'Miss Marston,' said the young Scotchman, 'I know you take some interest in Lutchmee. You remember I met you once at her house.'

Bella remembered only too perfectly, and recalled it blushingly.

'Well,' he went on, 'she has been very ill and very unhappy. Her husband is still in gaol, she is among total strangers, and if I might dare to mention it to one in your position, I think it is likely she is an object of some persecution from one or two of the overseers. I don't say anything against them; they have to deal with very cunning and unscrupulous work-people, and may believe that this poor woman is as bad as others, though I am convinced she is a good and worthy creature. If I did not think so,' said Craig, turning and fixing his fine grey eyes on those of his companion, 'I should not ask you to interest yourself about her.'

The young gentleman was improving, Bella thought. This compliment from so matter-of-fact a person was extra complimentary.

'What I have seen of her,' she said, warmly, 'has given me a very good opinion of her. I should like to see her removed from her present position; she is evidently quite unfitted for it.'

'I am glad to hear you say that,' exclaimed Craig, 'because I feel the same. She is far above the place. But I don't see how she can be rescued. Her husband is engaged to Mr. Drummond, who is not likely to let him off. Besides, he thinks the man, from real or fancied wrong, is inclined to be insubordinate, if not rebellious. The manager would scarcely listen to a word in his favour. Lutchmee is in the hospital, and of course anything I may do will be looked upon in the present state of affairs with suspicion; so,' said Craig, hesitating, but of course putting the thing with the most straightforward bluntness, 'so I – I thought I would ask you, as a woman, what you thought you could do, or if you could give me some advice as to what I should do for the poor girl. You know I owe her so much for her attention to me while I was ill.'

Now you, knowing Miss Marston's feelings about the intimacy between Lutchmee and Craig, will perceive that his candid question was of a kind to embarrass her. Lutchmee was all very well as an abstract object of compassion; but as a subject of interest to a young man like Craig, we may pardon Miss Bella if she looked upon the Coolie woman rather coldly. Yet on the other hand, liking Craig, anything that was interesting to him might be expected to interest this young lady. Between a nascent jealousy and an actual sympathy, however, there cannot be a very long struggle in a good heart. And her heart was a sound one. Miss Marston appreciated the overseer's manly candour, and her soul went with him in his self-imposed mission of charity.

'I think,' she said, quickly, 'it will be better for us not to talk about this any more, because I see papa is coming; and, as he is very friendly with Mr. Drummond, he might not care to hear about it. (Sweet opportunity to create a little inner circle of confidence with her companion!) I will come over and visit Lutchmee, and see what can be done for her. It is very kind of you, Mr. Craig, to trust me in a matter of this sort, for I am both young and inexperienced.'

'A woman's wit, my mother used to say, Miss Marston, was worth two men's wisdom.'

'But I am scarcely a women yet,' said Bella, blushing, 'even were that bold saying granted. However, I will do my best. Here is papa!'

The magistrate gave his hand to the young overseer, and probably excited by the news he had heard, and being chronically *ennuyé* on Sundays, he, to Craig's surprise, as well as to that of the young lady, invited him to go home with them to dinner. Though no further opportunity offered itself to resume this conversation, Craig felt a sort of satisfaction in Bella's presence, while her desire to please him increased with the taste of his company. The combined shrewdness and simplicity of his talk received a certain fascination from the natural gentleness, the tenderness of his manner. Mr. Marston, when the overseer had taken leave of them, was perilously frank in his approval of the young man's ability and modesty.

Thus it was that Miss Marston, on Monday morning, had taken Sarcophagus and gone over to the Belle Susanne hospital before breakfast; and Lutchmee, sitting in the women's verandah, was cheered by a musical voice, and a sweet, bright smile, and, what was an absolute absurdity for a patient in an estate hospital, with a cup full of delicious jelly.

Of course such a visit as that could not have occurred without being reported to Drummond's ears, even had it not met his eyes. He was now ceaselessly vigilant, and watched every part of the estate for indications of any threatening movement. Seeing Miss Marston and his old friend Sarcophagus enter the compound of the hospital, he followed them, and broke in upon Miss Marston's interview with the Coolie woman.

Fortunately the young lady, without any dishonourable prompting from Craig, had been quick to perceive the part she had to play, and she answered the somewhat sinister greeting of the manager by a frank smile.

'Miss Marston! You here? And without notice, miss? What can have so interested the belle of Demerara as to bring her into these poor premises?'

'Two things. One was to visit this poor woman, who I heard was ill.'

'How did such a rumour reach the ears of Miss Marston?'

'Oh, very easily!' with a slight blush. 'Papa asked Mr. Craig to come home to dinner with us yesterday, and he happened to mention her as the woman I had seen here once or twice before and taken an interest in. She seems really very ill and downcast.'

Drummond, glancing down at the Coolie, thought so too. With instinctive kindness he kneeled on one knee, and raising Lutchmee with one strong arm, with the hand of the other arranged her pillows in a more easy position. The woman shuddered, and turned her face away from him. His quick eye saw it, and it hardened his heart more than ever. He stood up with an altered manner.

'It is very kind of you indeed, Miss Bella, to come and look after her. But she is well taken care of here. And I can assure you your visit will be likely to be misunderstood. In the excited state of the Indians just now, it is almost dangerous for you to go about.'

Miss Marston felt that these words were very rude, and that they were intended to be rude, and to act as a veto upon any further interference with Lutchmee. But the deep reasons she had for pleasing Craig, and her own genuine and strong character, at once suggested to her a spirited reply.

'I am not the least afraid of the Coolies, Mr. Drummond,' she said, 'and I have a real interest in this poor woman. Do I understand you to say distinctly that you object to my showing any kindness to her?'

'Oh not at all,' said Drummond, biting his lip. 'My apprehensions on your behalf alone led me to speak as I did. It is the open attention which I think is likely to be misconstrued.'

'Well, Mr. Drummond, I will not intrude again while she is in hospital. But you will not mind her coming over to see me when she is better?'

Drummond assented to this with a bad grace, and Miss Bella took her leave. The manager was vexed at the whole affair, and more and more annoyed with Craig, whom he guessed to be at the bottom of this 'interference.' It was a reflection on himself to suppose that any of his Coolies wanted looking after by Miss Marston. But matters were not ripe for decided steps, and he kept his own counsel.

CHAPTER XXXIX

KNIGHT AND LADY

DILLOO had not been at home a week when, one afternoon, between four and five o'clock, Miss Marston arrived at the hut. Behind her the versatile Sarcophagus carried a basket of good things, few of which perhaps the Indian woman would care to eat. Lutchmee was sitting outside the house on the raised clay-floor, and when she saw Miss Marston, rose and received her with simple and graceful courtesy. The English girl's pleasant manner during her visit to the hospital had quite won the Indian woman's heart. In truth, her jealousy, such as it was, had been rather instinctive than moral. No more malevolent desire had crossed her thoughts than that of monopolising Craig's interest in herself. The refinements of Platonic affection or the temptations of lawless love were alike unknown to her. She was too child-hearted, too devoted to her husband, to give her fancies play in forbidden directions.

'Well, Lutchmee,' said Miss Bella, 'are you better now?'

'Iss, lady: well, well. Man come back too.'

She pointed inside the door, where Dilloo, sitting on a low stool, was engaged in cutting up some brilliant-looking papers.

'Why!' exclaimed Miss Marston, startled by the reminder, 'you are getting ready for the *Tadja!* I had forgotten it came so soon.'

Dilloo rose to his feet, and for the first time gazed upon the handsome young lady who stood there brightening the outlook from his door. She all fair and 'witching, and gay with the excitement of a kindly purpose, with the opaline lights through her sunshade playing around her: he in the shadow of his hut, darkly meditating on his wrongs, and, in rank luxuriance of passion, thinking of revenge.

'Iss,' said he, nodding his head moodily: '*Tadja* come!'

His fine form, naked from the waist upward, stretched and expanded, and his eyes glowed in the shadow. Even Miss Marston, who was an inexperienced observer, detected something sinister in his manner, which sent a slight thrill of alarm through her. But she was bold, and she held out her hand.

'Dilloo,' she said, not condescending to baby-English, 'I made Lutchmee's acquaintance when you were – were away from home. I am so sorry you have been so unfortunate, I feel so sorry too for poor Lutchmee. I hope there has been no mistake, and that you have not been punished when you did not deserve it.'

'Um!' said Dilloo, omitting to take the proffered hand, but making a low salaam. 'Mahitee send Dilloo prison. Dilloo good man. Mahitee punis Dilloo, Dilloo do no bad ting. *Tadja* come!'

If Bella could have misunderstood his language, she could not mistake his manner. Dilloo was not aware at the moment to whom he was addressing himself. Lutchmee instantly spoke in their own language.

'Oh, Dilloo!' she said, 'be not rude to the beautiful white lady. She is herself the daughter of the magistrate.'

The Hindoo started, and shot an angry glance at his wife.

'Do you tell me that!' he said, between his teeth. 'False woman, would you betray me to mine enemies? What does she want with us?'

Thus small injustice brought large suspicion, and suspicion ran to rage, and rage brought blindness to everything but the fell purpose of revenge; and in that absorbing aim, gentleness, goodness, love of wife, and manly courtesy, and all other graces, shrank back chilled and nerveless. How venomous and bitter are the fruits of rank iniquity!

But in a moment Lutchmee's native nobleness came out. Overlooking Dilloo's rough reproach, she rose, and after a brave, sorrowful look into his uneasy eyes, she took the still outstretched hand of the beautiful girl, and after holding it to her own bosom, laid hold also of the unwilling hand of Dilloo, and with a graceful gesture put them together.

'Dilloo,' she said, softly, 'thou art not just to thy wife, and thou art angry with thy wife's benefactress. Though this lady may be the daughter of Magistrate Sahib, who has done you so much wrong, she is not a party to it. Know that she came to visit me when I was sick, and she brings me now some generous gifts. Let one kind to me be treated by you with a grateful respect.'

Dilloo glanced doubtfully at his wife and at the young girl, and it was plain a strong struggle was going on within him; but taking away his hand, he walked out of the hut, and throwing a scowl at the grinning Sarcophagus, rapidly made off. Lutchmee hastened to offer excuses for her husband, and to try and remove from Miss Marston's mind any unpleasant feeling.

Bella Marston, of course, had not understood the conversation that passed between husband and wife, but she had divined in their tone and gestures enough to disquiet her. She sat down, however, beside the Indian woman, and with wonderful patience and skill gradually drew from her the whole story of her life, and especially of the mishaps of the unlucky pair at Belle Susanne. As she listened to the frankly-expressed complaints and sorrowful experiences of the Indian woman, the English girl's heart gave way to new sympathies, and her mind expanded to new ideas. There was a touch of compunction in her soul when she remembered how much of lazy life she had led, incredulous of these wrongs which she now began to perceive might be everywhere around her. In this way does not every generous and noble soul some day wake up to unacknowledged evils? Putting together Craig's disclosures about the management of the Indians with Lutchmee's simple story, the quick-witted young lady, for her own part, was not long in coming to an opinion. That facility is a privilege of her sex. It is true – and not astonishing, having regard to the methods of feminine education in vogue just now, and, with such monstrous injustice on the part of the stronger sex, permitted to go on unremedied – that to Miss Marston the effort of working out for herself the true meaning and bearings of all she had heard was rather confusing; but her mind was a vigorous one, if badly disciplined; and she had the aid of a pure, just nature, and of feminine wit. Her sympathies naturally went with the poor woman who, with infinite delicacy, had told a tale suggestive of evils, from which the ingenuous soul of her hearer started back in horror. Were such things going on around her, and was her father, as the Indian woman had implied, a part and parcel of the system by which those evils were sustained? Troubled by such thoughts, she took leave, enjoining upon Lutchmee if she should ever be in need of a friend, as in truth, from Dilloo's strange manner, seemed to be a thing that might well happen, she should come to the magistrate's and ask for Miss Marston.

'Sarcophagus,' said the young lady, pausing a few feet from the hut, 'there is a short way home from here, is there not, across Hofman's Lust?'

'Dere's a short way, Missa Bella, round by de cane-plot, all across de next dam, down along de dam to anoder dam, den up dat dam on de one side, and turn straight to de left, ober a lillie bridge and up anoder dam, and den round by Joel Jackson's, and troo Hofman Lust, ober two dams, and cross de bridge ob de big canal, den right along——'

'Stop, stop!' cried Miss Marston. 'Where is all this going to end? No matter: we will try that way for a change.'

'Oh, Missa Bella,' cried Sarcophagus, earnestly, 'do go round de straight way by de road! Jest about dis time all de Coolie come along de dams from dere work. Nebber do for young lady to go 'long dat way.'

Miss Bella reflected only an instant and came to a decision. If all the gangs were on their way home, might not all the overseers be upon the same track? There was a good half-mile of walking in Belle Susanne. They could (that is they would) take it leisurely. This was pure human nature. She had not seen Craig for so long.

Sarcophagus piloted the way. Presently, along the dam, came slowly dropping a few labourers, covered, on bare legs and arms, with dusty tokens of dusty toil. Some carried their hoes on their shoulders, some swung their cutlasses in their hands. They stopped and looked at the black and his fair mistress; and Sarcophagus felt a creeping in his flesh as he bethought him that these ill-conditioned people were armed, and, if they meant mischief, could do it. Let us not acquit these lowering Indians of evil thoughts. If they turned and gazed somewhat rudely at the graceful figure and proud bearing of the English girl, they had such wild wishes as come out of the bottomless depths of evil in uncultured natures. Bella did not like to find them lingering to watch her, and as she saw greater numbers approaching, began to wish she had gone 'round the straight way.' Sarcophagus being rather flurried missed a narrow, weed-covered crossing over the estate canal, and went on up the wrong side of it. The number of passing Coolies increased, and a small crowd of them, knowing that the path led nowhere but to the back of the estate, stopped to permit them to approach, and looked at them curiously. Some stood in the way, and when Sarcophagus, urged on by the boldness of terror, tried to pass them, they managed to hinder him without any violence.

The place where the young lady was thus checked was not a favourable one for escape.

On the left was a canal about twelve feet in breadth; on the right a square, which ought to have been filled with young sugar plants or well-hoed rows of hills, but was overrun with a thick fallow growth of bush of surprising height and closeness. Bella looked to right and left and onward, and could see no hope of succour if these sullen-looking people were really bent on mischief.

'Let pass!' cried Sarcophagus, brandishing his arm in desperation. 'Dis Miss Marston, magistrate's daughter.'

A quick-witted Coolie instantly caught the meaning of the latter part of the Negro's speech.

'The daughter of the Mahitee!' went round the circle in a moment, and angry glances were thrown at Bella.

'Oh, you idiot!' she cried to Sarcophagus; and the words were scarcely out of her mouth when the Negro was seized by three or four Coolies, who pinioned his arms: whereat Sarcophagus opened his vast mouth and gave forth a yell so mighty and so far-reaching that his astounded captors let him go. Almost at the same instant a lithe Coolie dashed out of the bush on the right, pushed through the group with powerful shoulders, and uttering a few low, angry words gave a sweep of his arm. It was Dilloo. Without a word the Coolies dispersed into the bush, and Dilloo, pointing up the dam, made a low salaam, and simply saying, 'Massa Craig,' leaped after his comrades, and vanished from sight.

Miss Bella, glancing along the dam, saw about half a mile off a white man on a mule, which he was urging onward at its best speed. In a few minutes he had come up.

'Miss Marston!' exclaimed Craig, jumping, all warm and breathless, off his mule. 'Pray what are you doing here, and in such times as these? You are quite pale. What has happened, and what were all those Indians doing around you?'

'Don't be alarmed, Mr. Craig,' said Miss Marston, trying to recover herself, but evidently much agitated. 'Really it was nothing, I suppose: but so many of them around us rather frightened me.'

'Dey already commence to kill me, sah!' said Sarcophagus: 'only I trow dem all off and yell out.'

'Ah, that was the shout I heard! You seem to have routed them completely. Take my arm, Miss Marston: you are faint. Sarcophagus, you can look after the mule.'

Craig, supporting Miss Marston, felt all the pleasure of a *preux chevalier* who had released his dame, and she all the bliss of rescued lady-lorn leaning on the arm of her deliverer. She soon recovered from her agitation, and then disengaged herself, for, pleasant as it was to be so near him, she had never given the overseer the privilege of thus supporting her, and she felt some bashfulness about parading with him in that position, though there was no one by to watch them. Craig, for his part, now that the excitement was over, looked pale and *distrait*. His talk was reserved, and, in truth, almost monosyllabic, so that by the time the young couple had arrived at the magistrate's house they had reduced themselves to a meditative silence. Miss Bella was mortified at Craig's coolness, and he, on his part, was agitated by conflicting thoughts.

What a soothing charm was there about this fair girl at his side, who looked at him so kindly and spoke in a voice so thrilling and so sweet! Under that sunny ray his soul warmed and expanded, but still could at first only raise its face bashfully toward the inspiring glow.

They paused at the foot of the steps of Mr. Marston's house. It then for the first time flashed across the young lady's mind that they had not considered what course they should take in regard to the incident of the afternoon.

'Pray come in and see papa about it,' she said to the young overseer; who straightway felt that it was an imperative duty to see the magistrate.

That worthy was much alarmed and annoyed by their story. It showed a more mutinous spirit among the Coolies than he had suspected, and it struck him as a very absurd position for his daughter, who really had a difficulty in accounting to him how she came to be there. A sharp-eyed mother would have accounted for it in a moment, – would have read the riddle in the blooming face.

'You should have asked the girl to come over here, if you wished to do her a kindness,' said he. 'If Drummond hears of it he will be very angry. He is bad enough as it is————'

He stopped. It had just occurred to him that he was speaking of Craig's employer, and, to the magistrate, Craig was only a patronised acquaintance. Mr. Marston bit his lip and looked more put-out than ever.

'Papa, you don't know what I have heard,' said Miss Marston, with animation. 'That poor Lutchmee has been persecuted most shockingly. And,' she added, bravely, 'I don't think, papa, that you ought to have convicted her husband. It was all a mistake, and the overseer told you lies about him.'

The awkwardness which these straightforward, impulsive people introduce into life, society, and politics! The insanity of ignoring the *finesse* of life, the stupidity of unreserve! Do not such people confound the counsel of the wise, and mortify sober and sedate judgments? What is a Dutch brick front with all its gravity before a cannon and a cannon-ball? And what is a most steady brickfaced Foreign Secretary, for instance, before one of your terrible eighty-ton political popular-movement guns with an impact of its shot to the tune of several hundred tons?

Marston looked at his daughter, aghast at her boldness, and scarce knew how to treat it in the circumstances. He was not going to argue with her the question of his own misjudgments and of an overseer's criminality, before another overseer, of whom, by the way, he only knew enough to feel a slight respect for him.

But the young people were both of them too straightforward for the elder. Said Craig: –

'I fear, Mr. Marston, it is true that Lutchmee has been a victim of unfair treatment. I have reason to believe that Chester and Hunoomaun, a Hindoo driver, are in a conspiracy to do her and her husband injury. Dilloo's conviction appears to have been obtained by misinforming you. Chester is a scoundrel!'

Horace was not more startled by that peal of thunder from the sunny sky, than were the magistrate and his daughter at the fierceness with which the Scotchman intensified this last expression.

'Hum!' said the magistrate, with increased vexation, as he jumped up, rubbed his hair with one hand and moved about restlessly. 'Mr. Craig, Mr. Craig!' he said, assuming a severe tone, 'do you know, sir, that it is very improper for you to speak to me in my peculiar position in that way? Here, you, – both of you' – Bella's heart leaped: it was the first time they had ever been so nearly associated – 'come and tell me that I have been the means of doing a man an injustice; and further, you, Mr. Craig, speak of one of your colleagues in a way which is more than reprehensible, sir: it is almost criminal – unless – unless, indeed,' added the magistrate, tempering his rebuke a bit, 'you have the clearest evidence, the very clearest evidence, Mr. Craig.'

'I am quite satisfied of it, Mr. Marston,' replied Craig, 'not that I have enough evidence, perhaps, to commit him in a court of justice; but I think, if we were alone, I could convince you in a short time that Dilloo has suffered from a wicked conspiracy.'

'But, good heavens, man!' cried the worried magistrate, 'don't you see that this is exactly what I ought not to listen to? I am the magistrate of the district: how can I hear from my daughter and you charges against people who are within my jurisdiction?'

'Well, papa,' retorted Miss Bella, ' you know Mr. Drummond has often come here and told you stories about his Coolies before you have gone to try their cases.'

Mr. Marston looked almost furiously at the daring young lady: and then, seeing how perfectly sweet and ingenuous was the air with which she received his glances, and in the bottom of his heart feeling that she was a sort of outside conscience to him, and not to be controverted, he shot a look at Craig, whose face held no riddles, and afterwards with a calmer aspect sat down.

'It is impossible to argue with young people,' he said, apologetically, to ease off his capitulation. 'But I thought, Mr. Craig, you were a practical Scotchman, and not given to romancing about people's wrongs. Now tell me what is this all about? And remember that I reserve the right of using any information you may impart to me.'

Thus it was that to Mr. Marston was gradually unfolded a story which did not so much surprise him, as it now aroused his mortification and his anger.

The truth was, hard words had that morning passed between him and Drummond. His native boldness made him less timorous than his more interested neighbours about the agitation among the Coolies. Hence his responses to their excited appeals were so calm as to exasperate them. In the midst of a current of passion, you will be deemed a traitor if you keep your balance and appeal to reason. Thus Mr. Marston was being rapidly isolated by his natural sense of justice, which had at length overcome his natural indolence, so that he was now ready to permit suspicion – which had long lain quiet, because there was every motive, and a constitutional inclination, to let sleeping dogs lie – to develope into proofs. And Craig's very definite statement, supplemented delicately by Miss Marston, made the magistrate supremely uncomfortable. He was puzzled how to treat the incident of the day at Belle Susanne. He did not doubt that the Coolies who had surrounded Bella and her attendant, had been tempted to mischief by the unwonted opportunity; and this was the most startling token he had yet received that there was a dangerous temper awakening amongst them. On the other hand he could not but recognise his obligation to Dilloo for his timely rescue, although he saw how evidently it showed an understanding between the Indian and his mates. Still, with all these indications before him, he hesitated about raising the alarm which would assuredly result from a publication of the adventure; and he was certain that in Drummond's present temper no effort would be spared to discover the culprits and make an example of them. Among them

Dilloo would be certain to suffer. In fine the magistrate was in one of the most difficult quandaries that can be imagined; for while duty seemed to demand that the occurrence should be made known, on the other hand there were weighty personal and general reasons for keeping it quiet. It would drag Miss Marston into needless publicity; it would aggravate Drummond's ill-feeling; and further it might hasten a collision between the Coolies and their employers. From all this it arose, naturally and involuntarily, that Mr. Marston found himself consulting with his daughter and the young overseer on something like confidential terms, and that the latter found himself taking up ground not altogether consistent with his loyalty to the estate on which he was employed. In the result it was decided that the affair should be overlooked, Bella undertaking that Sarcophagus should receive an instructive explanation of the circumstances from her. The magistrate felt mightily uncomfortable about the whole affair. At the bottom of his heart he was a little mortified that Craig should become a confidant of his family. Yet Marston's was not one of those natures that can rely upon itself, or is content to do so; there-fore he would fain have persuaded himself that this was a very sensible youth, and one to be trusted. What should come of the affair from without he did not like to think. Hence his discomfort. But in parting with Craig he was more candid than he had ever been with him, and he asked the overseer to visit them more frequently.

Craig, lighting his pipe, strolled home in the moonlight: a baneful radiance in those climates. He had the sensation that he had made a stride in manhood, but he could not exactly define why. It might be that he had played the cavalier, it might be that he had become the confidant of a magistrate. For some unowned reason he took the way home by which he had come with his sweet companion but a few hours before.

CHAPTER XL

A SHARP BLADE

WHILE that little conspiracy was being arranged at the magistrate's house, another convention was held, which narrowly concerned the parties to the first.

Hofman's Lust, the estate next to Belle Susanne, on the eastern side, was shaped like the letter L, only that in its relation to the latter estate the letter was reversed. The long limb ran between Belle Susanne and Guineatown, and the shorter limb eastward, between Guineatown and the shore road, which, by the way, turned inlandwards, and ran along the other side of Guineatown. Then the plantain grounds of the village extended as far back as cultivation was possible, being protected, as usual at the extreme rear, by a dam, to shut out the water of the interior in the rainy season. The Negro-yard of Hofman's Lust was situated at about the middle of the shorter or lower line of the estate, which was about half-a-mile in breadth, and for convenience sake it was habitual for the Coolies of Hofman's Lust, who were working on their estate at the back of the longer line, to take a short cut to and from their work across the Negro village, which straggled over nearly a square mile of swamp.

The manager of Hofman's Lust was a Creole Dutchman, named Fluyschutz, descendant of one of the marvellous old Hollanders who had helped to redeem this rich Colony from sea and marsh and wilderness. There was a clear mixture of the Negro in Mr. Fluyschutz's composition, evidenced not merely by his short curly hair and large lips, but by many other characteristic traces of manner and temperament. He was not a successful planter: his estate was ill-managed and deeply mortgaged, so that the means available for its improvement and for fulfilling his contracts with his labourers were stinted. His hospital had again and again been complained of by the Medical Inspector without result. His Coolies were in a state of chronic excitement, not likely to be assuaged either by the wretched staff of overseers who were needy enough to endure his poverty and his meanness, or by his own tyrannical disposition. Mr. Fluyschutz's position and habits were notorious in the Colony; yet no Governor would have dared to refuse the Creole's application for a batch of Coolies, although no one could doubt that they were being consigned to a lot of hopeless hardship, tempered only by an official serveillance which did not dare to be rigorous, and was unwilling to be keen. *Hinc illae lacrymae!* Hence so many of those sorrows which engage the sympathies of kindly people in Britain, and work their revenge upon the better class of planters in these odd communities. You may depend upon it that Drummond, whilst he was obliged to be civil to Mr. Fluyschutz, and felt it necessary on high planter grounds to defend him from too intrusive Governmental interference, felt that if all such men could be turned out of Demerara it would be far easier to make concessions to the clamours of reformers. It is bad men who handicap the good – not alone in Demerara.

An estate like that of Mr. Fluyschutz's was a standing nuisance to a neighbour. It was always in a state of discontent. Its slovenly management and continual troubles exerted a disastrous influence upon the adjacent labourers. If there were a conspiracy or a rising no one would be surprised to hear that it began or was fomenting at Hofman's Lust. And in truth among the supporters of the Memorial those who were most in earnest were the Coolies in its Negro-yard. Among them was a certain Ramsammy, who had been a Sepoy in India, and who prided himself on his military appearance and training. Without question Ramsammy had been a conspirator before, and was at best a Wahabee, wild and malevolent.

Ramsammy knew a good deal of English. Alert, adroit, cunning, – a wily actor, – he was a frequent visitor to Guineatown, and was pretty familiar to its lounging inhabitants, who knew him by the name of 'Indy Soldiah.' He was accustomed on *fête* days to emerge from obscurity into fame by adopting an old red uniform, wherein he blazed about fiercely in the fervid sun.

Akaloo had pitched upon Ramsammy as the best man to lead the Coolies at Hofman's Lust; and hence Dilloo, who was not abstractedly a likely man to cultivate Ramsammy's acquaintance, was thrown into association with him. They frequently met, like other politicians, to talk over the state of the country. Ramsammy knew Gonzales very well: perhaps he had been of service to the Portuguese in divers matters connected with the latter's trade, for Gonzales found it useful to have a sort of Coolie-agent on each estate, – it may have been to extract rum from the puncheons; it may have been to help to sell it. At all events the news of the brutal attack on Gonzales, which thrilled the whole community, aroused in the Sepoy a vivid indignation. And Dilloo, himself a victim of inconsiderate treatment, returned to his work in precisely that state of mind which would bring such a man under the mastering influence of a resentful passion to be prompted by an astute and unprincipled friend.

Dilloo and Ramsammy were engaged on this particular night in a low conversation in the latter's hut.

'Why should we wait for an answer from the Queen?' urged the Sepoy to Dilloo, who with all his boldness and resolve shrank from any precipitate step. 'They mean to draw the cord more tightly round us. It will not be possible soon for an Indian to be free, even after he is "unbound." They have passed a law ordering every free man to carry about with him his picture taken by the sun, for which he is to pay four dollars, or he will be arrested on the roads. Four dollars to prove that he is not bound!'

'Ay! what next?'

'What next ?' continued Ramsammy. 'I was in the village to-day. I went to see the man who sells for the Portugee Sahib, – our friend, you know, whom they beat so badly. Well, the man told me all the guns and pistols in the country have been bought up by the planters.'

'What?' cried Dilloo. 'How did you find that out?'

'I went to buy a pistol,' replied the other, coolly.

'They mean to massacre us,' said Dilloo, slowly, shaking his head. 'What then can we gain by delay? Let us at least have our revenge before they slay us.'

Thus in these dangerous communities comes action and reaction – then reaction against that – and then perhaps terrible action.

'I have vowed,' the Wahabee went on to Dilloo, 'before I die to dip this blade in the living blood of that accursed manager Sahib. He is worse than your manager. He once struck me: the Negro dog! He is not an Inglees.'

'And I, for my part', said Dilloo, 'made a vow while I was in prison, that if ever the chance is given to me, I will take the life of that magistrate who sent me wrongfully to gaol.'

'I know,' replied the other, nodding: 'magistrate and manager! One pays the other – the other helps the one who pays him. Well, *he* is easily got at. His house is not very far off, and he has no men to defend him. They do not like him, I know, in the village. But he is a strong man: what you do must be done secretly. You might get him poisoned. Do you know the Negro conjuror and doctor whom they call Obe?'

Dilloo shook his head.

'Well, you should know about that. The Negroes look upon him like a god. His power is terrible. He lives far back in a sort of island in the middle of the woods, some miles from Guineatown. He has a hut there in a large tree. His god is a huge cock's head cut out of wood, and hideously painted and smeared with blood. If he casts his evil eye upon you, you are lost. You have only to give him offerings and name the name of your enemy, and the Obe will kill him secretly and cunningly. Sometimes he strews poisoned thorns for naked feet. Sometimes it is a pin taken from a decayed corpse, with which if you scratch yourself you die in agony.'

Dilloo shuddered. It was too supernatural.

'But,' said the other, 'I do not know whether he would do anything for us. Get a knife like this, my friend.'

He held out a common horn-handled American bowie-knife, strong, and bright, and sharp. Dilloo taking it, firmly grasped the rough handle. It was not a weapon he cared for: but as he held it, and glanced at the glittering blade, and a sense of unrevenged wrongs rose within him passionate and powerful, his fingers played nervously round the corrugated haft. With such an instrument he could destroy his enemy. A nice thing for poor easy-going Mr. Marston to be the subject of a resentment so practical!

At that moment another Indian glided into the hut, which was lit only by a low-burning lamp. Dilloo's arm moved, and the blade flashed, but the other spoke

'Hold. It is Akaloo!'

'What, is this Dilloo?' cried the new-comer, who had been rather startled by his reception. 'Are you practising already? Put away those things: that is the last appeal.'

'It is you who have brought us thus far,' said Ramsammy, securing the knife: 'do you now desire us to go back?'

'No!' replied the estate trader. 'But I would have you act with caution. These planter-Sahibs are trying to get you into a false position, and, if you do not restrain yourselves, they will succeed. You have only to show some violence, and you put yourselves into their hands.'

'Can we not overpower them?' said Dilloo, bridling. 'We are twenty to one.'

'No!' answered the Madrassee. 'They are all armed, and few of the Coolies are as strong and brave as you two. You will only run your neck into a noose.'

At the dreadful word, they all shuddered. Hanging is very hateful to an Asiatic, – as indeed it is not pleasant to any race we know of.

'I hear from Mr. Williams, the lawyer-Sahib, that the planters are pressing the Governor very hard to arm the whites and make them all police. There are to be more soldiers sent for: all the roads are guarded already by police overseers. I had to make a long round to the back to get here. Every free man must carry a pass and a photograph. I shall get one tomorrow.'

The two Coolies looked at each other.

'We missed a great chance to-day,' said Dilloo: 'but I could not help it. The daughter of the magistrate, a beautiful white girl, was wandering in the middle of the estate with one of those Negro dogs. A party of our people surrounded them, and the opportunity was so good, that I believe they would have made the best of it; but the lady has been very kind to my Lutchmee, and was indeed going home from a visit to her, and I could never have permitted any injury to come to her in such circumstances. So I ran in and sent them all off, and fortunately the overseer Craig Sahib came up and took her home. He is the only kind man on the estate.'

'I know of him,' said Akaloo. 'Gonzales has told me of him as a true and honest young gentleman.'

'My wife nursed him,' said Dilloo, 'and she spoke of him always with kindness. But he sees her too often,' he added, darkly. The sad experience which these natives have of our countrymen destroys their confidence in the best.

'Fear him not!' said Akaloo, 'I beseech you. He is a friend at court. You are too hot and jealous.'

'Well I may be,' retorted the other, sullenly.

'I am going on farther to-night,' said the Madrassee. 'Mr. Williams begged me to warn you all to keep quiet and attempt no rising. In two weeks is the *Tadja*———'

– 'For which we are preparing!' said the others significantly.

'Give directions that it shall be the quietest ever spent. Have no brawls, no dissensions: give no opening for cruelty. When they strike, they will strike hard. Peace be with you.'

Shortly after Akaloo had gone, Dilloo set out to walk home by the short cut across Guineatown and through the estate of Hofman's Lust. Lithe and unencumbered, he got over the ground very rapidly. A bright moon shed its radiance over the melancholy flats, pieced out in vast square patches by the silvery lines of the canals, that seemed to stretch out into the infinite space. The village was all asleep. The only sounds were the deep bass roll of the billows on the shelving shore, a sound like distant thunder, and the bell-like toll of a single campanero in the woods some miles away, faintly rippling to the ear through the deathly stillness. Out of the ground and from the numerous canals rose up a sultry mistiness which was transfigured by the moon into lurid vapour. Suddenly a single bark from the most distant hut in Guineatown struck harshly through the dull air, and then up rose a terrible canine chorus from every part of the village, to which each hound and cur lent his voice with furious zeal, and beside which one would think the dead must be aroused from slumber. It did not startle Dilloo, and as for the inhabitants of the village, it was a music that lulled them into deeper repose.

As Dilloo passing along a dam of Hofman's Lust, silently trampling with his unshodden feet, was about to cross the main canal of the estate, his quick eye detected something moving alongside a dam that ran at right angles to the one on which he walked, about a hundred yards off. The figure was using the shadow of the dam, and of the long weeds which fringed it, to crawl along. At first he thought that it was a dog or some other animal; but every now and then it stopped and rose to an erect position: Dilloo at once dropped himself gently into the grass beside the road. Evidently the figure had not detected him, for its movements were not such as would have indicated suspicion of any one on this side of the dam. It must be stalking some object on the other side. Looking sharply before him, Dilloo then for the first time noticed a moving form, which, being clad in white, had not before attracted his attention: it was slowly walking onward to Belle Susanne. He guessed at once that this was Craig, and became curious to know why the overseer should be so suspiciously followed. Choosing the left side of the dam on which he was walking, the other figure gliding up towards it on the right, Dilloo, concealed by the embankment, ran quickly down to the point at which the two dams and the canals intersected. He had arrived just in time to lie down flat in the grass and draw it over him, when above the embankment came the head of a Coolie. The moonbeams beat brightly into the eyes and face of Hunoomaun. Dilloo tightly grasped his lattey and held his breath, as the Sirdar, resting on hands and knees, keenly watched the receding figure. The heart of Dilloo beat strongly and wildly; he could scarcely restrain the temptation to have it out once and for ever with his enemy. But for the fact that Craig must have heard any noise, Hunoomaun would have had to try dread conclusions that night with the man he had wronged.

As it was, however, Dilloo moved. The Sirdar looked into the grass, and seeing there the form of some animal, suddenly dashed off at his utmost speed. As Dilloo, smiling sardonically, stood up to watch the runaway, the moonlight flashed on a blade in the villain's hand.

'Aha!' said Dilloo to himself, as he quietly followed Craig home unobserved, 'there are knives in more hands than one. I shall stick to my lattey.'

CHAPTER XLI

UNEASY LIES THE HEAD!

THE man whose fortune it is to be a Colonial Governor ought to have his head screwed on tight and straight. Nevertheless it is too often found that Dame Nature has bungled it, and left even very capable official heads rolling and lolloping about, as it were, loosely on their trunks. The Colonial Office used to have a certain fatality in discovering and editing or publishing gentlemen who carried their brain power in this loose aristocratic sort of way, and so long as the patronage is left to the Colonial Minister of the day and there is no Colonial Service system, it is likely that very queer persons will again and again be found to be in the wrong place at critical junctures of Colonial history. Poor Thomas Walsingham, at this momentous period of his pro-consulate, felt particularly conscious of the flabbiness of his vertebral structure, and heartily wished his dear friend Danby at Barbados, or Hatton-Mainham-Denvers-Studley at Trinidad, or Sir Winky Wankey, the old experienced Governor at the Cape, or in fine any other Englishman except Thomas himself, were just then sitting in the seat of government in British Guiana.

The hot excitement played around his head like summer lightning, and scorched and dazed it. He knew well the dangers of that brilliant Colonial Service. If he made an obvious mistake, British public, Government, Colonial Minister and all, would be down upon him, fatally. If he did what was abstractedly right, he ran the chance of its never being recognised as anything but a blunder!

The legislature – ycleped Court of Policy – was a fair version of most of these Crown-colonial Governments. In one day, much against his judgment, though he did not like to oppose it with decision, an ordinance was passed changing the vagrant law, which had been severe enough before. The effect had been correctly stated by Akaloo to Dilloo and the Sepoy. No free Coolie could budge from his home unless he carried a magistrate's pass and a photograph of himself, – the price of which together was fixed by the ordinance at six dollars, – without running the risk of being seized, locked up, and if the precious documents were lost, committed to prison for a month.* A month's labour at least to procure the evidence of one's freedom under an English Government!

The planters had long desired to pass this ordinance. It would help to make the unindentured people still more uncomfortable than they were, and would drive them to seek indenture as an improvement upon freedom. Since all these free people had served five years at least, and had thus become acclimatised, their labour was more valuable than that of new Coolies; besides that, being in the free market, they were enabled, like the Negroes, to insist upon fair terms.

Outside the legislature there was extraordinary agitation among the planting community. The case was thus put by Mr. Ingledew at the Club: –

'THE PEOPLE OF BRITISH GUIANA, Sir, have risen in their might! Our rights are in danger. Our free constitution, which has existed unimpaired ever since WE wrested the colony from the Dutch, is threatened with extinction! Our franchises, our liberties, our property are menaced by revolutionary agitators! The Coolies are being inoculated with communistic fallacies, by intriguing conspirators. The fanatics of Exeter Hall will be called on to crush us. But we shall not succumb without a struggle!'

And so it seemed. It looked as if they meant to have a fight: yet no one had been attacked. There had been no riot. No conspiracy had come to light other than the simple combination promoted by Akaloo and others to get the Coolies' griefs fairly before the Great Queen.

– For, among all ingenuous native peoples in and out of our territories, the embodiment of British power and Government is

* If any reader believes such a thing incredible, let him read the Mauritius Blue-book.

THE BRITISH QUEEN! She is imagined as all-seeing and all-performing. The righteousness that is done, the vengeance that is wreaked, the reforms that are wrought, the blunders that befall, by or through her thousand-headed staff in any quarter of the world, are the righteousness, the vengeance, the reforms, the blunders of the distant and unseen Monarch. It is a glorious ideal – a sad unreality. Were it in fact true, fortunate were Her Majesty's dominions. If every man who administered in her name, from Prime Minister down to the resident at Falkland Island or Sherborrow, felt, and, feeling, showed that he was an humble partner or medium of that embodied Greatness of the realm's Majesty, Power and Righteousness; and were to strive for his part to maintain and transmit undimmed the glory of that Fountain-head of light and goodness, and thus helped to strengthen in all men's hearts reverence for the Impersonation of British Sovereignty, – how noble and how precious to all the earth would be the outgoing of the national majesty and might! Such a sentiment is not unpractical, – nay, it hath in it wholesome uses and blessed influences. When all executive power is working up to a high ideal of truth, justice and glory, it is a strong, though sensitive network of nerves which knits the whole system together into a vigorous and perfect national life.

It was the crime of the Coolies that they had appealed directly to this Majestic Person. Finding within reach of them no ears to hear or heart to be moved on Its behalf by their plaints, they were now going up to the foot of the throne, – and that was the place where their masters were least willing to meet them. For they must have thought that it was an impudent presumption on the part of such bondsmen, already, like Jeshurun, too well off; – a menace to the privileges of men who had been accustomed to look upon these people as outside the pale of social and constitutional regard. Else, why did Mr. Ingledew so candidly express the arrogant views of the planting community? Out of one hundred and fifty thousand inhabitants, it was a pleasant illusion of these gentlemen to think that a few hundred whites constituted 'The People!' Blacks, Madeirans, Coolies, all swarming in tens of thousands, what were they? Why, they were machines to make money for the people of Demerara – to provide cheap sugar to the world in general, and plenty of profit to speculating Britons in particular. Doubtless, candid reader, if you and I were there, making money through the existing system, and knowing that to change that system meant in any case less profit to be gained, nay, perhaps much money to be lost, although we knew it might also involve a more even distribution of wealth throughout the community, we should never see the falseness of our ground; we also should call ourselves 'The People,' and be ready to vindicate our privileges even to blood. Ministers of Christ in Apostolic and other Churches have been found thus blind, and how should we poor laymen escape? If you can only manage to put your conscience in your pocket, can you not be a most comfortable and honest thief, or a most gracious and gentlemanly scoundrel?

So vividly did the planters and their dependents feel the danger of exposing their system to the searching eyes of impartial justice, that they deemed it even wicked to submit it to such an inspection. What they – The People – had determined to be right and necessary for the good of them – The People – why should keen-eyed critics and quick-nosed philanthropists be permitted to subject to visual and olfactory tests? Why, those humanitarians live by smelling and spying! They see moles and smell smells when all other eyes and noses are quite insensitive. They really know nothing about the necessities of places many thousand miles away, – like the Mauritius, for instance, where a beneficent Providence has placed two hundred and odd thousand Coolies at the mercy of a precious oligarchy, – worthy, say, of Houndsditch! – and yet these busybodies have an impudent habit of discussing things they do not understand, worrying Colonial Ministers with deputations and memorials (signed, generally, 'F.W. Chesson,' – d—— him!), and of challenging God-ordained systems, or opinionating on human rights and other silly abstractions.

The course these planters took at this critical period laid them open to a fearful suspicion of Machiavelian policy. They went about armed, having emptied all the gun and pistol-shops. They noisily demanded of the Governor that he should swear in special constables, plant cannon commanding all the main dams into

Georgetown, proclaim martial law, and send to Barbadoes for more troops.

Whereto Governor Walsingham answered that there had been no riots, nobody had been killed or hurt; and, so far as he saw, the Coolies, though excited, were not disposed to fight, and he was not disposed to force them to it.

Upon this Mr. Ingledew called the Governor 'a temporising poltroon;' Drummond called him 'a baby;' the *People's Warder and Cock of Liberty* stated that he was 'a shallow nincompoop; the effete relic of a used-up family tree; a gubernatorial idiot,' and 'a political and moral eunuch.' These phrases were the invention of a clergyman, commonly called a minister of the Gospel, (though, evidently, not any one of the familiar Evangelical Gospels), and who was ostensibly more inspired in his utterances than ordinary mortals. In addition to loud, violent language – the *Cock of Liberty* termed it 'the majestic voice of the people,' – the planters and overseers went from plantation to plantation displaying their arms, and in some cases hectoring the Coolies. These sprang to the conclusion that there was to be a massacre. The wildest rumours were circulated, and as they began to tell each other of their fears they also began on the various estates to aggregate into groups prepared to act together. Thus the terror of the one party evoked the organisation of the other.*

The Governor of the colony was sitting in his private room, and was busy drafting for his Secretary one of the despatches to the Colonial Office, which was to go out by the monthly mail. Responsibility, want of sleep, a sluggish liver and mosquitoes had depressed and unnerved him. In such conditions men cannot condense, so they expatiate; and he was in the midst of an effort to embody in one vast paragraph a vivid picture of the state of affairs.

His Secretary announced the Roman Catholic Bishop. Mr. Walsingham winced when he heard the name. The 'affair Gonzales,' as the French would have termed it, still remained a hard nut for him to crack. The unlucky Portuguese had been

* See the Barbadoes Blue-books of 1876.

slowly recovering under the attentions of his gentle nurses, fever having supervened on the terrible bruising he had received. The Portuguese community, though inflamed to a high degree, had not as yet given any sign of action, – a reserve which the Governor regarded with suspicious alarm. And now the wily ecclesiastic, who entered with so deferential a bow, and pressed the Governor's hand with so velvety a touch, must have come, his Excellency thought, for the purpose of raising the unpleasant question.

'Your Excellency is quite disengaged?' said the Bishop, in English. 'If not, may I perhaps go, and return at some more convenient time?'

'I am always disengaged to you, my Lord,' replied the Governor, graciously; though he could not restrain a glance at the sheets of unfinished sentence. 'You so seldom do me the honour to visit me that I would forego much to enjoy this rare treat.'

'Ah, ah!' said the ecclesiastic, smiling. 'Your Excellency is flattering. I am, as you know, a most occupied man. Your Excellency also has much engrossing labours. So long as all goes well it is no occasion that we should meet, though always in my experience the entertainment is so agreeable.'

'Am I then to infer from your language, Bishop, that all does not go well, since you are here to-day?'

'Perhaps, yes. To be frank, your Excellency,' said the Bishop, looking anything but 'frank,' as his keen dark eye glanced from under his black eyebrows, and he played with his small brown hand on his full, smooth-shorn chin, 'it is already three weeks that a Portuguese, one of my compatriots and co-religionists, sir, has been flagellated almost to the death by a planter, named Harris. He has, grace to Mary, nearly recovered himself. The Portuguese community, which is much agitated and insulted by this circum-stance, has waited to see your Excellency take the means to punish this so great crime; but———'

The Bishop here stopped and shrugged his shoulders, as he raised his hands, by which pantomime he gently conveyed to the Governor a reminder that his Excellency had not taken steps to punish that so great crime.

Mr. Walsingham's manner under the influence of the Bishop's eye was not as candid and easy as might, for the sake of his English blood, have been desired.

'You know, my Lord Bishop,' he said, blinking his eyes in a vain attempt to baffle the episcopal gaze, 'that since that unfortunate occurrence, which I deeply regret, the colony has been agitated by a political excitement, demanding all the attention of the Executive, and we have not had time to inquire into the details of a street fracas.'

'What!' cried the Bishop, with a start. 'Do I hear your Excellency call a brutal assault on my countrymen a "street fracas"? You have not received, sir, the veritable information. The Portuguese do not so regard it. It is a very serious thing. My countrymen cannot conceal from themselves that justice most rigid is dealt out to them on the most slight infraction of the law. This man, Gonzales, for instance, has before this time been punished with severity for alleged breaking of excise laws; but when a planter has done an outrage most grave, so as nearly to destroy a man's life, there is no regard. Behold, your Excellency, from this, there naturally results discontent and irascibility!'

The ecclesiastic spoke ever so smoothly and glanced ever so quietly, but keenly, sidewise at the Governor, who stirred uneasily in his chair. The heat appeared to distress him. However, he made a gallant effort to charge the enemy.

'The public mind is greatly excited, my Lord. All my experience of you gives me the assurance that you will use all your powerful influence over your countrymen to get them to postpone agitation of their grievances until this danger has blown over.'

'I cannot accept the responsibility your Excellency so graciously imposes upon me,' cried the Bishop. 'The community of the Portuguese have restrained themselves until now, under my very strong counsel and injunctions, but they will not any longer remain passive. A very grave state of affairs arises if Mr. Harris is not early arrested and subjected to process.'

'Good heavens! my Lord Bishop,' cried his Excellency, in a stew; 'will you increase our complications at this critical moment?

Were Harris to be arrested we might have bloodshed. Consider, I pray you, the peace and prosperity of the colony are at stake.'

'Mr. Governor,' said the Bishop, and his soft purring enunciation gave his words greater incisiveness, 'behold! what is the peace and prosperity of the colony excepting supreme and undisturbed rule of the planters? All is regulated in their interest. Remember, your Excellency,' – here the Bishop pinned his man with steady eyes and a monitory finger, – ' remember how unjust to my Church the law has been in the process of the administration of the estate of the pious Don Diego. Years since has it been a testamentary *donum* to us, but from your Excellency has been no response to our demands so frequently reiterated.'

'I cannot interfere, my Lord, with the administration of the law,' argued the Governor.

'Nor any more with the Administrator-General, I am aware,' interposed the Bishop, in the gentlest tone, smiling the while. 'But the notorious incapacity and evil manner of administering his trust, of that official, may come under your Excellency's notice and perhaps receive your attention?'

'The matter has not been overlooked,' said his Excellency. 'It is partly due to the complications of the Dutch law———'

– ' Which complications, I regret to be obliged to remind your Excellency, do not appear to prevent very facile administration of estates, in which the English gentlemen planters are interested———'

'Permit me, my dear Bishop, – I was going to add – I have had a minute prepared on the subject for the Colonial Minister.' (His Excellency felt justified in this case in representing the deed for the will.) 'I will consult the Attorney-General. Let me beg you to postpone all these matters to a calmer season. You must really lend us your valuable help, as a minister of peace, to quiet the dangerous excitement which prevails. You may depend that at the earliest possible moment your affairs shall be satisfactorily settled.'

The Bishop externally looked the picture of polite credulity, but his words were sharper than a two-edged sword.

'I fear, Excellency, that nothing will satisfy my people but immediate recompense. Mr. Harris must be prosecuted, and it would very materially assist in calming the – *dangerous excitement* – do I not use your words so correct? – if you would be able to assure me that the administration of the Estate Don Diego, will be immediately facilitated. I am delighted to observe that you so favourably view it.'

The Estate Don Diego was a *bête-noir* to the Governor. Acres of paper had been wasted over it. It was a case in which a very admirable institution had been perverted in a very arbitrary way, to keep the Roman Catholic Church out of the enjoyment of a valuable property. In British Guiana the inhabitants have some advantages that greater and more civilized communities are stupid enough to forego. There is an official called the Administrator-General, in whom vests all property of bankrupts and intestates, to be administered for the benefit of all concerned, under an official scale of costs. In a free and large community, with a press and public opinion to keep him in order, such an official would seem to be a necessary boon, did we not see that in England, for instance, he does not exist; for a small but powerful coterie of legal monopolists manage to thwart almost every attempt to improve and cheapen laws and their administration. But in a close community like that of a Crown Colony, where the interests of officials and planters are so mixed up, you cannot always ensure, even with Her Majesty's representatives looking on, an honest discharge of public duty. The pious Don Diego had, without doubt, intended to leave all his wealth to Bishop Carvalho and the Catholic Church; but a slight informality in the will afforded the Administrator-General a pretext for stepping in to administer as for an intestacy, and for several years enabled him by clever lawyering to avoid stepping out. In the meantime the management of the estate involved a lucrative patronage and many fees.

The Governor just then wished the estate Don Diego in Hades, and the Bishop there in possession of it. But he knew that he was fairly cornered.

'Will you allow me to see what can be done?' said His Excellency. 'When would it be convenient for you to have another interview on these subjects?'

'To-morrow!' replied the Bishop, promptly. 'Not later than to-morrow, your Excellency, in consideration of the so *dangerous excitement* – which you most correctly have termed it.'

'Very well,' said the Governor, unable to suppress a grimace, the pill being bitter. 'Let it be to-morrow, my Lord. I am sure I can rely on your good offices.'

'Always, your Excellency, regarding with admiration your Excellency's ever so wise administration of the Government. Permit me, your Excellency, to offer you my salutations.'

The Bishop left the room, and the Governor turned with a shadowed face to his unfinished sentence. But he was not yet destined to have done with it.

In the ante-room the Bishop encountered the Intendant-General.

'Ha! me dear Bishop, is it yourself? We live in troublesome times. No doubt, with the public spirit which always distinguishes you, you have come to promise your influence in keeping order.'

'That, Major,' replied the ecclesiastic, smiling, 'is foreign to my office. It is the affair of the Executive,' motioning towards the Governor's room. 'But the Civil Power always has claim to the aid of the Church, when it discharges well itself its duty to the Church.'

He said this deliberately, and emphasized it with an uplifted finger. Then he went away.

'What's the old thief up to now?' soliloquised the Intendant-General, as he opened the door into the Governor's room.

'Good morning, Major!' cried His Excellency. 'Did you meet the Roman Catholic Bishop going out?'

'I did.'

'And what did he say?'

'Faith, he was enigmatic, to my fancy. He said the Church would help the State when the State helped the Church.'

'Ha! ha !' laughed the Governor. 'A good old principle of his Church. But do you know what he is driving at ? Sit down and listen.' –

'The property will have to be managed,' said the Major, when Mr. Walsingham had ended his recital. 'If he gets that, he can keep the Portuguese quiet. I'll see the Administrator meself. As for Harris, that is a more difficult business. I'd like to know where's the magistrate would commit him?'

'It must be done,' said the Governor, firmly. The Bishop's words had pierced far beneath his outer coat of policy, and had touched his honour.

'Have you heard the news, Excellency?' said the Major.

' No.'

'They've begun to put this new ordinance in force, and the police have taken up twenty men on the roads on the West Coast, before they could get a photograph at all. But better still, sir,' the Intendant-General went on with a radiant face. 'They captured this morning seven Coolie children crossing Guineatown from the buildings at Hofman's Lust, carrying their fathers' dinner to the back of the estate – it's the short cut, ye know, – and the infants are all locked up! Drummond just told me Fluyschutz took it before himself without consulting Marston.'

'The devil!' cried Mr. Walsingham. 'How can anyone govern such a contrary set of people?'

'Now, easy! me dear Governor,' said the Major, earnestly. 'I'll help ye out of the scrape. Sure couldn't we just arrange to have them little vagrants all committed for a year to the Orphan Asylum? 'Twill settle the thing beautifully now; and by the end of the time I'll make decent Christians of the lot.'

The Governor laughed consumedly.

'I admire your persistency, O'Loughlin,' he said, 'and it will no doubt be rewarded some day. You will get a shower of orphans. But of course you are not in earnest. It is really too ridiculous!'

'Ah, faith!' said the Major, ruefully, 'I'm heart-broken with that same asylum. Good-day, your Excellency. I'm off now straight to the Catholic Bishop! I'll sell it to him; he wants it for a convent, and he'll be paying for it with Don Diego's money!'

When the Major had gone the Governor touched the Secretary's bell.

'Send for the Attorney-General. Write "urgent" on your note to him. Prepare a minute ordering him to take steps to prosecute Mr. George Harris for the assault on Gonzales.'

And before the day was out the news was over the Colony like wild-fire, that a summons had been issued by the Georgetown magistrate against Mr. George Harris, of Bitter Marsh, for the assault on Gonzales.

CHAPTER XLII

A SUDDEN DISMISSAL

THE near approach of the *Tadja* was signified by extensive preparations on all sides. The Coolies, as was their wont before these festivals, were engaged on every estate in secret manufactures, which in ordinary times consisted of the paraphernalia, dresses, instruments and weapons of a great celebration. The whites, anxious and watchful, took every precaution fear could suggest to meet an outbreak.

Chester, now high in Drummond's confidence, arranged through Hunoomaun to have the Coolies of Belle Susanne carefully watched; but Dilloo, on the track of vengeance, was morbidly alert, and nearly every effort to discover anything in the manner or the proceedings of himself and his friends was foiled. The Barbadian took every opportunity of embittering Drummond's mind against Craig: and he happened to possess a piece of information which he knew would deeply incense the manager. He, however, kept it back for a few days, in order to make the blow against the object of his enmity the more decisive.

The Governor, in view of the peril that seemed to be impending, issued orders to the stipendiary magistrates of the various districts to hold meetings of the Justices, and send in reports of the state of affairs within their jurisdiction, together with such practical suggestions as the magistrates might deem it proper to make.

It was on the morning of this meeting that, as Craig was turning out of bed in the rough shanty inhabited by the overseers, Chester, from the other end of the room, called out to him that the manager wished to see him before he went 'back,' and would be waiting for him at the estate house.

There was something in the Barbadian's manner, in the glitter of his large teeth and the play of his mobile yellow face, that struck Craig – not a very acute observer – as rather sinister.

'Why did you not tell me that last night ?' he said to the Creole.

'Soon enough this morning,' replied the other, jauntily. 'Too soon for you, I guess.'

'What do you mean?' said Craig, a little fiercely. The other occupants of the room, Martinho and Loseby, sitting on the sides of their beds, watched the scene with attention.

'Oh, nothing!' said Chester, trying to look indifferent as he thrust a yellow leg into his canvas trousers. 'P'raps Mr. Drummond wants to know what you were doing at the back of Belle Susanne with the magistrate's daughter last Friday week.'

Across the room in a couple of bounds Craig jumped in an instant, and with a single grasp of his great hand on Chester's throat drove his head against the wall in furious anger.

'Did I not tell you,' he cried in a terrible voice, 'never to mention Miss Marston again? Eh! eh!'

Bump, bump went Chester's head against the boards, and the tears rushed from his eyes, and some inarticulate sounds from his lips. The other overseers pulled off Craig, who instantly felt ashamed of himself, while the breathless Creole fell on his bed and cried aloud with rage and pain.

The Scotchman dressed, listening to the threats and imprecations of the wretched overseer, and then took his way gloomily to see the manager. He asked himself whether anything could compensate him for the misery of such an employment in such company.

Mr. Drummond was waiting in the verandah, and, as was evident at once, in no good humour. He neither sat down himself nor permitted the overseer to do so.

'I have been waiting ten minutes for you, sir,' he said, sternly.

'I beg your pardon, Mr. Drummond. I have been giving Mr. Chester a lesson in manners, sir,' replied Craig, with unusual spirit. He was in a chafed and irritated state, admirably complementary to that of his employer.

'Oh, you have, have you? That will be another matter for the magistrates, perhaps. Will you explain to me why you did not report the occurrence of last Friday, in which you and Miss Marston seem to have played the principal parts?'

'There was really nothing worth reporting. The young lady was frightened no doubt by seeing a number of Coolies about her; but she was not hurt, and I saw her home. Neither she nor her father desired to make any fuss about it.'

'Do you mean to say that Mr. Marston was a party to concealing the matter?'

Craig hesitated.

'I think, sir, any questions about Mr. Marston's conduct ought in justice to be put to himself. I might do him a wrong by imperfect representation.'

'I daresay: though there seems to be a perfect understanding between you.'

'I am persuaded,' said Craig, 'that Mr. Marston would not do anything that was not strictly honourable.'

'Ah,' replied Drummond, with a sneer: 'he has a most influential backer. He would very likely say pretty much the same of you.'

'I should feel honoured by Mr. Marston's good opinion,' replied Craig, simply.

His coolness and steadiness worked Drummond's anger up to a high pitch. Unable to contain himself, he swore roundly at the overseer. Craig, listening and looking at his master, whom he overtopped by an inch, braced himself, with a dangerous restraint, which made his whole frame quiver visibly.

'Mr. Drummond,' he said, 'I once had a respect for you, but I am rapidly losing it. I came into your employment to be treated like a gentleman, and I will not take that language from you or any other man.'

The shadowy play of Craig's eyes, which looked manfully into those of the manager, warned the elder not to push his anger too far.

'Very well, sir,' he said, affecting a laugh. 'You shall not be subject to such degradation any longer. Here is an order on my Georgetown agent for three months' wages, with an allowance for board. Give him a receipt. You will be good enough to take yourself off to-day. The steamer sails next week. I presume you will not look out for another employment in the colony after being dismissed by me. I cannot have on my estate a man who connives at disobedience and encourages bad discipline, and who has not the sense to understand what is for his own interest. Good-day to you, Craig: your ingratitude has deeply disappointed me.'

And the manager, half-ashamed of himself and half-sorry for the young man, fairly turned and ran away before anything more could be said.

There can be no doubt that Drummond's expression of regret at Craig's 'ingratitude' was quite genuine. If he and his servant differed in their notions of honour or honesty, it scarcely mattered which was right or which was wrong: the master was sure to think himself ill-used. The temper which insists on more than legal or moral service to repay friendly or benevolent treatment is a very common one; and in proportion to the purity of a man's course sometimes will be the disappointment of a master who finds him too honest for his purpose. It not seldom happens that friends who rely on each other's honour as well as each other's amity, fall out when the latter succumbs to the former, and the sufferer in that case will almost invariably go about proclaiming himself to have been sadly abused!

Craig stood looking at the cheque in the early light and slowly realizing what had happened, with sundry meditations thereupon arising. But his reflections were interrupted by Missa Nina, who came to him softly, with tears in her eyes.

'O Mister Craig,' she said, 'I'm so sorry! He never was so bad as this. Sure the devil has got hold of him this time. Where will you go to, dear Mister Craig ?'

She even in her kind solicitude laid her hand caressingly on his shoulder; but Craig slipped away, though he felt touched by the poor woman's sympathy.

'Have you heard all?' he asked.

She nodded.

'I knew it was coming, Mister Craig. Chester was in here last night after supper, and told a long story. I was listening through the partition, but I could not get out to tell you. He said Hunoomaun had found out all about the thing, some way, and he followed you to Mister Marston's. They only don't know who the Coolie was that saved Miss Bella.'

Craig saw in a moment that he had been the victim of Chester's revenge, and he felt some wicked gratification in thinking of the wretched Creole with his head against the wainscot, and his rolling eyes and lolling tongue, under the grip he had given him. Then he thought of the magistrate's daughter, and of her father, and of Dilloo, – who was, as he could see, in great danger of being found out and ruined, – and of Lutchmee; and the result was a very miserable jumble of sensations, amongst which stood out one of extreme pain that he was going away from it all. Some of them needed aid and protection, – and one of them———?

'I must go and get ready,' he said. Good-bye, and God bless you, Nina. Ten thousand thanks for all your kindness to me!'

Nina sobbed. She held his hand and checked him.

'Are you not going to say good-bye to Miss Bella?' said she, slyly, recovering a little.

'I don't know,' replied Craig, hesitatingly. 'Perhaps I had better not.'

'Do go now!' urged Missa Nina, drying her tears again, and speaking very earnestly. 'You know she has been very kind to you. I am sure she will feel it very much if you don't.'

'Hum!' said Craig. He was really glad to have his own bashful wishes encouraged by Nina's counsel, and that counsel he resolved to take. But first he went off to the overseers' quarters and packed his small wardrobe; and having changed his working dress for a more presentable suit, was passing through the yard, intending to pay farewell visits to Lutchmee and then at the magistrate's, when he met Nina, who came up breathless. She had been running fast.

'Mister Craig,' she said, 'Simon Pety is to drive you into Georgetown. I ran all the way back to look for Mr. Drummond and ask him. He swore at me, and told me to mind my own business: but no matter – he said you could take the buggy.'

'My poor Nina!' cried the Scotchman, shaking hands again very warmly.

'Mr. Craig,' she said, earnestly, 'don't you go to Mr. Marston's until after twelve o'clock. Mr. Drummond let out that there is a meeting there this morning, and he is going. It will be over I

suppose before breakfast, and you will be safe to go after. Come
with me now and have something to eat.'

When Craig had fortified his inner man with the ample provision made by Miss Nina, he looked, as a healthy man should do,
with more cheery feelings on the world at large, – and on his own
case in particular. He was young and strong; he had done right, –
save that at the bottom of his satisfaction there was an uncomfortable feeling that he had hit Chester's head very hard and had not
consulted his own dignity.

'After all,' he said to himself, philosophically, 'this fellow is a
nigger, one ought not to expect too much from him.'

Whereupon, as the result of his reflections, this singular young
man set off to find the peccant Creole and beg his pardon; but an
inquiry made to Crampton at the buildings, who expressed his
hearty regret at Craig's dismissal, proved that Chester was too far
away to be looked up within a couple of hours, so the Scotchman
turned towards Dilloo's hut.

It happened that the Hindoo, who was devoting every spare
hour to preparations for the *Tadja*, was in the house; while
Lutchmee, in her light skirt and jacket, ran about on her small
bare feet, preparing some rice for breakfast. The overseer had
lately avoided her, and in a life which has no spiritual or mental
food, of books, or society, or religion, or art, or of the sight of
various and beautiful nature, to lose even the incidental pleasure
of meeting an agreeable friend causes a vast hiatus. So that when
Lutchmee saw Craig approaching she naturally uttered an exclamation of delight; and her husband, watching keenly from within,
saw her, with that elegant ease of which he had been so proud, run
up to the Scotchman and familiarly take his hand like a loving
child, – and there was really nothing more than this infantile feeling in the simple act. Then Dilloo, still watchful, saw Craig, who,
his heart being softened at the moment, was slightly off his guard,
lay his big hand gently on her tiny head as he would have done to
a little girl.

Not so very long since the Coolie would have regarded this
scene between Craig and Lutchmee with less suspicious eyes. He
liked and respected the overseer; he loved and trusted his wife.

But now how greatly had his frank, manly nature suffered from the scorching bars of unjust justice, and the withering influence of ungenerous treatment! His mind was diseased with the sense of wrong, suspicion, resentment, the craving thirst for revenge, and he regarded the incidents of this meeting between his wife and the overseer with jealousy and anger.

'See,' said he, to himself, 'she lets him touch her head! Is she then so much at home with an Inglees?'

But Lutchmee turned on the instant, with an innocent face, and said to Craig, –

'Man in house: come and see him.'

Whereon Craig came forward and looked into the hut.

'Come out, Dilloo,' he said, with his manly voice. 'I have come to say goodbye. I am going away to England.'

Dilloo jumped to his feet and came out.

'Craig-Sahib go away?' he cried, in amazement.

Lutchmee clasped her hands and looked the picture of distress. Dilloo's dark eye, settling on her for a moment, suddenly clouded over. The moodiness of his altered nature had its way, and he was angry that she should feel so intensely the loss of a stranger. And then there darted through his mind, all in a tithe of the time it takes to tell it, the terrible suspicion of jealousy. However, he commanded himself, and turned to Craig.

'Why Massa go? All Coolies like Massa. Always good to Coolies. All Coolies cry for Massa. No oberseah now good to Coolies. Manahee, oberseah, all de same bad to Coolies. *All right!*'

He nodded defiantly and significantly at these last words, and his eyes strayed into the hut and fell upon his *Tadja* preparations.

Craig looked at him earnestly a moment, and felt that something had come over the man which left a disagreeable impression.

'Dilloo,' he said, laying his hand on his shoulder, 'for your own sake, for Lutchmee's sake, take my advice: be careful what you do. Try and work out your time here quietly. You have money enough to take you back to India. Don't even *think* of doing any harm to anyone on this estate. You will be caught and sent to prison, or hung, as sure as you live.'

'Ha,' exclaimed Dilloo, with his eyes on fire, 'yes! I go prison two times for nossing: next time go, go for one good ting. Salaam!'

He dashed into the hut and shut the door. Craig shook hands with Lutchmee, and a weak mist dimmed his eyes, while she sobbed as if her heart would break. The overseer hastened away towards Hofman's Lust and the magistrate's house.

No sooner was he out of sight than Dilloo, in a rage at his wife's softness, took a thin cane and, for the first time in his life, beat her.

As her shrieks came forth from the hut, several women ran to their doors in the village and listened. One of them was a flabby-looking creature, much laden with silver and with a half-toothless mouth. She smiled as she heard the cries. She had been spying through the chinks in her house the interview between Craig and the two Coolies, and she put two and two together;

'Ha,' said she, with a chuckle, 'he has found out the sly woman at last, has he? I thought her day would come. Let us see if she will hold her head so high now!'

CHAPTER XLIII

JUSTICES IN COUNCIL

EVERY justice in the district put in an appearance at the meeting which had been called at the magistrate's house. Mr. Marston looked forward to that convention with some anxiety. He was too well aware of the character of some of the great unpaid in the colony; and he felt, moreover, that the planters were beginning to think of him with suspicion. Part of this feeling no doubt arose from a conscious change within himself. Of late, the things which had come to his knowledge through Miss Marston and the Scotch overseer had greatly disquieted his mind. The natural reaction of a dogmatic nature against the somewhat rudely expressed criticism of his recent conduct, not only in the horribly licentious press which disgraces most of our small colonies, – and some of our large, – but in private conversations, served to strengthen his determination not to be misled, while it quickened the keenness of his insight. He could not admit to himself that the Coolies had done any wrong in making a complaint by memorial to the Queen, or that Williams was as bad as a convicted felon or worthy of hanging, because he had taken a fee to draft the petition. So he had shaken hands with Williams in Water Street, and was reported to the Club, with opprobrious comments, and received an intimation from the Committee that if he should err so notably again, he would be asked to retire. Of course he immediately resigned. One incident leads to another. His irritation strengthened his resolution, and therefore when Mr. Fluyschutz committed to prison seven little Coolie children who had been caught on the short cut across Guineatown carrying their fathers' dinners to the back of Hofman's Lust, Mr. Marston, without consulting the Governor, promptly ordered their discharge, on several grounds, but one particularly which was incontrovertible, – namely, that these children were Mr. Fluyschutz's own labourers, and that therefore

Mr. Fluyschutz should not have tried this case. Nevertheless, Mr. Drummond was as irate as anybody at what Marston had done.

'Why the d—— should he be so punctilious at such a time as this?' quoth Drummond in all sincerity. 'It is only letting the Coolies see we are divided, and encouraging them to go on with their rebellion.'

A magistrate who is not a partisan in these chronic crises of the planting colonies, is genuinely regarded as an enemy. Your planter may repudiate that as a principle, but he could not contravene it as a fact. It is too patent to the visitor, it is written too glaringly on the pages of Commissionary evidence. *In mediis tutissimus ibis* is a Latin proverb, but privileged planters do not deal in Latin proverbs, if they should be able to understand them. 'At this supreme moment of the People's danger,' Mr. Ingledew had pompously declared at the Georgetown Club, 'he who's not for us is against us!' And one is obliged to admit that he was perfectly correct. If you are interested in abuses, how can you bear to have them disinterestedly criticised?

It was not surprising that when Mr. Marston received the assembled justices in his verandah, an air of coldness and constraint prevailed on all sides. Mr. Fluyschutz was there with his dignity grievously upset, and, as his manner showed, not easy to be set right again. There also was Mr. Dupree, of Colston, and Mr. Macginnis, a rough, vulgar Irishman, from a small place up the Mahaica River, called, in bitter irony, 'Brighton.' There also were Messrs. Mackintosh and Grant, of the estates of Van der Tromp and Galilee. Drummond of course attended; and Mr. Marston had taken upon him to ask Mr. Telfer, as the parish clergyman, to lend his benignant influence to the discussion.

Drummond and Macginnis arrived together; and as they slowly ascended the long steep of stairs leading to Marston's verandah, where all the jalousies were turned downwards to keep out the sun and left open to admit the air, they designedly or incautiously spoke in a tone which reached the ears of everyone in the gallery.

'No man has any business in these times, when all our lives are in danger, to be neutral. I say it is d—— cowardice for a fellow to make his living out of the planting community in quiet times and desert them in a pinch.' Thus spoke Drummond.

'By——, sir, that's true!' answered Macginnis; 'and I'd very soon tell him so, too, to his face. For meself, there's me, every night of me life, never knowing but what I'll be killed by a hunthered or two of rebels in me bed! Gad, I'd like him to go and sleep there for himself! Would I stand upon terms with them riff-raff? There's only one argument a nigger or an Indian under-stands, and that's buck shot, I tell ye.'

And if Mr. Macginnis's record could have been unfolded, as perhaps it never will be till the day of judgment, it might have been found that he had acted before now up to his opinion. He was one of those *mauvais sujets* whom Drummond would in ordinary times have treated with coldness, if not with contempt. But common danger, like misery with *its* bed-fellows, brings men cheek-by-jowl with odd characters. It was a very hard cause indeed which could gain anything by the advocacy of Fluyschutz or Macginnis.

Marston and the other justices overheard this conversation, and his blood coursed with painful rapidity through his veins, though no one could have discerned, except by the scintillation of his eyes, that a word had reached him. He gave Drummond his hand, and nodded to Mr. Macginnis.

'You, gentlemen, are the last to arrive,' he said. 'We will proceed to business. As a matter of form, shall I take the chair?'

And the magistrate sat down in his favourite seat by the table.

'His Excellency the Governor,' proceeded Mr. Marston, 'as I see by this letter, desires me to consult you, gentlemen, in regard to the state of affairs in this district, and the steps to be taken to preserve the peace in the agitated state of the Colony. You are more familiar with the feeling that exists among the labourers than I can be. But I would mention that there have been no assault cases before me for ten days, and so far as I know there is no immediate danger calling for extraordinary action.'

Macginnis, who had taken his morning dram, and was encour-aged by it, was about to speak, when Drummond forestalled him. The tension of all minds showed itself in his words and manner.

'I thought it would be taken for granted that there was "danger,"' he said. 'I did not suppose there was any white man in the Colony who required proof of that. When forty thousand labourers, surrounding a few masters and overseers on estates up and down the country, begin to put forward ridiculous and inadmissible claims, I should say a man must be a mole not to see danger.'

A general clearing of throats among the justices served as a sort of cheer to this speech. Marston, keenly sensitive to the delicacy of his position, held his mouth with bit and bridle, and answered quietly, –

'We are only differing about the meaning of the word "danger." I did not refer to the menace involved in the attitude of the Coolies under the Memorial, but to the "danger" of a physical outbreak.'

'Physic be d——— !' cried Macginnis, roughly, 'and the Memorial too! We'd all be murthered and killed before you, or the likes of you, would see any danger! It's not to split straws we came here today, but it's to settle how we can keep them devils in their proper places.'

Marston's eye grew dark and stern as he fixed Macginnis with his glance.

'Well,' he said, 'if all devils were kept in their proper places, it might be more convenient for the world. But I would remind you, sir, that if any good is to come of this discussion it must be conducted in a gentlemanly manner.'

Macginnis sulked, and Marston went on.

'But, gentlemen, as you all appear to be resolved that there is danger calling for preventive measures, let us consider what, in your opinion, are the arrangements necessary for the preservation of the peace.'

Drummond, holding a slip of paper in his hand, read as follows: –
'Proclamation of martial law.

'Restriction of all Coolies to their estates till after the *Tadja* time.

'Prohibition of the *Tadja*.

'Arrest and prosecution of Gonzales and Williams for inciting the Coolies to insurrection———'

'Good heavens!' interrupted Marston, who had listened astounded to these demands. 'On what grounds?'

'Do you know, Mr. Marston,' answered Drummond, angrily, 'that the Memorial drawn up by those two men contains false and malicious charges against the Legislature, the Executive, the Magistrates (including yourself), the police and the whole planting community? With such ignorant and excitable people, do you suppose that such charges could be concocted and put into shape without the risk of raising a rebellion?'

'I do not see that it need follow,' replied Marston, doggedly. 'That must depend, to a great extent, upon the way their representations are met and treated.'

Here little Mr. Telfer, who had been nodding and blinking in a corner, perched his small body well forward on the edge of his chair, and perspiring with excitement, gamely crowed a clerical challenge thus : –

'I agree with Mr. Marston!'

The justices looked at the little man with wonder and rage. He was pale, but his face shone with a certain earnestness which none of them had ever seen upon it before. Macginnis burst out upon him:

'Who the ——— asked your opinion? Have you turned traitor, too, against your bread and butter ? By –'

'Stop, sir!' said little Mr. Telfer, jumping off his chair, and holding up his hand towards the ruffian, as if he were about to exorcise a fiend. 'I am indifferent to your insolence to a humble person like myself, but I shall ask these gentlemen to protect me from hearing the name of God profaned, – and by such lips as yours.'

Drummond, looking at the little man with some admiration, was obliged to reach out his powerful arm and sweep him into safety, for Macginnis actually rose as if to make a dash at the courageous prophet. And from behind the great manager's chair the worthy parson watched the excited discussion which now arose. There was challenge and retort, blast and counterblast. As they all came down upon him harder and harder, Marston waxed more firm and explicit in his remonstrances. Drummond finally lost patience.

'It is useless to waste any more time, gentlemen,' he said, rising. 'If we are to take proper measures in this district we cannot expect the co-operation of our Stipendiary,' – he put an emphasis on the

word, – 'Stipendiary Magistrate. Before I go I wish to give the
meeting one piece of information which throws a further light on
Mr. Marston's conduct. You may judge of his fitness for the
important post he occupies in this grave crisis, when I tell you that
he concealed from every one an incident which happened last
week at Belle Susanne; when Miss Marston, walking home across
my estate, was actually threatened with personal violence by a
mob of my Coolies. She was rescued, I believe, by one of my
overseers, whom I this morning dismissed ——'

'You have dismissed Craig!' cried the magistrate.

'Yes, sir, I have. You seem to have an understanding with him. –
Gentlemen, will you believe it, Mr. Marston combined with one
of my overseers to keep this serious affair, which proves a rebellious spirit among the Coolies on my estate, a secret, and I only
heard of it by accident?'

All the planters rose to their feet, and looked at Marston, who,
however, without moving, said with dignity, –

'I had no reason to believe that Miss Marston was really threatened with any serious danger. Mr. Craig is a young man of good
character, and, I think, of sound judgment, and he agreed with me
that what happened on the occasion was not worth notice.
Besides, gentlemen, one thing will at once appeal to your good
feeling, – the person chiefly concerned was my daughter. –
However,' he said, rising, and speaking somewhat sharply and
curtly, 'I decline to discuss the propriety of my conduct here. I
shall be ready to defend myself in the proper quarter. I presume I
may say that this meeting is at an end.'

The justices and Mr. Marston parted without any stretch of
civility; and adjourning to Drummond's house to breakfast,
arranged for an immediate appeal to the Governor for Marston's
suspension. Mr. Telfer, whose ecclesiastical apple-crust had broken to let forth some evidences of warmth and sweetness,
remained to encourage the magistrate with a few not over-strong
though sincere words, and then, feeling that he had a mission,
went off to see the Governor.

CHAPTER XLIV

THE FIRST BLOOM OF LOVE

WHILE the magistrate was undertaking his disagreeable duty in the verandah, an experience which had in it something of an awakening and tutorial character for him, things were happening not far off which even more narrowly concerned his peace.

Miss Bella was not insensitive to the change that was taking place in the magistrate's views, and to the probably serious consequences of that change upon his position in the Colony. So long as she had lived content with things as they were, and in blissful indifference to the rights and wrongs of the relations between the privileged whites and the labouring blacks and browns, her mind had really nothing to develop it; but now, that mind, habitually indolent, naturally strong, had been roused to think upon a subject very difficult, very complicated, very wide in its bearings, very much apart from ordinary young-lady consideration; and the interest in which was intensified by its association with an object of pure but absorbing passion.

Perhaps we are not often conscious how much of our mental development is prompted or governed by mere sentiment. Could we only, in summing up the results of our education, rely upon the accuracy of our perceptions and of our memory, how much might we not be able to trace to the oddest and most unintellectual springs! You have learned a language because of your affection for one who spoke it, or you have shut up a whole set of faculties, like a Chinese nest of boxes, because of the powerful influence of some sentimental devotion. The fondness for a woman has quickened indolent minds to unwilling studies, and turned the current of life from one channel to another. A youth, bent by the force of another's likes or dislikes, may be diverted from the career of a Stephenson or a Brunel to that of a Gladstone or a Wilberforce.

Affection, or the want of it, – sentiment, or its absence, – how deep are their influences on that composite being called man, and how rarely are those influences truly gauged and recognised in that greatest of all artistic aims, a good education! How many a time does the strong affection for some true man stir up the fallow ground of a woman's mind (often so criminally neglected), and open and stimulate its fertilizing powers! When there is no set education at hand, the strong mind sometimes, by the chance of some such prompting, seeks out an education for itself. Miss Marston's mind was developing under an influence unconsciously wielded, and Craig might never have known, had he not paid his farewell visit, that he had been a tutor to so fair a woman.

But these remarks may be resented by the reader as rather tedious; however, now, having got to the end of them, he is at liberty to strike them out.

Miss Marston, we say, sufficiently appreciated the gravity of affairs to feel that the meeting which was going on in the magistrate's verandah was of grave importance to her father; wherefore it became her, as a young lady, to grow very much excited about it; and, unfortunately, there was no counter-irritant to relieve her anxiety. Extremely little housekeeping was required in the easy-going household. Miriam and Sarcophagus were always up and away to Guineatown by daybreak to purchase the day's meat and vegetables. There was hardly anything in the cooking to call for elaborate discussion. Miriam had been cook to the late Chief Justice, no mean gastronomist. Who could have tasted her crab-backs and not have felt that the singular creature was endowed with a divine genius? And what an exquisite idea of taste was evidenced by her salmis of that noble lizard, the iguana! There was no diversion, therefore, to be had for Miss Marston in the kitchen-yard; and none over the simple appointments of a Demerara house, so that the young lady, not finding a novel sufficiently distracting, and worried by the loud and angry tones of the discussion in the gallery, at length found it impossible to sit still, and taking her light sun umbrella went out to the garden. She had on a simple white morning dress, with a blue ribbon round her neck floating in bannerets behind: this was her only ornament. Her

object expressed to herself was to see if there were any ripe grana-
dillas or a good mango or two on her father's favourite Indian tree.

As she passed along by the bright-green thorny hedge, in a
careless reverie, her muslin dress caught upon what the old poets
would have called an 'envious' thorn. Stooping, umbrella on
shoulder, to extricate the flimsy material, she suddenly heard,
greeting her from the other side of the hedge, a well-known voice.

'Good morning, Miss Marston,' it said, in rather sober tones.

It was strange how, striking in unexpectedly on her high-strung
feelings, this voice yet played with a soothing and pleasurable
influence. But Miss Bella was very quick.

'Oh, Mr. Craig!' she said, rising immediately, 'how you frightened me!'

Craig was altogether too sedate a fellow to catch at the opportunity of making some happy repartee to this doubtful expression.
She stood there looking at him across the hedge, with a faint
blush, Aurora-like, flattering the pure, bright skin of her cheek;
and her quick eye, taught of love, saw anxiety in his face and a
shade of sorrow. But the sunshine in her countenance threw an
instant's reflective ray on his.

'I am afraid I am taking a liberty, Miss Marston,' said the
humble overseer. 'But I did not like to go away without coming to
say "good-bye" to Mr. Marston and yourself. He – you – have been
so kind ——'

She turned pale and red by turns.

'Good-bye, Mr. Craig! Why, where are you going?'

'Home to Scotland: Mr. Drummond has dismissed me.'

Almost before he had finished his words he had jumped the
hedge at a bound, and caught the falling girl in his arms. He had
seen her, with his keen grey eye, – he had seen her lids drooping
down, her face paling, the sun-shade sinking slowly in her passive
hand, and the pretty holder thereof slowly but gracefully following, and he leaped over just in time to catch her as she fell.

'You are ill, Bella, – Miss Marston I mean. – I will call for some
one.'

He hardly knew what he was saying. Her fair figure was resting on
his arm, her small white hand clutched his shoulder, her sweet and

noble face was there close to his, as he bent down looking eagerly at the pallid features, where the windows of life and sentiment were shut down. But when he proposed to raise an alarm, the young lady opened her eyes, and saying, 'Don't, please,' – quietly shut them again!

Only a few seconds passed, which seemed then, and seemed ever after to Craig and Bella, to have been a long, long interval, when Miss Marston's eyes suddenly opened again very wide, and she said, –

'Oh, Arthur, what are you going away for?'

She disengaged herself from his arm and stood before him, blushing, blooming, goddess-like. A little bright, round, tell-tale crystal had slipped from under the long-lashed lids. Craig was quite confused.

'Miss Marston! Bella!' he cried, his mind quickened by a sudden revelation, 'Do I? – Do you? – I mean, what do you ? – Do you really love me?'

'Well, sir,' said Miss Bella, rallying and assuming a quizzical air: 'What do you mean?'

'Bella,' he slowly answered, looking at her with puzzled eyes, and yet as she, quite keenly observant, thought to herself, such deep, fine eyes, 'I love you – if I dare.'

'Oh! and don't you dare?'

She coquettishly picked up the white umbrella and threw it over her shoulder, which she slightly turned away from the hesitating young giant.

Whereupon Craig, with practical decision picked her up, umbrella and all, and under that gracious shade gave her a kiss on either cheek, and then setting her down again, looked at her with a half-frightened triumph.

'Bella,' he said, 'if I may – I hardly dared to think I might – I will love you with all my soul!'

Bella did not say anything: she was too happy to speak. She began, indeed, to cry, covering her face with a bit of white cambric, and putting poor Craig into a terrible state for a moment or two. When she took away the little cloud it opened up a brilliant sunshine to the ravished swain. She gave him her hand, and he squeezed it so hard in that large grasp of his, that she could not check a little cry.

'There, let me go, Arthur: dear Arthur! – Wait at the back of the house until I wave a handkerchief out of the window. Drummond is in there. You will, of course, come and breakfast with us.'

And before he knew it, she was gone.

CHAPTER XLV

THE TADJA

THE day of the *Tadja* had come. From one end of the Colony to the other on all hands estate-work was laid aside. The night before had been one of general anxiety and preparation. The Coolies were engaged in getting ready for a festival – the whites, from the Governor downwards, were making arrangements for a fight. Mr. Walsingham, under the pressure of his responsibilities, had worked himself into a fever which confined him to his room. He was nevertheless obliged in his bed to hold conference, as intermittent and frequent as his heats and chills, with the Inspector-General of Police and the officer in command of the small garrison at Eveleery. From the Arabian Coast to Berbice the police, under their district inspectors and aided by special constables, were ready, armed with rifles and cutlasses, to take the field on the slightest indication of trouble among the Coolies. The Governor did his best to restrain the arrogant spirit of his advisers. He had issued very strict orders that the troops were to remain in their barracks, under arms, but without any open demonstration, and that the police, regular and irregular, should be confined to their stations and should make no movement except under the command of the local stipendiary magistrates. For he wisely shrank from entrusting to planter justices of the peace the responsibility of deciding when they ought to use force in their own interest. The stipendiaries, among them Mr. Marston, were directed to assume the superintendence of their respective districts.

In truth however there was at the time no danger of a general outbreak. Although the communication between the East Indians in these colonies is mysteriously rapid, and Akaloo's memorial had been so universally signed that the whole of the Coolies were in thorough accord, there had been no time to concoct a serious rebellion, or to ascertain on what local leaders and local forces such men as Dilloo and the Sepoy, even were they disposed to attempt a rising, could rely. The only real danger was that in some quarter, owing to the suspicions or terror of the whites, a local riot might occur, and set the match to a larger blaze. And of all places in the Colony where such a riot might happen, the estates of Belle Susanne and Hofman's Lust, with the seething questions of difference between men and masters, were the most likely. Accordingly at Belle Susanne, Drummond and all his overseers, aided by some friends from Georgetown, had joined with Mr. Fluyschutz of the neighbouring estate, to arrange a common defence. The Coolies of these two plantations were, as usual, to hold their festival together. The headquarters therefore of both parties was at Belle Susanne.

As early as four o'clock in the morning, when the inmates of the planter's house and the overseers in their cribs were starting up after short and troubled rest, at the call of sable women carrying cups of smoking coffee, the murmur of gathering people and the thrum-thrum of the Indian drums could be heard through the quiet darkness, from the Negro-yard a few hundred feet off.

In this singular holiday the Coolies of all religions indifferently join. The West Indian *Tadja* is said to be nothing more nor less than the Mohammedan feast of the Mohurrun, adapted to a new country and to novel circumstances. In those circumstances it apparently ceases to have any religious meaning, and becomes, like the Christian's Christmas, an excuse for a holiday, a carouse, and even a half-Carnival rout. Yet the Coolies are very jealous of allowing white people to witness its ceremonies or to inquire into their meaning. Hence they arise early in the morning and begin the chief rites before daylight, rites which probably vary on different estates.

At Belle Susanne, on this morning of alarm, the excitement in the village appeared to the listening whites in Drummond's verandah, where the overseers had been ordered to report themselves, to increase most ominously from moment to moment. This however was soon explained by the arrival of the manager of Hofman's Lust and his party, with the information that all their Coolies had marched off to join their friends at Belle Susanne. This was about an hour and a half before sunrise.

The spot where the preliminary ceremonies of the festival were to be performed, was an open space of ground behind the Negro-yard, such as is usually allotted by the manager to the Coolies for exercise and amusement. Parts of it were carpeted with grass, but most of its surface was simply clay, smooth-trodden by the frequent prints of naked feet. In one corner of this ground there always stood a tall pole, at the top of which, from a little cross-yard a couple of feet in length, there hung, for there was scarcely ever wind enough to blow it out, a streamer of white calico. A space of ground around this pole, about ten feet square, was fenced in with bamboos, and was usually kept inviolate by the Hindoos.

Near this, on the morning of the festival, stood a curious and prominent object, towards which the crowd of gathering Coolies, already showing signs of excitement, began to draw. The air was chill and heavy, and the blackness of the night, made deeper by the unhealthy mists that rose from the ground, was unrelieved except by a single torch of cotton dipped in oil, which swung in a half-cocoanut from the top of a bamboo stuck into the ground at one corner of the small enclosure. The flaring light played weirdly over the brown faces of the men and women, pricking out with its gleams their flashing eyes, glancing on their well-oiled skins, lighting up their fair white cambric and calico garments, or glittering now and then on their silver ornaments.

Within the enclosure, tied to the bottom of the pole, were two or three kids. Not far off a dozen Coolies or more, with drums of hide stretched over calabashes or hollow cylinders, thrummed monotonously with fingers and thumbs, and broke out occasionally into a dismal croon or chant, which appeared to make the poor kids eminently unhappy, for they struggled to get free and bleated piteously.

The light also fell dimly on the object before mentioned, which was the centre of attraction to the arriving Coolies. It was a huge pyramidal, or, perhaps more correctly, conical structure, arranged in stages, which rose from the ground at a diameter of six or eight feet, to an apex at the height of about twenty feet. The decoration was of tinsel and brightly-coloured papers. In form it resembled a pagoda, pierced with many windows, and fluttering with little flags of coloured cotton or silk or paper. This was the '*Tadja*,' which gives the name to the feast.

Before the dark shades of the sky began to be flecked with the first grey gleams of dawn nearly the whole of the Coolies of the two estates had assembled on the ground. Dilloo was there and Lutchmee, and Hunoomaun and Ramdoolah; and altogether nearly a thousand Hindoos, arrayed in their best attire, had come to the celebration. The drums now began to beat with increasing energy. The song of the drummers grew louder and more strident. The people, under the influence of natural and artificial excitement, moved uneasily to the measured beat and steady monotone of the music. An old man with a soft white beard, and robed in white from head to foot, walked into the enclosure followed by two young Indians, simply bound round the loins with their white babbas. One of these bore a sharp knife, the other a bowl of clay. For a moment there was a dead silence while the old man laid his hand on the head of one of the kids, and taking the knife from the youth, drew the blade dexterously across the victim's neck. As the other youth adroitly caught the spouting life-stream, the people set up a shout and the drummers yelled and thrummed with intenser energy. The kid was soon dead, and its body, along with the bowl of blood, was borne into the village. The other kids were killed in the same way. The victims were afterwards cut up and distributed to those who cared to buy flesh for the day's feasting, the ceremony not being regarded as of a sacred character.

By the time this simple performance had been concluded, old Phœbus, who in those equatorial latitudes gives short notice of his coming, began to throw long rosy streaks of light across the hemisphere, and very soon after his great ruddy shoulder came hurtling up above the long line of the distant horizon, darting the blinding rays with sudden fervour along the unobstructed landscape, and effecting a marvellous transformation in the scene. The Coolies looked round on one another, and chatting together admired their *Tadja*, which on this special day was a particularly splendid one. For the time there was a lull in the interest, and leaving a few to guard the sacred erection from hostile affront or injury, the rest turned to the always important, though common-place ceremony of breakfast. Some, crowding into certain houses, began already to partake of arrack, which was provided in large quantities. Every man had with him his long, trusty hackia-stick, and it could be seen by their swagger as they walked, and by the nervous balancing of their weapons as they moved to and fro, that they were all in a humour of conceit, dangerous to anyone who should venture to offend them.

Meantime important preparations were being made by some picked men. In Dilloo's hut, he and his Sepoy friend from Hofman's Lust were adorning themselves, while Hunoomaun, with Ramdoolah's assistance, prepared his big form for the part he was to play in the coming procession.

During two or three hours everything remained quiet, except that there was a good deal of lively intercourse going on, and that the excited state of the people developed some harmless quarrels. Drummond, accompanied by his head overseer, sauntered through the village and took a look at the *Tadja*; but seeing that all was going on as usual, and that there were no signs of trouble, he retired again to his house, and kept his garrison out of sight.

The Sepoy and Dilloo however were engaged on something far more serious than the decoration of their persons. Outside the hut, Lutchmee was cooking the rice for the morning's breakfast, which for this special occasion was to be savoured with curry of kid. The two men speaking low managed to carry on a conversation which she could not overhear.

Dilloo said, –

'I have sounded many of my matties. They all seem to think it is not a good day to make a fight. Akaloo sent me word last night from the big town that all the Inglees are ready for us. They have armed themselves: the soldiers are ready to march, and the police are waiting in the stations, to come forth on the slightest warning.'

'Yes,' added the Sepoy. 'And they are plainly afraid of something. Could we have been overheard at any time ? I told Samânee to wait behind us this morning, and watch the manager's' houses, at Hofman's Lust. He tells me that the manager-sahib and most of the overseers as soon as we were out of sight followed us over to this estate. Some of them have guns and others swords. They went into your buildings, and there I expect they are now, watching us very closely all this time.'

'I should like to burn them out!' cried Dilloo fiercely, grinding his teeth together. 'Ah! I daresay they would be glad of a chance to fire upon us. I had set my heart on burning down that magistrate's house to-night. But I fear we must keep quiet. We will wait our chance and rise when they do not look for it. But all our men say we shall have first to get rid of that rascal Hunoomaun, before we can safely strike a blow. He is a spy and a traitor. Do you know that he has volunteered to be a "tiger" to-day ? Hah! I should just like to kill him in his skin!'

'So you may!' said the other. 'See! You are a great man with the short-stick. Challenge him to fight you at the games to-night. If you look out you may get a chance to knock him on the head and finish him.'

Dilloo, who had taken a morning stimulant, caught up and clutched convulsively in his powerful grasp, a short, thick stick, about two feet and a half long, and whirled it about his head with surprising rapidity.

'There, there!' said the Sepoy. 'Stop. Your wife will hear you. Surely you are not going to practise on me?'

'No. But I shall have *him*! See. Do you feel the weight of that stick? I have made it heavy with metal at both ends.'

'It is too heavy for me,' replied the other, after taking it and poising it in his hand. 'I fear you will not be able to make quick play with it, and they say that Hunoomaun is a wonder at the game.'

'I don't care how good he is,' said Dilloo, stretching out his arm, along which the moving muscles under the shining skin glanced like the powerful coils of a boa-constrictor. 'There is no other man in the country who can use that stick so quickly and easily as I can.'

'Good,' cried the Sepoy. 'Then watch your opportunity: knock him on the head and settle him. It will be taken for an accident.'

'No. If I kill him, they shall never take me alive. These rogues of Inglees would never give me any mercy. They would be only too glad to hang me if they could get the chance.'

Dilloo undoubtedly said this in all sincerity, and if we feel assured that his suspicion was a foolish one, we cannot deny that his experience of English administration in the Colony had given him some reason to distrust it.

The two men looked at each other moodily. Life for them had lost its hope. They were in that critical state of despondency which leads to so many and such various outbreaks of evil among men.

'Whatever comes, let us meet it bravely!' cried the Sepoy; and they went out to breakfast.

Before noon the Coolies began to swarm again into the open space where the Tadja stood. The performers struck up at intervals a tremendous thrum-thrumming, and raised their discordant voices to the highest pitch, while the Coolies moved round in a sort of dance, every now and then uttering shouts and clapping their hands.

By noon the whole space was filled up by the moving crowd – the men in their white dresses and snowy muslin turbans, the women in brilliantly-coloured skirts and velvet jackets, or with white sarees and chudders, their bare arms and legs, covered with silver, flashing as they moved. Here and there little half-naked children, some brown as berries, others black as coal, danced around their parents, uttering sharp cries of pleasure.

Presently the old white-headed man came out from his house and approached the *Tadja*. Fifteen or twenty strong men, among whom was the Sepoy, stripped to their babbas, followed him. Then amidst the acclamations of the crowd two long powerful bamboos were run through rings on either side of the platform on which the *Tadja* was built, and the bearers, bending to the work, raised it to their shoulders. The drums struck up more frantically than ever; the people shouted and stirred about with wild excitement; the bearers, shaking the light structure into its place on their shoulders, moved forward, the great temple vibrating from base to pinnacle as the sun played brightly on its gaudy hues and flashing tinsel decorations.

The ancient took his place in the van, and then suddenly, with hideous cries, two figures rushed into the crowd, which gave way before them right and left with shrieks of real or feigned alarm. They were two magnificent men, stripped to the skin, with loin-cloths of coloured calico. Their bodies were painted in stripes of bright red and yellow. Over their heads were two frightful masks made to resemble the heads of tigers, and to ligatures bound round their waists were attached tails ringed and curled to resemble those of the animals they presented. The movements of these two figures were singularly soft, agile and graceful. Every play of their muscles was distinctly visible through the thin covering of paint, as they crouched, and leaped, now on all fours, now on their legs. They kept immediately in front of the Tadja, as if to make way for it. Behind came the whole body of Coolies in loose order; some of whom threw off part of their dresses, and wild with excitement or drunkenness danced round it, flourishing their latties. In this order they carried the *Tadja* to a spot where a tomb of plaster had been prepared to imitate masonry. This was intended to represent the tomb of the Prophet's sons. After further ceremonies of a simple character, around this object, the *Tadja* was again lifted, the drums and shoutings increased in their resonant and vocal intensity, and the procession moved off, passing slowly along the high road by the village of Guineatown, to the river which flows about a mile on the other side of it.

The Negroes of the village looked curiously on from a distance, as the excited Coolies passed along the road, many of them (both men and women) by this time far gone in intoxication. At certain intervals the bearers rested and sometimes were changed; but, always in front of the *Tadja*, never resting, running, creeping, leaping, imitating the stealthy and cat-like movements of tigers, went the two strong figures. They were Hunoomaun and Dilloo. In jumping about, neither of them very sober, they came sharply against each other by an accident.

'Devil!' said Dilloo, glaring through his mask at the Sirdar; 'I would I had you by yourself at this moment that I might kill you!'

'Were I alone with thee, O cowardly dog,' replied Hunoomaun, 'thou wouldst not say so.'

'To-night then,' cried Dilloo in the other's ear, 'let us try our strength before all the people, and let him who is beaten die.'

'Good,' answered the other, whose courage was at the moment up to the point.

On either side they leaped from each other, no one having noticed their altercation, and they continued to flash their gaudy colours with increasing activity before the slowly moving temple. In this way the procession approached a spot which had been selected upon the banks of the river. It was a point at which the deep, dark stream ran round a bluff or elevated platform, which rose not more than fifteen or eighteen feet above it – a rapid, brown-tinged, eddying stream, rolling on strong though silent, with the ribbed and roving muscles rising up upon its surface. Here the people arranged themselves near the bank to watch the last of the *Tadja*. The scene was strange. The sultry day was beginning to darken towards its close. The crowd, with its bright and varied dresses, was stirring with restless motion. Above them towered the tinsel pagoda, which quivered on the backs of the weary bearers. The huge sun from afar just peeping over the horizon tinted all the scene with magic hues, while beneath lay the weird and polished darkness of the gliding river. Suddenly the old man, standing out before the people, raised his hand. The bearers, aided by many bystander's, braced themselves for a great effort. There was an instant of deathly stillness. Then the drums struck up – the huge *Tadja* swung to and fro. Another instant and it was thrown over the bank sheer out into the deep, dark, whirling water. The crowd gave a long acclamation, and rushing to the edge watched the floating wreck. The main part, whether weighted by stones or by the plaster tomb, before described, one cannot be positive which, had sunk out of sight.

While every one crowding upon the bank was breathlessly watching the spot where the temple had disappeared, a loud shriek suddenly startled every ear, and a woman, either drunk or frenzied, was seen to cast herself from the bank into the silently seething waters. She instantly disappeared. There was a groan of surprise and horror.

'Who is it ? Who was it?'

'She was heavy with silver – she will never rise.'

'Ramdoolah! Ramdoolah!' shouted those who had been near the miserable woman, when she rushed forward to take her fatal leap.

One of the tigers bounded into the air.

'Are you sure it was Ramdoolah?' he cried through his tigerish mask.

'Yes, yes!' cried a chorus of voices.

Hunoomaun groaned. Not a little of his savings had gone down on the woman's body, irredeemable from the clutch of the insatiable river. He drank a draught of arrack supplied by a friend, and then approached his fellow-actor.

'She has taken all my money with her!' he said through his teeth. 'Cursed be the body of the she-dog! I am ready for anything. To-night we fight to the death!'

'Be it so,' replied Dilloo. And gambolling away he ranged himself near his wife and danced around her, with an activity and skill that won the plaudits of the spectators. Ramdoolah was very soon forgotten.

CHAPTER XLVI

A FIGHT

WHILE these events occupied the Coolies during the day, the managers and overseers at Belle Susanne passed their time in a restless suspense. Mr. Marston had sent his daughter into Georgetown, to the house of a friend. Not giving any credit to the idea of a projected outbreak, he was content to rely for his own protection upon Craig and two black policemen, with such aid as could be rendered by the mercurial Sarcophagus. In the morning, accompanied by the Scotch overseer, he walked over to Belle Susanne to view the scene of the festival, and was received with no unfriendly demonstrations. Late in the afternoon, hearing the shouts of the returning crowd as it passed Guineatown in the dusk, the magistrate with Craig went out again to see the people go by. The procession had then broken up into a loose and disorderly rout. The Indians were hastening back in small bodies. The bottles which some of them were flourishing amply accounted for the irregularity of their order and the noise of their progress. It was almost dark as the magistrate and his companion stood a few paces from the main dam, upon the road leading to his house, and took note of the straggling crowd.

'I see no signs of wickedness there,' said Mr. Marton, *sotto voce*. 'They are just the same as usual, most part drunk, the rest looking at them, all hurrying back to their evening games.'

As he said this a body of Coolies, among whom were several women, approached, in the gloom. Before them danced a tiger-like figure. The Scotchman's quick eye picked out from among them the lithe form and stately step of Lutchmee.

'Ha!' he said. 'There's my nurse Lutchmee. I wonder where her husband is?'

As he spoke one or two of the crowd approached and recognised them. An exclamation instantly went round. 'See! there is the Magistrate Sahib!' Both Dilloo and Lutchmee heard it. She felt a quick, instinctive thrill of alarm. The truth was that Lutchmee would fain have been safe at home, for the rude fun of her companions terrified her. And when she saw the magistrate standing so near the road, she immediately appreciated the danger of a collision. Dilloo's quick eye seeing Mr. Marston, his heart beat furiously within him. His lattey had been left at home, being out of keeping with the character he was playing; and the knife – alas! the knife of the Sepoy was upon that worthy's person, and where that person was at the moment who could say? While this was passing through Dilloo's mind, Craig advanced and shook hands with Lutchmee. The people knew him well, and regarded him not unkindly, while Lutchmee greeted him with intentional warmth. She called to Dilloo, –

'Here is Craig Sahib.'

This broke Dilloo's reverie, and with a rather shambling gait for a tiger, he came up and put out his paw to the Scotchman. Craig looked with admiration at the supple and powerful form of the Coolie, which he could fairly distinguish in the dusk. At this moment a number of others joined the crowd. Among them was the Wahabee. Craig's eyes were all round him, and Marston, standing close by, keenly watched every motion. The Sepoy was well known to both of them. As his tall form came up his eyes flashed with quick intelligence, and pushing through the crowd he drew up close to Dilloo. He was intensely excited.

'See!' he said, in their own language, but in a loud whisper. 'There is your enemy. Let us take him now while we have him.'

Only a moment passed, when Lutchmee uttered a loud scream, and Craig's quick, nervous grasp had seized the Wahabee's hand at the wrist with an iron clench that left it powerless. The Sepoy's knife dropped to the ground. Before Dilloo could stoop to seize it Lutchmee had caught it up and thrown it towards the magistrate, who instantly secured it. At the same time he drew a revolver, and the click of the lock was heard, but he immediately restored it to its pouch again.

'Let the man go, Craig,' he said. 'He is only drunk.' Then addressing the Sepoy he said, 'I know you, and shall see you again.

You must not carry knives. Go home quietly all of you and finish your games, but take care not to make any row.'

The Sepoy and Dilloo, abashed, rapidly pushed on homewards. The crowd followed. Lutchmee remained behind. A great cloud was over her. The fire that shot from her husband's eyes at the instant when she had put beyond his reach the means of vengeance, told her of love driven out by injury not of her inflicting, to make way for a rage that threatened to fall upon her innocent shoulders. She shuddered as she recalled Dilloo's deadly look, and then covering her face she sat down and sobbed aloud.

The two men conversed apart.

'It will not be safe for her to go home to-night,' said Marston. 'The fellow is drunk and excited. To-morrow he will have forgotten it.'

'I almost fear not,' replied Craig, who knew the man better. 'It is most unfortunate that he should have suffered such injustice. He is wonderfully changed of late. I cannot help feeling, Mr. Marston, that he and the Sepoy are quite capable of something desperate. We must take Lutchmee to a place of safety, and I earnestly advise you to have a few more police up to your house. Meantime I will go over and warn Mr. Drummond.'

It was now so dark that moving figures looked like shadows. The magistrate raised Lutchmee kindly and supported her towards his house, as Craig took the shortest path to Belle Susanne.

By this time, Dilloo and the Sepoy, who as they went had been engaged in animated talk, had reached the Negro-yard, and the former looked eagerly round for Lutchmee, among the Coolies that came dropping in. She did not appear, so postponing his wrath with a curse, he turned to get ready for his evening engagement with Hunoomaun. He washed off his gaudy stripes, doffed the tiger-head, abandoned the sinuous tail, and once more appeared with his babba round his loins, a coat above it, and a white turban on his head, – a man worthy to take his part in the athletics of the evening. His evil spirit, the Wahabee, aided these preparations. When all was ready, and the two friends had refreshed themselves with a little food and too much arrack, Dilloo seized the short thick stick, and a small round shield of strong wickerwork, and proceeded to the scene of the Indian sports.

The night was dark, although the sky was spangled with innumerable stars. From horizon to horizon throughout the vast glimmering concave not a single speck of cloud veiled from sight one gem of all the magic constellations of the equatorial hemisphere. A warm, hothouse air, unstirred by a breath of wind, made every object clammy with its moisture. Old Ocean, not very far away, went on dribbling out his majestic forces in fretting the unresisting beach. On the other side, the swampy forest, with all its amazing life of brute and growing things, stretched far and on in immeasurable silence. But, nigh at hand, sharp cries and acclamations and drunken shouts and occasional shrieks of women and strange wild songs disturbed the stillness, while an upward glow of light, which cut a sphere of radiance out of the gloom, was thrown out by a large number of torches fixed upon poles in a large circle, which had been formed in the middle of the exercise-ground of Belle Susanne.

Here an extraordinary scene met the eyes of the armed guards who, under cover of the night, had turned out of Drummond's house and the estate-buildings, to watch the proceedings of the immigrants. The light threw its weird illumination over the masses of excited and chattering Coolies, many of whom squatted in the front ranks of the circle, while behind them row upon row of dark faces and glistening eyes impatiently waited for the commencement of the proceedings. In the middle of the circle two or three well-known athletes, who were to open the proceedings by going through some exercises, and who afterwards were to act as judges of the succeeding trials of skill, were standing and conversing together. The conversation in the crowd was very animated. Its main topic was the approaching combat between Hunoomaun and Dilloo. Though Hunoomaun still retained many of the friends whom he had made during his voyage, he was not a favourite on the estate either among the men or women; while Dilloo was kindly esteemed on every hand. The antipathy between the two men had been necessarily marked by their fellow labourers, and for this reason a peculiar interest was taken in the trial of skill about to take place. Of course the mob were unacquainted with the deadly nature of the proposed conflict, but they expected that very hard blows would be given and received, and that neither of the tigers would be likely to succumb without some cruel marks of the other's power.

Drummond with two or three others had succeeded in ensconcing himself unnoticed behind the Chinese barrack more than a couple of hundred yards away from the scene, and by climbing up some steps to the edge of the roof was able through a glass to command distinctly all the countenances which came fairly under the light. Craig had seen and warned him, and after taking a glance at the crowd was soon on his way back to Mr. Marston's house. Drummond, keenly watching through the glass, said to Fluyschutz, who was beside him, –

'I wonder what those fellows in the centre are whispering about? There is a tall man, your Sepoy I think, and a d – d rascal he is too! – going through the crowd and talking to some of the men. Chester, where is Hunoomaun? And what has become of Dilloo?'

'I have not seen Hunoomaun, sir,' replied the overseer, 'nor have I heard from him. It was arranged that Ramdoolah should meet me beyond the hospital just after dusk, if she had any news, but I waited half an hour and she did not come.'

'Drunk, I suppose,' said Drummond.

'No, I scarcely think that,' replied the Barbadian. 'She is on the track of some one. I do not see either Lutchmee or Dilloo among the people, sir.'

'No, nor Hunoomaun either.'

At this moment there was a movement among the people. Ramsammy left the crowd and went out of the circle of light to meet some one. Scarcely noticed by Drummond, several strong men to whom the soldier had been talking had slipped out of the circle and followed him. He had heard the voice of Dilloo. He checked the latter a few yards beyond the reach of the light, and whispered in his ear, –

'I have arranged with ten or twelve good men to stand exactly behind you. I shall be among them. If you succeed, fall back at once among us, and we will carry you off. We are to go up the dam and turn along the road towards the village, and then you can get up the path by Hofman's Lust to the forest. Try and find the track that leads to the Obe's house. If we give him money he will protect us.'

Dilloo nodded, and drawing a deep breath walked steadily forward. It was a crisis – indeed the most terrible crisis – of his life. He faced it with the boldness of an ignorant fatalism. The only feeling that might at the moment have tended to soften or unnerve his heart, namely, a sense of anxiety and love for Lutchmee, had been suddenly quenched by her act in saving the magistrate. Dilloo's wrath at this want, on her part, of concert and of obedience had blazed so strongly that, as he stepped into the arena which was to settle for him a question of life and death, his only regret in facing his doom was that he had not been able before he did so to despatch his wife! It is hardly possible to conceive how the scientific or unscientific – it matters little what we term them – arrangements of an artificial system of indenture, with the laws that defined and regulated it, had succeeded in moulding out of a manly, tender, generous and loving character, a hard, unnatural and ferocious savage. We have not been without instances in Christian lands where circumstances and conditions have thus distorted most promising natures.

But now the lookers-on from the Chinese barrack had seen Dilloo, equipped as we have described him, march into the circle amidst the acclamations of the spectators. Not many steps behind came Hunoomaun, whose big form, the effect of which was heightened by the large white scarf he had twisted in turban fashion around his head, loomed up gigantic, and caused not a few of the friends of Dilloo to shake their heads. In truth, the Sirdar had never shown himself to such advantage. The loss of, and, with Ramdoolah, the aggregated envies and hatreds of years, and the decisive nature of the issue he had undertaken to face in the approaching fight, all lent to Hunoomaun a nerve and courage which his naturally coward heart had never felt before. And therefore, as he stalked firmly into the middle of the light, with his basket shield hung on his arm, and his hand grasping a strong truncheon, he was able to give Dilloo a fair look of defiance.

'There's our man, sir,' said Chester, who had been looking through the glass. 'But I don't see his wife. Can it be possible that he is going to have a bout with anyone? He is all ready for it, at all events.'

A great shout from the crowd, a great noise of beating drums and squeaking pipes, drowned for the moment Chester's observations.

Then ensued a dead silence.

The crowd settled down steadily. All those in front sat on the ground or squatted on their hams, while those in the rear packed themselves tightly together, until, looking round the circle, it showed in the flaring light of the torches a belt of eager faces and flashing, restless eyes. On one side, the two or three men we have spoken of, quietly dropped off their upper garments, and with nothing but a cincture round the waist, two of them, taking up some heavy Indian clubs, began a series of graceful though powerful exercises. These over, with great applause, two well-known wrestlers stepped forth, and after a little fencing succeeded in getting a grip of each other's brown and slippery bodies. Long and stern was the struggle, eager the interest, and noisy the partisanship of the crowd, until at last, after a prolonged and anxious agony, one went over the other's head and was carried off senseless by his friends. The agitation had now worked itself up to an almost uncontrollable degree. Here and there the arrack had been freely used, and many found it difficult to sustain their standing or sitting positions. The crowd from behind pressed more closely upon those in front. The flare of the blazing torches, renewed by watchful Coolies after each bout, the close moist air of the night, the heat of nearly a thousand bodies rising in such an atmosphere, made the scene appear like a round sphere of luminous mist, in which dark figures stood out strange and almost awful to the unseen lookers-on. Drummond was eagerly gazing through his glass.

'There is something strange going on,' he said to his friends. 'Dilloo and Hunoomaun are both stripping.'

'Then they are going to fight,' said Chester. 'Mr. Drummond, you ought to put a stop to that. If Dilloo gets a chance at Hunoomaun he will kill him.'

'Oh! nonsense,' said Drummond. 'He is not so easily killed. He is big and strong, and looks uncommonly like business. By Jove, I never saw him undressed before. He has limbs like a bull. Ha!' he continued, 'the Sepoy has just taken off Dilloo's coat. He's a tidy man too, and every inch an athlete. We shall see some fun. I shouldn't wonder if he took the wind out of the big fellow after all.'

'Won't you interfere?' asked Chester, anxiously.

'No,' replied the manager. 'They won't hurt each other. There! They are about to begin.'

With the naked eye the whites could see the two figures step out into the arena, and cautiously approach each other.

We will watch the fight from the inner circle. When the rivals moved forward, the practised eyes of the athletes, who might be called the bottle-holders, were unable to determine to which of them should be awarded the palm of promise. Hunoomaun, with long and powerful limbs, great hands and feet, strongly-knit and rather ungainly joints, a broad chest and powerful ribs, in addition to his superior height, looked a most formidable antagonist in a combat, wherein the sole protection was a wicker-work shield, and the adroitness and quickness of the parry and defence. But then it was clear that under his black and deeply-pitted skin, there were layers of fat which, however they might contribute to give a better contour to his form, were not likely to lend him any advantage in a prolonged struggle.

On the other hand, every eye that turned to Dilloo as he stepped forward easily and lightly upon the beaten ground, was instantly captivated by the perfect proportions of his form, the smooth brightness of his skin, the clear, easy-going play of his powerful muscles, and all those evidences of good condition which are the delight of connoisseurs. There did not seem to be an ounce of unnecessary flesh over the broad brawny shoulders and breast, or on the strong ribs, over which his well-oiled skin played smoothly. His arms and legs, so finely formed and so firmly moulded, promised rapidity, intensity and exhaustless power of motion. He stood forth, poising in his right hand the heavy truncheon which had won the Sepoy's admiration, and on his left arm bearing the little shield which was his only protection. His head was uncovered, but his hair, short as it was, had been bound up by the Sepoy with a thin strip of calico. Hunoomaun, on the contrary, had come forward still wearing the large turban which gave such additional importance to his height. Dilloo, keenly watching his antagonist, said a few words in a low tone to Ramsammy, who addressed the judges.

'Hunoomaun must take off his turban. It is not fair that he should protect his head.'

The judges nodded. With very bad grace the Sirdar lifted the white bundling from his head. He inadvertently threw it on the ground, where it fell with a thud. What made it so heavy? He had carefully lined it with some strong iron wire. Dilloo and his friend smiled significantly.

And now the two men, standing within two yards of each other, each with his left arm carrying the wicker shield advanced a little before his chest, each leaning lightly forward on the left foot, which was thrust before the right, each glowering over the edge of his shield keenly into the other's eyes, as if to read in advance the thoughts and intents of each passing movement of the brain, and each very silently, dexterously, but deliberately twirling his truncheon in his hand, began a series of slow passes, in regular and alternate order. As they did this stepping round and round, every one in the circle could note with admiration the play of every muscle, and the trained science of the two athletes. The music, which had struck up as they commenced, gave the time to these preliminary motions, which were of a singularly graceful character. Gradually the music became more and more impatient, and with its quicker movement the steps and passes of the players increased in activity. Their eyes began to glow with excitement and their limbs to be bedewed with the heat. Sharp and distinct through the musical brawl could be heard the regular cracks of the sticks as they struck together or fell upon the wicker shields, which had need to be strong to bear such blows. Still more rapid grew the music, yet more speedy the interchange of movement, sharper and quicker the rattle of the truncheons and the clashing of the shields, until at last so vehement and quick were the motions of the men that the passes could scarcely be distinguished one from another, and the cracking of their weapons gave forth an almost uninterrupted sound. It was then that suddenly Dilloo gave a sharp cry, and a thud was heard to break the monotony of the rattling chorus of blows. Another sharp cry, this time from Hunoomaun; another, and another, and each time it was clear to the spectators that one or other of the combatants had been severely hit. Yet neither stayed his hand a moment. Each kept his dark eye fixed on the other. Each seemed possessed with a serpentine quickness of movement and glance. So fierce and frequent had the blows become that it was impossible to distinguish them, or to guess even where or when a wound had been given. And now from both the combatants began to rain not only a dew of perspiration, but dark spots of blood, some of which, in their rapid evolutions, sprinkled the white dresses of the men and women who were nearest the arena. But so wild had the excitement of the crowd become that this was all unnoticed. There in the midst of the lights was something twirling, rattling, loudly breathing, occasionally crying out sharply, but like one single monster all arms and legs and having the velocity of a machine. Round and round it spun with untiring clatter and action. More frequent and copious were the sprinklings of the crimson rain. When now and then out of the whirling fray a face gleamed for an instant under the light, men fancied they could see nothing but features of gore, with eyes flashing white and deadly. It gradually became clear to every one of the thousand spectators that this was no mere bout of amusement, but that the two men were fighting to the death. The effect of this conviction was only to intensify the agitation. The blood that now dyed the ground, and flew so freely about, appealed to the savage nature in every breast. The musicians became so excited that they ceased to play, and a dead silence fell upon the wondering crowd, as they listened to the regular tattoo of the heavy truncheons on wood, and shield and skin, – rattle and crack and thud, then crack and rattle and thud, in cruel and monotonous sequence. The fight had gone on so long that both the men were becoming fatigued. The passes were less swiftly made, the blows less frequently given; but this gave the onlookers the opportunity to observe that the strokes when they did fall were more determined and deadly. Further, it was gradually made manifest that Hunoomaun was suffering most. He was drawing back before the rain of Dilloo's blows on his stick and shield and skin, and was acting more on the defensive – an attitude in which his superior height gave him an advantage. Moreover he was obviously distressed for wind. Seeing this Dilloo pressed him more ardently, and being a little incautious, gave the Sirdar an opportunity. Intending to finish the conflict, he brought his stick down with fearful force, directing it at his adversary's head. Dilloo was only just able to turn his head aside, when the cruel weapon fell upon his shoulder, making a savage indentation in the skin, and disabling his left arm. But the Coolie scarcely felt the pain. Before Hunoomaun could recover himself, the terrible heavily-primed truncheon of Dilloo had struck him on the temple, and, while he was falling, a second blow crashed through his skull, and in an instant he lay on the ground, dead – and weltering in his blood.

CHAPTER XLVII

THE ESCAPE

DILLOO, overcome by loss of blood and by the prolonged and terrible exertions of the struggle, fell back into the arms of the Wahabee.

It is very difficult to relate, with due regard to chronological order and artistic realisation, what then occurred. The reader must remember that nearly a thousand Coolies, of whom more than three fourths were men trained to labour, most of them excited by drink, were gathered in a dense mass around the arena of the conflict. Within a couple of hundred yards of them, and keenly scrutinising all their proceedings, were Drummond, Fluyschutz, and some overseers, every one armed to the teeth. Farther off, at the estate-buildings, keeping a good look-out, was a large party of whites, mostly overseers. Another armed party, consisting of Martinho and two Georgetown clerks, guided by Simon Pety, the latter furnished with an old gun, dangerous chiefly to the bearer, who regarded it with wholesome suspicion, had made a wide detour, and were ensconced in a cane-piece, some four or five hundred yards up the dam on the land side, thus commanding the regular approaches to the Negro-yard from the 'back,' or from Guineatown and Hofman's Lust. Their position allowed them to see little but a great sphere of illumination and men as trees moving within it. The circumstances of the fight between Hunoomaun and Dilloo were equally unknown to them and to the men in the estate-buildings.

Both these parties were startled into instant watchfulness and alarm by a sudden outcry from the mob of Coolies, followed immediately by a flash and a shot. What had happened?

Drummond had been closely watching the marvellous movements of his two Coolies. From a distance, and in the doubtful light, he could not detect the severity of the conflict or observe the free flow of blood. Knowing that the Indians were accustomed on these occasions to have exhibitions of prowess in the game of single-stick or truncheon, he supposed that the two men were simply intent on exhibiting their superior skill; and, a strong man himself, he could not withhold exclamations of admiration at the pluck and persistency of the two rivals. But his quick eye, aided by the glass, saw in a moment the meaning of Hunoomaun's last tremendous effort; and even though the cracks of Dilloo's blows on the skull of the unhappy Sirdar had not sounded clearly to his ear, the manner of Hunoomaun's fall, and the second terrible stroke, delivered as he was in the act of succumbing, carried a quick conviction to the manager's brain that the driver had been seriously and intentionally hurt. The yell that followed from the crowd, their terrible outcry and agitation as they surged round the fainting Dilloo, quickened the manager's rapid suspicion that this was a pre-arranged affair and perhaps a preliminary to an out-break. Lifting his hand in the air he fired one of the chambers of his revolver as a signal to his forces, and then, descending from the barrack, moved forward towards the crowd seething under the glare of the torches. But the Coolies were too quick for him.

The moment Drummond's shot was fired, a voice in the crowd – it was the voice of the Sepoy – uttered a command. In an instant every flaring torch was extinguished, and the scene which had been a moment before so vivid was suddenly swallowed up by the darkness. Drummond at once checked his men, and, stopped to deliberate.

In the crowd, now deprived of light, everyone was talking and everyone had a different idea. They shouted for Dilloo, they cried out against the manager, they proposed to fire the buildings. The women, rudely pushed about, and half crushed in the struggling mass, shrieked dismally, and some of the Chinese, drawing their knives, were in two minds whether they would not let go their savage natures, and, like Malays, 'run a muck.' But amidst it all a body of about a dozen kept their heads, and had a definite purpose. They were guided by Ramsammy. He, supporting Dilloo, whispered to those nearest him to force a way through the crowd in the direction of the back-dam and to get off the estate as rapidly as possible. Dilloo, though terribly wounded, was by this time recovering breath, and able to walk. The band keeping together succeeded in

breaking through the press, but it was easier to do this than to separate themselves from the people, who were ready to take any direction given to them. Thus it happened that, although Dilloo and his
body-guard went on quickly, they drew after them a comet-like tail
of excited Coolies. The Sepoy saw the danger. He knew that they
must now be followed by Drummond's forces, and that there was a
risk of a collision. Of course he had no knowledge of Martinho's
ambush in the cane-piece. Therefore, as his company were directing
their way, hampered by their mates, along the right bank of the
estate canal straight on towards the spot where Martinho and his
party lay *perdus*, the Wahabee seized Dilloo's arm, and evading the
agitated Coolies, slipped deliberately but quickly into the canal; and
crossing it, proceeded, as rapidly as Dilloo's state would allow, up the
other bank. This took them towards the point where the footpath to
Guineatown crossed the canal and the estate dams. As they were
nearing this point, Dilloo, faint from loss of blood, stumbled, and fell
upon the ground.

'Leave me,' he said hoarsely to his companion. 'You must
escape. I shall die here.'

'No, no,' cried the other, earnestly, trying to rouse him. 'If you
are found you will be hung. Come a little way farther, and I can get
you help.'

While he was speaking, there was the flash and loud report of
firearms a few hundred feet off on the other side of the dam,
succeeded by a vast hubbub. Martinho's party, supposing that they
had been discovered, and that the mob coming in their direction
meant to attack them, had fired off their weapons to stop the
advance, and had then discreetly run away. The Coolies, checked for
a moment, but furious at this unexpected reception, which naturally
seemed to them to be a wanton offence, charged into the cane-piece
with loud cries, and becoming disordered in the eagerness of their
search, soon spread themselves far into the estate, with no other
result than to wear out their strength and their excitement.

But while this was going on, the Sepoy and Dilloo had a diversion
of their own. The noise disturbed some one who was keeping guard
at the narrow board which served as a bridge over the canal. And
while Ramsammy, alarmed by the events which had occurred on the

other side of the water was endeavouring to get his friend to rouse himself and escape, a noise of footsteps running in their direction disturbed him. He was just about to rise when, some twenty feet off, a shadow could be discerned swiftly coming through the gloom; there was a sudden blaze of light, a prodigious noise, the whistle of shot, and then a yell, all sufficiently frightful. The Coolie, whose stooping position had probably saved his life, saw a few feet off a body rolling on the ground, and heard a voice which sent a thrill through the frame of Dilloo.

'Oh – oh – oh! Pety, you smote hip and thigh. Dis time de Lord call you home, I reckon. Oh, Susey, Susey, nebber see you 'gain! Dis yere gun gone off spontaneous, and fixed me up. Oh – oh – oh! hit 'im in de belly – all de bowel gush out! Oh———.' Splash rolled Pety into the water. The Sepoy, running along the bank, searched eagerly for the Negro's gun, in order to brain him. Fortunately, after going off unexpectedly and by the force of its recoil, as he was running along holding it loosely in front of him, hitting him in the region he had alluded to, the gun had gone under water with Simon Pety, and did not come to surface again when he scrambled up the bank, puffing and blowing like a small rhinoceros. Before the poor fellow could catch his breath or pull his wits into order, he was seized by the throat. But Pete was not to be choked off like a dog, and grappling at his adversary he gave him an unexpected kick with his knee in the wind, which made the angry Sepoy let go. Then, fearful lest the Negro should be backed by other estate-people, the Indian, soldier as he had been, turned and fled. Simon, ejaculating, 'Ha! I put to flight de army ob de wicked!' shook off the water, and feeling in his pocket for a small flask of rum, which Susey had supplied to solace his night watch, was about to prescribe it to himself, when he was startled by a groan which seemed to come from the ground only a few feet from where he was standing.

'De Lord deliber us!' he cried. 'Yere's anoder ambush. No! yere's a living being on de ground. You ain't dead yit, are you?'

He knelt down beside the figure, which now lay motionless. Then putting his hand upon it, he found the body was half-naked, still warm, and wet with something the touch of which instinctively made Pety shudder.

'Dis yere's a case of wilful allyby. Dat oder fellow gone and done dis *felo de se*. – Hallo! dis yere man agoin' to move! Ki! you got to surrender to me, General Simon Pety, or I kill you!'

Dilloo groaned.

'Please, yes, you go kill me – please,' said the Coolie.

Pety jumped a couple of yards off. He knew the voice. This was the formidable Dilloo, most likely laying an 'ambush' in real earnest. But finding he was not followed, mingled curiosity and kindness drew Pety back to the side of the wounded man. The Negro was a very different being now from the hypocritical missionary and iconoclast who had sought to convert Rambux No. 2.

'Dilloo!' he said, kindly, 'dis ain't you?'

'Iss,' replied Dilloo. 'Coolie die.'

'No – no die!' cried Pety. 'Stop! yere's rum. Wait a minute! Getty water.'

He reduced the strength of the spirit with water from the canal, and then poured some down the Coolie's throat. This revived him.

'What you do yere?' asked the Negro, as the Coolie sat up. 'Stay, you not goin' to move yet.'

'Kill Hunoomaun!' said Dilloo, savagely. 'Hit 'im head dis stick.' The truncheon was still in his grasp.

Pety shuddered. He knew that the two men were enemies. And here was the very Dilloo, who had once given him a beating, a murderer, and completely in his power. But he hardly thought of that.

'Dou shalt not kill!' said Pety, solemnly.

'Dilloo no kill Hunoomaun, Hunoomaun kill Dilloo,' said the other, simply.

'Hum!' reflected Pete. Then he gave Dilloo his hand and helped him up gently. The other was greatly refreshed. Pete administered a little more rum and a piece of biscuit.

'Dilloo gib Pety licking one time,' said the Negro. 'But de Lord say, "If dine enemy hunger, feed him; if he dirsty, gib him drink." I guess I go to heap coals ob fire on your head dis time! Take some more. Now, Dilloo, dis gentleman not agoin' to hurt you. You get away off quick, oderwise Massa Drummond ketch you – you go hang.'

Dilloo shook at the idea of that. He took Pety's hand and squeezed it gratefully. The Coolie was not mortally wounded, and his spirit was recovering. Then he turned to go.

'Stay!' said the Negro, in a whisper, 'dere's someone coming. Come in yere!' and he dragged Dilloo by the arm into the cane-piece on the left, and going on his hands and knees made along one of the rows for fifteen or twenty feet. Dilloo followed. They crouched down each behind a sugar-plant. Voices were heard of persons coming along the canal, and on the nearer side of it. It was Drummond's party, now joined by Martinho and others.

When, just as he was advancing on them, the torches had been put out by the Coolies, the manager turned and retreated a little to form his plans. He saw the uselessness of throwing himself into a crowd in which no one could distinguish friend from foe. Chester was sent round to order the buildings-party to remain in their place, and to keep strictly on the defensive; while Drummond resolved to wait, and ascertain before moving what the labourers meant to do. In a few minutes the noise and move-ment beyond the exercise-ground indicated that the crowd had gone up the canal towards the back-dam. The manager knew that Martinho was on the look-out in that direction, and presently he saw the flashes of the guns fired from Martinho's station, and then could discern the scattering of the immigrants over the estate. He resolved to retire and send for a body of police, and meantime to await any attack that might be made on the buildings. Immediately after his arrival, Martinho came in with the whole of his party except Simon Pety, who had been detached to watch the cross-path we have so often mentioned. Martinho's companions had heard the report of the Negro's gun, and as by this time the sounds of the pursuing Coolies showed that the great body of them had penetrated far into the estate, Drummond resolved to make a dash to rescue Simon Pety, if he were yet alive.

Thus it was that the two men crouching in the canes heard the manager's voice as he came along the dam. His quick eye, now ac-customed to the darkness, detected signs in the long grass on the side of the path which led him to stop.

'See here, Martinho; uncover the lights, and let us have a look.'

'Ha! see!' he continued. 'Somebody has been lying here, and there is blood on this grass!'

'Yes, sir,' said another of the party, who had gone on a few steps, and who now distracted the manager's attention from what might have led to a discovery; 'and there seems to have been a scuffle here.'

The lantern was brought to bear first on the scene of Pety's struggle with the Sepoy, and then of his involuntary gyrations with the gun. It was clear that some one had gone down the bank into the water, and equally clear that some one had come out of the water. On the hasty survey in the imperfect light, it was the general opinion that the person who had come out of the water had entered it again, voluntarily or involuntarily, and as drowning was out of the question he must, they concluded, have passed over. Therefore the party resolved to get across by the bridge and examine the other side.

This search after Pety, occupying as it did all Drummond's attention, probably saved the manager from a serious collision with his labourers, and the Colony from a dangerous outbreak, for before long the Coolies, finding no opposition, and having been uninjured by Martinho's fire, dropped quietly back to their homes and went to rest.

No sooner was his master fairly on the other side of the water, than Pety, taking Dilloo's hand, and whispering to him to keep perfectly quiet, cautiously made his way through the canes towards the path leading to Hofman's Lust. It was pitch dark, but both of them knew the way perfectly. They had nearly reached the road when Pete, who was in advance, caught his foot in some soft body lying on the ground and fell over head first. He could not restrain an exclamation. Fortunately it was inarticulate, for Drummond's quick ear heard the noise. He instantly fired in the direction from which it came. But for that the Sepoy, who was in fact Pety's stumbling-block, might have come to a quarrel with the Negro, which would have been fatal to Dilloo's escape. The sense of common danger kept the three fugitives perfectly quiet; and Drummond, after shouting Pete's name, and listening in vain for any movement, thought it discreet not to tempt the danger of an ambush, and withdrew with his small party to the buildings. Dilloo had quickly passed some explanations with Ramsammy, and told him of the kindly part the Negro was playing. They lay quiet for some time, until they heard by the retreating voices that the danger of discovery was over, and then the three men debouched on the track to Guineatown. There Pety handed over to the Sepoy the remains of the flask of rum and some bread, that is to say, biscuit. He advised the two fugitives to go up the dam of Hofman's Lust to the edge of the wilderness, and then strike across to the plantain-grounds, and follow the path through the forest and swamp to the house of the Obe man. That person would, if properly propitiated, cure Dilloo's wounds and conceal the two men from pursuit. In sending them away, Pety drew out of his belt sundry pieces of silver, which he forced on the unwilling Coolies.

The simplicity of Pety's moral views can alone account for his omission to note that while he was doing a good turn to an enemy, which seemed to be in strict accord with Scriptural injunction, he was rendering himself accessory to a felony and amenable to human laws. To his mind the refinement was inappreciable. And he would probably, if challenged, have taken pretty much the same ground as an Irish monk at Verona, who had been a prize-fighter. This person observing one day an Italian soldier behaving cruelly to a poor man, interfered, and advised the soldier to stop. On this the fellow struck him a buffet in the face.

'My friend,' said the friar, 'the Saviour saith, "If thine enemy strike thee on the right cheek, turn to him the other." Here is my other cheek.'

'Well!' ejaculated the soldier, 'there!' giving him another buffet.

'Now,' said the friar, slipping off his cloak, 'having enjoined thus far, the Scripture saith no more. Wherefore I conclude it leaveth the rest to the judgment of the saint, and my judgment is to give thee a thrashing.' Which he duly performed.

Shaking Pete's hands and thanking him warmly, the Coolies made off as quickly as possible; while the Negro slipped down the dam, and running into his house in a state of well-affected terror, nearly frightened Susey into very serious consequences. Everyone connected with the estate was too glad to see him back, and too occupied with the apprehensions of this exciting night, to examine narrowly into his account of his adventures. It was most readily believed that he had run away, and, like the fight related by the American humorist, 'His subsequent adventures interested them no more.'

CHAPTER XLVIII

ACCESSORIES AFTER THE FACT

PETY'S safe return and the escape of the two Coolies ended the second stage of the proceedings of the eventful night of the *Tadja* festival. Hunoomaun's body still lay weltering upon the ground. But Drummond, as soon as he had convinced himself that there was no danger of an attack by the Coolies, bethought him of the necessity of holding an immediate inquest, and in the middle of the night sent over to Mr. Marston a messenger with an account of what had occurred. The magistrate was on the alert. The report of several shots had reached his ears during the evening, but unwilling to move from his post until he had been duly summoned, he had waited for news with deep anxiety. He ordered a detachment of police to Belle Susanne, with an inspector, who was directed to make the arrangements for the investigation. Mr. Marston and Craig, with another detachment, set out by way of Hofman's Lust, with the view of learning, if possible, something of Ramsammy's whereabouts. The dangerous demeanour of the Sepoy, on his way back from the immersion of the *Tadja*, added to his evident friendship for Dilloo, led the magistrate, when he came to reflect on these matters under the light of the startling news he had received, to suspect the Sepoy of complicity with the accused. His suspicions were intensified when a search of the Sepoy's quarters yielded no sign of him, although the night was far advanced and all the other Coolies had retired to their beds. As soon as he had assured himself of Ramsammy's elopement, Mr. Marston went on to Belle Susanne. As Lutchmee was the wife of the accused, the magistrate deemed it right that she should accompany his party in charge of Craig.

Meantime, the scene of the Sirdar's death had been examined by the police. His body was found frightfully bruised, not only by

Dilloo's blows, but by the trampling of the Coolies in making their escape from the ground. No one, indeed, had thought it worth while to take charge of the dead Sirdar. His corpse was carried to the open space under the hospital, and there laid out to be viewed by the magistrate and jury. Three or four of the visitors from Georgetown, who were not connected with the estate, were then sworn in as a jury, and the Guineatown doctor, who came and conducted an autopsy with commendable rapidity, certified in the usual technical terms as to the cause of death. There could be little doubt what the verdict would be. It was one of 'Wilful Murder.'

In the course of the inquiry, for which several Coolies were summoned from their beds, it came out that Ramdoolah, the reputed wife of the deceased, had committed suicide, that the Sepoy had absconded, and, lastly, that Lutchmee had not returned to the estate with her husband, but had spent the evening at the magistrate's house. This last piece of intelligence enraged Drummond to a high degree. Marston very frankly related the passage between the Coolies and himself, admitting that, regarded in the light of later events, it bore a significance greater than he had at the time attached to it.

'I supposed they were merely drunk,' he explained; 'and when I had secured the only weapon I saw, I thought it better to take no further notice. I retained Lutchmee, because I hoped that when her husband's intoxication was over he would have forgotten the incident.'

But Drummond refused to see any justice in these explanations. The truth was, that at the bottom of his heart he was persuaded that a collision with the immigrants, followed by swift, relentless punishment, would have a salutary effect which years could not undo. The peace of the Colony, in his view, depended on some signal example. Now, the day had passed without a rising. The preparations had been useless. The forty or fifty thousand Indians in the Colony were given time to work out those deep insidious plans of which their employers dreamed. If any one has a difficulty in conceiving how a man with any ordinary sense, not to say of humanity or justice, but of simple selfish policy, could work himself into such a frame of mind as this, let him peruse the speeches, the letters, the expressions of feeling, which gave such vivid force to all the doings of those who, in the year 1876, called themselves the 'People of Barbados' ; – I mean not the words merely of obvious ruffians, but of putative gentlemen.

Lutchmee, when she had answered the few questions which were put to her by the jury, retired and rejoined Craig, who, talking apart with one or two friendly overseers, had thought it discreet not to intrude on Drummond's notice. Daylight was by this time not far off. As the young Scotchman was about to leave the ground, he was intercepted by Simon Pety, with a whispered invitation to his cottage, coupled with a hint that he had something important to tell. Craig assented, and he and his companion followed the Negro to his house, the shutters of which were carefully closed. In the sitting-room Mrs. D'Orsay was waiting with coffee and food supplied by Missa Nina, to which Craig's hunger enabled him to do sufficient justice. When he had finished, Pete beckoned him into the back room, and confided to him all his adventures of the night before.

'Why should you help Dilloo to run away?' asked the Scotchman, when the Negro had finished.

'"If dine enemy hunger, feed him" – "it shall be an excellent ile dat shall not break his head." Dat's de reason, Massa Craig.'

Craig smiled grimly; but, not being very credulous of the Negro's good-faith, added, 'Nothing else?'

'Yes, Massa Craig,' replied Pety, in a low tone, and with a confusion of manner not natural to him; 'dis de true reason, Massa Craig. Before I get complete sanctification I go and tell Massa Marston a big lie about Dilloo. Dat always heavy like a piece ob lead on my conscience. So, when I see Dilloo purloining away from pursuit, you see, Massa Craig, I want to try to help 'im off.'

'Yes, I see,' replied Craig, dryly. 'But you know, Pety, you have made yourself liable to be had up before Mr. Marston for being an accessory to the murder, if it was one, and you *will* be had up, if they find it out, unless you tell at once what has become of Dilloo.'

Pety's face grew terribly long, and assumed a strange leaden tint; but after a short struggle with himself the natural colour and expression began to revive.

'Well, Massa Craig,' he said, solemnly, 'by de help ob de Lord I risk it! I swear dat time before de magistrate Dilloo beat me for noting, when he only come in and save Rambux from a beating. – Rambux bad man, you know, Massa Craig. He bow down to a graven image ob de debbil. – But I tell lie about Dilloo, and now I nebber gib up de knowledge where he gone to!'

'Hum!' said the Scotchman. 'But, my friend, what am I to do? Does it not strike you that if I keep this quiet, I shall be doing exactly what you have done, and be in the same position, if not worse?'

Pety was astounded at this view of the transfer of moral responsibilities by a law which, like the familiar example of the transmission of force through a row of billiard-balls, operated to carry criminality through a number of intermediates to the farthest end of a series.

'Oh, Massa Craig!' he said, however, 'sure you nebber go tell on de poor man, – sartain you nebber do dat!'

And truly, when Mr. Craig had to face the duty fairly, he was agitated by conflicting emotions. But when he turned and looked into the room where Lutchmee, gathered up in a corner, sat, a picture of the most terrible suffering and sorrow, his mind was made up. With all the firmness of his nature he said to himself, 'I will die before I give up the secret!'

It was arranged that Lutchmee should remain for the day at the Negro's house, awaiting any information that might be received of her husband; while Craig joined Mr. Marston, who was setting out to report to the Governor the incidents of the night. There was a good deal of excitement in Georgetown over the intelligence, but, fortunately, in all other parts of the Colony, with the exception of a few drunken broils, the *Tadja* had passed off without an insurrection.

CHAPTER XLIX

MASSA DRUMMOND'S GOD

THE sun had risen. His long rays traversed the flat and silent land – silent save where with sharp strident cries troops of the white and scarlet ibis sought the shore, or in the sedgy meadows the handsome clean-limbed cattle rose and shook themselves, and hailed the god of day with pious lowings. Swiftly before his burning glances mist and dew went up, like the incense of prayer, unseen to heaven. The same sun brightened the scene of bloodshed, and licked up the drops that testified of a human life ebbed out for ever. The same sun lit up the active examination and pursuit of avenging law and the flight of guilty fugitives. The same sun woke up discontented labour and terrified capital. No work was done or attempted to be done anywhere in the Colony that day.

The Coolies gathered together and talked in anxious whispers, while the managers, overseers and police kept coming and going as if the whole country were in rebellion.

In the meantime, the two fugitives, following Pety's directions, had passed beyond cultivation and penetrated the forest and jungle. Here and there were open swamps or dry sandy strips; then came close undergrowth, and over it the shadowing foliage of large thickly-growing trees. The path which had been described to them as the route to their destination – the lair of that strange African wizard and impostor, the Obe man, – was quite undiscoverable in the darkness, and the fugitives pursued their way guided by a brilliant star which they had noticed in the direction which they desired to pursue. Spurred on by fear, they pressed painfully forward. In the darkness they tripped over treacherous vines, or caught their arms or necks in swinging loops of the 'bush-ropes,' or canoned against prickly trunks of the tree-ferns, or tumbled over and into vast nests of ants, whose action and sharp vengeance on Dilloo's wounds gave him fearful discomfort. At length, when they had pushed on for several miles, and were secure from any immediate capture, the Coolie gave way, and sank upon a ridge of sand, which happened to occupy an open space in the forest. He had only reached thus far by using up the remains of Pety's flask, and now, between his wounds, his exertions and the previous day's intoxication, he was in a fever and delirious.

The morning was just about to break. A dull light began to steal through the vast forest and up into the overhanging sky. The deep, strong darkness seemed to move about, and to be transformed into strange shapes, among which there opened up, as in a black fog, awful, mysterious vistas. Laying his friend in as comfortable a place as he could find, the Sepoy began to explore in every direction, in the hope of finding some trace of a path, but in vain. The sun had been up an hour, and he was still wearily pursuing his search when he heard at some distance through the woods a loud, clear voice, that rang beneath the arches of the huge trees with a wonderful gush of sonorous melody. Startled by the sound, which seemed to come from a woman, the Coolie rapidly stalked from trunk to trunk, until he came in sight of a tall handsome Negress, who was following an almost imperceptible path in the forest. On her head was a basket containing fruits and provisions. Keenly glancing round, the Coolie saw that she was alone, and with cautious movements followed her. After passing through the forest for some distance, she reached a spot in its densest part, where the dampness of the ground and the luxuriance of the vegetation warned off human beings by its deep gloom and its fetid atmosphere. It was a home of poisonous plant and teasing insect and deadly snake, and of the rankest luxuriance of vegetation. Towards the thickest part of this close the woman directed her way, and while the Coolie was wondering how she would get through the tight and tangled undergrowth, she suddenly disappeared. Following quickly on her steps, Ramsammy found himself opposite a scarcely discernible opening through the otherwise impenetrable bush, and dropping on his hands and knees glided silently onwards for ten or fifteen feet. As he crawled along, he suddenly touched with his naked body a large smooth object, which snatched itself away with startling vigour, and hissed a challenge that thrilled through his heart. It was a snake – a huge bush-master, and if it had been in the humour to tackle the Sepoy it would have saved law and administration any further trouble on his behalf. As it passed away he could hear far away through the bamboos the sway and noise of moving pythons and other snakes, disturbed by his entrance. He glided on, and found himself on the edge of a wide cleared space of considerable size, shut in with splendid vegetation, around and above. High up, supported in air by the majestic pillars of the mora and the greenheart, and tall, slender palms, and ribbed with huge branches, hung a vast canopy of dense foliage, which the rays of sunshine vainly strove to penetrate. The branches and trunks and stems of the palms and other trees below were trellised and looped all round with swinging lianas. Beneath was the dense protective circle of forest undergrowth, – mixed bamboos and tree-ferns and young palms, and all the quick wild luxuriance of a tropical bush. The dimness of the outer forest here gave way to a deeper and more awful gloom. The chatter of paroquets and monkeys, the cry and clatter of gorgeous huge-billed toucans, did not disturb this dismal scene. It seemed fitted to be a home of silent-creeping reptiles and of death. A shudder ran through the Coolie's veins, and striving to accommodate his sight to the darkness, and to discover the movements of the woman, he observed that, in the middle of the enclosure, at the foot of a huge mora tree, which might be called the central pole of this terrible tabernacle, there was a hut of large dimensions, constructed of timber and bamboos and thatched with the leaves of the *trooly*. Out of this hut there had moved silently a large dark figure, before which the woman had prostrated herself in presenting the basket. On a motion from the figure she rose, and they conversed together in a low voice. The Sepoy's inspection of the man from a distance had no reassuring effect. His size was extraordinary, and his vast shoulders and long arms impressed Ramsammy with the feeling that, even if this huge Negro did not possess supernatural powers, it would scarcely be desirable to engage in a struggle with him on natural grounds. Indeed, Ramsammy began to wish himself out of the place, which chilled him by its dreadful and mysterious circumstances. The gloom, the size, the silence – broken only by the uncertain movements of the reptiles, – the awe of the woman – all shattered Ramsammy's usual confidence.

The Negress and the figure, which Ramsammy did not doubt was the Obe whom the Negroes dreaded so much, disappeared into the hut. Thereupon Ramsammy turned to flee, but no sooner had he begun to creep through the foliage, than on all sides there arose a commotion among the snakes that swarmed in the under-wood about the enclosure. They were indeed the wizard's body-guard. In an instant his quick ear detected the sensation, and guessing there was some stranger in the neighbourhood he rushed out of the hut.

'Who dah? who dah?' he cried, in a terrible voice, running to-wards the entrance.

The Coolie, in desperation, jumped to his feet, and, facing the Obe man, made an Eastern salaam, and stood silent before him.

'What you man do heah? – You Coolie, – you no niggah!'

The woman had run out after him, and was looking on. It was no other than Simon Pety's friend, Miss Rosalind Dallas. She at once recognised the Coolie as 'Indian soldiah,' familiar to her in Guineatown. In truth, having gone to consult the Obe with the ob-ject of revenging herself on Simon Pety, she had been induced to become a slave of the brutal impostor. As the latter was about to stretch out towards the poor Coolie his finger, one touch of which would have turned him in a few minutes into a corpse,* Miss Dallas intervened.

'Know dis man,' she said to her ugly lover. 'Only Coolie man. – You want Obe?' she inquired of the Sepoy.

'Iss,' responded Master Ramsammy. 'Coolie man, Dilloo, ober dere, go die. Obe sahib come medicine 'im?'

He pointed out of the enclosure, and the Obe, seeing that it was a genuine demand of help, said, –

'Coolie man hab money?'

'Iss, iss!' replied Ramsammy, but cautiously as regarded him-self. 'Plenty cash ober dere.'

This necessitated going for it, at all events, and the huge Negro accordingly set off at once with the Sepoy. Rosalind, out of curiosity, followed.

* See Charles Kingsley's 'At Last.'

When they reached Dilloo, the Obe, empiric as he was, saw at a glance that there was little to be done for the patient. He had lost a great quantity of blood; the juice of poisonous shrubs had entered through the open wounds; ants and flies had already begun to pasture on the helpless patient. In a few words the Coolie explained, as best he could, that Dilloo had killed a man, and was running away from justice; and then he gave the man all the money Dilloo had, not disclosing the fact that in his own babba there was hid away an adequate store of silver pieces.

The Obe was an African of the lowest type. His receding forehead, huge broad face, with its baboon-like features, enormous ears, weighed down with large metal rings; lips like those of a hippopotamus, his great trunk and powerful arms and legs, altogether made a creature whose physical characteristics were worthy of the terror inspired by his infernal profession.

He ordered Miss Rosalind and the Coolie to carry the delirious patient to the enclosure, and in a short time Dilloo was lying outside the hut, upon a bed of dried grass. Then the Negro, who had been preparing a warm fomentation, directed Rosalind to wash the Coolie's wounds with it, while he himself, retiring again to his hut, concocted with muttered incantations a draught to be administered to the patient. The effect of the draught was to put Dilloo to sleep.

Miss Dallas then offered Ramsammy some food, and, entering into conversation, managed to extract from him an account of the events of the night before. Among other things she learned the part that Simon Pety had played. She also found out that Dilloo had a wife living.

'Dis man die,' said she, nodding towards the sleeping Coolie. 'No want to see woman before die?'

'No,' replied the Sepoy. 'No see woman. She bad woman to dis man.'

Ramsammy, having finished his meal, began to bethink him of his own safety, and consulted the Negro, who came out in an hour to take a look at his patient. The black assured him that he was perfectly safe there, that no Negro policeman would think of coming within a mile of the place on any hostile errand. So terrible is the superstition about these fellows that the very mention of them sends a thrill of horror through a Negro's frame.

The Sepoy thereupon sat down to watch beside his sleeping friend – a task which is admirably suited to the Indian temperament. Rosalind, having cleaned up the few cooking utensils and extinguished the fire, loosened the solitary robe of calico which enwrapped her robust form, and went out to seek some sunny opening in the woods where she could bask and sing without disturbing the morose quiet of her dangerous mate. He remained inside the hut, the door of which was kept closed.

And now through the deep repose far away in the woods could be heard the scream and chatter of birds. The notes of Rosalind's voice just penetrated to the ear of the listening Coolie. The mysterious shadow which surrounded him seemed to be alive with the gentle motions of gliding reptiles, or sometimes a hiss could be heard, as they crossed each other's path. The only other sound was the breathing of the sleeping man, and a portentous sound from the interior of the hut, which struck awe to the soul of the lonely Sepoy. It was, however, nothing more supernatural than the snoring of the African. Thus the day passed on until nearly four o'clock. Rosalind had sung herself to sleep in the sun-glow. The Sepoy, overcome with his fatigues, had snatched some restless repose. Suddenly Dilloo woke. His mind was perfectly clear. He was astonished at the gloom and the strange aspect of the place in which he found himself. He soon discovered and awakened his friend. He was very feeble. They conversed together in low tones. It seemed impossible to raise one's voice in such a place. The Negro, who had the instinct of an animal for sound, hearing conversation, quickly came out, and, after examining the sick Coolie, gave a peculiar whistle. In a few minutes Rosalind entered the enclosure, going on her face before the Obe man as the Sepoy had seen her do in the morning. From this it may be supposed that Miss Dallas was in mortal fear of her companion; but, in truth, the Obe was madly devoted to her, and as she was a woman of no small nerve and acuteness, she was able to have pretty much her own way with him. Her chief ambition was to learn the secrets of his wicked craft, in order that she might succeed to his influence and power.

The couple consulted together, and she set to work to prepare some soup. Meantime, Dilloo, conscious that his strength was failing him, and now recalling only the tenderest reminiscences of the past, bethought him of Lutchmee. He earnestly begged his friend to send for her. Ramsammy was at his wits' end what to do. He knew that for him to go and seek out Lutchmee was to run the risk of a long imprisonment, if he were to escape being found guilty as an accomplice of the capital crime. He therefore tried to explain to Rosalind, whose kindly manner encouraged him as much as the brutal appearance and strange ways of the Obe man repelled him, his friend's wish. When Miss Dallas at length succeeded in apprehending the difficulty, some residuum of good feeling which lay beneath her evil nature was stirred up. She left the Coolie and entered the hut. We have not yet described its interior. It was built of a frame of rough timber, with a pitched roof, the apex of which was about twenty feet from the ground. In the centre, elevated upon the trunk of a tree, was a huge figure roughly resembling the head of a cock. At the end, a great black idol, which had been smeared from time to time with blood, and which was lit up by a floating wick in a glass of oil, added a grotesque horror to the wretched scene. The atmosphere of the place was close and stifling. In a corner, lying like a pig on a couch of grass, was the African. Rosalind approached him.

'De Coolie man go die?' she asked.

'Yes, die sartain,' he replied.

'He ask to see wife – Coolie woman at Belle Susanne.'

'Belle Susanne! Dat Simon Pety's place – eh?'

'Yes, Mister D'Orsay lib dare,' replied Miss Rosalind, with a gulp.

'Hah! you want go see Mr. D'Orsay, eh?' cried the savage sharply.

'No, I don't care 'bout it. But de big Coolie man 'fraid to go; and you berry kind dis poor Coolie. Let him see de woman before he die. You be good man. I go look out de Missionary man, tell him to go and bring de Coolie woman. While I go, you carry de Coolie out dere in de woods, and den dey all talk togedder.'

It took all Rosalind's tact, and a good deal of time, before she could get the man to give way. At length, on her solemn assurance that she would only go to the 'Missionary' – no other than that worthy clerk, the Reverend Adolphus Telfer, – the African assented, threatening her with supernatural vengeance if she failed to keep her promise.

Without giving him time to change his mind, the big girl tucked up her skirts and swiftly made her way to the home of the clergyman, which was on the edge of Guineatown, and not far from the house of Mr. Marston. The little parson was greatly disturbed by the information she brought; but, quietly pocketing his excitement, he directed her to wait in the verandah, and, seizing his hat and stick, set off by the shortest route to Belle Susanne. It was dark, but the little minister went on as if he saw clearly before him. A kindly zeal lightened his way and braced his not over-strong limbs to active energy. He had a curious struggle with himself as he went along. Was he right in what he was doing? He had learned where an accused murderer was lying in a condition to ensure his capture, and here, instead of running off with the information to his next-door neighbour, the magistrate, he was on his way to help the criminal's wife to an interview. The little man had not satisfactorily settled the question with his conscience when he arrived, breathless and very warm, at Pety's door. Communing never so closely, he had, notwithstanding, managed to keep clear of a meeting with any of the white people of the estate. Now, early as it was in the evening, and hot as was the air, Mr. D'Orsay's door was closed. The clergyman knocked, and to him, almost immediately, Simon himself answered the summons.

'Massa Telfer!' cried Pety, astounded. The parish minister was not of Pety's persuasion.

'Hush – sh – sh – sh – !' said the little man, darting past Mr: D'Orsay, and motioning to him violently to shut the door. The petroleum lamp disclosed to him there assembled within Mr. Craig, Mrs. D' Orsay and Lutchmee, who looked upon him with amazement.

'Oh! Mr. Craig!' he cried, shaking hands with an enthusiasm he never threw into his services; 'I am so delighted to see you here! Just the man we want! A most providential coincidence. I wish to find Lutchmee, the wife of a man named Dilloo – Eh? – Oh yes! – this must be – How do you do? Eh? Quite well, I hope. Keep up! The Lord help you, my poor woman! Oh! Mr. Craig!'

While he was delivering himself of these scattered sentences, the Reverend Adolphus Telfer was spinning round the room like a cockchafer on a pin. Craig conceived that he had lost his wits. But presently he showed signs of recovery. He drew Craig into a corner.

'Mr. Craig,' he said, 'I have heard of the runaway Dilloo. There is a woman at my house – Rosalind Dallas. I know her. She is now, I believe, in the bonds of iniquity. But just at this moment, no matter. She may be useful. Dilloo is dying out in the woods, some miles beyond Guineatown, where that infamous Obe is said to lurk. He wants to see his wife. If this is the woman, as I suppose, will you get her to come? – and perhaps you will not mind accompanying us. I shall go. There may yet be a few hours of grace given him by a merciful God.'

In a very short time the party set out. A somewhat awkward interview took place between Pety and Rosalind. She, however, insisted on his returning home, as her ferocious master would have become uncontrollable at the sight of him; and Pety, not insensible to the danger of the expedition, discreetly went back to his wife.

Poising on her head a large lanthorn, supplied by the clergyman, Miss Dallas stalked along at a rapid pace in front of the party, which consisted of Craig, Mr. Telfer and Lutchmee. They made their way in perfect silence. Each was overpowered with thought. Lutchmee could not weep. She was in a fever of sorrow and expectation. As they passed so quietly through the still scene, in the gloom of which the lanthorn shed its small gleam like a will-o'-the-wisp, the only sound that broke the charm of the silence was the far-off knell of the campanero – the strange bell-bird of the Guianian woods.

Rosalind found that the Negro had not removed the wounded man from the enclosure, to which accordingly she led the way. They were guided by a glare which, rising from behind the lower bushes, sent up under the high roofing of the shadowy foliage an awe-inspiring glow. The light came from a large fire which Ramsammy had kindled, under the African's direction. The resinous wood threw out a balmy fragrance, and the light brought out in clear relief every object within the enclosure – the hut, the figures, the graceful form of the surrounding growth, the trellised bush-ropes and the far-up sombre arches of the majestic trees, ribbing the thick roof of leaves. Even Craig felt a sudden thrill of wonder as he entered this mysterious place, and took in all the circumstances of the scene – the dying man stretched out beside the hut, the Sepoy watching beside him, the huge Negro leaning against the door and eyeing the flames of the huge fire as if he could feed upon them. But at sight of the visitors, the sable wizard, after exchanging a word or two with Rosalind, vanished into the house, barring the door.

Lutchmee, with a beating heart, drew near her husband. She knelt beside him and wrung her hands.

'Oh, Dilloo, Dilloo!'

He held out his hand. She kissed it and pressed it to her bosom. They said little. They looked into each other's eyes, and there was a world in their glances. Sorrow, compassion, mutual forgiveness, the old love that at this final parting takes new life and grows young again, the tender passion of these last moments of earthly intercourse – all this there was in every word and gesture of that brief interview, and one thing more – the pang that comes of the doubt 'Shall we ever meet again?'

At length Craig and Mr. Telfer, who had remained apart, approached. Dilloo recognised them both. He was perfectly himself. He tried to muster words to thank them. The clergyman, touched by the evident nearness of the departing soul to the dark postern of death ventured to say a few words in vindication of his office. He tried in simple language to tell the dying man of a long life, an endless and possibly blest hereafter; of forgiveness of sin done here; of a balm for the sorrows, weaknesses and agonies of time, a rescue from the bondage of evil, a lasting freedom of joy – a Saviour, Jesus Christ, who had opened the gates from death into life, from pain to bliss.

The Coolie listened impassive, silent. He held Lutchmee's hand tightly in his own. The moments flew by. Lutchmee watched the ebbing, dribbling life.

'See, Dilloo!' cried the Missionary, stirred to earnestness. 'There is good and life ready for you even now. Believe in Jesus Christ – trust your soul to Him!'

'No!' cried the dying Coolie, loudly, almost fiercely, and with unconscious but terribly pointed satire, as he half raised his body. 'No! No! Jesu Kriss Massa Drummond's God – Massa Marston's God – all Inglees God. No God for Coolie!'

And turning his face away from the Christian, the Coolie breathed out his soul into the bosom of the Unknown God.

THE END